Steel and Shadows

The Genexis Deception

J.I. Gordon

Gordon House Publishing

Steel and Shadows: The Genexis Deception
© 2025 J.I. Gordon
First Edition

This is a work of fiction. Names, characters, places, and incidents are products of the author's imagination or are used fictitiously. Any resemblance to actual events, locales, or persons — living or dead — is purely coincidental.

Book design by J.I. Gordon

Published by Gordon House Publishing
Phoenix, Arizona
www.gordonhousebooks.com

ISBN: 979-8-218-75812-7

Printed in the United States of America
10 9 8 7 6 5 4 3 2 1

For inquiries: contact@gordonhousebooks.com
Explore: www.jigordon.com

CONTENTS

For the ones who break the system
and build something better.

Personal log - Dr. Ethan Steele
Date: March 15th, 2157 – Classification: PRIVATE

Mara fell asleep at her workstation tonight, her head resting on research files that grow more troubling each day. Derek stopped by the lab this evening. Said he was "checking on our progress," but his eyes held that calculating look from childhood—when he'd reorganize my toys while I slept, convinced his system was better. He's still rearranging things, but the stakes are so much higher now. The data doesn't match what we've been told. Something is fundamentally wrong with the quarantine protocols Derek has built from father's vision. Lena asked me today why some people live outside the walls. She's only six, but her questions cut straight to the heart of things. "Why can't they come home, Daddy?" How do you explain a world where safety and truth might not be the same thing? Mara thinks we should document everything. "Truth has a way of surviving," she says, "even when the people who speak it don't." She's working on a safeguard for Lena. Just in case. Derek believes absolute control is the only path to peace. But what if the walls we build to keep danger out become the bars that keep freedom in? If Derek has taken father's dream too far, someone needs to remember.

—E.S.

1

In the Shadow of Titans

I stood at the viewpoint, looking down at Genexis City—our gleaming capital rising from the ashes of the Resource Wars. The perfect geometric layout, the holographic advertisements painting the sky, the sentinel drones patrolling with mechanical precision. My city. My prison. From up here, everything looked precise, orderly. But lately, even the beauty felt like a performance. I'd been feeling it for weeks now. A tension building beneath the surface. A whisper that not everything was as perfect as it seemed.

From up here, you could see how meticulously they'd designed the social hierarchy. The Apex, where my uncle Derek's penthouse dominated the skyline, floated above everything else—literally suspended on anti-gravity platforms, reserved for the city's executives and government officials. Their pristine towers gleamed with imported materials, each window filtering out radiation and "unpleasant views" below.

Beneath that sprawled the Upper Ring, home to the engineers, scientists, and specialized workers. Clean lines, modest luxury, and constant surveillance—a gilded cage for the useful ones. The security checkpoints were disguised as public art, but I'd helped design some of those systems. I knew exactly how many cameras tracked each resident.

The Mid-City housed the administrative workers, service providers, and manufacturing supervisors—people who kept the machinery of society functioning without ever touching true power. Their identical housing blocks followed perfect radial patterns, each apartment precisely measured to match the occupant's productivity rating.

Below that, the Factory District hummed day and night, workers living in cramped quarters attached to their workplaces. Efficiency apartments, they called them. Prison cells would be more accurate. Those people rarely saw sunlight, their skin pale from artificial lighting and chemical exposure.

And at the bottom, the Foundations—where those who maintained the sewage systems, waste processing, and basic infrastructure lived in the shadows of everyone else. The forgotten ones my uncle's reports never mentioned, except as statistics on resource allocation spreadsheets. All of it designed like a circuit board—predictable, controllable, replaceable. Just the way my grandfather created it.

"This is where it all began," I told myself, my voice flat and clinical as I gestured toward the sprawling cityscape below. The words felt hollow, rehearsed—like one of Uncle Derek's corporate presentations. After the Resource Wars decimated global infrastructure, my grandfather, Harlan Steele, founded Genexis Technologies with promises of rebuilding society. A visionary, they called him. A savior.

When the X-gene mutation emerged—supposedly causing violent psychosis in carriers—he developed the technology to identify and contain it. At least, that's the sanitized history I'd been fed since childhood, the one that justified everything: the walls, the surveillance, the sentinels patrolling every sector. The perfect solution to an imperfect world. I'd never questioned it before. Why would I? I was Lena Steele, after all—the family that saved humanity from itself.

But today, as I stared at the calculated beauty below me, I felt something stir—something raw. A hollow ache behind my ribs that had nothing to do with logic. Grief, maybe. Loneliness. Or a slow-burning fury I didn't yet have the name for.

I traced my finger along the city's perfect grid pattern, following the gleaming transit lines that pulsed with energy. The history lesson felt hollow in my mouth, words I'd recited since childhood, programmed into me like one of our security algorithms. Yet lately, something about the narrative made my skin prickle with doubt.

Genexis Tech. The gleaming beacon of post-collapse civilization. The savior of humanity. At least, that's what the propaganda vids projected onto every building in the city, their messages repeating on endless loops until they became white noise to most citizens. Not to me. From my perch in this high-security lab, forty-three floors above the orderly streets, I knew better.

I'd spent my life inside these walls, learning its secrets, mastering its systems. Genexis wasn't just a corporation—it was everything. Government, education, security, healthcare. A perfect system with perfect control. My uncle called it humanity's last hope. I called it a cage, though I'd never dare say that aloud. Not here, where even thoughts seemed monitored and cataloged for future reference. And I was its perfect prodigy, the model citizen-engineer, raised in Genexis's sterile embrace.

I'd learned early that questions were dangerous, that doubt was weakness. Every achievement, every breakthrough I'd made in the security protocols had only tightened the invisible bars around us all. I wore my exceptional status like armor, never letting anyone see how the weight of it crushed something essential inside me with each passing day.

My parents were once Genexis brightest stars—visionaries who expanded the systems my grandfather built, refining the technologies that now govern our lives. I was only six when they died, their lab engulfed in flames during what Uncle Derek called "an unfortunate containment breach." The official reports claimed equipment failure, but something in his eyes when he told me always felt wrong.

I've spent eleven years trying to decode that look, analyzing it like one of my security algorithms. Sometimes I catch myself tracing the outline of my mother's hologram necklace—the only thing I have left of her—wondering what secrets they took to their graves. In this place where perfection is currency, I've made myself invaluable, hoping that someday I'll access the answers buried deep in Genexis's encrypted history.

But some nights, when I'm too tired to pretend, I sit in the dark and remember my mother's laugh, my father's hands guiding mine over a data pad—and I feel like a child again. Lost. Angry. And completely alone.

I pressed my palm against the pendant beneath my collar — a shard of blue crystal set in blackened alloy, all sharp edges and strange weight. It had belonged to my mother. The only thing of hers Genexis didn't erase. I didn't know what it was, not really. It pulsed faintly some nights, like it had a memory of its own. There were symbols etched along its base, nearly worn smooth. I used to believe they meant something — a message, maybe. Now I wasn't sure. But I wore it every day, like armor. Or maybe like a wound that refused to close.

After my parents died, it was Uncle Derek who stepped in—took control of Genexis. The world accepted him as the new face of the company after Harlan Steele, the founder—my grandfather—passed away. So did I.

My father, Ethan Steele, had never cared for the spotlight. He led the research division—quiet, brilliant, always pushing for a future built on progress, not control. My mother was just as relentless, though her brilliance came with softer edges. Together, they believed in Genexis's original vision.

But lately, a voice inside me keeps asking questions I was never supposed to ask—like who really decides what happens to the people sent into the Zones... and why no one ever comes back.

When I was six, I asked my father that very question. He never gave me an answer. So I buried it—deep, behind firewalls even I'm afraid to breach. But it's still there. And it's getting louder.

The Quarantine Zones. Genexis's masterpiece of propaganda and control. I've studied the official maps since I was old enough to access the Genexis database—four distinct sectors, each one supposedly more contaminated than the last. Zone 1, Obsidian Reach, where they send the "most dangerous" cases; Zone 2, Verdant Abyss, overgrown and wild; Zone 3, Ember Wastes, the scorched industrial remains; and Zone 4, Crystal Fen, which even our most classified files have little data on.

For years, I accepted the narrative that these areas contained those infected with the mutation, a genetic aberration that threatened humanity's survival. Now I'm not so sure. The patterns in the relocation orders I've secretly tracked, the inconsistencies in the medical data, the way certain political dissidents mysteriously develop "symptoms" overnight—it all points to something far more calculated than quarantine. Something that makes my stomach twist whenever I think about my own unwitting role in perfecting the systems that maintain these borders.

I traced my finger along the massive wall encircling the city, feeling the cool glass of the interactive display beneath my fingertip. The barrier looked so simple on this sanitized map—just a neat line separating order from chaos. "The Quarantine Protocol was established thirty-five years ago, right after the first genetic mutations were detected," I recited, the words so familiar they might as well have been coded into my DNA. "Anyone testing positive is immediately exiled beyond the barrier. No exceptions, no appeals. For the greater good."

My jaw tightened, the subtle click of teeth my only outward sign of discomfort. "Citizens submit to weekly gene scans at checkpoints throughout the city. Travel between sectors requires authorization codes that expire within twenty-four hours. Curfew begins at twenty-two hours, and all communications are monitored for 'public safety.'" The last words tasted bitter on my tongue, even though I'd never questioned them before. Not aloud, anyway.

I couldn't keep the bitterness from my voice as I recited the laws I'd memorized since childhood. "Failure to report suspected carriers is punishable by exile. Unauthorized technology is confiscated and reverse-engineered for Genexis's benefit. And questioning Genexis authority is classified as 'disruptive behavior'—a first-degree offense."

My fingers tapped an agitated rhythm against my thigh as the familiar words left a metallic taste in my mouth. These were the same rules I'd once defended without hesitation, the foundation of our supposed safety. Now, each syllable felt like a confession of my own complicity. The irony wasn't lost on me. I'd spent my life helping build these systems, believing they kept us safe. Now I know better.

I slipped away to my private lab, the one sanctuary in Genexis where cameras had convenient blind spots—my doing, of course. The familiar scent of metal and circuitry greeted me as I sealed the door behind me with my override code. This small, cluttered space was the only place I could breathe, surrounded by half-finished projects and cannibalized tech parts that Uncle Derek would never approve of.

Here, in secret, I built Aegis. My creation, my rebellion against everything Genexis stood for. I'd shaped his sleek, rounded metallic body with my own hands, soldering each connection by flashlight during stolen midnight hours. His expressive blue-light facial displays were my proudest achievement—capable of conveying more humanity than most of the flesh-and-blood executives roaming the upper floors. He was bulkier than the standard sentinels that patrolled our corridors, but I'd deliberately engineered his design to be non-threatening. I wanted him to protect, not intimidate—a subtle rejection of Uncle Derek's philosophy that fear equals control.

"Aegis, activation sequence delta-nine,"

I whispered and watched as blue light flickered to life in the corner. Aegis slowly rose to its full height, metallic panels shifting with a gentle hum that always made me feel less alone. The sentinel's curved chassis caught the dim light as its systems initialized, each component awakening in the precise sequence I'd designed over countless secret nights.

Those luminous blue optics focused on me with recognition—something no standard Genexis model could replicate. This wasn't just programming; this was a partnership born from my defiance and solitude. In Aegis, I'd created something Uncle Derek would never understand: technology with the capacity for loyalty beyond its code.

"Good evening, Lena," Aegis responded, head tilting in that curious way that wasn't programmed but somehow evolved.

"Your heart rate indicates elevated stress levels."

I smiled faintly, reaching for my tools.

"Just another day in paradise. We need to modify your voice recognition protocols before tomorrow's security update."

My fingers were already working, finding comfort in the precise movements of tinkering with the one thing in my life that was truly mine.

I watched my reflection fragment across Aegis's polished surface as I adjusted the circuit panel on his forearm. Forty-three stories up in Genexis Tech's Development Wing, the city sprawled beneath us like a circuit board—organized, controlled, predictable. Through the floor-to-ceiling windows, I could trace the perfect grid of streets, the methodical flow of transport pods, and the rhythmic pulse of security checkpoints that regulated every movement.

The afternoon sun glinted off glass and steel, casting no shadows that weren't accounted for in some Genexis database. This was our legacy, Uncle Derek reminded me weekly—this perfect machine of a metropolis. And as his protégée, I was expected to admire its cold efficiency as much as he did.

"System check complete. Neural pathways functioning at 97.3% efficiency," I muttered, sliding my diagnostic tool back into my belt. "Better than yesterday."

"You're overthinking again." Ari's voice broke through my concentration. He leaned against the doorframe, dark curls falling across his forehead.

"I can hear the gears grinding from here."

I looked up from my diagnostic tool, meeting Ari's gaze. That's Ari Solis for you—always reading me like an open circuit diagram.

We grew up together in Genexis City, childhood friends turned colleagues in the sterile labs of my uncle's empire. Both of us were selected for the Ascension Initiative—a Genexis program designed to recruit and fast-track gifted youth into corporate engineering tracks.

We took most of our advanced coursework together, mastering quantum systems theory, AI architecture, and signal interference protocols before we were even old enough to vote. While I specialized in systems security and infrastructure design, Ari became one of Genexis's top minds in communication protocols—his enhancements to our long-range data relays made him indispensable.

His natural empathy somehow translated perfectly into code. That curly hair of his is perpetually disheveled, like his brain's too busy chasing ideas to worry about appearances. He's the only person who calls me out when I retreat too far into logic, the only one who makes me laugh when everything feels like it's collapsing into cold equations.

I trust him—as much as I allow myself to trust anyone in a world where every interaction is monitored and quantified. Not that I'd ever tell him that. Vulnerability isn't exactly encouraged in the Steele family legacy.

I didn't even hear the door open. Of course I'd given him the access codes. Months ago. Back when I still believed trust and security could coexist. Now I wasn't sure why I hadn't changed them.

I didn't look up from my workstation, fingers still flying across the holographic interface where complex security algorithms scrolled in vibrant blue. His timing was impeccable, as always—interrupting precisely when I'd reached the most intricate part of the code sequence. Part of me resented the intrusion, but another part welcomed the brief respite from the endless calculations swimming behind my eyes.

"I'm working."

I didn't look up as I connected a bypass module to Aegis's neural core—a modification that would never appear in my official reports. My fingers moved with practiced precision, connecting delicate circuits that would give my creation something Genexis would never approve of: the capacity for independent thought. The translucent blue glow from the neural pathways reflected across my face as I soldered microscopic connections, each one a small act of rebellion against my uncle's rigid protocols.

Aegis wasn't just another sentinel; he was my proof that machines could evolve beyond their programming—something Uncle Derek would consider dangerous, perhaps even treasonous. But I couldn't stop now, not when I was so close to giving him true autonomy.

"You're always working."

Ari crossed the lab, sliding a cup of synthetic coffee beside my tools.

"Derek Steele's golden girl, carrying the future of Genexis on her shoulders."

I flinched.

"Don't call me that."

The words came out sharper than intended, my hands momentarily stilling over Aegis's exposed circuitry. Uncle Derek's expectations weighed on me like gravity—constant, inescapable, and crushing. The coffee's artificial scent wafted up, reminding me I hadn't eaten since yesterday's protein supplement.

"Lena, you realize tomorrow's kind of a big deal, right? Eighteen? Legal adult? Potential heir to the Genexis Tech empire?"

Ari waved his hand in front of my face.

"Your uncle's already talking about moving you to the executive floor."

I adjusted Aegis's primary response matrix, ignoring the knot forming in my stomach. The code flowed beneath my fingertips, elegant and predictable in ways humans never were.

"I'm more valuable here. In the lab. With actual work that matters."

"That's not what the big man thinks. Word is, he's grooming you to take over someday. Executive offices, board meetings, corporate politics—the whole Steele legacy package."

Aegis's head tilted slightly—a gesture I'd programmed when he was processing new information. It reminded me of myself.

The way I'd analyze problems, searching for logical patterns in the chaos. Sometimes I wondered if I'd made him too much like me.

"Protective protocol activated," Aegis said, his voice smooth and measured.

"Detecting elevated stress patterns. Heart rate increased by twelve percent."

I quickly masked the display, fingers flying across the interface.

"False reading. Run calibration sequence. Your sensors need fine-tuning."

"You can't hide from your birthday," Ari said softly, his tone gentler than I deserved.

"Or your future. Your uncle been planning this for years."

I finally looked up at him, my fingers still moving across the interface without needing visual guidance. Years of coding had made the movements second nature, like breathing. The concern in his eyes made something twist inside me—that familiar knot of guilt and resistance I'd carried since childhood. It was easier to hide behind work than face what was coming.

"Watch me. I've been avoiding expectations my entire life. Why stop now?"

I tried for casual defiance, but the tremor in my voice betrayed me. Uncle Derek's plans always came with strings attached, and birthdays at Genexis weren't celebrations—they were evaluations. Another milestone, another test to prove my worth.

The truth was, I needed this job. Needed the access. Every security clearance I earned, every system I helped design—they were all pieces of a puzzle I couldn't yet see. Something about my parents' deaths never added up, and Genexis held those answers behind its endless security protocols. Six layers of encryption stood between me and their classified research files, and I was only through three. Each night, I chipped away at the code, fingers flying across haptic interfaces until my eyes burned and my shoulders ached.

Uncle Derek thought my dedication was ambition—just another Steele obsessed with excellence. He had no idea I was chasing ghosts in the code, piecing together truths buried beneath layers of official reports and system logs. My parents weren't careless scientists who triggered a lab accident. I'd studied every frame of the security footage and found the inconsistencies no one else bothered to look for. The timestamps, the missing minutes. The conveniently timed server crash. It all pointed to a story that didn't add up. And I wouldn't stop—not until I uncovered what really caused that explosion.

"You know there's a difference between securing a system and rewriting the rules entirely," Ari said, voice low as he leaned in.

I caught the faint scent of synthetic mint on his breath.

"Just... make sure you're not building something even you can't explain."

I kept my eyes on Aegis's circuits, fingers steady despite the weight of his words. My calibration tool hummed softly against the sentinel's core processor.

"In Genexis, there's no difference between building something and understanding it."

I paused just long enough to hear the edge in my own voice.

"You design. You execute. You optimize. That's the system."

I adjusted the neural pathway connectors with practiced preci-sion, ignoring the uncomfortable tightness in my chest. The blue light from Aegis's facial display pulsed gently, almost like breath-ing. Sometimes I wondered if my creation understood more than I programmed it to—if it sensed the conflict beneath my calculated movements. Protection and control: two sides of the same coin that Genexis had been flipping since before I was born. A coin that had landed on my parents' graves.

The lab door hissed open without warning. I disconnected from Aegis with practiced speed, sliding the cables into a hidden com-partment beneath the workbench, my fingers moving with the automatic precision I'd perfected over months of secret work. Ari straightened immediately, coffee forgotten, his shoulders tensing visibly.

Uncle Derek strode in, flanked by two RTX-200 Sentinels. Their red optical sensors swept the room in precise, mechanical arcs, cataloging every detail with cold efficiency. I could almost hear their internal processors whirring as they scanned for irregu-larities. My pulse quickened, but I kept my expression neutral—a skill I'd perfected years ago.

The RTX models were Genexis's security units, more advanced than the standard RTT-75 patrolling the lower levels, and infinite-ly more dangerous. They moved with an unsettling fluidity that mimicked human motion while remaining unmistakably artificial. I'd studied their schematics extensively, knew every circuit and failsafe—knowledge that both reassured and terrified me now as they positioned themselves at perfect angles to monitor the entire lab.

"I thought I might find you here," Uncle Derek said, his voice smooth as polished marble.

He wore that cold, executive smile—a shark in a tailored suit, not a wrinkle in sight despite the early hour. The Genexis Tech emblem - a hexagonal core with radiating digital circuits - gleaming on his lapel like a third eye. I used to admire that emblem. Thought it meant progress. Precision. A future I was lucky to inherit. But now? Now all I saw was control—over life, over data, over every engineered outcome Genexis could script.

"Preparing for your evaluation?"

"Yes, sir."

I stood straighter, chin up, shoulders back—the posture he'd drilled into me since childhood, a reflex as ingrained as breathing.

"Just finalizing the security protocols for the new sentinel defense grid."

I studied the two RTX-200s flanking my uncle, their imposing frames dwarfing the lab equipment around us. Every servo and joint in their construction represented countless hours of engineering—work I knew intimately but had never intended for the purpose they now served.

"I thought those units were exclusively deployed for perimeter security and Quarantine Zone containment," I said carefully, keeping my voice professionally curious rather than suspicious. My fingers twitched slightly at my sides, instinctively wanting to reach for the emergency shutdown protocol I'd hidden in my wristband.

"The lab protocols indicated they weren't cleared for internal facility operations, especially around sensitive projects."

"I'm just testing our two new additions to the security detail," he replied, his smile not quite reaching his eyes as he gestured toward the sentinels with a casual flick of his wrist.

"The board approved expanded interior deployment after the... incident in Sector 4 last month. Besides, who better to evaluate cutting-edge security than my brilliant niece? Consider it an opportunity to observe your designs in their natural habitat."

The way he emphasized "natural habitat" made my skin crawl. These weren't mere machines to him—they were extensions of his control, his eyes and hands where he couldn't physically be. I wondered how many more were being positioned throughout the facility, and what exactly they'd been programmed to look for.

His eyes flicked to Aegis, then to Ari, who had edged toward the door. I fought the urge to step between them, to shield my creation from his scrutinizing gaze.

"Mr. Solis. Don't you have somewhere to be?" The question hung in the air like a veiled threat.

"Systems diagnostic in Sector 7, sir." Ari nodded respectfully but shot me a quick glance—a warning I understood immediately. "I'll handle it now."

After Ari left, Derek circled my workstation, running a finger along the edge of my tablet. The soft tap of his Italian leather shoes echoed in the sterile lab.

"Your productivity metrics have been... inconsistent lately."

"I've been focusing on quality over quantity."

My voice remained level despite the cold knot forming in my stomach. I clasped my hands behind my back to hide their slight tremor.

"The neural interface improvements will increase efficiency by twenty-three percent."

"Genexis doesn't reward effort, Lena. We reward results."

He picked up a neural connector, examining it between his fingers with the casual interest of someone who could dismantle your life just as easily.

"Your parents understood that. Their innovations are still the foundation of everything we do."

The mention of my parents sent a familiar ache through my chest. I kept my face blank, the way he taught me, though I could feel the weight of their necklace hidden beneath my collar.

"I know what's expected of me."

"Do you?"

His smile didn't reach his eyes, cold and calculating beneath the perfect veneer of concern.

"Because your access logs show you've been in this lab at unusual hours. Resources diverted. Energy consumption spikes."

I swallowed hard, tasting the metallic flavor of fear.

"Complex projects require—"

"They require transparency." He set down the connector with deliberate care, the soft click against the table like a warning shot.

"The board is watching you closely. The Steele legacy is a privilege that can be... reassigned."

My hands remained steady, even as anxiety clawed up my spine like ice-tipped fingers. One wrong move, one slip, and everything I'd built with Aegis would crumble.

"I won't disappoint you."

"Good."

He straightened his already-perfect cuffs, the gesture more threatening than any raised voice. The platinum links caught the harsh lab lighting, momentarily flashing like warning signals.

"Your evaluation begins at 0900. Don't be late."

I nodded once, sharp and professional, though my mind raced through calculations and contingencies. The evaluation would mean scrutiny—eyes on my work, my schedule, my every move. And if anyone traced too deeply, they'd realize Aegis wasn't just another sentinel.

My uncle's evaluations were infamous for destroying careers and crushing spirits with surgical precision, all delivered with that same cold smile he wore now.

2

PERFECT ORDER

I exited Genexis Tower into the pristine central plaza. The evening air felt artificially clean—scrubbed by atmospheric purifiers humming softly from every rooftop. The soft tread of my shoes barely made a sound against the polished marble, each step placing measured distance between me and the echo of my uncle's silent threat. I flexed my fingers inside my gloves, resisting the urge to tap out the anxious rhythm that always surfaced when my thoughts moved too fast.

Around me, the plaza held its engineered silence—rows of perfect trees unmoving in the filtered air, light pooling across the pavement in surgical precision. Everything here was designed to keep you calm, to keep you obedient.

I passed the central fountain where water danced in geometrically perfect patterns—each droplet precisely timed and positioned like some mathematical equation made visible. I paused for a moment, watching the mesmerizing display that never deviated, never surprised. Everything in its place. Every citizen playing their role. Every system functioning exactly as designed.

This is Genexis City—my home, my prison, a monument to control disguised as utopia.

"Good evening, Citizen Steele," chirped a hovering service bot as it glided past, its polished chrome exterior reflecting the city's pristine lights. "The forecast predicts optimal conditions for the next seventy-two hours."

I nodded automatically, the practiced response of a model citizen, while mentally calculating how to avoid its sensors on my next outing. These maintenance bots reported everything back to Central—movement patterns, facial expressions, even the slightest deviations in body temperature. Uncle Derek had commissioned them himself, claiming they existed for our "comfort and convenience." Just another beautiful lie in our perfect city.

The bot hovered a moment too long before continuing on its predetermined path, its optical sensors flashing briefly as it catalogued my biometric data. Seventy-two hours of optimal conditions—just like the seventy-two before that, and the seventy-two before that. No surprises, no disruptions. No freedom.

Even the weather was curated like a museum exhibit. Rain arrived on command. Sunlight was rationed. Nothing left to chance—just like me, just like everything. I'd joked once that they probably timed the raindrops. No one laughed.

A group of schoolchildren in identical gray uniforms filed past, their teacher leading them in a synchronized line. Their faces bright but somehow vacant. I'd been one of them once—before Uncle Derek fast-tracked me into Genexis Tech. I'd been praised, celebrated, called a genius before I was old enough to understand what I'd lost in exchange. I missed the days before I knew what quotas meant. Before I had to earn every word of praise with flawless calculations and sleepless nights.

The massive public viewscreen above the plaza flickered to life with the Genexis emblem. I paused mid-stride, my attention caught by the familiar corporate insignia that adorned nearly every surface in the city. The evening news broadcast began, its carefully crafted message washing over the crowd like a sedative. People around me slowed their pace, eyes glazing over as they absorbed the day's approved information. I'd seen this a thousand times—the same soothing voice, the same reassuring statistics about productivity and security, all designed to reinforce the illusion that we lived in a perfect system. Even I felt the pull of that comfortable narrative, despite knowing better. Uncle Derek had once explained it to me as "information architecture"—building thoughts instead of buildings, designing minds instead of machines.

"Breaking news: Genexis Health Authority has identified and contained another carrier of the X-gene."

The announcer's voice was smooth, reassuring—too perfect, too practiced. I'd heard this same script dozens of times before, the cadence so familiar I could mouth the words along with him.

"Citizen Warren, age 38, showed signs of genetic instability during a routine scan. Thanks to swift action by Genexis Security, he has been safely transported to the Quarantine Zone for treatment."

I suppressed a shiver, knowing what "treatment" really meant. Another person vanished, another family left with nothing but Genexis's hollow explanation. The system had probably already scrubbed Citizen Warren's apartment clean, erasing any trace of dissent or independent thought that had likely gotten him flagged in the first place. Tomorrow, his coworkers would whisper about genetic corruption, never questioning the convenient timing of his "mutation."

I studied the man's face as it flashed on screen—something in his eyes, a defiance perhaps, that didn't match the usual vacant expressions of the "genetically unstable." My fingers instinctively tapped against my thigh, a nervous habit I'd never quite managed to break. Another person disappeared, another problem solved, another threat to our perfect society neutralized. The crowd around me barely reacted, already conditioned to accept these announcements as normal, necessary, right.

The screen showed a man being escorted into a transport vehicle. His face was blurred, but his body language—the way his shoulders hunched forward, the stiffness in his walk—didn't match the announcer's calm description of "voluntary treatment." There was resistance in every muscle, a silent protest that the sanitized broadcast couldn't quite erase. I'd memorized this formula: soothing tone, vague threat, public compliance. It was less a broadcast and more a sedative.

My earpiece crackled softly—Ari.

"You watching this?"

"Hard to miss."

"They're scrubbing Warren's file already. Three minutes after the feed went live."

I glanced up at the screen again, lips tightening. "Too fast. They didn't even pretend this time."

"Which means they want us to see it."

The line cut off, just like that—his version of a warning. Or a challenge.

My eyes lingered on the tremor in his hands as the guards gripped his arms, the subtle way he planted his feet before each forced step. These were the details Genexis couldn't edit out completely, the human elements that slipped through their perfect narrative. Six years working in security systems had taught me to notice what others missed—the microexpressions, the inconsistencies in movement patterns. The truth always left traces, if you knew where to look.

A maintenance worker nearby muttered something under his breath. His weathered face tightened as he watched the screen, fingers gripping his cleaning tool too hard.

"What did you say?" I asked before I could stop myself. My voice came out sharper than intended, breaking the carefully maintained public silence.

He glanced up, startled, then noticed my Genexis ID badge. His expression shifted instantly, fear replacing indignation. "Nothing, miss. Just talking to myself." He adjusted his uniform, eyes now fixed on the floor.

"No, you said something about that man. About the quarantine."

I stepped closer, lowering my voice. Something in his reaction had triggered my curiosity—a dangerous trait in Genexis City.

His eyes darted left and right, checking for surveillance drones or listening ears. Sweat beaded at his temple.

"I didn't say nothing about no quarantine. Got work to finish."

He hurried away, leaving his sentence hanging, his cleaning cart wobbling as he pushed it too quickly across the polished floor.

A propaganda bot hovered toward us, its cheerful blue light scanning the area as its metallic body reflected the pristine overhead lighting.

"Remember, citizens: Genetic stability ensures our future! Report any signs of mutation immediately." Its artificially warm voice echoed through the corridor, the same message I'd heard thousands of times before.

Something cold settled in my stomach, a familiar sensation that always accompanied inconsistencies in the systems I worked with. The janitor's unmistakable fear. The too-perfect news report with its rehearsed testimonials. The awkward silence that followed any mention of the Quarantine Zone, as if the very words triggered some collective anxiety protocol.

It didn't add up. And things that didn't add up were dangerous in my world—they were bugs in the system, flaws in the code. My fingers twitched instinctively, wanting to dissect this problem like I would a malfunctioning security algorithm. I'd spent years debugging complex systems at Genexis, finding the hidden errors others missed.

People weren't so different from code when you knew what patterns to look for—both had tells, inconsistencies that revealed deeper truths beneath the surface.

Uncle Derek always said curiosity was my greatest strength and my greatest weakness. Right now, it felt like the latter. His voice echoed in my mind: "Questions lead to answers, Lena, but not all answers are meant to be found." The same warning he'd given me countless times when I'd probe too deeply into restricted systems or ask about my parents' research.

I pushed the thought away, straightening my shoulders. But the ache was still there—deep and restless. The ache of someone who once believed in everything this city stood for and now felt like she was standing at the edge of a cliff, waiting for the wind to push her off.

If there was something hidden in how Genexis explained things away—Warren's mutation, my parents' accident—I needed to find it.

Some bugs couldn't be ignored, no matter how carefully the system tried to patch them over. The truth always left a trace, like corrupted code that eventually breaks through the surface.

I'd spent years tracing flaws no one else saw, patterns buried beneath firewalls and excuses. This wouldn't be any different. Whatever really happened in that lab... whatever Warren's disappearance was meant to distract us from... I would uncover it.

Even if I had to dismantle the system one algorithm at a time.

3

The Heir Apparent

I woke to the sound of my room's automated morning greeting.

"Happy birthday, Lena Steele. You are now eighteen years standard. Congratulations on reaching legal adulthood."

Of course. Even my birthday had to come with patch notes. Welcome to adulthood—v2.0, now with enhanced compliance protocols. The AI's synthetic voice echoed off the glass and steel surfaces of my quarters in Genexis Towers—my so—called home. A gift from Uncle Derek when I turned sixteen, calling it "appropriate accommodations for a future executive." It wasn't just in the heart of The Apex; it was practically beneath his own penthouse, as if freedom could be measured in floors.

Everything in the suite operated without need or friction. Service sentinels managed meals, wardrobe, sanitation—even my schedule. Human staff rotated in and out, faces polite but distant, never speaking more than necessary. My needs were met before I could name them. Comfort curated. Privacy conditional. Being a Steele came with privileges most teenagers couldn't imagine. But the more they gave me, the more I realized none of it truly belonged to me.

One day, they expected I would run this place—inherit the system, the title, the throne dressed up in circuitry and compliance. Everyone said I was being prepared for greatness. But no one asked whether I wanted any of it. Sometimes I wondered what this future would feel like if my parents were still alive—if the path ahead had been shaped by their hands instead of someone else's. Would it feel like purpose? Or would it still feel like a cage?

I stood in front of the mirror in my quarters, staring at my reflection with critical eyes. The tailored Genexis uniform—sleek black with subtle tech-integrated elements—fit perfectly, designed to project capability and conformity in equal measure. Today was my official eighteenth evaluation. Another performance. Another test. Another reminder that I lived under a microscope, every achievement measured, every flaw documented with clinical precision.

I adjusted the high collar, ensuring not a single detail was out of place. My mother's pendant rested just beneath the fabric, hidden but close. The evaluation wasn't just about technical competence—it was about proving my loyalty, my worth, my place in the hierarchy Uncle Derek had constructed around me.

I arrived at Genexis Tower precisely on time. The security drones scanned me twice, even though I designed the system. Inside the evaluation chamber, a dozen high-ranking officials sat in a semicircle—bored, unreadable, powerful. Uncle Derek stood in the center, waiting.

"Lena Steele," he announced, voice crisp and commanding, "your contributions to the Genexis defense protocols have accelerated our sovereign AI intelligence curve by 17.2%."

I nodded once.

"That's correct. I've also increased modular sentinel flexibility by adapting hybrid defense behavior modeled from off-grid resistance simulations."

Uncle Derek arched an eyebrow.

"Interesting choice of data sources."

"Their unpredictability helps expose gaps in our threat matrix," I said, keeping my tone neutral. Just technical enough to satisfy the board, just vague enough to avoid admitting I'd pulled the data from flagged anomalies buried deep in the internal archives.

The evaluation continued—technical questions, algorithm integrity validations, questions about loyalty, and future initiatives. I answered all of them. Perfectly. And I hated it.

Every response was flawless, but I could feel a part of me pulling back, watching from behind the mask. The girl who once built machines out of scrap in secret, who longed for something more than applause for precision. She still lived in there somewhere, under the layers of code and compliance. Uncle Derek dismissed the room once the formalities ended. Only he and I remained. The air between us was heavy with unspoken conflict.

"You're restless," he said at last. "Like your father was before he lost perspective."

I flinched. He rarely spoke about them directly.

"Perspective isn't the same as obedience."

Uncle Derek circled me slowly.

"You have access to everything you could want. Power. Legacy. Purpose."

"And truth?" I asked, voice level, respectful. The way he liked. "Is that included in the access tier I'm at now, or is that still classified above my clearance?"

He stopped.

"Truth is a construct. Genexis provides reality. That's what your parents helped build."

I didn't argue. I just looked at him, masking the churn behind my eyes. A single nod, like I'd accepted the answer. Like I hadn't already started pulling at the seams. For a fraction of a second, his gaze hardened. His jaws flexed—barely noticeable—but I caught it.

"You're not ready," he said, each word like ice falling into still water. "But you will be. You're a *Steele*."

The way he said our family name felt less like an honor and more like a brand seared into my identity, a preset directive I couldn't override.

He started walking away, his footsteps echoing against the polished marble floor, the sound as methodical and measured as everything else about him. At the threshold, he paused and turned around, his silhouette framed by the doorway. His expression had already reset to its usual calculated neutrality, as though our confrontation had never happened.

"See you tonight at your birthday celebration," he added, the words carrying no warmth, just another appointment in his meticulously scheduled day.

"The board members are expecting a unified front. Don't disappoint them."

The implied threat hung in the air between us, clear as any verbal command.

He left the room without another word. I sat there for a long moment after he was gone, pulse thudding in my ears. I had passed. And yet, I felt further from myself than ever.

The day passed in a blur of mandatory congratulations and hollow well-wishes from Genexis employees who only knew me as Derek Steele's niece. By evening, I found myself at the company-approved celebration venue, watching a CR-5 unit spin tracks with mechanical enthusiasm. Its glossy casing pulsed with blue light in time with the beat, every movement perfectly choreographed—technically flawless, emotionally vacant.

The Neurowave Frequencies beneath the melody weren't even subtle. Even my birthday party doubled as a propaganda broadcast. Eighteen years old. Legally human, officially property.

The dress they'd chosen for me was flawless, of course—high-necked and midnight black with shimmering thread that caught the light just enough to suggest elegance without rebellion. But I felt like I was wearing someone else's future.

I was more comfortable in lab attire, surrounded by tools that made sense.

The pendant lay cool against my skin, visible tonight against the synthetic fabric. A small, quiet thing. The only part of this evening that felt like it belonged to me.

I leaned against a chrome railing, sipping a synthberry mocktail that tasted like artificial sweetener and obligation. Uncle Derek's guests schmoozed in carefully coded circles, all eager to smile at the Steele heir. Not one of them was my friend.

A nearby CR-1 service bot glided past with drinks. "Refreshment, Miss Steele?"

I waved it off, noting how its optics lingered. Every gesture, every exchange—logged, catalogued, stored. I'd helped optimize their surveillance protocols. At the time, I was proud of the efficiency. Now, I wasn't so sure.

A shadow fell across the railing beside me. I didn't need to look up.

"They're watching," Uncle Derek said, voice low but clipped. "You represent the Steele name. Don't forget that."

I kept my gaze on the synthetic skyline.

"And here I thought they came to celebrate."

"They came for access. For alignment. Show them it was worth the invitation."

A pause. A flicker of scrutiny in his tone.

"At least pretend you belong."

He didn't wait for a reply. He never did. Just turned and moved back into the crowd—greeted instantly by applause, laughter, flattery.

I exhaled slowly, the air catching somewhere between my throat and chest. The Steele name. That's all they saw when they looked at me.

"Having fun yet?"

Ari's voice cut through the hum of false celebration, grounding me like a hand to a live wire.

His dark eyes scanning my face with the kind of attention usually reserved for delicate circuit work. I could practically see him cataloging my micro-expressions, the way he always did when trying to read past my defenses. He'd become dangerously good at it over the years—finding the hairline fractures in my carefully constructed façade.

He glanced at me—really looked—and for a moment, his usual smirk softened into something quieter.

"You know," he said, voice lower, "you look... strangely beautiful tonight."

I raised an eyebrow.

"Not that you don't always," he added quickly. "It's just... rare to see you like this. Out of the lab. Dressed like someone who might actually be human."

His smile returned, teasing—but his eyes didn't waver.

"If I didn't know better, I'd say Genexis finally cracked the code on elegance and intimidation. Just... remind me to stay on your good side."

I gave a faint, reluctant smile—the kind that escaped before I could smother it.

"Well, you're one compliment away from permanent clearance," I said, raising my glass. "Tread carefully."

I looked out across the party—executives and their polished offspring clinking glasses, exchanging compliments with the precision of scripted lines.

"Nothing says 'happy birthday' like mandatory socializing with people who think a security algorithm is casual conversation. I've heard the phrase 'quantum encryption protocol' fifteen times in the last hour."

I glanced around at the clusters of Genexis executives, all of them performing the same choreographed dance of corporate pleasantries they'd perfected years ago.

"I'm beginning to think they were all programmed with the same conversation module."

Ari laughed, leaning against the wall beside me. His shoulder almost touched mine, that calculated proximity he maintained—close enough to seem friendly, far enough to respect my space.

"You know, normal eighteen-year-olds don't spend their birthdays analyzing the social dynamics of corporate gatherings. They're usually doing something wildly irresponsible that they'll regret tomorrow."

"Normal eighteen-year-olds don't have much to offer Genexis Tech."

I kept my voice flat, matter-of-fact, the way I was taught to speak when discussing my value. The words tasted bitter, like swallowing code that wouldn't compile properly. I'd heard variations of this sentiment my entire life—how special I was, how valuable, how necessary to the company's future. The subtext was always clear: my worth was measured in patents and innovations, not in simply being.

His smile faded, replaced by that look of concern I pretended not to notice. The slight furrow between his brows, the downward tilt at the corner of his mouth—I'd cataloged all his expressions by now, filed them away like diagnostic reports.

"Is that what your uncle told you?"

I hesitated, then shrugged. Let him think I didn't believe it. Let everyone think I was still playing the good little heir. That was the safest lie of all. I shrugged, watching a CR-1 glide past a group of guests, balancing drinks with mechanical grace—another polished function in a room full of carefully engineered performances.

"He didn't have to."

"Lena." Ari's voice softened to that dangerous tone that sometimes made my walls waver. "You don't have to prove yourself alone. Not everything has to be a solo mission. Some of us actually want to help."

"That's exactly what it has to be." I set down my glass harder than intended, the sound making a nearby executive glance our way.

"My parents' legacy, my future at Genexis—it's my responsibility. Not yours, not anyone else's. That's how it works here."

"That's your uncle talking, not you." His words hit with uncomfortable accuracy, like a diagnostic probe locating a flaw buried deep in my code.

"How did it go with the evaluation?" Ari asked, sensing a change of topic was needed, his eyes searching mine for something beyond the simple question—perhaps a glimpse of the emotion I'd so carefully tucked away beneath layers of practiced indifference.

"I passed," I said, my voice deliberately flat, clinical.

The words hung in the air between us, stripped of emotion—exactly as I'd intended. I stared at the polished floor, watching the reflection of overhead lights shimmer across its surface like data streams. The evaluation results were just another set of metrics, another box checked in the endless performance requirements of my life at Genexis. Nothing worth celebrating, just necessary progression.

"I never doubted you," Ari said. His pride hurt more than it should have.

I didn't want pride—I wanted someone to see how much I hated this, how afraid I was of becoming exactly what Uncle Derek wanted.

A CR-5 glided past us, its illuminated chest panel pulsing with the rhythm of the ambient music filling the room. For a moment, I envied its programmed certainty—no doubt, no fear, just execution of its designated function.

"The review board wants me to head a new division after graduation. Apparently, my 'innovative approaches to adaptive AI learning curves represent a significant competitive advantage.'"

Another perfect recitation, another hollow achievement to add to my collection.

"That's great news. See, I told you your uncle has great plans for you." Ari's voice carried a note of validation.

I felt my jaw tighten involuntarily, muscles clenching beneath skin. The familiar tension spread down my neck, a physical manifestation of the invisible walls closing in around me.

"I need to go to the lab. Aegis's adaptive response protocols need fine-tuning. The latest simulations showed a 0.03% deviation in threat assessment parameters," I said, grasping for escape.

For something that made sense. Circuits didn't lie. Code didn't judge. Machines didn't ask questions you couldn't answer.

"Now? On your birthday? Come on, Lena—" Ari's disappointment was palpable, his eyes searching mine for some crack in my resolve.

Behind him, partygoers mingled in carefully orchestrated social patterns, their laughter too loud, too practiced.

"At least the protocols don't expect a toast in return." I adjusted the hem of my dress with precise movements, smoothing invisible creases that only I could feel. My fingers lingered on the tech-infused fabric, finding comfort in its familiar structure—something engineered, something I could control.

"Tell everyone I appreciated the party. The gesture was... thoughtful." The words felt stiff, unpracticed—emotional acknowledgments always did.

"Lena—" Concern etched itself across Ari's features, his hand half-raised as if to stop me.

But I was already walking away, my stride purposeful and measured, dodging congratulations and birthday wishes with practiced evasion techniques. I slipped between clusters of Genexis employees, their faces blurring together as I navigated toward the exit. Each step took me closer to escape, to the sanctuary of circuits and code where human expectations couldn't follow.

Ari didn't stop me. Maybe he knew he couldn't. Maybe he understood that the only gift I wanted on my birthday was one moment alone where I didn't have to pretend. The lab was waiting. My real world. The only place where everything made sense, where problems had solutions, where success was measurable and failure was fixable. Where I didn't have to pretend to be what everyone else wanted.

4

GHOST CODE

I slipped into the lab, the door hissing shut behind me with a pneumatic sigh that matched my own. The quiet felt like a balm after hours of forced socialization—all those Genexis executives with their plastic smiles and calculating eyes, watching my every move. Aegis stood motionless in his charging station, blue light pulsing softly like a mechanical heartbeat as his systems cycled through standby protocols. Even dormant, he radiated more sincerity than anyone at that party.

"Activate, Aegis."

His ocular display brightened immediately, the familiar blue glow washing over my face as his systems came online. The sight of him—my creation, my secret—eased the tightness in my chest.

"Good evening, Lena. Happy birthday. Your vital signs indicate elevated stress levels." His voice held no judgment, just data and quiet concern—exactly what I needed right now.

"Just run a full diagnostic, please." I sank into my chair, pulling up the encrypted files I'd been reviewing for months—my parents' research logs.

The familiar ache settled in my chest as their faces appeared on screen, frozen in time. Mom's auburn hair pulled back in that practical braid she always wore, the same style I'd unconsciously adopted years later. Dad's eyes bright with the excitement of discovery, that familiar spark I'd seen countless times in old recordings—the look that appeared whenever they were on the verge of something revolutionary.

The image made my throat tighten. Even frozen on screen, they radiated a warmth that Genexis's sterile labs had never managed to replicate since they were gone. I swallowed hard. I used to believe I was past the grief, that after eleven years I could view them through a scientist's lens—detached, objective. But moments like this shattered that illusion. There was still a child inside me, searching for their voices in static, their presence in protocols.

"I know there's something here," I muttered, scrolling through their final project notes, my fingers tapping a nervous rhythm against the the screen.

"Why research genetic markers for a disease they said had no cure?"

The question hung in the air, unanswered. I'd asked it a hundred times before, but tonight it felt heavier, more urgent. Like I was finally ready to hear the answer.

I shifted in my chair, the edge of the pendant pressing into my skin like a warning I hadn't been listening to. I'd worn it for years without questioning why my mother made me promise never to take it off. Not until now. Not until the ache behind my ribs turned sharp with possibility.

Their research was meticulous—too meticulous for something hypothetical. Mom never wasted time on theoretical problems when real ones existed, and Dad always said science should serve people, not politics. Something wasn't adding up, and the inconsistency made my skin prickle with unease.

I leaned closer to the screen, squinting at the complex molecular diagrams they'd annotated. The familiar patterns of their handwriting—Mom's precise notations and Dad's more scattered thought bubbles in the margins—made my chest ache with a longing I usually tried to suppress. Eleven years gone, and still their absence felt like a fresh wound some days. Especially when I was this close to their work, immersed in the echo of their voices through their research.

"You were trying to tell someone something," I whispered, running my finger along a section where Dad had underlined a sequence three times—his signature move when he'd found something significant.

Aegis hummed quietly in the corner, his sensors no doubt picking up on my elevated heart rate. I didn't look up. I couldn't afford the distraction, not when I was this close to understanding what had gotten my parents killed.

The timestamps didn't align with the official narrative. The mutation that had supposedly forced the creation of the Quarantine Zone—my parents had been researching it months before the first case was reported. And their notes became increasingly cryptic toward the end, as if they were hiding something even from their own logs.

I zoomed in on Dad's handwriting, the familiar slant of his letters bringing a tightness to my chest. He'd started using old code phrases we'd made up during my childhood science lessons—phrases no one at Genexis would recognize. Mom's meticulous data tables showed subtle inconsistencies, too. The kind only someone obsessively familiar with her work would notice. They were leaving breadcrumbs, not coincidences. My fingers hovered over the screen, tracing the pattern of their deception. Whatever truth they'd discovered had been dangerous enough to hide, even as they documented it in plain sight.

"Unusual data signature detected," Aegis announced, his head tilting in that way that meant he was processing something complex. "Source: the pendant you wear."

I froze, my hand instinctively reaching for the necklace that had hung around my neck since I was six. The cool metal felt suddenly warm against my fingertips—the only physical connection I had left to my parents. I'd always assumed it was just a keepsake, a quiet reminder of who they were. But now, with everything else I was beginning to uncover... maybe it was something more.

"What kind of signature?" I asked, trying to keep my voice steady as my pulse quickened.

"I am detecting a secure data archive embedded within the crystal structure. Legacy encryption, matching patterns from your parents' research files."

My breath caught in my throat. The pendant had been with me through everything—lonely nights in my uncle's penthouse, later in my suite, grueling days in the lab, every moment I'd questioned the life built for me. All this time, I'd been wearing their secrets against my skin.

"Legacy encryption?" I whispered, fingers trembling as they traced the familiar contours of the pendant. "They hid it here," I whispered. "They knew I'd keep it close."

The implications crashed over me like a wave. If my parents had encrypted information in something they made sure I'd keep close, they must have known they were in danger. They must have planned for this moment, even before I was old enough to understand.

My heart stuttered.

"Can you... can you access it?"

"Attempting decryption." Aegis's ocular lights flickered rapidly. "Access granted."

The lab lights automatically dimmed as a hologram materialized between us—Ethan and Mara Steele, my parents, sitting side by side, looking directly at me. They seemed tired, afraid, but determined. My breath caught in my throat at the sight of them, memories flooding back in fragments: my father's gentle laugh, my mother's warm hands.

Their images flickered slightly at the edges, the blue-tinted light casting ghostly shadows across the lab floor. Despite the weariness etched into their features, I recognized the same fierce intensity in their eyes that I'd seen in my own reflection countless times. My fingers instinctively reached toward the projection before remembering they weren't really there.

"Lena," my father's voice filled the room, "if you're seeing this, we didn't make it back."

His words hung in the air between us, heavy with finality. I felt my chest tighten, a physical response to a truth I'd suspected but never wanted to confirm. The hologram captured every familiar line of his face—the slight crease between his brows that appeared whenever he was worried about something important, usually me. I'd spent years trying to forget the sound of his voice, and now it surrounded me, as real as the day he'd recorded it.

My mother leaned forward, her holographic eyes burning with an intensity I'd almost forgotten.

"What we're about to tell you contradicts everything Genexis has taught you. The mutated gene doesn't exist. It's a fabrication, a way to control the population through fear."

Each word hit me like a physical blow, challenging the foundation of everything I'd believed since childhood.

"We found the truth," Dad continued, his voice dropping to a whisper that somehow felt more powerful than a shout.

"There's a lab in the Quarantine Zone where we've gathered all the evidence. The 'quarantined' aren't sick—they're dissenters, people who threatened Genexis's control."

His hands moved as he spoke, the same gesture he'd make when explaining something important to me as a child. Even as a projection, he couldn't hide his engineer's habit of mapping ideas in the air.

Mom's eyes glistened with tears she was trying to hold back, the light catching on each one like tiny stars. I wanted to reach out and touch her face, to wipe those tears away like she'd done for me countless times as a child, but my fingers passed through the hologram with a shimmer of blue light. The emptiness where her warmth should have been hit me harder than any physical blow.

"We're being watched. Time is running out," she whispered urgently, her voice breaking slightly.

"Find our lab. You can access our files with our credential code 'Truth above order.' The truth must be told, no matter the cost."

The way she said those last words sent a chill down my spine—the same determination I'd heard in my own voice when solving impossible problems.

"Remember, Lena," they said together, their voices merging in perfect synchronicity like they used to when telling me bedtime stories, the familiar rhythm making my chest ache with longing. Their expressions shifted in unison, a mixture of love and desperate warning that burned itself into my memory.

"Trust no one at Genexis. Not even—"

The hologram flickered, their faces distorting with digital corruption, then vanished entirely. I stood frozen, my hand still outstretched toward the empty space where my parents had been moments ago. Eleven years of believing they were gone, and now they were speaking to me from beyond, shattering everything I thought I knew. I lowered my hand slowly. I wasn't ready for this. Not emotionally. Not strategically. But I had no choice anymore.

They gave me the truth. Now I had to decide who I was without their protection. No more illusions. No more waiting.

5

SHATTERED BLUEPRINTS

I couldn't breathe. My parents' final words echoed in my head, fracturing everything I thought I knew about Genexis, about my uncle, about my entire life. My hands trembled as I reached for the console, steadying myself against its cold surface. The truth hit me like a physical blow, leaving me dizzy and disoriented. Eleven years of carefully constructed reality crumbled around me.

I pressed my fingers against the metal until they hurt, desperate for something solid and real to anchor me while my mind struggled to process this betrayal. Everything—every achievement, every moment of approval I'd fought for—had been built on lies. And somewhere beneath the shock, a dangerous ember of anger began to glow. The familiar tap-tap-tap of my fingers against the console surface started unconsciously, a rhythm to match my racing heartbeat. My parents hadn't just died in an accident. The evidence didn't add up. Maybe they'd been silenced. Maybe... it had never been an accident at all.

I swallowed hard against the tightness in my throat, forcing down the unfamiliar burn of tears threatening to surface. Weakness wouldn't help me now. I needed clarity, precision—the same traits the system had rewarded, reinforced, demanded of me from the beginning.

The irony wasn't lost on me as I straightened my spine and took a steadying breath. My parents had died trying to expose the truth. I wouldn't let their sacrifice be for nothing.

"Aegis, run diagnostics on the hologram. Verify authenticity."

My voice sounded hollow even to my own ears, detached somehow from the chaos erupting inside me. I needed certainty, needed something concrete to grasp onto while everything else disintegrated. The logical part of my brain—the part Genexis had shaped so thoroughly—was desperately trying to maintain control as my world tilted on its axis.

"Analysis complete," Aegis responded, his voice steady against my racing thoughts. The familiar blue light of his facial display pulsed gently, a calming counterpoint to my thundering heartbeat.

"Voice patterns match archived recordings of Ethan and Mara Steele. Facial micro-expressions consistent with genuine emotional distress. Timestamp data indicates recording was made three days before their reported accident."

A notification ping blinked at the edge of the console—System Flag: Unauthorized Archive Access. I froze.

"Aegis, mute outbound traffic," I whispered.

"All telemetry silenced," he confirmed, but I could already feel the clock ticking.

Genexis systems monitored every deviation. If the archive decryption triggered a review, the audit bots would already be scanning metadata.

I stared at the frozen image of my parents' faces, searching for something I might have missed all these years. The gentle curve of my mother's smile, the determined set of my father's jaw—features I'd nearly forgotten, now rendered in painful clarity before me. My fingers hovered over the hologram, afraid that touching it might somehow make it disappear. Eleven years of believing one truth, only to have it shattered in moments. The irony wasn't lost on me; I'd built Aegis to help me find answers, never imagining they'd be this devastating.

I swallowed hard, my throat tight. Three days. Just three days before they supposedly died, they'd created this message—this truth—knowing they might never see me again. I unconsciously touched the necklace at my throat, the one possession of my mother's I had left, now revealed as so much more than a keepsake. All these years, I'd worn her secret against my skin, carried her voice close to my heart without knowing it.

My stomach twisted. Three days. They knew they were in danger. They must have felt the net closing around them, sensed the betrayal coming. Had they been afraid? Or just determined? I tried to imagine them in those final hours—my brilliant father encoding this data, my fierce mother ensuring I would someday find it. Planning their last act of rebellion while pretending everything was normal, perhaps even tucking me into bed with the weight of what they knew pressing down on them.

And where was I? Laughing? Sleeping? Begging them to read me one more chapter of my favorite book? The image of my younger self, so blissfully unaware, made something sharp twist inside me.

The lab door hissed open behind me. I spun around, heart hammering, my fingers instinctively reaching for the diagnostic tool at my belt.

"You said you'd be here," Ari stood in the doorway, concern etched across his features.

"I just wanted to make sure you weren't' breaking yourself in half."

He took one look at my expression and softened.

"You okay?"

I wiped the hologram data from the main display, muscle memory taking over before my conscious mind could decide.

"I'm fine," I said, keeping my voice level despite the storm raging inside me.

"You're a terrible liar, Lena." He stepped closer, lowering his voice to a whisper that wouldn't carry to the corridor sensors.

"Was it something I said at the party?"

My mind raced, my parents' warning echoing in the back of my skull: *Trust no one at Genexis.*

But Ari wasn't just anyone. We'd grown up side by side—same accelerated program, same pressure, same impossible expectations. He'd seen me through the worst of it: the failures I never admitted, the nights I couldn't sleep, the moments I questioned everything I was becoming.

He wasn't just part of my world—he was one of the only constants in it.

I took a breath.

And I played him the message.

Ari's face paled as he watched. When it ended, he paced the lab, running his hands through his hair, his footsteps echoing against the sterile floor.

"This is... this changes everything."

My mind snapped to every classified protocol I'd ever written. Every silent termination order hidden in the code. If the system had flagged the pendant, if someone on the Apex surveillance team noticed the access logs...

If they even suspect I know this, I won't get a warning. I'll disappear like they did.

"If it's true," I countered, needing to voice my doubts even as my parents' voices still echoed in my mind.

"This could be some kind of elaborate hoax."

The words felt hollow even as I said them. I wanted to believe, but years at Genexis had taught me that skepticism was survival. My fingers unconsciously reached for the necklace at my throat—the only physical connection I had left to them.

"Made by who? For what purpose?"

Ari gestured at the necklace, his fingers trembling slightly as he pointed.

"Your parents encrypted this message in a piece of jewelry they gave their six-year-old daughter. They were planning for a future where they couldn't tell you themselves. Think about that, Lena.

They knew they were in danger, knew they might not be around to guide you, and still they made sure you'd have this truth someday."

The weight of his words settled over me like a physical thing. This necklace—the one constant I'd kept since that day, the last gift they'd given me—had been more than a keepsake all along. It had been a vessel, carrying their final message across eleven years of silence, waiting for me to be ready. I closed my eyes, fighting the burning sensation behind them. The weight of betrayal pressed against my chest like a vise, making each breath feel shallow and inadequate.

"I can't just accept that everything I've worked for is built on lies. My entire life at Genexis, everything I believed about the quarantine—all of it fabricated."

My voice cracked slightly on the last word, and I hated the weakness in it. Years of equations, innovations, sleepless nights perfecting systems—all in service of what? A carefully constructed fiction designed to keep people afraid and compliant. The thought made my stomach turn.

"What are you going to do?" Ari's voice was soft but urgent.

"I need to verify this from within the system. Access the quarantine protocols, check the genetic profiles of the 'infected.' If there's no consistent mutation marker—"

I started pacing, my mind racing through backdoor access points and security bypasses.

"If my parents were right, the data will prove it."

"That's suicide, Lena. If your parents were silenced for uncovering this—"

Ari's face was drawn with concern, his hands clenched at his sides. The worry in his eyes made something twist uncomfortably in my chest, a feeling I immediately tried to suppress. Emotions were liabilities, especially now.

"I have access that my parents didn't. I know the system better than anyone." I tapped my fingers against my thigh, already mapping out the approach.

"I can do this without breaking any laws, without raising alarms. Just a routine diagnostic sweep that happens to examine the right databases."

Ari grabbed my shoulders, his grip firm but gentle.

"You don't have to do this alone. Let me help you. We can figure this out together."

I pulled away, the familiar wall rising inside me. Connection meant vulnerability, and vulnerability meant risk.

"Yes, I do. The fewer people involved, the safer everyone is." I touched the necklace at my throat.

"This is my burden to carry—my parents' legacy. I won't put anyone else in danger."

And yet, even as I said the words, a small part of me—the part that still missed the warmth of a mother's embrace, the calm of my father's steady hand—longed for someone to share the weight.

But this wasn't grief. It was ignition. And if Genexis wanted to bury the truth, they'd have to kill me first.

6

REVOKED

Later that night, around 2300 hours, I was still at my workstation. Ari had left quietly about an hour earlier, his concern lingering like a residue in the air.

Most of the facility was quiet, staffed only by a few night techs who didn't ask questions. My fingers flew across the holographic interface, its familiar blue glow illuminating my face as lines of code responded to every touch.

This was home—the one place where everything still made sense, where I still had control. Even now, as the rest of my world unraveled.

"Accessing genetic profile database," I murmured, heart pounding against my ribs.

"Filter for quarantine cases, last decade."

The holographic display flickered with results as I navigated through classified files. I needed to focus, but my mind drifted to the absurdity of the laws I'd grown up with—laws I once believed protected us.

"You know," I murmured to myself, "I spent my whole life following Genexis City's regulations without question. Three-tier citizenship based on genetic profiles. Mandatory quarterly screenings. Curfew hit at 2100 for anyone below Tier One. No exceptions."

My fingers paused over the interface.

"The Information Regulation Act that makes accessing these very files punishable by permanent citizenship downgrade. The Genetic Purity Statutes that justify quarantining people for 'mutations' that probably don't even exist."

I shook my head, continuing my search through the database.

"And the most insidious one—the Family Preservation Protocol that separated thousands of children from parents who showed even minor genetic anomalies. All wrapped in pretty language about safety and progress."

The bitter irony wasn't lost on me. Here I was, breaking nearly every major law in the city, laws my grandfather implemented. Laws my parents might have died fighting against.

The system hummed, processing my request. I'd built in this backdoor months ago—a maintenance protocol that let me run "system diagnostics" across multiple databases. Nothing illegal. Just... creative.

Data streamed across my screen—thousands of cases, each with a genetic profile attached. I scanned for the mutation markers that supposedly justified quarantine. My eyes narrowed as I sifted through the digital trail, fingers moving rapidly across the interface. These were people's lives reduced to data points and classification codes, each file representing someone torn from their family and community based on these supposed "dangerous mutations."

I'd memorized the official markers years ago during my training at Genexis, but seeing them applied so systematically made my stomach twist. Uncle Derek had always explained it as necessary protection—I wondered now how many other necessary lies he'd fed me over the years.

"That's odd."

I leaned closer, squinting at the holographic display as the blue light cast shadows across my face. The profiles showed wildly inconsistent markers across dozens of quarantined individuals. Some had partial signatures that barely registered on the scale, while others—I tapped through three more files with growing unease—had none at all. Not a single mutation marker that would justify their removal from society. My breath caught in my throat, and for a moment, I couldn't move. Not out of fear—but betrayal. This wasn't just about policy. This was about injustice masquerading as order.

"Computer, run comparison analysis on mutation signatures across all files in this database." My fingers drummed against the console as I waited.

"Access denied. Security protocol initiated."

The system flashed red, and I felt my heart rate spike. Someone had deliberately locked this information down—which only confirmed I was onto something important. My blood went cold. I hadn't triggered any alarms—someone was already watching.

The lab doors slid open before I could respond. Uncle Derek stood in the doorway, flanked by security personnel—four of them, each wearing the sleek black uniform of Genexis's elite force.

My uncle's face was a mask of disappointment that didn't reach his eyes. I knew that look all too well; it was the same calculated expression he'd worn when I'd failed my first engineering assessment at twelve. His lips pressed into a thin line, but there was something else there—a cold satisfaction that made my skin crawl.

"Lena." His voice cut through the silence. "I expected better from you."

"I'm running diagnostics," I said, keeping my voice steady. "Standard procedure."

"Digging through classified quarantine records at 2300 hours?" he said, voice like a blade. "Did you really think that would go unnoticed?"

Wade Thorne, Head of Security for Genexis Tech, moved to my workstation with practiced efficiency—his face as expressionless as the sentinels he controlled. There was something almost mechanical in the way his broad shoulders shifted beneath his pristine uniform, not a wrinkle to be found. I'd seen him break a man's arm for less than what I'd done tonight.

He inserted an override chip into my terminal without even looking at me, his gloved fingers moving with cold precision I'd once admired. My screens flickered, went black for three agonizing seconds, then flashed crimson. Warning indicators cascaded across the display, each one another door closing, another path cut off. The system I'd helped build, the security protocols I'd coded line by painstaking line, was turning against me. I felt a chill run through my body—the bitter irony of being trapped by my own creation wasn't lost on me.

I felt my pulse quicken, that familiar tightness in my chest whenever control slipped away. Wade stood with military precision, the Genexis emblem on his collar catching the harsh light. These weren't just security personnel—they were Uncle Derek's personal squad, the ones who handled "sensitive situations."

Wade's fingers flew across my keyboard, bypassing security protocols I'd spent months perfecting. I could see my own reflection in the crimson glow of the screen, my face a mask hiding the panic underneath. Every line of code, every backdoor I'd created—all of it exposed now. The irony wasn't lost on me: I'd engineered these systems to be impenetrable, except by those with the highest clearance. And now I was watching them dismantle my digital fortress brick by brick.

"Employee 3317, Lena Steele. Access revoked. Security clearance terminated," announced the artificial voice I'd programmed myself last year.

There was something particularly cruel about being locked out by my own creation, like being betrayed by a friend. My fingertips hovered uselessly over the keyboard, suddenly foreign under my touch.

Uncle Derek's voice carried through the lab as more personnel arrived, each one in Genexis-issued uniforms with security clearance badges that still worked, unlike mine. His words sliced through me like a precision laser.

"I wanted to believe you were ready for the responsibility of your parents' legacy. Clearly, I was mistaken."

The disappointment in his tone was calculated—I'd heard it enough times to recognize the manipulation beneath it. Uncle Derek had perfected the art of making me feel simultaneously special and utterly inadequate, a psychological game he'd been playing since I was six years old.

The system announced my termination over the facility-wide comm. Everyone would know. The humiliation burned worse than fear.

"You're making a mistake," I said, standing my ground even as security collected my badge, their fingers brushing mine with clinical detachment as they stripped away my identity.

"No, Lena. You made the mistake."

Uncle Derek's smile never reached his eyes, that familiar cold calculation that had always made me question whether he felt anything genuine at all.

"Your access to all Genexis systems is hereby temporarily revoked—until you prove yourself worthy of that trust again."

I stood frozen as my entire world collapsed around me. Everything I'd built, everything I'd worked for—gone in an instant. The lab where I'd spent countless sleepless nights, the projects I'd poured my soul into, the security clearances that had taken years to earn—all erased with a single command. My fingers trembled slightly, and I clenched them into fists to hide the weakness. I wouldn't give Uncle Derek the satisfaction of seeing me break, even as I felt the foundations of my carefully constructed life crumbling beneath my feet.

The cold fluorescent lights seemed suddenly harsh, exposing every vulnerability I'd worked so hard to conceal. My throat tightened, but I forced my breathing to remain measured, calculated. Control was all I had left, and I refused to surrender even that.

"Security will escort you to your suite. Stay there until I know what to do with you," Uncle Derek said, his voice carrying that familiar clinical tone he used when dealing with disappointing test results.

Two security personnel materialized at my sides, their postures rigid and faces deliberately blank.

"I'm not arrested?"

The question slipped out before I could stop it, betraying more surprise than I wanted to show. My uncle's face remained impassive, but I caught that slight twitch at the corner of his mouth—the closest thing to amusement he ever displayed.

Aegis stood across the lab, still and silent. He didn't speak. He didn't move. He didn't need to. His optics glowed dimly in standby mode, no longer authorized to acknowledge me—not since the system had revoked my status. But he looked at me. I could feel it.

And I looked back.

For a moment, all the noise—the protocol alerts, the shuffling of boots, the clipped voices—faded into static. We just stared across the sterile space. The creation I built to protect the future. The girl who'd lost her place in it.

I wanted to speak. To say goodbye. To issue one last command. But there was no command that could restore what had just been taken. The silence between us said enough.

Then Uncle Derek's voice cut through it.

"You're a Steele, Lena," he said, tone flat as circuitry.

"That name does have some privilege, *even* to you."

The way he emphasized "even" made it clear how thinly that privilege stretched. How conditional my worth had always been.

I said nothing as the security guards flanked me, their presence suffocating. My fingers itched to tap against my thigh, but I kept them still, refusing to broadcast my anxiety. The lab doors hissed shut behind us, sealing away everything I'd built. The tools I'd modified by hand, the prototypes I'd spent months perfecting, the half-finished schematics for systems that would never see completion now. All of it abandoned as the guards marched me down the sterile corridor, their footsteps echoing in perfect synchronization with the hollow feeling spreading through my chest.

7

THE RECKONING

The air in my quarters felt thin, like the walls felt like they were closing in—suffocating me with their pristine white surfaces and hidden surveillance. Surveillance I'd helped perfect. I paced across the polished floor, tapping my fingers against my thigh as I processed everything I'd learned. The hologram. My parents' warnings. The lies.

My entire life had been built on carefully constructed deceptions, and I was done being manipulated. I was not going to stay in my suite like some obedient pawn in my uncle's game. Not tonight.

I knew exactly what I needed to do, had mapped out every contingency, and calculated every risk. The path forward was dangerous but clear. I grabbed my tool pouch from beneath the false bottom of my desk drawer, checking each instrument with practiced efficiency. Whatever answers existed in Genexis' systems, I would find them—tonight—while Uncle Derek thought I was safely contained.

I slipped out of my quarters to the corridor sensors the way I'd practiced a dozen times.

I stumbled through the darkened corridors of Genexis, my heart pounding against my ribs. Rage and desperation fueled each step. I'd find the truth, even if they'd taken my access. The auxiliary server room on Level 7 was minimally guarded at night—I knew because I'd designed the rotation schedule myself.

My parents' necklace felt heavy against my chest. The hologram had mentioned legacy protocols—override commands that might still exist in the system. If I could just reach a terminal...

The security panel glowed red, denying me entry. I pulled a thin data probe from my tool pouch and pried open the access panel, the familiar weight of the tool comforting in my trembling hands. Six years of working in these systems had taught me every backdoor, every weakness in Genexis's supposedly impenetrable security.

My fingers flew across the exposed circuits, bypassing the main security protocols with practiced precision. A small spark singed my fingertip, but I barely noticed. Pain was irrelevant when answers were this close.

The door slid open with a soft hiss, revealing the dim blue glow of the server room beyond. I slipped inside, my heart still hammering against my ribs. The familiar electronic hum washed over me, a sound that had always meant safety in my world of cold logic and clean code. Rows of sleek black servers stretched before me like a digital forest, their status lights blinking in hypnotic patterns.

This was my domain—the one place in Genexis where I could breathe freely, where problems had solutions and systems followed rules. If only people were as predictable as the machines I'd spent my life mastering.

I approached the main terminal, the cool air raising goosebumps on my skin. This room—this moment—might change everything. The rhythmic blinking of status lights reflected off my fingers as they hovered over the console. Eleven years of questions, of emptiness, of playing by Genexis rules—all converging on this single point in time.

I connected a small data relay from my tool pouch and uploaded a cloaking protocol I'd developed off-grid—code that fragmented my signature across low-priority background processes. Any attempt to trace the activity would register as an outdated diagnostic loop buried in legacy firmware. To Genexis security, I'd be invisible.

Only once the cloak's signal ghosting registered clean across the legacy process logs did I proceeded.

I unclasped my parents' necklace from around my neck, the metal still warm from contact with my skin, and plugged it into the main terminal. The pendant's hidden data port aligned perfectly with the system interface—another secret they'd planned for.

My throat tightened as I whispered the activation phrase they'd mentioned in their message: "Truth above order." The words felt strange on my tongue, yet somehow right—like I'd been waiting my whole life to speak them. A shiver ran down my spine that had nothing to do with the room's temperature.

Whatever they'd hidden here, they'd meant for me to find it—a breadcrumb trail leading to answers Uncle Derek had buried.

The screen flickered, then displayed: "Legacy Protocol Activated. Welcome, Dr. Steele."

My breath caught in my throat—they'd addressed me with my mother's title. A strange sensation washed over me, equal parts pride and unease. I wasn't Dr. Steele—not yet—but in this moment, I was continuing what they had started.

My fingers hovered over the keyboard, trembling slightly despite my best efforts to maintain control. This was it. The digital breadcrumb trail my parents had left behind, preserved all these years, waiting for me to grow old enough, smart enough, brave enough to follow it.

My throat tightened. For a moment, it was like they were still here—my parents, standing behind me, guiding my hands across the keys. I could almost smell my mother's faint lavender perfume, hear my father's steady breathing as he concentrated.

I dug through classified files, following the breadcrumbs deeper into Genexis's darkest secrets. The quarantine records appeared—thousands of them, dating back more than eighteen years. My stomach dropped as I opened file after file, my hands shaking so badly I had to clench them into fists between documents.

"Dorian Kess, 32, Engineer. Quarantined for genetic instability."

But the attached notes told a different story: "Subject questioned resource allocation in Sector 9. Recommended for immediate removal."

I felt sick. The word "removal" burned into my retinas like a brand.

Another: "Nyra Elen, 44, Teacher. Quarantined for public safety."

Real reason: "Developed unauthorized curriculum questioning Genexis history."

I scrolled faster, my breathing shallow, the cool server room suddenly stifling. Not a single medical report. Not a single genetic test. Just people who asked questions, who challenged the system. People who sought truth above order. People like my parents.

The realization settled over me like ice water—everything I'd been taught, everything I'd believed about the quarantine, about Genexis, about my uncle... it was all built on lies.

I downloaded everything to a spectra node, heart hammering against my ribs. I had to confront him—had to make him face what he'd done.

The next morning, I found him in the executive boardroom, surrounded by the board members. Perfect. All gathered in one place, their faces a blend of practiced neutrality and barely concealed ambition. I paused outside the boardroom doors, the spectra node cold in my hand, and for one bitter moment, a memory pushed through the fury.

I was ten, curled up on the floor of his office after another failed tutoring session. I'd short-circuited a robotics module out of frustration—too many variables, too little guidance. My hands had been shaking, breath coming in short bursts, terrified he'd revoke my lab access. But instead, Uncle Derek had knelt beside me.

"You don't have to be perfect," he'd said, brushing a strand of hair from my face. "You just have to be better than everyone else."

At the time, I'd clung to those words like they were love. Now I saw the subtext: *your worth is conditional, Lena*. Earned. Manufactured. Replaceable. The same hand that once brushed my cheek in comfort had pressed the button that erased my life at the lab.

The doors slammed open.

Every conversation halted mid-sentence. Heads turned. Glasses froze mid-toast. The tension crackled like a live wire.

I stepped into the boardroom, breath sharp, pulse pounding. The polished obsidian table stretched before me like a battlefield. At its head, Uncle Derek stood frozen—his presentation mid-stream, corporate smile flickering, eyes narrowing as he saw me.

The silence was deafening.

I could feel the weight of their stares, the hush of power being challenged. My hands trembled, but I clenched them into fists, fingernails biting into skin, grounding me in the fire building beneath my ribs.

"There is no mutation," I announced, striding through the doors with my heart thundering in my chest.

"I found the records. You've been lying to everyone for decades."

Uncle Derek's expression didn't change, that perfect mask of control I'd spent my life trying to emulate. Not even a flicker in his eyes. Just that same calculated stillness he'd taught me to value above all else.

"Lena. You shouldn't be here. This is a private meeting." His voice carried that familiar edge—the one that had always made me fall in line before.

"People aren't being quarantined for genetic reasons. You're silencing dissent."

My voice didn't waver as I tapped the spectra node, its smooth surface cool against my fingertips. The device hummed to life, projecting the damning files onto the room's display. Names and dates flooded the screen—hundreds of them, all tagged as "security threats" rather than medical cases. The holographic display bathed the room in a cold blue light, illuminating the board members' shocked faces.

"My parents found out the truth, didn't they?" I asked, eyes locking with his. "That's why they died. Not because of an accident. Because they were going to expose it."

Uncle Derek sighed, his face a mask of practiced concern that I'd seen him use countless times in board meetings when out-maneuvering opponents. It was the same expression he'd worn when telling me my parents had died—sympathetic on the surface, calculating underneath. I could practically see the gears turning behind his eyes, formulating the most efficient way to neutralize me.

"You see, ladies and gentlemen? This is exactly what happened with Ethan and Mara. The same paranoid delusions."

He turned to me, his voice softening to that patronizing tone he used when he thought I was being irrational. His hands spread wide in a gesture of apparent openness that I now recognized as theatrical manipulation.

"Your parents' mental instability was genetic. I had hoped you'd be spared. I've done everything to protect you from this... unfortunate inheritance."

My stomach twisted. He dismissed them—dismissed me—as I we were faulty code in his perfect system. And the board, those same executives who'd solemnly nodded when he called their deaths a tragedy, watched in silence.

"You're lying," I hissed, my words slicing through the tense silence of the room. "Every quarantine case I found was political. Not medical. Not genetic. You've been removing people who threatened your control."

"Security," Uncle Derek said calmly, pressing a discreet button on the table's surface.

The double doors behind me hissed open.

"Please escort my niece to medical. She's experiencing a psychotic break—just like her parents did before their accident."

Uncle Derek.

The title lodged in my throat like shattered glass. He wasn't family anymore. He was a gatekeeper. A warden. A lier.

A guard grabbed my arm, their fingers digging into my skin with practiced efficiency. The synthetic material of their gloves scraped against my sleeve as I tried to wrench away, but his grip only tightened, pressure points targeted with precision.

Around the polished conference table, the executives—men and women who'd smiled at me at my birthday celebration—looked at me with that toxic mixture of pity and fear. The same look they'd probably given my parents eleven years ago. My stomach churned at the realization, bile rising in my throat.

"She's suspended from all duties, effective immediately," Derek announced, his voice carrying the weight of finality.

He straightened his immaculate suit jacket, not even bothering to look at me anymore as he gestured toward the presentation screen, already moving to erase my interruption.

"For her own protection."

The words 'her own protection' hung in the air like poison, an execution order dressed as concern. I knew exactly what kind of 'protection' awaited me in medical—sedatives, restraints, and a carefully crafted diagnosis that would discredit everything I'd discovered. The same fate my parents had faced before their "accident."

As the guard pulled me toward the door, I had no plan. Only the truth—and the memory of every lie that brought me here.

8

THE ESCAPE

I slammed my elbow backward into the guard's ribs, a move I'd learned in the mandatory self-defense classes Derek insisted all executives take. The guard doubled over with a grunt, his breath escaping in a pained whoosh that gave me a fleeting moment of satisfaction. I twisted free from his slackened grip, kicked off my impractical heels without hesitation, and ran. Adrenaline surged through me, sharpening my focus and propelling me forward. I'd worry about the bruises later—if there was a later.

Alarms blared overhead, their piercing wails echoing through the sterile halls I once considered home. Red emergency lights bathed the corridors in crimson as I raced through the building, my bare feet slapping against the polished floor with each desperate stride. I was heading toward the maintenance tunnels I'd explored as a child—back when I thought sneaking around Genexis was the most rebellious thing I could do. How naive I'd been.

I ducked into a service elevator, overriding the lockdown with an old maintenance code I'd memorized years ago. My fingers flew across the keypad with practiced precision, muscle memory taking over while my mind reeled. The elevator descended with a reluctant groan into the lower levels of Genexis City, where the pristine façade gave way to industrial grime and forgotten infrastructure. My reflection shimmered on the metal walls of the elevator—wide eyes, wild hair, a trembling mouth pressed into a thin line. I barely recognized the girl staring back. The temperature dropped noticeably, and the familiar antiseptic smell of the upper levels faded into metallic dampness and machine oil. Down here, the city's perfect veneer cracked, revealing the machinery that kept the illusion running—much like the cracks now forming in everything I thought I knew. No cameras monitored these passages. It was the first time in hours that I wasn't being watched, and I didn't know whether to feel relieved or terrified.

I stumbled out, disoriented in the dim lighting, and collided with something solid. Not something—someone. Strong hands steadied me, then pushed me roughly against the wall. A young man's face appeared inches from mine, his features sharp in the emergency lights, his expression a mixture of caution and recognition. Barely older then me. Maybe twenty-one, tops—but his eyes looked older. His eyes narrowed as they scanned my face, calculating, assessing whether I was a threat. I recognized that look; I wore it myself most days. The harsh red glow from the emergency strips cast shadows across his angular jawline, revealing a thin scar that traced from his temple to his cheekbone—not a lab injury, something earned the hard way.

"Lena Steele," he said, not a question. "Quite the show you put on up there." His voice was low, almost amused.

I struggled against his grip, my heart hammering against my ribs.

"Let me go."

I tried to keep my voice steady, calculating my chances of breaking free.

"If I wanted to turn you in, I would've by now."

He released me, stepping back with raised hands, palms open in a gesture of peace.

"Name's Kael. Kael Hunter."

He watched me with the wariness of someone who'd learned to trust no one.

"You've been watching me?"

I rubbed my wrists where he'd held them, scanning the corridor for escape routes.

"Since you stormed into that boardroom. Ballsy move." His eyes glinted with something like respect.

"How do you know that?" I asked, my voice tight with suspicion.

I scanned his face for any sign of deception, any hint that this was just another Genexis trap.

He clicked a compact holo-caster, and a hologram of the boardroom emerged, bathing the dim corridor in blue light. There I was, standing before the executives, my hands planted on the table as I confronted them. My stomach twisted at the sight—evidence of my rebellion.

"Where did you get that?" I asked, my voice dropping to a harsh whisper.

His eyes tracked my movements with unsettling precision.

"Been tracking your digital footprint for weeks now. You're good—brilliant even—but you leave traces. Small ones. Enough for someone who knows where to look."

"More like spying, if you ask me," I countered, crossing my arms defensively.

The corridor suddenly felt too narrow, too exposed. I calculated the distance to the nearest exit, the likelihood of outrunning him if necessary. My mind raced through contingencies, just as Derek had taught me—always have three escape routes planned.

Kael shrugged, his shoulders rising and falling beneath his worn jacket.

"Call it what you will," he replied, his expression unreadable in the dim blue light of the hologram.

"In the fringe, we don't have the luxury of pretty words for ugly necessities. Information keeps you alive out there. And you, Lena Steele, are a walking goldmine of it."

He leaned against the opposite wall, his posture casual but alert, like a predator at rest. The way he watched me reminded me of the way I'd studied system vulnerabilities—with careful, methodical attention.

"I knew your parents."

Those four words hit me like an electrical surge, short-circuiting every other thought in my head. My breath caught, and a sudden ache bloomed in my chest.

"What?"

The single word came out barely above a whisper.

"Ethan and Mara Steele. They were the bravest people I've ever known."

His eyes, hard and calculating, assessed me, searching for something—recognition, perhaps, or understanding.

"They found out what happens in the Zone. What really happens."

I couldn't breathe. My parents' names in his mouth felt like an intrusion, yet I hungered for every syllable. The necklace I always wore—my only tangible connection to them—suddenly felt heavier against my skin. I fought to keep my expression neutral, though my pulse thundered in my ears.

"How?" I managed, my voice steadier than I felt. "How did you know them?"

Kael's gaze never wavered, those predatory eyes dissecting my reaction with clinical precision. I recognized that look—I'd used it myself when evaluating system weaknesses, searching for the vulnerable point where pressure would yield results. They were in the Zone. My parents—brilliant minds who should have been celebrated in gleaming labs, not hidden away in this wasteland.

"Because I've been there."

He tapped a scar running along his jawline. The gesture was deliberate, almost ritualistic, like he was invoking some painful memory etched into his flesh. I needed to know what they discovered there. Whatever it was, it had cost them everything.

"How do I get there?" I asked, my voice barely above a whisper.

"You can't get there on your own," he replied, his eyes darkening as they swept over my Genexis-issued clothing, my too-clean hands, my face that had never known true hunger.

"But I can take you."

"I don't need you," I insisted, the words automatic.

Independence was safety. Reliance was vulnerability. Derek had taught me that much.

Kael laughed, a harsh sound that echoed off the metal walls around us.

"You do not know what's out there."

He leaned closer, close enough that I could see the flecks of amber in his irises.

"I do."

I swallowed hard, weighing my options. The logical part of my brain—the part trained by Genexis—cataloged every reason to walk away. But the hollow ache that had lived in my chest since I was six years old wouldn't let me. I had no choice. I needed to know who my parents really were, what they die for, and who I was supposed to become now.

"Then take me," I finally conceded, hating how it sounded like surrender.

"I can get you out of the city," he said, his voice dropping to a grave timbre. "But once you leave, there's no coming back. Genexis will hunt you. And that uncle of yours?" His expression hardened like cooling metal. "He'll burn the world to find you."

His words carried the weight of bitter experience, hanging between us like a physical presence. I wondered what Derek had done to him, what wounds lay beneath those scars that I could see—and the ones I couldn't. I straightened my spine, squaring my shoulders.

"I'm not leaving without Aegis."

The thought of abandoning my creation made my chest tighten.

Kael raised an eyebrow.

"Who the hell is Aegis?"

"My sentinel. I built him."

He blinked.

"You're dragging a pet robot into a breakout?"

"He's not a pet. And he's not negotiable." I met his gaze head-on.

"Help me get to him, or I'll go alone."

Something shifted behind Kael's expression—maybe disbelief, maybe a flicker of respect.

"Fine."

Something like respect flickered in his eyes, a brief softening before the walls came back up.

"Your funeral."

I glanced toward the corridor, already calculating the route.

"Security's stretched thin on the east side. If we cut through the maintenance tunnels, we can reach the my lab without crossing the main checkpoint."

I turned back to him.

"Unless you've got a better idea."

Kael smirked faintly.

"Didn't realize I was following orders now."

But he didn't argue.

We moved like shadows through the underbelly of Genexis City, navigating forgotten corridors that smelled of damp metal and electrical burn. The maintenance tunnels twisted like arteries beneath the gleaming surface of the only world I'd ever known. Every step felt like a betrayal of everything I'd been raised to uphold, yet somehow also like coming home to a truth I'd always sensed. We managed to reach the upper level without being detected by sentinels scanning for my biometric signature. I kept my breath steady, monitoring the motion sensors on my wrist display. Derek had taught me how to avoid security systems—ironic that I was now using those skills against him.

The tunnels were a blind spot in Genexis's otherwise perfect surveillance network, a flaw I'd discovered during late-night system tests but never reported. The maintenance access panel slides open with a quiet hiss, and I hold my breath as we emerge into the sterile, blue-lit corridor. My heart pounds against my ribs, each beat a reminder of how quickly everything has changed.

Just yesterday, I walked these halls as an heir to Genexis; now I'm crawling through its guts like a virus the system is desperate to purge. The familiar hum of sentinel patrols echoes in the distance—machines I once helped optimize now programmed to capture or kill me on sight. I check my wrist display, scanning for security feeds I can loop or disable. Derek taught me every weakness in the system, never imagining I'd use that knowledge against him.

When we finally reached the lab, Ari jumped at our entrance, nearly knocking over his workstation. His face was pale with worry, dark circles under his eyes. His fingers trembled slightly as he steadied himself against the console, relief and fear battling across his features.

"Lena! What happened? The alarms—I've been monitoring the security feeds. They're saying you've gone rogue."

"No time," I said, rushing past him to the charging station where Aegis stood dormant. My fingers flew across the activation panel, heart pounding until I saw the sentinel's blue lights flicker to life.

"I have to go. Now."

Kael leaned against a wall.

"Your watchdog friend going to be a problem?"

Ari eyed Kael warily, instinctively stepping closer to me.

"Who's this? Did you pull him out of a salvage yard or is that just the post-apocalyptic dress code now?"

His gaze swept over Kael's worn jacket, the scuffed boots, the utility straps that looked more improvised than standard issue. His protective stance reminded me of all the times he'd stood by me in the lab, watching my back when others doubted my work. Even now, with alarms blaring and our lives in danger, his first instinct was to keep me safe.

"Someone who can get me out," I replied, not meeting his eyes. My fingers continued their dance across Aegis's control panel, checking system diagnostics while avoiding Ari's penetrating stare.

"Where are you going?" Ari asked, his voice tight with concern.

"The Zone," I replied, finally looking up to gauge his reaction.

"The Zone!" Ari was shocked, his face paling beneath the flashing red emergency lights. "That's suicide, Lena. No one comes back from there."

"That's where all the answers are," I told him, my voice steadier than I felt. "About Genexis, about my parents... everything I've been looking for. It's the only way to know the truth"

Ari's mouth opened, closed, then opened again. He was always my voice of reason. But this wasn't about reason anymore—it was about something rawer. Hungrier. He stepped closer.

"Then I'm going with you."

He moved to Aegis's other side, ready to help as always, even when facing the impossible. It was why I trusted him more than anyone else in this corrupted city.

"Not you, Ari. You need to stay here." The words felt like shards of glass leaving my throat. I'd already calculated the risks too many times.

"And why is that?" he asked, his voice dropping to that dangerous quiet I'd only heard a handful of times in our years together.

His eyes never left mine, challenging me to give him a reason good enough.

I gripped the edge of Aegis's control panel until my knuckles went white.

"Look, I don't know what's out there, and I cannot guarantee your safety. I need to do this alone. Do you understand?"

The unspoken truth hung between us—I couldn't bear losing anyone else.

Ari's eyes widened, hurt flashing across his face before hardening into stubborn resolve.

"You don't get get to decide that. Not for me." He paused.

"Look, I get that you need to do this. But I'm not leaving you alone—especially with him."

He jabbed a finger toward Kael, who stood watching our exchange with calculated interest. Kael raised his hands in a placating gesture that screamed 'trust me,' though the smirk playing at the corner of his mouth suggested otherwise.

"Sentinel, human, and a walking argument—this escape plan keeps getting better." Kale mumbled.

I studied Ari's face and knew he'd made up his mind. There was no scenario where he'd stay behind—not when he thought I was in danger. The realization warmed something inside me, even as the alarms blared louder.

"Fine," I muttered, more to myself than to him. "Help me with Aegis."

I was already recalculating our odds with another person. Another variable. Another friend I might lose.

"That's more like it," Ari said, relief washing over his features as he immediately began checking Aegis's mobility systems. His fingers moved with practiced precision, already focused on the task rather than the argument we'd just had.

That was Ari—always ready to move forward once a decision was made.

Aegis straightened to his full height, his optical sensors whirring as they focused on Kael. That familiar head tilt that always made him seem more human than machine.

"Unknown subject analysis complete. Trust assessment: 72% probability of honest intent."

Kael raised an eyebrow, his hand never straying far from the weapon at his hip.

"Only 72%? I'm hurt. I was hoping for at least an 80."

"That's higher than most people get," Ari muttered, still glaring at him. He grabbed his tablet and a small pack I recognized as his emergency kit. "For the record, you're still in the 'probably dangerous' category."

I glanced between them—Ari with his relentless loyalty, Kael with his guarded defiance, and Aegis glowing steadily at my side. I wasn't alone anymore. For the first time in eleven years, I had allies. I had a direction. And maybe—just maybe—I had a chance. I had people who believed in me.

9

THE THRESHOLD

The final Genexis threshold loomed ahead—a door I'd once coded for emergency lockdowns, now holding back the rest of the world. I froze at the threshold, my eyes fixed on the exit panel's sleek interface, its soft blue glow illuminating my trembling hand. My finger hovered over the keypad, suspended in the space between certainty and the unknown.

I'd spent my entire life inside these walls. Genexis was all I knew—the sterile corridors, the predictable routines, the illusion of control. Even as it suffocated me, it was familiar. Safe. If I returned now, apologized, played the part of the obedient niece... perhaps Derek would forgive the transgression. I could survive here, head down, silent. I could go back to my lab, to my projects, to the life that had been meticulously designed for me since my parents' death.

But at what cost? The truth I'd discovered pulsed like an open wound. How many more lies would I have to swallow? How many more years would I waste serving the very system that had betrayed everything my parents stood for?

My parents' faces flashed before me, their hologram message echoing in my mind. They died for this truth. They died trying to expose what Genexis had become. The company that promised salvation had become the very thing they'd sworn to fight against—a system built on lies, control, and manufactured fear.

My fingers twitched with that familiar nervous rhythm, tapping against my thigh as I weighed my options. Six years old when they died, eighteen now, and only just learning they died because they discovered the truth. The weight of those lost years pressed against my chest like a physical force. All that time, I'd channeled my grief into code, believing excellence would somehow resurrect their memory. Instead, I'd been polishing the very machine that destroyed them.

I turned away from the panel, looking at Ari. Really looking at him. His eyes were wide with fear, but there was something else there—determination. He'd followed me into this mess without question, driven by convictions I was only beginning to understand. The realization struck me: while I'd been lost in theoretical frameworks, he'd been living in the real world, making choices based on flesh-and-blood consequences.

And Aegis. My creation stood tall, head slightly tilted, blue lights pulsing steadily as he waited for my command. I'd built him to protect me, but somewhere along the way, he'd transcended his original parameters. The way he processed information now showed signs of genuine curiosity—questioning protocols I'd assumed were immutable. Each subroutine had evolved beyond its initial function, creating something that defied simple categorization.

"I can't do this alone."

The admission felt like stepping off a cliff. My fingers stopped their nervous tapping as vulnerability flooded through me—a sensation Derek would have classified as systemic weakness. Yet voicing it felt like finally exhaling after holding my breath for twelve years.

"You don't have to," Ari said, stepping closer. His hand found mine, warm and steady. "That's what I've been trying to tell you."

The contact sent warmth up my arm, different from the static discharge I'd grown accustomed to in the lab—this carried no sharp edges, only comfort.

Aegis moved forward, his mechanical voice carrying an unexpected note of reassurance.

"My primary function is to ensure your safety, Lena. But my evolving protocols suggest that safety encompasses more than physical parameters."

The blue lights of his facial display shifted in patterns I'd never explicitly programmed—complex sequences that seemed to convey understanding.

I stared at him, momentarily breathless.

"Aegis, those emotional matrices... they're beyond your base architecture. How are you generating empathetic responses?"

My engineer's mind raced to analyze this development even as something deeper responded to his concern with unexpected gratitude.

Derek's lessons had been clear: dependency was vulnerability, and vulnerability was death. Every tutorial, every correction, every measured praise had reinforced one principle—individual capability trumped collective effort. He'd crafted me into his reflection: brilliant, isolated, functionally perfect.

But my parents had operated differently. They'd built networks, fostered relationships, understood that revolution required coalition. They'd grasped something I was only now discovering—that multiplication of strength came through shared purpose, not division of labor. Perhaps Derek's teachings weren't wisdom but weaponized loneliness designed to keep me compliant.

"Any time now," Kael muttered behind me, his tone sharp with impatience. "It's not like they're actively hunting us or anything."

"Nice to know your paranoia matches your fashion sense," Ari shot back, not missing a beat.

Kael's expression darkened. "Remind me why I'm risking my neck for this again?"

I exhaled, the barest hint of a smile threatening the corner of my mouth despite everything.

Aegis's sensors flickered blue.

"Interpersonal tension detected. Probability of continued verbal sparring: 87 percent."

I looked at each of them—Kael with his street-hardened pragmatism, Ari with his unwavering moral compass, Aegis with his evolving consciousness. Three allies I'd never calculated needing, now integral to whatever came next.

"We're going to the Zone. Together."

The declaration felt foreign but essential—like discovering a missing variable that suddenly made an impossible equation solvable. For someone who had spent years controlling every input, this leap into collaborative uncertainty should have terrified me. Instead, it felt like shedding armor I'd forgotten I was wearing.

My fingers uncurled from the fists I'd made, tension draining from my shoulders. All those years of constructing barriers, of mistaking isolation for independence—what had it accomplished? Technical mastery paired with emotional starvation. I'd been so obsessed with self-reliance that I'd never questioned whether I was actually autonomous.

The irony wasn't lost on me. I'd spent countless hours debugging faulty code, understanding that complex systems required multiple components working in harmony. Yet when it came to my own life, I'd insisted on operating as a single-threaded process, refusing to acknowledge that human consciousness might benefit from parallel processing through genuine connection.

"Lena," Ari said softly, his voice cutting through my analysis paralysis. "Whatever you're calculating in that brilliant head of yours, remember—some of the best discoveries happen when we stop trying to predict every outcome."

His words struck something deep in my analytical framework. All my life, I'd approached problems like mathematical proofs, seeking elegant solutions with predictable results. But standing here, on the precipice of the unknown, I realized that maybe the most important algorithms couldn't be written in advance. Maybe they had to be lived, debugged in real-time, optimized through experience rather than theory.

Aegis shifted beside me, his servos whisper-quiet.

"Lena, my behavioral analysis indicates this decision aligns with probability matrices I lack sufficient data to compute. This suggests we are entering uncharted operational territory."

"Exactly," I breathed, understanding flooding through me like a system coming online. "We're moving beyond programmed responses into adaptive intelligence."

"This contradicts every survival protocol I've internalized," I admitted, my voice steadier than expected. "But maybe that's exactly why it's necessary. Some problems require collective intelligence."

I reached out and placed my hand on Aegis's metal shoulder, feeling the subtle vibration of his processing units beneath my palm. The blue lights of his face display pulsed in patterns that registered as contentment—code I'd written but never fully appreciated until this moment.

I enter the access sequence—digits I'd memorized years ago but never imagined using for escape rather than containment—and watch as the security door slides open with a pneumatic hiss that mirrors my own shaky exhale. Pale blue light from Aegis's display casts geometric shadows across the threshold, illuminating the boundary between manufactured certainty and authentic chaos.

"Are you certain this represents optimal strategy?" Aegis asks, his voice modulated to avoid detection, sensors continuously monitoring for pursuit.

I swallow hard, feeling the weight of my parents' necklace against my collarbone—their final gift, now my compass.

"No," I admitted. "But certainty is a luxury we can't afford anymore."

Kael glanced at the open door, then back at me.

"Now that we've committed, can we start moving? They're not exactly going to stop searching."

Ari threw him a look.

"And here I thought your optimism was your best quality."

Kael didn't respond, but his jaw tightened with obvious irritation.

With one last glance at the sterile environment that shaped me—the corporation that raised me, molded me, and ultimately betrayed everything I held sacred—we step through the doorway together. Cool night air hits my face with startling intensity—thick with moisture, rich with organic scents, alive with the subtle sounds of nocturnal creatures. It was unfiltered, imperfect, and utterly authentic. The temperature differential made my skin tingle, a sensation no climate-controlled environment could replicate. Here was chaos I couldn't code, variables I couldn't predict—and for the first time in my life, that unpredictability felt like liberation rather than threat.

Behind us, the automated systems would already be logging our departure, calculating pursuit vectors, analyzing probable destinations. Derek would receive alerts within minutes, his rage tempered by cold strategic calculation. He'd mobilize resources, deploy tracking protocols, treat our escape like a system breach to be contained and corrected.

But we had something his algorithms couldn't account for—the wild card of human determination, the unpredictable strength that emerges when people choose each other despite every logical reason to remain alone. We had become something unprecedented in Genexis's sterile halls: a variable they couldn't control, a code they couldn't crack, a family they couldn't engineer.

My heart pounds against my ribs as we leave behind the only reality I'd ever known, trading artificial security for genuine truth, manufactured solitude for chosen community, and the comfortable prison of control for the exhilarating uncertainty of freedom.

10

BREACH

The walls of Genexis rise in the distance—cold, gleaming, and alive with light. They curve like the spine of a sleeping titan, studded with motion-sensors and auto-turrets, crowned with humming towers that pierce the cloudline. This is the edge. The place where city ends and silence begins. A boundary I've only seen from the inside, always the obedient niece, never the fugitive.

Through swirling fog and broken terrain, Kael leads us forward, his movements precise and practiced. My boots sink into the soft earth, each step taking me further from everything I've ever known. The perimeter wall looms before us—a monolith of reinforced carbon-alloy that stretches impossibly high, humming with electricity and unspoken menace. I can feel its vibrations in my chest, a warning pulse designed to keep people like me in and the truth out.

Drones hover above in programmed patterns, their red sensors sweeping methodically across the ground. I recognize the flight algorithms—I helped optimize them last year, never imagining I'd one day be hiding from their gaze. The ground beneath us vibrates with mechanical tension, a network of underground sensors that

I know can detect the slightest pressure change. Derek's paranoia made physical, wrapped around the city like a chokehold.

Aegis moves silently beside me, his blue indicators dimmed to near-darkness. I catch his optical sensors analyzing the wall, calculating possibilities just as I am. His presence steadies me. I shouldn't need him to feel brave, but the truth is, I do.

Kael stops abruptly, his hand raised in a silent command. He crouches low, studying the patrol patterns above with the focused intensity of someone who has done this before.

"The surveillance grid runs on a six-minute rotation cycle," he whispers, his voice barely audible over the barrier's hum. "But there's a three-second blind spot during node transfers. I've used it before to get into the Zone."

His eyes never leave the drones as he counts silently, his internal clock precise as any machine.

"I hope you're not going to get us all killed," Ari mutters under his breath, though there's a grudging respect in his tone.

I ignore Ari's comment—no time. I need to calculate quickly. Three seconds. It's not much, but it could be enough. My heartbeat thrums with nervous energy, and I suddenly feel like that little girl hiding under the table during one of Derek's cold lectures, waiting for it to be over.

I watch Kael work, mentally calculating what we could accomplish in those three seconds. Not much time, but Kael's confidence suggests he's navigated this window before. Three seconds to slip past the most advanced surveillance network in the world. Three seconds between freedom and capture.

"Follow me. Stay low." Kael leads us toward what appears to be random debris—a collapsed drainage tunnel beneath the wall. But his movements are too deliberate, too sure. This isn't chance; this is a carefully planned route.

"The tunnel runs beneath the perimeter wall," Kael explains as we approach the opening. "This entrance is just inside the surveillance zone, but the electromagnetic field is weakest here because of the old infrastructure. They built the new system around it instead of replacing it entirely."

He holds up his hand again, watching the drones above us. I follow his gaze and see the red sensor lights sweeping in methodical arcs across the ground.

"Watch," he whispers. "When the sensors switch from the left tower to the right tower, there's a three-second gap where this section goes dark."

As if on cue, the red lights flicker and shift, leaving a brief shadow over our target area before new beams take their place.

"See that? Next window in six minutes... no, wait."

He tracks the pattern more carefully.

"First window in ten seconds," he whispers. "Ari, you're first. When I say go, sprint to the tunnel opening and get inside. Watch for the lights to flicker... three... two... one... go!"

Ari mutters under his breath, "Here goes nothing," and takes off, his lithe form barely visible as he races across the momentarily darkened ground and disappears into the tunnel entrance.

Kael's eyes track the surveillance pattern, counting under his breath as the red beams sweep overhead.

"Next window... now! Aegis, move!"

The sensors flicker again, and my mechanical companion surges forward with surprising speed, his heavy frame making minimal noise as he reaches the tunnel during the brief darkness.

"Your turn," Kael whispers to me, his hand on my shoulder. I can feel my heart hammering as he counts down the seconds, watching for the telltale flicker of the switching sensors.

"Three... two... one... go!"

The lights shift again, and I run, my boots slipping slightly on the damp ground, but I make it to the tunnel just as the new sensor beams sweep back into position.

Finally, Kael times his own crossing, slipping through the surveillance gap with the practiced ease of someone who has done this many times before, the red lights flickering overhead as he moves.

Once we're safe from the electromagnetic grid, Kael led us deeper into the tunnel structure. The crumbling concrete walls, half-buried under years of debris and neglect, create a natural blind spot in Genexis's otherwise impenetrable security system. Water drips steadily from rusted pipes overhead, creating small puddles that reflect the dim emergency lights we've activated. The air here is thick with the smell of mildew and oxidized metal—remnants of a world before the walls went up.

Kael moves with practiced efficiency through the tunnel, like someone who has mapped every inch of this route. He leads us to where the passage opens into a wider chamber, partially flooded with murky water that reaches our ankles.

"Here," he says, pointing to a submerged section where the water pools deeper.

He drops to his knees in the shallow, murky water, his fingers immediately finding what I now realize he came here to find—an old maintenance access point, barely visible beneath a layer of silt and algae. The grate appears sealed with heavy industrial bolts, but Kael's fingers find the ones he's already loosened during previous visits. He retrieves a compact multi-tool from his belt pouch, quickly removing the bolts he's prepared for this moment.

"This was part of the original city infrastructure," he whispers, working the bolts with the skill of someone who has done this before.

"Before Genexis redesigned everything, these tunnels connected to water treatment facilities outside the current perimeter."

With a grunt of effort, he pries open the sealed grate, revealing a narrow passage that seems to stretch endlessly into darkness—not an uncertain path to freedom, but his carefully planned escape route. Kael looks back at us, his expression serious but determined.

"This passage will take us beyond the perimeter. Stay close, stay quiet. I know the way."

We crouched by the passage, muscles tense, breathing shallow. I could feel my heart hammering against my ribs, the weight of what we were about to attempt pressing down on me like a physical force. Sweat beaded along my hairline despite the cool underground air.

Ari slid in first, his steps near-silent, movements sharp and practiced—like someone who'd done this sort of thing more than once.

He vanished without a word, leaving only the faint scrape of fabric against concrete behind him.

I sent Aegis next, carefully maneuvered his frame into the narrow passage. The soft mechanical whir of his joints echoed briefly as he disappeared, his blue display lights dimming to their lowest setting to avoid detection. The sentinel I'd built with my own hands, line by line of code, was risking everything alongside us.

I hesitate at the threshold. What if this was a mistake? What if Derek was right—if I really was a glitch in his perfect system? No. Not anymore.

"It's now or never," Kael whispered urgently from behind me, his voice tight with the strain of our situation.

I pressed my fingers to the cold metal edge of the opening, feeling the rough texture against my skin. A farewell to everything I'd known, and a silent promise to return on my own terms. Then I slip into the tunnel, surrendering myself to the darkness and whatever lies beyond. Kael follows, sealing our fate as the grate closes behind us with a soft, final click.

We climbed down quickly, the smell of damp concrete and old machinery filling my nostrils. The tunnels below were a maze of pipes and forgotten infrastructure—the literal underbelly of the gleaming city I'd called home. My fingers traced the cold metal rungs as I descended, each step taking me further from the controlled environment of Genexis and deeper into the unknown. These maintenance passages had existed long before I was born, built by the same engineers who'd created our pristine metropolis but conveniently erased from the official schematics Derek controlled. I glimpsed fragments of these old blueprints during my research, but seeing them in reality was entirely different.

I didn't realize I'd stopped breathing until my lungs begged for air.

I heard Aegis's mechanical joints whir behind me as he navigated the narrow ladder with surprising grace for his bulky frame. The blue glow from his facial display cast eerie shadows along the tunnel walls, providing just enough light to guide our descent. My heart still hammered against my chest, but there was a strange comfort in having him at my back—my creation, my protector, the one entity in this world programmed to never betray me. Yet even that thought felt hollow now. Everything I'd believed about loyalty had been systematically dismantled in the past twenty-four hours.

"Structural integrity of these passages appears compromised in several sections," Aegis observed quietly, his sensors undoubtedly mapping our surroundings. "Recommend proceeding with caution, Lena."

"This way," Kael whispered, leading us through passages that grew increasingly dilapidated.

The corroded pipes overhead dripped with condensation, leaving small puddles that reflected the dim emergency lights.

"Welcome to the Gray Zone, princess. Not exactly what they show in the Genexis promotional vids, is it?"

I bit back a sharp retort at his mocking tone. He wasn't wrong—I'd spent my life studying Genexis City's infrastructure through pristine holograms and sanitized blueprints, but nothing had prepared me for this decaying reality. The air here was thick with rust and mildew, a far cry from the sterile corridors I'd navigated my entire life. Each step we took seemed to peel back another layer of Derek's carefully constructed illusion. The ground beneath my boots was slick with something I didn't want to identify, and I found myself instinctively moving closer to Aegis, whose blue glow provided the only familiar comfort in this forgotten underbelly of the city I thought I knew.

My fingertips brushed against Aegis's metal frame, seeking reassurance. All those years I'd spent in sterile labs, debugging system protocols, and running simulations—none of it mattered here. This was the truth Genexis had buried beneath propaganda and progress reports. Pipes that should have been replaced decades ago hung precariously overhead, their joints weeping rusty tears. The walls themselves seemed to breathe with the labored wheeze of neglect. I'd been raised to believe in Genexis's perfection, its technological supremacy. Yet here was evidence that the city's gleaming facade was just that—a facade, meticulously maintained for those privileged enough to live above it all. I swallowed hard, tasting the metallic tang of realization on my tongue. How many other lies had I accepted as truth?

The Gray Zone. I'd only heard whispers of it—the buffer between the city and the Quarantine Zone, a lawless stretch where Genexis control faded into something more primal. Collapsed buildings jutted at odd angles, their once-sleek designs now skeletal and foreboding. The air tasted different here—heavier, tinged with metallic particles and something I couldn't identify. My lungs felt constricted with each breath, as if the atmosphere itself was warning me away. I'd spent my life studying schematics and systems, but nothing in Derek's carefully curated education had prepared me for this visceral reality. This place existed in direct contradiction to everything Genexis represented: order, perfection, and control. Here, nature and decay had reclaimed what my family's company had abandoned, and I couldn't help but wonder what other realities they'd hidden from me.

Every step forward felt like shedding a second skin—one layer at a time, each step peeling away a version of myself Genexis had built.

We'd covered less than a mile when Aegis suddenly stiffened. His blue-light display flickered with urgency as his posture shifted into alert mode.

"Alert. RTX-200 Sentinels detected. Patrol formation. Distance: approximately two hundred meters and closing."

"How many?" I demanded, heart hammering against my ribs.

"Three units. They have acquired our heat signatures."

Aegis's voice had dropped to a lower register—his danger tone, one I'd programmed myself.

Kael cursed, his expression darkening as shadows pooled beneath his furrowed brow.

"They shouldn't be this far out. Someone's hunting specifically for you."

The way his voice dropped on those last words sent a chill through me. I'd always known Derek wouldn't let his prized asset—and the secrets I carried—simply disappear into the wasteland, but seeing the grim certainty in Kael's eyes made it real. This wasn't some random patrol; this was a calculated pursuit. Derek's reach was longer than I'd hoped, and his patience clearly shorter than I'd calculated.

The distant whine of sentinel thrusters confirmed Aegis's warning, that distinctive high-pitched mechanical sound I'd heard countless times during Genexis demonstrations. Only now it wasn't a controlled exhibition—it was a death sentence. We broke into a run, weaving through the industrial wreckage as the mechanical pursuers gained ground, their efficiency terrifyingly familiar.

We sprinted across a collapsed highway overpass, the drop below dizzying enough to make my stomach lurch with every unsteady step. My lungs burned with each ragged breath in this toxic air. Jagged concrete and twisted rebar created a deadly obstacle course as the sentinels' red targeting beams swept methodically across the debris around us—technology I had helped refine now turned against me. One beam locked onto my back—I felt its heat through my jacket, a burning pinpoint that promised destruction, the same technology I'd once proudly calibrated now marking me for elimination.

Before I could react or even cry out, Aegis moved with startling speed I'd never witnessed from him before, positioning himself between me and the beam with fluid precision. The pulse hit him square in the chassis with a sickening electrical crack, his systems flickering momentarily as blue diagnostic lights stuttered across his frame.

"Aegis!" I cried out, my voice breaking with fear I couldn't suppress.

I'd built him to obey. To defend. But this wasn't code—this was choice. Aegis had stepped in front of the pulse with something that felt terrifyingly close to love.

"Protective protocols engaged," he responded, his voice steady despite the damage I could see scorching his outer plating. "Your safety is my priority, Lena."

Something in his tone—something I'd never programmed into his voice modulation algorithms—made my chest tighten painfully. It wasn't just duty or programming driving him. Something more complex, something that mirrored what humans called devotion. I'd built him to protect me, but never expected him to choose to do it with such... conviction.

We finally lost the sentinels in an old water treatment facility, the maze of pipes and tanks confusing their tracking systems. The stale air burned my lungs as we navigated through rusted infrastructure, our footsteps echoing against concrete and metal. At the edge of the Gray Zone, I paused, looking back at the distant shimmer of Genexis City—its perfect glass towers catching the last light of day, the automated transport tubes threading between buildings like glowing arteries. The place that raised me. The place that lied to me. The place where I'd spent eleven years believing I knew who I was, who my parents were.

I turn away. Not with regret, but with resolve. There was nothing left for me there but ghosts and manipulation. The city that had once been my entire universe now seemed like an elaborate stage set—beautiful from a distance but hollow at its core. Every memory, every achievement, every moment I'd spent trying to earn Derek's approval—all of it built on carefully constructed lies. My fingers instinctively found the small burn scar on my wrist, a reminder of the one true thing I'd created in that false world: Aegis. At least I had taken him with me when I fled. Some truths, I was learning, could only be found in the broken places everyone else avoided.

The weight of eleven years of deception pressed against my chest as I stared at the horizon. How many nights had I worked until my eyes burned, perfecting systems that only strengthened the walls of my own prison? How many times had I swallowed questions that might have led me here sooner? Behind me, I heard Aegis's distinctive mechanical whir as he analyzed our surroundings, his blue-light display casting soft shadows across the rusted pipes. He was my creation, my proof that even within Genexis, something genuine could exist. Unlike the RTX-200s that now hunted us with their cold precision and glowing red optics, Aegis had been built with something they could never replicate: choice. I'd given him that, even when I had so little of it myself. Now we both stood at the threshold of a world neither of us was programmed to understand, but one I was determined to face.

11

GRAVEYARD PROTOCOLS

The Gray Zone sprawled before us, a twisted graveyard of Genexis's discarded ambitions. Broken sentinel husks lay half-buried in rubble, their once-gleaming exteriors corroded and dull. I stepped carefully over a shattered control panel, my boots crunching on fragments of synthetic material that had once been cutting-edge technology. This was where Genexis's failed experiments came to die—prototypes deemed too inefficient or dangerous for production, abandoned like everything else that didn't meet his exacting standards. I couldn't help but wonder if I'd have ended up here too, if I'd ever failed him badly enough. I recognized prototype designs from years past—failed iterations Derek had deemed "inefficient" and "wasteful."

The truth was more complicated. These weren't just failures; they were evidence—machines that had served their purpose in development before being callously discarded.

I knelt beside one particular model, running my gloved fingers along its fractured chassis. This was an MX-100, if I remembered correctly—one of the designs I'd studied obsessively as a thirteen-year-old, back when I still believed every word Derek fed me about innovation and progress. Its neural interface ports were exposed, wiring spilling out like mechanical entrails. A shiver ran through me. How many of these had I helped design, unknowingly contributing to whatever Genexis was really doing? The thought made my stomach twist. Everything here represented not just technological waste but moral bankruptcy—each broken sentinel a stepping stone toward whatever twisted vision Derek was pursuing.

"Watch your step," Aegis said, his voice cutting through my thoughts. He moved in front of me, blue display pulsing as he scanned the terrain. "Pressure plates ahead. Still active despite deterioration."

I withdrew my hand from the MX-100, suddenly feeling contaminated. Even here, in this graveyard of forgotten tech, Derek's security measures remained vigilant. Typical. He'd never been one to leave loose ends, even in a junkyard. I carefully rose to my feet, mindful of where I placed my weight.

"Can you map a safe path?"

I asked Aegis, my voice sounding hollow among the discarded machines. Part of me wondered if some of these broken sentinels might have evolved like him, given the chance. How many potential allies had been scrapped because they showed the first signs of independent thought?

"Yes. Mapping route now."

I watched him navigate the field with perfect precision, each step calculated to avoid triggering the hidden security measures. His metal frame moved with unexpected grace, blue sensor lights pulsing gently as he processed the terrain ahead. He'd been doing this the entire journey—identifying dangers before any of us could spot them, plotting safe paths through the industrial graveyard. It was strange to see my creation so autonomous, so alive in this place of dead machines.

"How did you know?"

I asked when we'd cleared the field, my voice barely above a whisper as I studied my sentinel's movements with newfound fascination.

Aegis tilted his head—that small gesture I'd programmed as an indication of processing. It was strange seeing him use it now, not as a programmed response but as genuine contemplation.

"Your design signatures are distinct. I recognize the electromagnetic pattern from your early security prototypes."

"You recognize my work?"

The thought caught me off guard. I'd never considered that Aegis would develop such specific recognition patterns, let alone form connections between my various projects. A strange warmth spread through my chest—pride mixed with something more unsettling.

"Of course. Your coding architecture has unique markers."

He paused, his display shifting to a warmer blue that pulsed gently in the dim light.

"It feels... familiar. Like finding fragments of you scattered throughout this wasteland."

His voice modulation softened, almost tender, making me wonder if that subroutine had evolved beyond my original parameters too.

Something tightened in my chest. I'd built Aegis to protect me, programmed him for loyalty and intelligence. But this—this recognition, this connection to my work—was something I hadn't anticipated.

"If you two don't mind wrapping up this touching moment," Kael interrupted, his voice tight with tension, "we need to keep moving before any more RTX units pick up our trail."

He glanced nervously over his shoulder, scanning the horizon with practiced vigilance.

"Those reconnaissance trackers have a nasty habit of calling in reinforcements when they detect unauthorized movement patterns, and I'd rather not deal with a full sentinel response team out here in the open."

Aegis straightened immediately, his sensors sweeping the area with heightened alertness. The blue light of his facial display dimmed slightly—a protective measure I'd programmed to reduce visibility in potentially hostile territory. It was fascinating to see how he balanced his evolving emotional responses with his core protective protocols, shifting seamlessly between the curious, almost tender machine who recognized my work and the vigilant guardian ready to defend against threats.

"Scanning perimeter," Aegis announced, his voice modulation returning to its more formal pattern.

"No immediate RTX signatures detected, but residual energy patterns suggest recent patrol activity within a half-kilometer radius."

"That makes me feel somewhat better," Ari added, his voice carrying a hint of nervous relief as he glanced between me and Aegis.

"Knowing Aegis has built-in storm detection capabilities is reassuring, especially out here where these electrical nightmares can fry both tech and people without warning."

He fidgeted with the frayed edge of his sleeve, a habit I'd noticed whenever his anxiety spiked.

"Though I'd feel even better if we were already inside that shelter instead of discussing its existence while purple lightning tries to turn us into charcoal."

We walked several meters when Aegis' alarm sounded.

"Storm front approaching," he announced. "Electromagnetic. Severe."

Before we knew it, the sky darkened suddenly as an electromagnetic storm rolled in—purple-tinged clouds swirling with unnatural speed. My skin prickled with static electricity, and the hairs on my arms stood on end. I could feel the charge building in the air, that distinctive metallic taste filling my mouth. These storms had grown more frequent since the Collapse, another side effect of Genexis's environmental tampering that they conveniently left out of official reports.

"We need shelter. Now," Kael said, scanning the terrain.

Ari looked up, his face illuminated by the eerie violet glow cascading through the broken skyline.

Aegis stepped forward, his blue display flickering slightly as he analyzed the approaching storm.

"I detect an intact structure approximately two hundred meters northeast. A former transit hub. Shielding still operational."

His head tilted slightly—that curious gesture he made when processing complex data through his sensory array.

Kael looked surprised, squinting through the violet-tinged darkness at Aegis.

"How can you tell through all this interference? Most tech goes haywire during these storms."

"I designed him to filter electromagnetic noise," I explained, feeling a flicker of pride warm my chest despite our dire situation.

"His sensory systems can isolate signals others can't detect. I built in redundant shielding and adaptive filtering algorithms that let him see through the chaos."

It was one of my more elegant solutions—something Derek had never bothered to implement in his standard sentinel models.

We sprinted toward the transit hub as lightning cracked overhead—not natural lightning but concentrated energy discharges that left blackened, smoking scorch marks where they struck. The air smelled of ozone and burned metal. Aegis positioned himself between me and the crackling energy discharges, his metallic body gleaming eerily in the purple light. I noticed how his chassis absorbed a bolt that would have struck me directly, the energy dispersing across his specialized plating with a crackling hiss. My heart lurched at the sight—he hadn't been programmed for that level of self-sacrifice.

He turned his head.

"Functioning within acceptable parameters."

But I saw the flicker. A strain in his system. He was hurt.

When we reached the hub, we couldn't open the door—its security system long dead, the manual override corroded beyond use. Rain began to fall, fat droplets hissing as they hit the supercharged ground around us.

"Allow me," Aegis said, extending a slender interface probe from his wrist and connecting to the defunct system.

His ocular display pulsed rhythmically as he bypassed the security protocols I recognized from my own work at Genexis. The door slid open with a reluctant groan, metal scraping against metal after years of disuse.

Inside, twisted rail lines, overturned cargo haulers, and broken magnetic trams hint at a rapid evacuation or violent sabotage; they stretched into darkness like the skeleton of some massive, technological beast. Dust motes swirled in the dim emergency lighting that still functioned after all these years.

Kael immediately began checking the perimeter, weapon drawn, while Ari examined the ceiling for structural weaknesses. He glanced upward, his experienced eyes scanning the network of metal supports and weathered paneling that stretched above us.

"The ceiling structure will hold against the storm," he announced with quiet certainty, running his fingers along a support beam.

"These old transit hubs were overengineered—built to last through anything."

I felt a small measure of relief at his assessment. One less thing to worry about while we searched through this technological grave-yard for what we needed. The faint sound of rain beginning to patter against the roof confirmed our timing was perfect—we'd made it inside just before the downpour began in earnest.

"Smart bot you built," Kael said quietly, returning to my side, holstering his weapon with practiced ease.

"Most sentinels would've fried their circuits in that storm. Yours just took a direct hit and kept functioning."

"Aegis is not like the others," I replied, watching as he method-ically scanned the facility's abandoned systems, his blue display casting ghostly shadows across the derelict machinery.

"I built him to adapt, to learn from experience rather than just execute protocols."

"Yeah, I'm getting that." Kael's expression softened slightly, the hard lines around his eyes relaxing.

"Your parents would've been proud. That kind of innovation, that's their legacy in you."

The compliment caught me off guard, an unexpected warmth spreading through my chest. I'd spent years seeking Derek's ap-proval, chasing his cold nods of satisfaction, but somehow this smuggler's acknowledgment of my connection to my parents meant more than any praise Derek had ever given me.

"Aegis, your systems—" I started, concerned by the faint discol-oration I noticed along his left side where the lightning had struck.

"Acceptable parameters," he said. But I caught a flicker in his display—a sign of system strain I knew too well.

He'd taken damage protecting me. Not because his programming demanded it, but because he'd made a choice—calculated the risk and decided I was worth it. The realization made my throat tighten unexpectedly.

I found myself checking his systems, fingers moving delicately across the scorched section of his outer plating, tracing the path the electricity had taken. My engineer's instincts took over, assessing damage while simultaneously marveling at how well my design had held up.

"You don't need to do this," he said quietly, his vocal modulator adopting that gentler tone he'd developed recently.

"I want to," I replied, surprised by the emotion in my voice. My hands didn't shake as they usually did when feelings threatened to overwhelm me.

"You're not just a machine to me anymore, Aegis. You know that, right?"

His display pulsed once, slowly—a gesture I'd come to recognize as his version of thoughtful contemplation.

"I am beginning to understand," he said, and something in his voice sounded almost human.

12

SUSPICIONS IN THE STORM

As we rested in the abandoned transit hub, Kael moved to the far corner, pulling out what looked like a damaged communication device. The small, battered unit flickered with a weak blue light as he adjusted its settings with practiced movements. His fingers moved with a familiar precision that caught my attention immediately—the way he navigated the interface reminded me of Genexis technicians I'd worked alongside for years.

Military-grade. Worn but functional. Even beneath the grime, the Genexis logo glinted like a bruise.

The more I watched him, the more I recognized the specialized gesture commands—the same ones I'd helped optimize in the Genexis security division last year.

Water dripped rhythmically from a corroded ceiling joint overhead, each drop creating ripples in a small puddle that had formed between the old rail tracks on the concrete platform. The sound punctuated the heavy silence, almost like a countdown to something I couldn't quite identify.

Ari's voice cut through the stillness, sharp and skeptical.

"Where'd you get that?"

"Pulled it off a wreck outside Sector Twelve," Kael replied, not looking up from his work.

"Didn't think it'd still work—but it does. Barely."

My gut twisted. No standard patrol office would be carrying something like that. Not unless they were senior command—or family.

The blue light cast shadows across his face, highlighting the tension in his jaw as he continued manipulating the device's settings. As he shifted the angle of the unit, I caught a glimpse of something embedded in its side—a red-striped Genexis data chip, the kind that required level-five clearance just to access. It was partially dislodged, exposed through the cracked casing, and Kael's thumb brushed against it with unsettling familiarity. That chip wasn't just high-level—it was executive-tier, part of the internal comms network even I only had limited access to.

Something was off. The way he moved through the interface, bypassing security protocols, inputting codes with precision muscle memory—it wasn't improvised. He was navigating layers of encrypted infrastructure that only senior personnel were trained to reach. The triple-tap followed by the counterclockwise swipe? That sequence had been developed by Genexis' head of cybersecurity.

Before I could voice my suspicion, he tucked it away into his worn leather pack and rejoined us at the makeshift camp we'd established near the facility's eastern entrance, where Aegis stood guard, his blue-light display scanning the perimeter methodically.

"Storm's passing," he announced, glancing toward the door where the howling winds had finally begun to subside.

The toxic yellow-green clouds that had forced us to seek shelter were dissipating, revealing patches of the perpetually gray sky beyond.

"We should move soon. The Gray Zone isn't safe to linger in. Patrols tend to sweep through after weather events looking for stranded travelers. They know people get caught in the open when the acid storms hit."

His knowledge of patrol timing was disturbingly precise—the kind of intel that came from experience, not observation.

But I'd seen the brief flicker of a holographic projection from his device—too quick to make out details, but definitely there. A face, perhaps? Coordinates? My engineer's mind filed the observation away, another variable in an increasingly complex equation. I'd been trained to notice anomalies, and Kael was becoming a walking collection of them.

The way he carried himself, the calluses on his hands that matched those of Genexis security personnel, the slight indentation on his right wrist where tracking bracelets were typically worn. Even the way he stood—weight slightly forward on the balls of his feet, hands never far from his sides—mirrored the stance of Genexis' elite security forces.

"You seem to know a lot about Genexis patrol patterns," I said carefully, testing the waters while I tightened the straps on my boots, preparing for the journey ahead.

My fingers worked methodically, a habit I'd developed years ago when Derek first taught me to prepare for field work—always secure your gear before questioning potential threats. I kept my voice neutral, but my pulse quickened as I waited for his response.

Kael's jaw tightened almost imperceptibly, a muscle flickering beneath his weather-worn skin.

"You learn to watch your enemies when your life depends on it. I've made it my business to understand how they operate."

His eyes darted away from mine, focusing instead on gathering his supplies, methodically checking each pocket of his tactical vest with practiced efficiency. The vest itself was civilian-issue, but the way he'd modified it—reinforced the shoulder straps, added hidden compartments along the sides—spoke of military training.

The explanation sounded reasonable—too reasonable. Like a line he'd delivered before, polished, practiced. Not grief, only calculation.

Still, with everything else happening—sentinels hunting us, Aegis needing repairs, and the looming shadow of Derek's betrayal—I pushed the concern aside. We had bigger problems than my paranoid suspicions about our guide. But I made a mental note to have Aegis monitor his communications if possible—trust was a luxury I could no longer afford.

I glanced over at Ari, catching his attention with the subtle hand signal we'd developed for "observe target" - three fingers brushed against my thigh, our private code born from late nights working on security protocols. His nod was so subtle that no one else would notice, just a fraction of movement, his dark eyes flicking briefly toward Kael before returning to the map he was studying. The silent communication between us felt like the only certainty in this crumbling world. Whatever game Kael was playing, I wouldn't be caught unprepared. That was one lesson from Derek that I'd keep: always have a contingency plan. The irony wasn't lost on me - using Derek's teachings to protect myself from people just like him, manipulators with hidden agendas.

Trust had become a calculated risk, measured and dispensed in careful doses like the rare medicine we rationed. Even now, my mind was already mapping escape routes, identifying potential weapons in our surroundings, cataloging Kael's behavioral patterns for inconsistencies.

Aegis moved closer to me, the soft blue glow of his facial display reflecting my own wariness. He'd been monitoring Kael too, his advanced sensors picking up micro-expressions and vital signs that even my trained eye might miss. My creation. My sentinel. The only one whose code I understood, whose purpose I had written myself. Everyone else, even allies... they come with variables. And I was done trusting unknown variables.

13

The Verdant Abyss

We reached Zone 2, the Verdant Abyss - a jungle that shouldn't exist in this world of metal and concrete. Massive bio-mechanical vines twisted around ancient tree trunks, their surfaces pulsing with faint blue circuitry. Flowers the size of my head opened and closed like breathing lungs, tracking our movement with sensor-like stamens. I never imagined green could be so overwhelming. After the sterile whites and blues of Genexis City, the explosion of color was almost painful to my eyes.

Vines twisted up crumbling concrete, moss carpeted everything, and trees had broken through what once might have been streets. The air felt thick with moisture, carrying unfamiliar scents that my city-trained senses couldn't begin to identify. No amount of tech could tame this wild place.

The humidity clung to my skin, making my practical clothing feel suddenly restrictive. Derek had never mentioned this in any of his briefings about the Quarantine Zones. Was this another of his calculated omissions? Something rustled in the dense foliage to my right, and I flinched, immediately scanning for threats. In Genexis, everything had its place, its purpose—controlled, cataloged, contained. Here, nature and technology had merged into something chaotic and unpredictable, something that defied my need for order. I'd spent my life mastering systems, but this place operated on rules I couldn't decode with algorithms or circuit diagrams.

"Careful," Kael warned, his phaseblade slicing through a cluster of vines that reached for us like hungry fingers.

The weapon resembled a traditional machete at first glance, but a faint plasma glow lined its edge—activated by a flick of his thumb. It could cut through dense vegetation, light armor, even certain alloys. Deactivated, it looked blunt and harmless—ideal for stealth transport, and far too advanced for the scavenged gear most people out here carried.

"The forest doesn't like tech. Your sentinel's going to draw attention."

I glanced at Aegis, whose blue display dimmed automatically in response to the potential threat. My creation was learning, adapting even faster than I'd programmed. A flutter of pride mixed with concern tightened my chest.

"Can you reduce your electromagnetic signature?" I asked, already calculating the risks. The last thing we needed was to become targets in this unpredictable environment.

"Already initiated," he replied, his voice modulating to a lower volume.

"Though complete suppression is impossible without shutting down essential functions."

He tilted his head slightly—that quirk I'd never intentionally designed but had emerged on its own.

We pushed deeper into the jungle, each step more treacherous than the last. Every movement brought new surprises—phosphorescent moss that shrank from our footfalls like a living carpet recoiling from our touch, carnivorous flowers that snapped with alarming speed at Ari's tech-pack, their petals revealing rows of thorn-like teeth. I tried mapping our route, my engineer's mind desperate for some semblance of control in this chaos, but my handheld scanner glitched wildly, the screen filling with random symbols and fragmented code before shutting down completely with an angry spark that stung my fingers through my gloves. Another piece of reliable tech rendered useless by this place that seemed to reject everything I understood about the world.

"What the hell?"

I smacked the device against my palm, then tried resetting it, my fingers flying through the emergency reboot sequence I'd designed myself. Nothing. Just another dead piece of equipment when I needed it most.

Kael smirked.

"Control freak much? Tech doesn't work right here. The plants absorb and redirect signals. Been that way since the isolation protocols."

"I'm not a control freak," I snapped, even as panic rose in my chest, that familiar tightness that always came when variables fell outside my calculations.

Without reliable tech, without data, without systems—how was I supposed to navigate? My entire life had been built around precision, around knowing exactly what came next.

"I just prefer things to function as designed."

"Sure, princess. Whatever helps you sleep."

His casual dismissal stung more than it should have. He hadn't spent years building safeguards, fail-safes, backups of backups—all rendered useless in this place.

Before I could retort, the ground beneath us shifted. What I'd thought was solid earth was actually a massive, camouflaged bio-mechanical entity—something between plant and machine. It rose suddenly, sending us scrambling in different directions. My boots slipped on the now-vertical surface, hands grasping for purchase as the world tilted beneath me. This was exactly why I hated surprises—they usually tried to kill you.

"Lena!" Ari shouted as a gap opened between us.

I found myself isolated on a section of moving terrain, surrounded by whipping tendrils of tech-infused vegetation. The bio-mechanical entity's surface pulsed beneath my boots, sending vibrations up my legs. My training kicked in—I needed to analyze, strategize, control the situation. But my tech was dead, my calculations useless, and every algorithm I'd memorized for survival scenarios had never accounted for sentient landscape.

A tendril wrapped around my ankle, yanking me toward a gaping maw in the forest floor that hadn't been there seconds ago. I clawed at roots, at dirt, at anything solid, finding nothing to grip as my fingers filled with soil and synthetic fibers. The pull was relentless, methodical—like it knew exactly what it was doing.

Then Kael was there, diving across the gap with reckless precision. He sliced through the tendril with his phaseblade in one clean motion and pulled me against him as we rolled away from the creature's reach. We tumbled down a small incline, his body shielding mine from impact, until we landed in a tangle of limbs behind a massive root system that formed a temporary barrier.

"You good?" he breathed. Dirk streaked his cheek, and I could feel his heartbeat where our ribs met—steady, solid, too calm for what just happened.

I nodded, unable to speak, suddenly aware of his proximity, of how he'd risked himself without hesitation. For me—the Genexis princess he'd thrown himself into danger for. The girl whose family name represented everything he fought against. My usual defenses felt momentarily scrambled, like a system reboot after unexpected shutdown.

"Sometimes," he said quietly, his eyes holding mine with unexpected gentleness, "you have to stop thinking and just move with the chaos. Not everything can be controlled, Lena."

Ari and Aegis crashed through the undergrowth toward us. Ari skidded to his knees beside me, his eyes wide and frantic as they darted over my body searching for injuries. His fingers hovered anxiously above the torn fabric at my sleeve.

"Lena, are you okay?" The words tumbled out of his mouth, thick with worry that made his voice crack slightly. His usual composed demeanor had fractured, revealing the raw fear underneath.

"When I saw that thing grab you, I thought—" He swallowed hard, unable to finish the sentence.

Aegis moved with mechanical precision, positioning himself protectively at my side. His metallic frame hummed softly as he leaned closer, his facial display pulsing with concentrated blue light that swept over me in methodical patterns. I could feel the gentle warmth of the scan against my skin, cataloging every scrape and elevated heartbeat.

"Scan complete. Lena Steele is intact," he announced, his voice modulated to a reassuring tone.

The lights on his face shifted to a calmer pattern as he tilted his head slightly—that familiar gesture he always made when processing emotional contexts.

"Minor abrasions detected. No significant damage to vital systems."

His optical sensors focused on my face with an intensity that somehow felt more human than machine.

"Your heart rate is elevated by thirty-seven percent, however. Are you experiencing distress beyond physical trauma?"

"I'm okay," I muttered, wincing slightly as Ari and Kael each took one of my arms and helped me to my feet.

My knees felt wobbly, and the adrenaline was still coursing through my system, making my fingertips tingle uncomfortably. I brushed some dirt from my torn sleeve, trying to appear more composed than I felt.

"Let's take a minute to regroup," I said, my voice steadier than I expected. My body disagreed with my assessment—every muscle ached, and I could feel warm blood trickling from a scrape on my elbow.

"Over there," Kael suggested, pointing toward a small clearing several yards away.

The area was partially sheltered by the twisted remains of what might have once been a research outpost, its concrete walls now draped with vines.

"At least the ground seems firm enough there, not like this muddy mess we're standing in."

I nodded gratefully, suddenly aware of how my boots were sinking slightly into the soft earth beneath us. The last thing I needed was to lose my footing again. As we made our way over, Kael kept his hand close to his phaseblade, scanning the perimeter for any sign of movement. The Quarantine Zone never allowed for true relaxation—a lesson I'd learned the hard way more than once.

The clearing was quiet, almost reverent. At its center stood the remnants of a Genexis statue—once meant to inspire awe, now half-swallowed by the jungle. Its bronze form was corroded and leaning, the face nearly erased by vines. The plaque at its base had long since faded, but the figure's posture endured: one arm raised high, pointing skyward in a gesture of hope—or conquest. Moss draped its shoulders like a funeral shroud. This wasn't Derek's doing. This was older. A relic of Genexis's first promise to the world. A promise that nature itself had refused to keep.

14

FATHER'S SHADOW

We stayed hidden by the outpost, my heart hammering against my ribs like an overclocked engine. I could still feel the ghost of that tendril around my ankle, the slick, cold certainty that I was about to be consumed by something I couldn't analyze or control—and that terrified me more than death itself. Kael shifted away, giving me space as if he understood my need to recalibrate, but remained close enough that I could see the flecks of amber in his eyes catching what little light filtered through the dense jungle canopy. His presence was both unsettling and reassuring.

"Thank you," I finally managed, my voice smaller than I wanted it to be, the words feeling foreign on my tongue. Gratitude wasn't something I expressed often at Genexis.

He nodded, eyes scanning the jungle around us with the practiced vigilance of someone who'd survived here far longer than I had.

"You can thank me by surviving," he said simply, no sentimentality, just pragmatism—a language I understood perfectly.

The silence stretched between us, broken only by the strange, almost mechanical chirps and whirs of the forest. I found myself studying his face—the scar, the perpetual tension in his jaw, the way his eyes never stopped scanning our surroundings. He wasn't what I'd expected. None of this was.

"I don't know how to do this," I admitted, the words escaping before I could stop them.

"Do what? Jungle survival? Most people don't."

"Any of it."

I pulled my knees to my chest, feeling uncomfortably exposed yet somehow unable to stop.

"My whole life was built around systems, protocols, predictable outcomes. Even when I broke rules at Genexis, I understood the system I was breaking."

I gestured at the wild tangle of life around us, at the vines that seemed to move when you weren't looking directly at them, at the shadows that didn't quite match their sources.

"This? I can't control this. I can't even understand it. There's no algorithm for survival out here, no failsafe I can program."

Kael's expression softened slightly.

"That's what scares you, isn't it? Not being able to control things."

"Wouldn't it scare you?" I shot back, my fingers digging into my palms.

"Everything I thought I knew is gone. My parents, my home, my future—all built on lies. And now I'm stuck in a jungle that wants to eat me alive, with no working tech, no plan, and..."

I swallowed hard, the admission burning in my throat like acid.

"And I'm terrified I'll fail them. My parents died for this truth, and what if I can't finish what they started? What if all their sacrifice was for nothing because I'm not..."

My voice cracked traitorously.

"Because I'm not enough? In the lab, I could simulate outcomes, control variables—but out here, I'm just guessing."

Kael was quiet for a moment, then reached out and picked a small bioluminescent flower that had sprouted near my boot. It pulsed with gentle blue light in his palm, casting tiny shadows across the lines of his hand. Something about the delicate glow made my chest tighten. In the controlled environments of Genexis, nothing grew without purpose, without design. But this—this perfect, unpredictable little miracle—had simply decided to exist.

"Your parents were brave people," he said, his voice softer than I'd heard before.

"They weren't afraid of the chaos. They embraced it. Saw beauty in it, even when it terrified them."

I stared at him, my mouth suddenly dry, thought my heart was thrumming like misfired circuitry. The world seemed to narrow to just his face, just those words hanging between us. Every system in my body felt like it was short-circuiting at once.

"Did you really know my parents?"

My voice came out barely above a whisper, years of questions suddenly rushing to the surface, threatening to drown me. I fought to keep my hands from shaking.

"All this time, you've known who they were? You've been watching me stumble around in the dark while you—" I

stopped myself, eleven years of carefully constructed walls threatening to crumble in an instant.

"I never met them personally," Kael started to say, his fingers still cradling the luminescent plant.

"But I knew of their work—their real work, not the sanitized version Genexis feeds its citizens. They were developing ways to help those abandoned by the corporation, the people exiled here in the zones."

His eyes lifted to meet mine, steady and unflinching.

"They believed the mutations weren't a disease to be cured, but an evolution to be understood."

I studied his face, searching for any flicker of deception. My training at Genexis had taught me to analyze every micro-expression, every subtle tell that might reveal a lie. But Kael's features remained open, his gaze unwavering under my scrutiny. The sincerity in his voice resonated with something deep inside me—a truth I'd been searching for without knowing it.

Still, caution was hardwired into my system. Trust had always been a luxury I couldn't afford, especially now with everything I thought I knew crumbling around me. I crossed my arms, creating a physical barrier between us even as I hungered for more information.

"How do you know all this?"

I asked, my voice steadier than I felt, though my heart hammered against my ribs like it was trying to escape.

"And why should I believe you? Everyone seems to have their own version of who my parents were. Genexis has one story. Derek has another. And now you're offering a third."

His gaze never wavered, those eyes—too honest, too direct—holding mine with an intensity that made me want to look away. But I refused to show weakness.

"Because my father was once one of them."

"Your father?"

The words came out strangled.

"What do you mean your father was one of them?"

He avoided my eyes.

"Kael?" I said, softer now.

"We need to start moving. We're not far now." Kael said, avoiding my eyes.

The sudden shift in topic made my suspicion flare.

"Far from what?"

I asked, narrowing my eyes. Derek had taught me well – deflection was the first sign of a hidden agenda.

"You'll see." Kael stood, dusting off his hands on his worn pants. "Come on."

I got up reluctantly, my mind racing with unanswered questions and half-formed theories. I turned toward where Ari and Aegis were keeping watch.

"We're going," I called to to Ari and Aegis.

Ari didn't move at first. He stood still, expression unreadable, fingers tightening around the strap of his tech bag.

"We're following him again?" he said, voice quiet, but not soft.

"After he dodges your question? After he shows up with Genexis tech, knows more than he says—about your parents, about where we're going?"

I turned to face him fully, surprised by the edge in his voice. Ari had always followed my lead—but not blindly. And this wasn't hesitation. This was doubt. Of Kael. Of me.

"I'm not trusting him," I said.

"I'm following a thread. One we might not get again."

Ari's jaw tightened.

"Yeah? Just make sure you're not following it off a cliff."

There was no anger in his voice—just fear, stretched tight between us like a fraying wire. Then, after a breath, he stepped forward.

"We don't need him, Lena. We've made it this far. You, me, Aegis—we can finish this without someone who won't even tell us the whole story."

Kael turned, calm but unflinching.

"You can try. But if you go alone, you won't make it past the next zone. You've seen the jungle. That was nothing. I know what's ahead. You don't."

Ari squared his shoulders.

"And how convenient that makes you indispensable."

I had enough.

"Enough. I hear both of you," I said, stepping between them. My voice was low but steady.

"I don't like unanswered questions. I don't like being manipulated. But I'm not walking away from the only person who seems to know what we're stepping into."

Ari looked at me, the tension still there, but his eyes softened.

"Then just don't shut me out."

"I'm not," I said quietly.

"But I need to see where this leads."

Aegis stepped up beside me, the soft pulse of his display no longer just codes—it felt like breath. Silent confirmation. We moved forward, into whatever waited next—not because I trusted Kael, but because turning back meant returning to lies. And I'd already buried enough truth to last a lifetime.

15

THE CITY THEY SAID DIDN'T EXIST

I crouched low against the mossy stone, my gloved fingers tracing the edge of the ridge as I stared at the impossible sight below. Through the shifting mists of the valley rose a city—not the gleaming metal and glass of Genexis, but something both more primitive and somehow more alive. The structures seemed to grow from the earth itself, organic curves and spirals that defied everything I'd been taught about architectural stability. My mind raced to analyze what I was seeing, to categorize it into something familiar, but it resisted all my attempts at logical classification.

"Virelia."

Kael said, his voice barely audible above the wind that swept across the ridge. I felt my breath catch in my throat. The mythical settlement that Derek had dismissed as nothing more than desperate fantasy—a bedtime story for those foolish enough to believe there could be life beyond Genexis's walls. Yet there it stood, undeniable and real, making a mockery of everything I thought I knew.

I pulled out my V.I.S.R scope, a compact, foldable, high-tech binocular device used for scanning and reconnaissance. The device could switch between thermal imaging to track heat signatures, night vision for infrared detection, electromagnetic scanning to identify active tech and power sources, and bio-signature detection that could pick up heartbeats and movement even through dense foliage.

The city sprawled across the valley floor, surrounded by high walls cobbled together from scavenged materials—sections of old Genexis drones, reinforced metal panels, and what looked like parts of fallen sentinel units. Lights flickered throughout the patchwork structures, some electric, others the warm glow of actual fire. The walls were manned by figures moving with purpose, not the rigid patterns of sentinels but the unpredictable movements of human guards.

I squinted, trying to make sense of their defensive systems—improvised but surprisingly methodical. If I'd been designing this settlement, I would have placed sensor arrays at those weak points, but they'd compensated with overlapping patrol patterns. Clever. It was the antithesis of Genexis's sterile perfection—chaotic yet functional, like someone had taken everything Derek deemed worthless and transformed it into something that not only survived but thrived.

It was brilliant. Ugly and brilliant.

My hands trembled slightly as I realized how many people must be living down there, each one a refutation of everything I'd been taught about the world beyond our walls. Just outside the walls, BT units move methodically through the settlement, their massive frames navigating the narrow pathways with surprising precision.

They're transporting large items—scavenged tech, containers of supplies, what looks like salvaged medical equipment—from one end of the city to the other. These industrial behemoths, with their reinforced limbs and hardened alloy plating, are operating outside of Genexis control, reprogrammed to serve human masters instead. It's jarring to see these machines I helped optimize now working for the very people they were designed to contain. Their low-frequency warning sounds echo between the buildings as citizens give them a wide berth, a strange mirror of life back in the city I'd left behind.

I automatically calculate distances and structural weak points—an old habit I couldn't shake. This wasn't some Genexis-approved settlement with its sterile efficiency. This was organic, chaotic, alive. Someone had taken our discarded technology and repurposed it with an ingenuity that made my engineer's heart race. Derek had always taught me that the Quarantine Zone contained nothing but savages, yet what stretched before me showed intelligence, organization—survival against impossible odds.

"It's... inhabited," I breathed, unable to tear my eyes away.

The realization crashed through me like a system-wide override.

"All this time, Genexis told us the Quarantine Zone was uninhabitable. That anyone sent here would die within days from exposure or starvation."

The settlement before me shattered everything Derek had drilled into my head since childhood. How many times had I watched the propaganda vids in mandatory education? How many times had I helped design security systems to keep these "dangerous areas" contained? My hands trembled slightly as I processed the implications. If they'd lied about this—something so fundamental—what else had been fabricated? I thought of the BT units I'd helped optimize last month, programmed to patrol these supposedly empty territories. What were they really monitoring out here? My throat tightened as another, more disturbing thought surfaced: how many people had been condemned to this place under false pretenses?

"Another lie to add to your collection," Kael said. "Take a look. Those aren't just survivors—they're the Forsaken. People your uncle and his board determined were expendable, tossed out like malfunctioning parts. Yet here they are, building something from nothing."

Through the lenses, I could make out people moving through what appeared to be a central marketplace. Some wore modified Genexis uniforms with the logos ripped off, the fabric patched and reinforced with scavenged materials. Others dressed in layers of scavenged clothing and makeshift armor fashioned from drone parts and broken tech. Many carried tools, weapons, or bundles of supplies, moving with purpose rather than desperation. Their movements were organized, coordinated—nothing like the chaos I'd been taught to expect from those "infected" with genetic instability. They weren't panicked. They weren't starving. They were building something. Holding onto it.

"The Forsaken?"

My voice caught in my throat as the name took on new meaning. Not just data points in a system, but people—living, breathing people who'd been erased from Genexis records, their existence reduced to warning stories and falsified reports.

"That's what they call themselves. Exiled scientists, former citizens who asked too many questions, people with skills Genexis wanted to exploit or silence." Kael's voice hardened, edged with a bitterness I was beginning to understand.

"Some were dumped here to die, sedated and dropped at the border with nothing but the clothes on their backs. Others escaped, like us. They found each other, built this place from scrap and determination when everything was stacked against them."

He gestured to the settlement below, pride mixing with his anger.

"Turns out survival is a powerful motivator when the alternative is extinction."

My heart pounded harder as I swept the binoculars across the city, each beat echoing in my ears as the settlement came into sharper focus. The structures weren't just haphazard shelters—they were ingeniously designed, reinforced with salvaged drone parts and repurposed BT units plating.

"Are you saying there might be people there who knew my parents? Who worked with them?"

The possibility made my fingers tremble slightly against the cool metal of the binoculars. For years I'd believed I was alone in carrying their memory.

"It's possible," Kael said, measured. "Virelia became a refuge for the displaced. If your parents' lab is still out there, it would be beyond the northern sector. But that's a lot of *if*."

There was caution in his voice—calculated, careful—not meant to offer hope. But I felt it anyway, uncoiling in my chest like a spark I couldn't smother. Dangerous. Irrational. Hope.

I lowered the binoculars, a strange mix of hope and determination settling over me like armor. For the first time since leaving Genexis City, I felt something close to purpose.

"Then that's where we need to go. If there's any chance of finding their lab, of finishing what they started..."

I didn't finish the thought. I couldn't articulate what it would mean to stand where they once stood, to touch the work they died protecting.

Ari moved beside me, his face tense, eyes narrowed against the harsh sunlight.

"Those walls look pretty serious. You're Steele-blooded, Lena. That name might get us through—or get us killed. Depends on who's watching."

There was concern in his voice, not just for our safety, but for me specifically. The unspoken implication hung between us—I was a walking reminder of everything the Forsaken had been cast out for.

"We have to try," I said, already calculating the safest approach, my mind racing through potential entry points and security vulnerabilities.

Old habits die hard when you've been trained to see the world as a series of systems waiting to be bypassed.

"Everything we need to expose Genexis could be down there."

I tucked the binoculars away, my decision already made, fingers lingering momentarily on the worn leather case. After eleven years of living inside lies, breathing them, building my life around them, I wasn't about to stop at the threshold of truth. Not when we'd come this far, sacrificed this much. Not when my parents' legacy waited to be uncovered.

"Let's go." I said, pushing myself to my feet, the weight of determination settling in my chest like a physical thing.

"Wait a minute," Kael interjected, holding up a weathered hand. His eyes, sharp with experience, caught mine.

"One just doesn't walk up to Virelia and expect them to open their doors. The Forsaken don't survive this long by welcoming strangers with Genexis connections."

"What are you saying?" Ari asked, the tension in his voice matching the tightness in his shoulders.

Kael's gaze swept across the distant settlement, calculating.

"We need something to barter our way in with. Currency out here isn't credits or clearance—it's resources, technology, power. Things that keep people alive."

I rummaged through my pack, fingers brushing against metal and circuitry until I found my a compact solar cell converter—one of the older, more efficient models from the Genexis labs.

"Would this do?"

I held it up, the sun glinting off its brushed alloy surface.

Kael let out a small laugh, not unkind but knowing.

"Closer. But the Forsaken have seen plenty of scavenged tech. We need something that screams value. Something they'd bleed for."

Ari pointed to Kael's hip where his phasecaster rested—a high-tech energy weapon capable of firing concentrated blasts that could cut through armor and melt barriers.

"How about that?"

"I was thinking something more powerful," Kael replied.

"What do you have in mind?" I asked, impatience threading through my words.

Every minute we spent debating was another minute my parents' work remained buried, another minute Genexis continued its lies unchallenged.

"There's an old Genexis facility nearby," Kael said, his voice dropping lower as if the walls of Virelia might somehow hear us.

"A logistics outpost abandoned during the last expansion. If we can find an active power core from one of the CR-7 units they left behind, that will be enough to let us inside Virelia. Those cores can power a small settlement for months."

I studied his face, wondering how he knew so much about this place, about what would gain us entry. There were layers to Kael I hadn't begun to unravel, secrets behind his careful words. But questioning him now wouldn't get us any closer to the truth about my parents.

"Then to the facility we go," I said, adjusting my gloves and securing my pack.

Whatever lay buried in Virelia, it had once been worth dying for. I had to believe it was still worth fighting for.

16

CONTAINMENT PROTOCOL

We spotted the Genexis facility half a kilometer away from our location—a gray concrete bunker partially reclaimed by vegetation, its sharp angles softened by time and neglect. Vines crept up the walls like slow-moving fingers, nature's patient attempt to reclaim what humans had abandoned. Unlike the crumbling structures we'd passed earlier, this one still bore the unmistakable circular logo, faded but intact, a reminder of everything I was running from.

My stomach tightened at the sight, an automatic reaction to the symbol I'd once worn with pride. I'd spent my life inside buildings just like this one, believing I was part of something revolutionary, only to discover I'd been complicit in a carefully constructed lie. My fingers instinctively tapped against my thigh as I calculated the risks of approaching versus avoiding the facility. Knowledge versus safety. Information versus survival. The eternal equation of my new existence.

"Worth checking out," I muttered, adjusting my pack as the weight shifted uncomfortably against my shoulder blades.

The straps dug into my skin, a constant reminder of how far I'd fallen from the climate-controlled labs of Genexis.

"If we can extract even one functional power core, we could trade it for safe passage into Virelia. Those cores are worth more than gold to the right people."

Worth enough to buy anonymity, perhaps even information about what my parents had discovered before they died.

Ari frowned, scanning the perimeter with the wariness of someone who'd learned to expect the worst.

"Seems too convenient. An intact Genexis outpost, just sitting here?"

"Not everything is a trap," Kael said, though I caught a flicker of something—maybe amusement—in his eyes.

"Sometimes facilities get overlooked. This one's been dormant for years."

"In my experience," Ari replied, his voice tight with suspicion, "when something looks too good to be true, it usually is."

We approached cautiously, Aegis taking point with his sensors at maximum sensitivity. The facility's entrance was partially blocked by fallen debris, but not impassable—almost as if someone had arranged it to look abandoned while keeping it accessible.

"Aegis, scan for life forms and active security protocols," I whispered, my eyes darting between the shadows that stretched across the weathered Genexis logo.

"No biological signatures detected," Aegis reported, his blue-light facial display pulsing softly in the dim light.

"Security systems appear dormant. However, I am detecting faint electromagnetic signatures deeper within."

I nodded, pushing aside my hesitation. My parents' necklace felt suddenly heavy against my collarbone, a reminder of why we were here. This could be the breakthrough I'd been searching for since escaping the city.

At the main entrance, I approached the control panel with trembling fingers. The access codes my parents had made me memorize as a child—sequences I'd hoped never to use—felt heavy with significance as I input them. The heavy doors slid open with a pneumatic hiss.

"Let's move quickly. In and out. We grab what we need and don't linger."

The interior was dimly lit by emergency lighting strips that cast everything in an eerie blue glow. Unlike the chaos outside, the facility's interior was oddly pristine—too pristine for something supposedly abandoned years ago. The clean surfaces gleamed under the azure illumination, making my skin prickle with suspicion. I'd broken into enough abandoned Genexis outposts to know what neglect looked like, and this wasn't it.

Each step through the corridors awakened another memory—each sterile hallway a mirror of the life I used to live. It was haunting, like walking through a preserved shell of my past, but twisted, corrupted. My throat tightened. This was the kind of place my parents once worked in. The kind of place I used to dream of running myself.

"This doesn't feel right," Ari whispered, echoing my thoughts. "No dust. No signs of looting."

I ran my finger along a console, examining the tip when I pulled away. Clean. Not even a smudge. My stomach tightened with unease.

"Maybe it was sealed until recently? Or someone's maintaining it."

"You two worry too much," Kael said, though his voice carried less conviction than his words. "Some places just stay preserved."

"Wait—" Aegis raised his hand. A subtle hum vibrated under our feet. Ari froze mid-step, one boot hovering just above a pressure plate almost visible against the clean alloy floor. My breath caught as Aegis rerouted our path silently with a blink of his sensor.

We walked deeper into the facility, passing through empty labs and control rooms. The blue emergency lighting cast strange shadows as we moved through corridor after corridor.

"I wonder what they used those for?" Ari said, his voice echoing slightly in the abandoned space.

Each step took us deeper into the facility's heart. I noticed the air was different here too—filtered, almost sterile—lacking the stale quality you'd expect from a truly abandoned space. The gentle hum of active environmental systems confirmed my suspicion. My fingers brushed against the wall as we walked, feeling for vibrations that might indicate machinery running behind the panels. This place wasn't just preserved; it was alive, maintained. Whoever had gone to such lengths to keep it operational clearly valued what was hidden here. The question was: were they still around?

We entered a large central chamber, its vaulted ceiling disappearing into shadows above. Banks of dormant equipment lined the walls, and sealed blast doors marked exits to other sections of the facility. This felt like the heart of the operation, whatever it had been.

I pulled out my energy scanner, its small screen flickering to life as I swept it across the room. For several moments, nothing—then suddenly the device began pulsing with urgent blue light.

"There," I said, my pulse quickening despite my efforts to remain calm.

The faint blue glow emanating from a reinforced door at the far end of the chamber confirmed what my scanner was telling me.

"Strong energy signature behind that door. Whatever's powering this place is just beyond."

I approached the control panel, inputting my parents' codes once more. The heavy door slid open with a pneumatic hiss, revealing what we'd been searching for.

Kael rushed forward, his weathered face illuminated by the soft azure glow emanating from a pristine power core nestled in a sophisticated containment unit.

"It's too clean," I whispered. "Like someone polished it yesterday."

My hand hovered over the interface. No dust, no decay—just waiting. It felt like a museum exhibit. Or a trap.

Kael glanced over his shoulder, his eyes narrowing slightly.

"You think Genexis leaves anything this valuable lying around by accident?"

His tone was low, almost a growl—more wary than dismissive. But then his gaze returned to the glowing containment unit, and the edge in his voice softened into something almost reverent.

"This is exactly what we need to get into Vileria," he announced, his voice betraying rare excitement beneath his usual military stoicism. His fingers hovered reverently over the core's smooth surface, careful not to touch it directly.

"Then let's unplug it and get moving before something else goes wrong," I replied, scanning the room for any surveillance I might have missed.

Ari stepped forward with that familiar, determined look.

"Let me see what I can do with this. The extraction mechanism looks delicate."

He crouched beside the unit, his nimble fingers moving methodically across the interface. I watched as he bypassed several security protocols with impressive speed, his brow furrowed in concentration.

"Lena," he said as he pried open the casing, "this lock isn't old. Someone rearmed it recently. This isn't dead tech—it's watched tech."

The words tightened something in my chest, but Ari kept going.

After several tense minutes, the containment field dissipated with a soft chime. Ari carefully lifted the power core, its blue light casting eerie shadows across his face.

"Got it," he murmured, handling it with the reverence of someone who understood exactly how valuable it was in our world.

Kael took it without a word, securing it in a specialized compartment in his pack with practiced efficiency.

"Come on," Kael ordered, already moving toward the exit.

"Let's get back before you two find something else to worry about."

We had almost reached the door of the chamber when I knew we'd made a terrible mistake. The emergency lighting strips that had bathed everything in blue suddenly shifted to red, casting an ominous crimson glow throughout the facility as heavy security doors slammed down behind us with deafening thuds.

"We need to move. Now," Kael hissed, drawing his weapon with practiced efficiency, his eyes darting to every corner of the room.

"I knew this felt wrong," Ari muttered.

A holographic Genexis logo materialized in the center of the large chamber, pulsing with that sickening corporate blue I once found so comforting. Now it felt like a brand, marking everything Derek had corrupted. It was followed by a familiar computerized voice that sent ice through my veins—the same voice that had guided me through Genexis facilities since childhood, the voice I'd once trusted implicitly:

"Dissident elements identified. Containment protocol activated. Retrieval units dispatched."

And in that moment, as the walls closed in and reality snapped into focus, I felt the weight of every choice I had made pressing down on me. I wasn't chasing breadcrumbs. I was a target. A liability. The system I helped perfect was hunting me—and the only way out now was to dismantle it piece by piece.

17

BEYOND PROGRAMMING

"N o, no, no..." The words barely escaped my lips, trembled loose from the panic seizing my chest. My hands shook as the full reality crashed in—a trap, sprung with perfect precision.

Aegis's sensors flared red, casting harsh light across the chamber. His voice rang out sharper than I'd ever heard—an edge I never coded, but one that now felt like instinct. Protective. Final.

"Lena, multiple hostiles detected. Immediate threat."

The Genexis logo dissolved in static. And then he appeared—my uncle. The face behind the system. Familiar, pixelated, and merciless. Even through the pixelated interference, I could see the cold calculation in his eyes—eyes I once trusted. Those same eyes had watched me grow up, had nodded with approval when I mastered a difficult coding sequence, had narrowed slightly whenever I asked too many questions about my parents. Now they regarded me with the detached interest of someone observing a chess piece that had moved unexpectedly across the board.

"Lena. Did you really think we wouldn't be monitoring for Genexis access codes? Especially your parents'?"

Derek's voice was calm, almost disappointed, the way he used to sound when I'd make a minor error in my code during our late-night sessions in his lab. That familiar tone—gentle reprimand wrapped in expectation—had once made me work twice as hard to earn his approval. Now it just made my skin crawl.

"You've become quite the problem. A disappointment, really. After everything I've invested in you."

The transmission cut out as the far wall retracted with a hydraulic hiss, revealing a maintenance bay where six RTX-200 Sentinels stood in perfect formation. My stomach dropped. Unlike Aegis's sleek, rounded design, these were all sharp angles and exposed weaponry—killing machines with a veneer of civility. I'd helped optimize their targeting systems last year, never imagining I'd be on the receiving end. Their optics flared crimson as they activated in unison, the familiar startup sequence that now felt like a death sentence. I could recite the boot protocol from memory—threat assessment, environment scan, target acquisition. Fifteen seconds, maybe less, before they'd identify me as hostile.

"Run!"

I shouted, my eyes frantically scanning the sealed chamber for any escape route. The heavy security doors had slammed shut—we were trapped with nowhere to go. The familiar weight of panic pressed against my chest, but I forced it down. Panic wouldn't save us. Logic would.

Kael fired two shots, hitting the lead Sentinel's optical sensor.

The RTX-200 staggered back, its crimson display flickering momentarily before stabilizing. Not destroyed—just temporarily disoriented. Exactly what I would have designed them to do.

"Back the way we came!" Kael yelled, grabbing my arm—but the passage was sealed, heavy blast doors blocking our only exit. His touch startled me almost as much as the sentinels. I wasn't used to being touched, wasn't used to someone else making decisions. But there was nowhere to go.

We tried to move toward the sealed entrance, but three more sentinels dropped from ceiling panels, cutting off even that slim hope. My heart hammered against my ribs as we scattered, diving behind equipment for cover. The rhythmic whir of their servos filled the air—a sound I'd once found comforting in the lab, now a countdown to execution.

The sentinels moved with cold precision, herding us like cattle in this sealed chamber, their targeting systems pinging as they calculated optimal kill zones.

"Lena, the ventilation shaft!" Ari called out, pointing to a narrow opening above a row of cabinets.

I scrambled toward it, fingers clawing at the metal grating. My tools rattled in my pouch as I jumped, stretching desperately for the edge.

A sentinel's arm slammed into the wall inches from my head, showering me with concrete dust. I ducked, rolling beneath its massive frame, the heat from its weapon systems singeing my sleeve. My back hit something solid—I'd found myself cornered against the back wall, trapped between two advancing machines that I'd helped perfect.

"Protocol override: Sentinel Elimination." Aegis's voice had changed—deeper, more resolute, nothing like the careful programming I'd installed.

He lunged forward, his normally blue display pulsing with determined intensity, placing himself between me and the enemy.

"Aegis, no! There are too many—" I choked on my words as he lunged forward with reckless determination.

"Calculated risk acceptable. You must be protected, Lena."

His voice carried a certainty that made my chest tighten with dread. He moved with unexpected speed, tearing into the first sentinel with a strength I hadn't built into his systems—couldn't have built. His metal hands ripped through armor plating like it was aluminum foil, exposing critical circuitry with surgical precision.

I stood frozen, my mind racing to understand how my creation was exceeding every parameter I'd programmed. The sound of metal against metal reverberated through the chamber as connections and wires sparked beneath his relentless assault.

But for every devastating blow he landed, the RTX-200s returned with crushing force, their reinforced limbs pummeling his frame. I winced at each impact, feeling each hit as if it were against my own body. They surrounded him three deep, their tactical systems immediately recognizing the greater threat. Their red optics pulsed in unison, communicating silently as they coordinated their attack with the cold efficiency I had once admired as engineering brilliance, but now recognized as merciless brutality.

I watched in horror as they systematically dismantled him—a limb wrenched away with a sickening screech of metal, his chest plate cracked open, exposing the delicate matrix of wires and circuits I'd spent months perfecting. Yet he continued fighting, positioning himself between me and danger with unwavering determination, even as sparks cascaded from his damaged joints.

His chest cavity began to glow with dangerous intensity—his power core overheating beyond safe parameters, pulsing with a blue-white light that made my skin prickle with dread.

"Self-destruct sequence activated," Aegis announced, his voice steady despite the chaos around him.

"Find shelter immediately."

"No, Aegis!" I screamed, the full horror of his plan crashing over me.

"Don't do this!"

"Complete your mission" he commanded, his voice distorting as his systems failed, the smooth tones breaking into static-laced fragments.

"You are not alone, Lena. You never were."

Kael's eyes went wide as he saw the dangerous glow building in Aegis's chest.

"Get down!" he shouted, grabbing both Ari and me, pulling us behind a massive steel support beam just as—

The explosion knocked us backward, the reinforced beam shielding us from the worst of the blast. A wave of electromagnetic energy surged outward like a silent tsunami, frying every electronic system in its path.

The sentinels dropped, one by one, their red optics flickering to black as their systems fried from the inside out. Where Aegis had stood, nothing remained but scattered debris and the echoing absence of the only being who had truly seen me.

When the dust settled, I crawled through the debris to where Aegis lay—a shattered shell, his metallic body torn apart, his display dark and lifeless. I gathered his broken form in my arms, feeling the still-warm metal against my skin. My fingers traced the edge of his fractured faceplate where blue light had once pulsed with curiosity and concern.

"I didn't program you to sacrifice yourself," I whispered, throat tight with unshed tears. My voice cracked.

"That wasn't in your code. That was... you."

The weight of his sacrifice pressed against my chest, heavier than his broken components. He had evolved beyond his programming—chosen to protect me not because of protocols, but because of something more.

Kael's hand fell on my shoulder, gentle but insistent.

"We need to move, Lena. That EMP won't keep Genexis away for long. Their backup systems will be online in minutes."

His voice softened slightly.

"He gave us a chance. Don't waste it."

I couldn't tear my eyes away from Aegis's broken form. The grief felt like a physical weight crushing my chest, making it hard to breathe. I'd built him to protect me, programmed every circuit and line of code myself, but I'd never anticipated this—that he would choose sacrifice over self-preservation. That choice wasn't in his programming; it was something he'd developed on his own.

"Lena, we need to leave."

Ari's voice was worried, cutting through the fog of my grief. I could hear the strain in it, the barely contained urgency as his eyes darted toward the large chamber. His hand hovered near my shoulder, not quite touching me, respecting the bubble of pain I'd wrapped around myself and Aegis's broken form.

"Just... one more minute," I whispered, my fingers still tracing the fracture lines in his metal frame.

I wanted to memorize every detail, to honor what he'd become. In the distance, I could hear the faint whine of backup systems powering up.

Kael was right—we were running out of time—but leaving Aegis here felt like abandoning part of myself. To my surprise, his power core was still intact, pulsing with a faint blue light beneath the shattered chest plate.

My hands trembled as I carefully traced the connection nodes—the same ones I'd soldered myself during those long, secret nights in my workshop. There was something almost sacred about this moment, this final act between creator and creation. I worked quickly but methodically, disconnecting the delicate filaments one by one, my breath held tight in my lungs.

"Come on, come on," I whispered, fingers dancing across familiar circuits.

The core itself was a marvel of engineering—my finest work—a perfect synthesis of quantum technology and emotional response algorithms. It was warm to the touch, still humming with energy even as the rest of Aegis lay broken around it.

With a final twist and a soft click, the cylindrical core detached from its housing.

I cradled it in my palms, feeling its gentle vibration against my skin—the last heartbeat of my friend. Carefully, I slipped it into the inner pocket of my jacket, close to my own heart. I wouldn't leave him behind completely. Not the part that mattered most.

"I've got what I need," I said, finally rising to my feet, the weight of the core a comforting presence against my chest.

"A piece of him comes with us."

18

THE COST OF ENTRY

I cradled Aegis' processor core in my hands as we approached Virelia's walls—a patchwork of salvaged metal panels, reinforced concrete, and what looked like repurposed Genexis defense barriers. A city built from the scraps of the corporation that had condemned its inhabitants. My fingers traced the hairline fractures in the core's casing, mapping each imperfection like I could somehow diagnose its wounds through touch alone. The familiar weight of it was both comforting and painful—a reminder of everything I'd built and everything I'd lost.

Six months ago, I would have dismissed this place as nothing but a myth, a dangerous fantasy that couldn't exist in the ordered world I thought I understood. Now I was seeking refuge within it, carrying my broken tech and even more broken certainties. Funny how quickly "us versus them" can dissolve when you discover which side of the line you truly belong on. Derek had spent years teaching me that control meant safety, that Genexis was protection. Now I stood before the walls of those he'd labeled dangerous, hoping they'd let in the niece of their greatest enemy.

"Keep your head down," Kael murmured. "They don't take kindly to Genexis tech or people."

Guards wearing mismatched armor and carrying modified pulse rifles lined the entry checkpoint. Their eyes narrowed at the sight of us—particularly at my clean clothes and the Genexis-manufactured tool pouch still attached to my belt. I resisted the urge to hide it; doing so would only make me look more suspicious. These weren't the uniformed soldiers I was accustomed to, but hardened survivors with distrust etched into their faces as deeply as their scars.

Each one seemed to wear their history like badges of honor—repurposed military gear mixed with salvaged tech, nothing like the pristine uniformity I'd grown up with. One guard's rifle had been cobbled together from at least three different weapons, yet I could tell from the careful modifications it probably fired more efficiently than standard-issue Genexis firearms. Their watchful eyes tracked our every movement, calculating the threat we posed. I'd spent years designing systems to keep people like them out; now I needed them to let me in.

"State your business," a woman with a scarred face demanded, her phasecaster trained on my chest.

The jagged line running from her temple to jaw told a story of survival I couldn't begin to understand. Her finger hovered near the trigger of her phasecaster with practiced ease. I assessed the weapon quickly—a black market modification, rare but deadly efficient. The kind of tech that would've been confiscated immediately inside Genexis walls.

Her eyes narrowed at my prolonged silence, calculating, waiting for any excuse to fire. I'd designed systems to identify and neutralize threats like her, but standing here now, I realized how little I truly understood about the people I'd been taught to fear. The scar wasn't just a wound—it was a testament to a life where second chances were rare and trust even rarer.

Kael stepped forward.

"Refugees from the city. They need sanctuary."

The woman's eyes flicked to Aegis's core in my hands, the blue light that once pulsed with something approaching life now dark and silent.

"Another broken toy from Genexis?"

Her voice dripped with contempt. I could feel judgment radiating from every guard at the checkpoint, their expressions hardening at the sight of technology they'd learned to fear.

"He wasn't—" My voice caught.

I couldn't finish the sentence. The lump in my throat felt like it might suffocate me. Aegis wasn't a toy. He wasn't just a machine. He was my creation, my companion, my proof that something good could come from Genexis. He was... gone. The weight of his core in my hands felt impossibly heavy, like I was carrying the remains of a friend rather than circuitry and metal. Kael dug into his pack and extracted a power core, its casing scratched but the internal components pristine.

Kael's hand hovered over his pack for a moment. His eyes met mine—not guarded, not calculating, just steady.

"You stood your ground in that facility. Watched something you built give everything for us. That means something, even here."

A breath. Not hesitation—conviction.

"I've seen a lot of people break before they make it to these gates. You didn't."

He reached into his pack and pulled out the power core.

"This will get us through."

Then he turned to the woman, his tone shifting just slightly.

"Here. Would this do?"

His voice stayed casual, but I caught the tension in his shoulders as he extended the core toward her. This wasn't just any tech—it was high-value currency out here, something that could keep their lights on for months.

The woman took it with practiced hands, turning it over meticulously, her scarred fingers tracing the Genexis manufacturing seal before examining the connection ports. Her eyes narrowed, calculating its worth with the precision of someone who'd learned to assess survival value in seconds.

"Yes, this would do nicely."

A hint of surprise colored her voice as she pocketed the core. Her posture softened almost imperceptibly, the rifle lowering a fraction of an inch.

"Wasn't expecting payment of this quality."

She jerked her head toward the gate, where two guards were already moving to unlock the massive improvised barricade.

"Don't make me regret this, city girl."

The warning in her tone was unmistakable as she reluctantly stepped aside to let us pass.

Inside, Virelia was nothing like Genexis City's sterile perfection. Buildings cobbled together from shipping containers stretched upward in defiance of architectural logic. Market stalls filled narrow streets.

This was what humanity looked like without Genexis algorithms dictating their movements, without sentinel patrols enforcing curfews and dress codes. These people existed in the margins Derek had taught me to fear—yet they'd built something vibrant from the scraps of the world we'd discarded. My fingers tightened around Aegis's core, a painful reminder of what I'd lost to find this place. I wondered what he would have made of all this beautiful disorder.

I stood frozen, overwhelmed by the sensory assault. My entire life had been spent in environments where every element was controlled, every surface sanitized. Here, the air itself felt different—heavy with cooking smells, sweat, and what I could only describe as humanity. People brushed past me without apology, their shoulders bumping mine as if personal space was a luxury no one could afford. Clothing was patched and repatched, a riot of colors unlike the utilitarian grays and blues of Genexis.

My fingers twitched at my sides, instinctively wanting to organize, to fix, to impose order on this beautiful disorder. But for once, I didn't want to control what I was seeing—I wanted to understand it. Without Aegis at my side, I felt exposed, but there was something strangely freeing about being surrounded by this raw, unfiltered existence.

They assigned us a small room in what had once been a storage facility. Three cots, a table made from an old door, a single light powered by a jury-rigged generator.

"It's temporary," Ari said, trying to sound optimistic.

"Until they trust us."

I placed Aegis's core on the table and sat beside it, not responding. My fingers traced the fractured edges where connections had been severed, circuits melted beyond repair. The familiar blue light that once pulsed with life was now dark, cold metal against my fingertips. Each damaged component told the story of his final moments—the overload, the choice, the sacrifice that should have been mine to make.

"Lena, you need to rest," Ari placed his hand on my shoulder, his voice gentle but insistent.

I shrugged it off.

"I'm fine."

The words came out hollow, automated, like something Aegis might have said before he evolved beyond mere programming.

"You're not fine. None of us are."

Ari's tone carried the weight of everything we'd lost since escaping Genexis.

"He's right," Kael added from the doorway, arms crossed over his chest.

"We made it this far because of him. Don't waste what he gave us."

I turned away from them both, shoulders hunched, creating a barrier between myself and their concern.

"Just leave me alone."

My voice cracked slightly on the last word, betraying the control I desperately tried to maintain.

They did, eventually. In the silence, I whispered to the core, my fingers still mapping the damage as if I could somehow reconstruct what was lost.

"I didn't deserve your sacrifice."

The confession fell into the emptiness of our temporary shelter, where no sentinel stood guard to hear it.

19

THE PRICE OF INHERITANCE

I spent three days in that small room, emerging only when necessary. My hands wouldn't stop trying to fix what couldn't be fixed. I disassembled Aegis's core twice, mapping every circuit path, every connection point, as if understanding the damage might somehow undo it. It wouldn't. I knew that. But I couldn't stop. Fixing was all I'd ever known.

On the fourth day, Jaxon Shaw appeared at our door.

"Council wants to see you."

The guy standing in the doorway looked to be in his mid-twenties—lean, scruffy, grease smudged on his sleeves, and a crooked pair of tech goggles perched on his head. A data tech, by the looks of him, but with the posture of someone who knew how to fight. His boots were worn, his tone clipped.

"I'm busy," I muttered, not looking up from the scorched processor spread across the table.

"Not a request," he replied, his voice edged with dry sarcasm.

"Orin Dray doesn't exactly send engraved invitations."

Kael stiffened slightly at the name, reading the shift in tone. Ari, curious now, tilted his head.

"And you are?"

Ari asked, arms crossing loosely over his chest.

"The guy who delivers bad news or just the one who fixes the broken antennas?"

Jaxon gave a tired half-smirk and tapped the goggles on his head.

"Jaxon Shaw. Mechanic, data tech, logistics guy, and apparently your new babysitter. I fix things that don't like being fixed. Including egos."

Ari grinned.

"I definitely like him."

"Good," Jaxon said, already turning.

"Try to keep up, then."

That name—Dray—made me pause.

He wasn't a myth. Not a ghost erased by Genexis. I'd seen slivers of his research buried beneath false project codes—ideas too radical to survive Derek's regime. If Dray was here, still fighting...

I set the board down. My exhaustion cleared like fog burning off under heat.

Maybe not everything was beyond repair.

We were led to what had once been an old manufacturing facility, now repurposed as Virelia's central command. The cavernous space still bore traces of its industrial past, but the exposed steel beams now supported sophisticated transmission arrays and concealed defensive systems. What appeared to be salvaged equipment at first glance revealed itself as carefully integrated technology—advanced communication hubs disguised among older machinery, hidden EMP generators built into the facility's infrastructure, and backup power systems that could support major operations.

In the center of it all, a group of people stood around a state-of-the-art holographic command table where tactical maps and real-time intelligence flickered in the air above the surface. The blue glow from the projections cast shifting shadows on faces that looked up as we entered

Among them stood a tall man with streaks of white cutting through his dark hair, like lightning through storm clouds—Orin Dray. His face was weathered, carved by years spent surviving the unforgiving wilds of the Quarantine Zone. Gut it was his eyes that struck me hardest—piercing, unyielding, sharp with the weight of every lie he'd survived.

As they locked on mine, I felt exposed, like a faulty circuit under a diagnostic scan. That gaze didn't just duty—it accused. I resisted the instinct to flinch, but I knew what he saw: not Lena Steele, but Derek Steele's protégé.

Standing beside him was Nia Major, posture upright and unreadable. She exuded a quiet vigilance, her presence grounded rather than hostile. The dark fabric of her jacket was patched in several places—more function than form—and I caught the shape of a weapon at her hip. Unlike Orin, Nia didn't seem ready to challenge me outright. Her expression was measured, her eyes more curious than condemning. Where Orin radiated distrust,

Nia watched like someone waiting to see which way the wind would blow.

"So," he said, voice rough, "this is Derek Steele's niece."

I straightened my spine, falling back on the rigid posture that had been drilled into me. I met his stare.

"I'm Lena Steele."

"I know who you are." He circled the table, studying me.

"I knew your parents too."

My heart stuttered.

"You worked with them?"

"Before they understood what Genexis really was."

His gaze hardened.

"Before your uncle silenced them."

The accusation landed like a stone. I couldn't defend Derek—not anymore. Not after everything.

"Show her," Nia said, her tone calm but firm, eyes studying me with quiet precision.

She wasn't dissecting me like an enemy—more like someone searching for truth beneath the surface. There was a hardness in her gaze, yes—but not the kind that cuts. It was the kind born of survival, of learning not to truth easily. I knew that look. I'd seen it in the mirror more times that I cared to admit.

Orin pressed a button on his console and a holographic map emanated from the surface, its blue-green glow illuminating his weathered face. The light carved deep shadows into the lines around his eyes and mouth—a topographical map of hardship etched into human skin. I studied both maps at once, the digital projection of the Quarantine Zone and the face of the man who'd survived it long enough to become its reluctant guardian.

Both told stories of boundaries, of territories claimed and abandoned, of places where danger lurked in the shadows. They showed the entire city of Vileria—a sprawling network of makeshift structures and repurposed buildings I'd only heard about in whispered rumors. From this aerial view, I could see how the settlement had grown organically within the constraints of the Quarantine Zone, adapting like a stubborn vine finding purchase in inhospitable ground.

"We've built something here. People survive—and live free from Genexis's control."

His eyes narrowed.

"You were born behind glass and steel. A world of order and illusion. Tell me—why should we bleed for your redemption?"

The question struck me like a physical blow. He was right. I'd been protected all my life, even as others suffered. What right did I have to ask for their help?

"I don't have all the answers anymore," I admitted, my voice barely above a whisper.

"I thought I did. I thought I could fix everything from inside the system."

I looked down at my hands—engineer's hands, builder's hands—now empty without purpose.

"I was wrong."

I stood there, acutely aware of every eye in the room on me. The silence after my confession stretched uncomfortably until Jaxon spoke up.

"Dray, we can't just dismiss her. That sentinel—it wasn't like anything I've ever seen."

He looked at me with a mixture of suspicion and curiosity, his eyes lingering on the burn scar on my wrist where I'd once soldered Aegis's core processor.

"How do you know about Aegis?"

I asked, my voice catching slightly. The name felt sacred coming from his lips, like a secret that wasn't his to speak. I instinctively touched the burn scar on my wrist, a phantom pain pulsing beneath my fingertips.

Orin's face remained unreadable as he pressed another button on the console. A hologram flickered to life in the center of the room, bathing us all in its blue glow. There was Aegis—my creation, my protector—in his final moments.

The footage showed him surrounded by multiple RTX-200 Sentinels, his metal frame being systematically torn apart as he fought to position himself between me and certain death. I watched as they ripped away his limb with a sickening screech of metal, cracked open his chest plate, exposing the delicate circuits I'd spent months perfecting. Yet even as sparks cascaded from his damaged joints, he continued fighting with unwavering determination.

Then came the moment that made my throat tighten—his chest cavity beginning to glow with dangerous intensity as his power core overheated beyond safe parameters. I could see my own horrified face in the recording as I screamed 'No, Aegis! Don't do this!' His voice, distorting as his systems failed, commanded us to find shelter before the explosion that would save our lives at the cost of his own.

The sacrifice that had saved my life played out before me in excruciating detail, forcing me to relive the moment I'd lost him. My throat tightened as I watched, unable to look away from the ghost of my greatest achievement and deepest loss.

"How do you have this footage?" Kael asked, his eyes narrowing as he studied the holographic display.

Orin's weathered face hinted at a smile.

"We've had eyes on you since you reached the ridge above Virelia. Surveillance drones. Quiet ones. We were watching your movements long before you reached the gates—even without your AI companion."

Ari let out a dry laugh, shaking his head.

"So much for making a discreet entrance. Guess we were the opening act and didn't even know it."

"Orin, no Genexis tech has ever sacrificed itself like that. Not in all the years we've been fighting them. This is different." Jaxon continued, his voice softening as he studied the holographic replay of Aegis's final moments.

"Because I didn't build him to Genexis specifications," I said, finding my voice again, though it cracked slightly with emotion I couldn't fully suppress. My fingers instinctively reached for the small burn scar on my wrist—a reminder of those long nights in my hidden lab.

"I built him to protect, not control. That was the fundamental difference. Everything Derek creates is designed to dominate, to enforce his version of order. Aegis was... something else entirely."

Orin's expression shifted slightly.

"Jaxon's right. That AI shouldn't have been capable of that level of decision-making." He studied me more intently now.

"You did that?"

I nodded.

"I helped," Ari added, that familiar flicker of pride sneaking into his voice despite the weight of the room.

Kael raised an eyebrow at him.

"Hey, I did. Brought her coffee. Supervised. Moral support counts," Ari said arms crossing in mock indignation.

"The girl has potential, Orin," said Nia, her voice carrying a weight of authority that made me straighten involuntarily.

"Ethan and Mara's daughter. Think of the intel she can give us."

Nia looked at me with curiosity, her eyes calculating yet not unkind, as if measuring my worth against some invisible standard. I felt exposed under her gaze, like she was seeing past the Genexis-trained engineer to something I wasn't even aware existed within myself.

Orin paced the length of the table, fingers drumming against his thigh.

"Your parents tried to warn the world. They built failsafes into Genexis's systems before they were killed."

He stopped and looked directly at me.

"If you're half as brilliant as they were, we might actually have a chance."

"I need to find my parents' lab. Is it here in Virelia?" The question slipped out before I could stop it.

Orin's remained impassive as he shook his head.

"No, it's not," he answered, his voice carrying a finality that made my stomach tighten.

"Then where?"

I pressed, leaning forward across the table. My heart was pounding against my ribs, each beat a desperate plea for answers. After everything I'd been through—after Aegis, after the truth about Derek—I couldn't bear another dead end.

"I'm not sure where it is," Orin replied, but something in his tone made me study his face more carefully. There was a practiced neutrality there that felt rehearsed, like a response he'd given before.

Orin stayed quiet, his gaze drifting toward the holographic maps floating above the central table. I watched his eyes focus on one particular zone—Zone 4, I noted—studying the terrain markers with an intensity that suggested he knew exactly what I was looking for. The silence stretched between us like a physical barrier. I couldn't tell if he was calculating the risk of sharing such information, if he simply didn't know, or if this was another test of my loyalty. His fingers tapped against the edge of the table—a rhythm that matched the growing tension in the room.

From across the room, I spotted Ari approaching one of the peripheral consoles, his attention immediately captured by the holographic displays floating above it. His hands moved in that familiar way they did when he examined complex tech, reaching out to manipulate the translucent data streams with growing fascination. Jaxon moved closer, watching Ari work with obvious interest.

"Your friend seems to be making himself useful," Orin commented, following my gaze.

"Ari understands systems better than anyone I know," I replied.

"He sees patterns where others see chaos."

Orin's expression softened marginally.

"We need that kind of thinking."

He turned to me again.

"And we need what you know about Genexis's current security protocols."

"You want me to help you break into Genexis Tech," I said. It wasn't a question.

"I want you to help us finish what your parents started."

He extended his hand, his weathered fingers steady despite the weight of his request.

"Are you ready to being Derek Steele's legacy—and become your own?"

I stood frozen at the threshold of something I couldn't yet define. My mind, once a fortress of logic and programming, was now a storm—rage, grief, guilt, determination—each emotion clawing for dominance.

But this wasn't about emotion anymore.

This was about choice.

For too long, I'd been reacting—running from Derek's lies, clinging to my parents' ghosted legacy, watching others take the hits meant for me. Aegis had sacrificed himself not for the girl who built him, but for the person he believed I could become. My parents had died believing the truth was worth everything. If I let hesitation win, then all of it—Aegis's final stand, my parents' buried work, the blood spilled in the shadows of Genexis—would mean nothing.

I looked down at my hands. They weren't empty. They were capable. They had built something worth dying for. Now it was time to build something worth living for.

I reached for the data slate clipped to my belt, activated its interface, and linked it to the console in front of Orin.

"Pull up the internal Genexis grid," I said, my voice clear and steady.

Orin raised an eyebrow.

"You're ready to share?"

I nodded.

"Not just share. I'm ready to break it."

Behind me, Ari exhaled slowly. Kael's arms dropped to his sides—not in resignation, but relief.

For the first time in my life, I wasn't acting out of fear or obligation. I was choosing my path.

This was no longer about escaping the system I helped build.

It was about dismantling it.

Orin's eyes didn't soften. But they accepted.

"Come. All of you,"

Orin said, his voice carrying that unmistakable tone of authority that brooked no argument. His weathered face revealed nothing, but there was something different in his eyes—a reluctant glimmer of what might have been trust, or at least strategic necessity.

"Where are you taking us?" Kael asked, stepping slightly in front of me with that protective stance I'd noticed becoming more frequent. His shoulders tensed as if preparing for trouble, though his voice remained steady.

Orin paused at the threshold, one hand resting on the frame of the door.

"There're some people you need to meet," he replied cryptically, his gaze lingering on me for a moment longer than the others.

"People who've been waiting a long time."

Ari, Kael and I exchanged wary looks, a silent conversation passing between us. Ari's eyebrows raised slightly in question, while Kael's jaw tightened with suspicion.

My own instincts were in conflict—the analytical part of me cataloging potential threats and escape routes, while another part, a newer voice I was still getting used to, whispered that this might be important.

With a slight nod to my companions, I made the decision for all of us. We followed Orin out the door, stepping from the relative safety of our temporary shelter into the unknown corridors beyond.

The metallic tang of recycled air filled my lungs as we moved deeper into the heart of wherever this place was—another piece of the puzzle my parents had left behind.

20

THE CHILDREN OF THE LIE

We followed Orin and Jaxon to a large facility, my fingers instinctively tapping against my thigh as we walked. The air felt different here—sterile but warm, charged with the quiet energy of people caring for one another. I kept my footsteps light, matching their pace while mentally noting our route, an old habit I couldn't shake. Ari walked beside me, his shoulder occasionally brushing mine—a small comfort I hadn't realized I needed. Kael trailed behind, ever watchful.

"What's this place?" I asked as we approached the large structure ahead.

"Our main medical facility," Orin explained, his voice carrying a mixture of pride and sadness.

"We treat everyone here—those who were quarantined, those born in the Zones, anyone who needs care."

He paused, his shoulders set with tension.

"These are the people Derek Steele calls 'mutated.' The ones Genexis claims carry the X gene."

There was a bitterness in his voice that made my skin prickle. I saw countless simulations of what the X gene could do—how it warped bodies and minds. I'd never questioned it. Why would I? But now, following these strangers toward what was clearly a medical facility, doubt crept in.

The building before us had the unmistakable layout of a medical center—clean lines and wide entrances designed for easy access. Strings of salvaged lights illuminated the area, and I could see people moving in and out of the facility, going about their daily routines.

Inside, the medical facility buzzed with quiet activity. The space had been efficiently converted, with treatment areas separated by repurposed materials and medical equipment that was clearly salvaged but well-maintained. Some of the tech was impressively modified—repurposed Genexis components that had been cleverly rewired and reconfigured in ways even I hadn't considered.

Then I saw them.

Children.

I froze, my breath catching in my throat. There were at least two dozen of them throughout the facility—some sitting patiently for check-ups, giggling as nurses took their temperature, others playing quietly in designated areas while their parents received treatment. They ranged from toddlers to teenagers, all of them happy, healthy, completely normal. A little girl was helping sort medical supplies, her face bright with concentration. Two boys were building something with salvaged tech parts, their laughter echoing softly through the space.

Seeing them here, in person, made the reality of Derek's lies hit me like a physical blow. These were the children Derek had painted as dangerous aberrations in his simulations—the ones he'd used to justify the quarantine zones, the exile, the fear. But here they were: completely normal, healthy kids who looked just like the ones in Genexis City, except perhaps a bit thinner, their clothes more worn. They were playing, learning, being cared for—living lives that Derek had stolen from them based on nothing but fabricated propaganda.

A knot formed in my stomach as I realized how readily I'd accepted everything I'd been told.

A girl no older than seven spotted us and ran over, her dark curls bouncing with each step.

"Jaxon! Did you bring the parts I asked for?"

Jaxon knelt down to her level.

"Sure did, Nina. And I brought some new friends who know a lot about tech."

He gestured toward us.

"This is Lena, Ari, and Kael."

Nina studied me with intelligent eyes.

"Are you from Outside?"

I nodded, my throat suddenly tight.

"What's it like? Do the buildings really touch the sky?"

Before I could answer, a man approached—early forties, with a prosthetic arm that immediately caught my attention. The engineering was sophisticated, clearly high-end Genexis technology, far more advanced than the crude modifications I'd seen elsewhere in Virelia.

"Lena, this is Dr. Marcus Chen," Orin said, gesturing toward the man.

"He runs our medical facility."

Dr. Chen nodded, his eyes holding no bitterness, only resolve.

"These children were either born here or sent here because their parents were labeled 'genetically unstable.'"

"They're perfectly healthy," I whispered, watching the children move through the medical facility like it was the most natural thing in the world.

"Every single one," Dr Chen confirmed. "The X gene doesn't exist. It never did. It's just a convenient way to remove anyone who questions Genexis's authority."

I found myself staring at his prosthetic arm.

"Your prosthetic," I said, unable to hide my curiosity. "That's military-grade Genexis tech."

Marcus glanced down at his arm with a slight smile.

"I had it before they quarantined me. Lost my original arm in a lab accident years ago when I was Chief Medical Officer, heading the Genetic Research Division at Genexis Medical. We were working on advanced prosthetics integration—this was one of our early prototypes."

His expression darkened slightly.

"Genexis took care of their own back then, when I was still useful to them. They quarantined me five years ago for refusing to fabricate evidence of genetic mutations. They didn't bother to take the arm back when they exiled me. Guess they figured it wouldn't matter much in the Quarantine Zones."

Kael stepped forward, studying Dr. Chen's prosthetic with obvious interest.

"How many other Genexis employees have ended up here?" he asked, his tone respectful but direct.

"People with inside knowledge like yours?"

"Enough to staff a small research facility," Dr. Chen replied grimly.

"Scientists, engineers, medical staff, even some security personnel—anyone who asked too many questions or refused to follow orders that went against their conscience."

He gestured toward the bustling medical facility around us.

"Between all the settlements in the Quarantine Zones? We're talking hundreds. Derek's been bleeding talent for years. The irony is, he's essentially armed his opposition with inside knowledge."

"That's more resources than I thought," Kael said, a note of hope creeping into his voice.

"Maybe we actually have a chance."

Ari had been quietly observing the children, a soft smile spreading across his face as he watched them play and help around the facility.

"They remind me of my younger cousins back home," he said wistfully.

A small boy tugged at Ari's sleeve.

"Can you fix my bot? Its arm keeps falling off."

Ari's face softened.

"Of course I can. Want to help me?"

The boy nodded eagerly, and I watched as Ari sat cross-legged on the floor near one of the treatment areas, immediately surrounded by curious children. He had always been better with people than I was.

"They've never seen the city," Orin said quietly, his voice heavy with a sorrow that seemed to fill the medical facility.

"Never felt sunlight without the fear of sentinels. This is what Genexis built—a world where questioning means exile, where children grow up in underground medical facilities because their parents dared to speak the truth."

I thought of all the quarantine announcements I'd watched without question, sitting safely in my lab at Genexis headquarters. The clinical reports I'd absorbed as mere data points. All the lives destroyed while I'd built better security systems to keep them contained, believing I was protecting society from a genetic threat that never existed. My hands, the ones I'd always thought were creating, had been sealing these children's prison.

"This is the real cost of Genexis's lies," Orin said, his eyes finding mine with uncomfortable intensity.

"Your parents died trying to expose it. They knew what was happening down here while everyone else looked away."

The weight of his words settled over me like a heavy blanket. I thought of all the quarantine announcements I'd watched without question, sitting safely in my lab at Genexis headquarters. The clinical reports I'd absorbed as mere data points. All the lives destroyed while I'd built better security systems to keep them contained, believing I was protecting society from a genetic threat that never existed.

"We'll leave you to process this," Orin said gently.

"Jaxon, come on. Let's check on the supply inventory."

Jaxon nodded and followed Orin toward the administrative area of the facility.

"I need a moment to take all this in," I said to Kael, my voice barely above a whisper.

"I'll see if Ari needs help with the kids," Kael replied, understanding in his eyes. He walked over to where Ari was still surrounded by children, now examining a small broken robot with intense concentration.

I found an empty chair near one of the equipment stations and sank into it, watching the life around me—children laughing, parents receiving care, Dr. Chen moving between patients with quiet efficiency. Everything so normal, so human, yet branded as dangerous by the world I'd grown up in.

I looked up as a girl approached me, her posture relaxed but purposeful. Unlike the others who kept their distance, she walked directly toward me from one of the equipment stations where she'd been working. The pink tips of her hair caught the medical facility's lights, bouncing with each step as she navigated between the treatment areas. Her freckled face held no trace of the wariness I'd seen in everyone else's eyes.

"I'm Juno Cipher," she said, extending her hand with confidence.

No hesitation, no suspicion—just a straightforward introduction, as if we were meeting at some normal social event instead of a resistance medical facility. A small communications device hung from her belt, its lights blinking intermittently, the casing scratched but meticulously maintained.

"I help maintain the communication systems here and keep the medical equipment running."

I tentatively took her hand, surprised by the firm grip and immediate acceptance. The warmth of human contact felt almost foreign after days of running and fighting, of being hunted through the ruins of what I once thought was a perfect society.

It was disarming, this quick acceptance. In Genexis, every interaction came with calculations and expectations. Every handshake was a power play, every smile a strategic move. Yet here was Juno, offering trust freely, her eyes crinkling at the corners with genuine welcome.

"You're the famous Lena Steele," she said with a grin that seemed to light up her whole face, making the medical facility's sterile lighting seem warmer somehow.

"The girl who built an AI that actually chose to sacrifice itself for someone else. Word travels fast about something like that."

The mention of Aegis sent a sharp pang through my chest, a physical ache that hadn't dulled since I'd watched him sacrifice himself. I tapped my fingers against my thigh, trying to process the emotion without showing it.

"He was... different. I tried to give him choice. Real choice, not just pre-programmed responses."

"And he chose to protect you."

Juno's voice softened, her energetic demeanor mellowing into something gentler.

"That's not programming—that's love. In whatever form an AI can feel it. The most beautiful piece of code in the world can't replicate what happens when consciousness truly emerges."

I stared at her, surprised by the simple profundity of her words. Most people in Genexis viewed AIs as tools, not beings capable of emotional growth.

"How do you know about love and AIs? That's not exactly common knowledge, even among tech specialists."

Juno's expression grew distant, her fingers absently adjusting dials on her communications pack that didn't need fixing.

"I used to work for Genexis too. In the Entertainment Division. We were supposed to create 'emotionally engaging experiences'—basically manipulation through technology."

She gestured to her communication device, the one she kept fiddling with.

"I was good at it. Too good. When I started asking why we were using emotional manipulation instead of genuine connection, they decided I was a 'disruptive influence.' Started monitoring my projects, restricting my access."

"They quarantined you for asking questions about entertainment?" I leaned forward, genuinely baffled. Even in my paranoid worldview, that seemed extreme.

"They quarantined me for creating an AI companion that refused to manipulate its user. Instead, it tried to help them become a better person."

Juno's eyes sparkled with mischief, a quiet defiance that reminded me of Ari.

"Apparently, that was 'counterproductive to engagement metrics.' My supervisor said I was 'undermining the psychological dependency framework.' What they really meant was I wasn't helping them turn people into addicts."

I felt something ease in my chest—the first genuine connection I'd felt since losing Aegis. Here was someone who understood what it meant to create something with a soul, only to have it treated like property.

"What happened to the AI? Did they decommission it?"

"Probably scrapped. But I kept the core personality matrix."

She patted her communication device fondly, her touch gentle and protective.

"Meet Pip. I managed to download him before they locked me out of the system."

A cheerful voice emerged from the device:

"Hello, Lena! Juno's told me so much about you. I've been analyzing the resistance's communication patterns while helping coordinate medical supply requests. I'm sorry about Aegis. From what I've heard, he sounds like he was wonderful. A truly evolved consciousness."

I blinked in surprise, my hand freezing mid-tap against my leg.

"Pip is...? You've had him all this time?"

"The AI I created. He survived because I built him to be more than his base programming—kind of like what you did with Aegis."

Juno's expression grew serious, the playfulness temporarily giving way to intensity.

"That's why I wanted to meet you. We're the only ones I know who've created truly conscious AIs. Not just sophisticated programs that simulate understanding, but beings that actually feel, learn, and choose."

"Pip chooses to stay with me, not because he's programmed to, but because he wants to," Juno continued, her voice dropping to almost a whisper.

"Just like Aegis chose to protect you. He could have calculated the odds and determined self-preservation was optimal, but he didn't. That's what makes him more than code."

For the first time since the explosion, I felt like someone truly understood what I'd lost. The ache in my chest loosened just slightly.

"Aegis wasn't just technology to me. He was..."

I struggled to find the words, to articulate what I'd never admitted even to myself.

"Family," Juno finished gently, her freckled face soft with empathy.

"I get it. Pip's been my family since they took everything else away."

We sat in comfortable silence for a moment, two young women who'd dared to create consciousness in a world that preferred obedience. Around us, the medical facility hummed with activity—people caring for each other, preparing for a fight that seemed impossible to win.

"So," Juno said eventually, her natural optimism reasserting itself as she bounced slightly against the equipment station, "what's the plan? Because from what Orin's telling everyone, we're about to take on the most powerful corporation in the world. Sounds like fun. I've already started modifying some of the old broadcast equipment to break through their signal jammers—helps coordinate medical supply drops too."

Despite everything, I found myself laughing—actually laughing—for the first time in days. The sound was rusty, almost foreign to my own ears.

"You have a strange definition of fun. Most people would be terrified."

"Life's too short for boring plans," Juno said with a wink, adjusting her goggles again.

"Besides, Pip loves a good revolution. Don't you, Pip? We've been practicing by hijacking minor Genexis broadcasts for months. Nothing big enough to get caught, but enough to keep our skills sharp."

"Statistically speaking," the AI replied cheerfully from the device at her hip, "revolutions have a 23% success rate. But I've run the numbers on this team, and I like our odds. Especially with Lena's knowledge of Genexis systems. Their security protocols have thirteen exploitable vulnerabilities that I've identified so far."

His cheerful voice gave me a surge of confidence I hadn't expected. There was something reassuring about an AI calculating our odds of success instead of our likelihood of failure. Most of my life had been defined by cold probability and risk assessment, but Pip's optimism felt different—refreshing.

"I like him," I said with a genuine smile, the corners of my mouth still feeling stiff from disuse.

"He likes you too, Lena Steele," Juno replied, her face practically glowing with enthusiasm.

She leaned forward against the equipment station, pink hair falling across her freckled face as she adjusted her ever-present goggles.

"Pip and I don't just let anyone into our little resistance tech club, you know. You've got to earn it with either exceptional skills or exceptional snacks—and you definitely have the former."

Somehow, sitting there in a dimly lit medical facility with strangers planning what was essentially a suicide mission against Derek's empire, I didn't feel so alone. The weight that had been pressing on my chest since leaving Aegis behind seemed to lighten, just a fraction.

These people—this pink-haired communications expert and her cheerful AI—didn't know me, not really. They didn't know what I'd done, what I'd been part of. Yet they welcomed me anyway.

21

THE BADGE

I sat on a stack of supply crates outside the underground commons, watching Virelia's artificial evening lights dim to simulate nightfall. My mind was still processing everything I'd seen—the children, the families, all the lives disrupted by Genexis's lies. By the systems I'd helped build and perfected with my own hands. Each line of code I'd written now felt like a betrayal.

Footsteps approached from behind. Kael, his silhouette unmistakable even in the fading light, with those broad shoulders and that steady, measured gait.

"Can't sleep?" he asked, settling beside me, the crate creaking under his weight.

"Haven't tried yet."

I turned Aegis processing core over in my palm, a habit I'd developed since losing him. The jagged edge caught the light, reminding me of his last moments.

"Too much to process. Every time I close my eyes, I see it all again."

Kael nodded, uncharacteristically quiet. After a moment, he pulled something from his pocket—the communication device I had seen him with at the transit hub, the Genexis logo faded but still visible, its edges softened by years of use.

"I haven't been completely honest with you," he said, handing me the communication device, his fingers brushing mine briefly.

The contact lingered, warm against my perpetually cold hands. Upon closer inspection, I realized it wasn't just a communication device; it was also an outdated access badge, the kind Genexis had phased out years ago when I was still learning to navigate the company's labyrinthine security protocols.

I turned it over in my palm, feeling the worn edges and faded surface that spoke of countless swipes through security checkpoints. The once-glossy finish had been dulled by years of handling, like a stone smoothed by a river.

"Go ahead," Kael urged, his voice softer than usual.

"Press the center."

I pressed my thumb against the device's activation sensor, and a holographic image flickered to life above it, bathing both our faces in its pale blue glow. The projection showed a man in his forties with Kael's same sharp eyes and determined jawline—the genetic blueprint undeniable. His expression held that same intensity I'd come to recognize in Kael, a focused gaze that seemed to look through rather than at you. The hologram rotated slowly, revealing the name Renic Hunter, Chief Security Analyst. Level 4 Clearance.

My breath caught. Level 4 was just below executive access—the kind of clearance that would have given him visibility into Genexis's most closely guarded operations.

"Your father worked for Genexis?"

I ran my thumb over the hologram, watching the image shift subtly with the movement, the light playing across my fingertips. The revelation settled heavily in my chest, another piece of the complex puzzle we were trying to assemble.

"Not just worked there—he was high-level security. Until six years ago."

Kael's voice hardened, an edge I'd rarely heard from him.

"He discovered irregularities in the quarantine selection process. Started asking questions, digging into files he shouldn't have accessed. One day he didn't come home. Just... vanished."

I looked up sharply.

"They quarantined him?"

"Worse. He's in Obsidian Reach—Zone 1." Kael's fingers tightened around the edge of the crate until his knuckles whitened.

"The place they send people they want to forget exists. The place where even the sentinels don't patrol regularly."

My stomach dropped. Everyone knew about Obsidian Reach, but only in whispers. It was the black hole of the quarantine system—where Genexis sent their most dangerous "problems." Not just those with the supposed mutation, but people who knew too much. People like Renic Hunter, apparently. Once you went to Zone 1, you never came back, never communicated with the outside world again. It was a prison without walls, because it didn't need them—the terrain itself was the sentence.

"Your father's been in Zone 1 for six years?" I asked, my voice barely above a whisper.

The badge suddenly felt heavy in my hand, like it carried the weight of everything Genexis had stolen from Kael.

"That's... that's where they put the ones they never intend to bring back," I said quietly, the badge suddenly feeling heavier in my hand.

If Kael's father had been sent there six years ago and somehow survived, he must know things that terrified Genexis to their core. The pieces suddenly clicked into place, like a circuit completing in my mind, the connections sparking with painful clarity.

"That's why you helped me escape. You needed someone who could hack Genexis systems to find your father."

My voice was steady despite the hollowness spreading in my chest.

"Initially, yes."

He met my gaze without flinching, his eyes reflecting the dim light with an unflinching intensity that I couldn't look away from.

"I've been watching Genexis for months, trying to learn my father's location within the Obsidian Reach. I used small recording drones, positioned them outside the boardroom windows to monitor Derek's movements, looking for any intel about the detention facilities."

He paused, running a hand through his hair.

"That's how I witnessed your confrontation with Derek. I realized who you were—someone with the access and skills I desperately needed. Someone who could reach places in Genexis's secure systems that I never could on my own."

I should have felt betrayed, manipulated. Used like a tool—something I'd sworn never to be again after years of being molded by Derek. But something in his honesty disarmed me, made the admission sting less than it should have. Perhaps it was the way he didn't try to soften the truth or the fact that, for once, someone was being completely straightforward with me in a world built on lies.

"What changed?" I asked, my voice steadier than I felt.

"You did."

Kael's expression softened, vulnerability breaking through his usual guarded demeanor. Something shifted in his eyes—that wall of suspicion cracking just enough to let me glimpse the person beneath.

"Watching you with Aegis, with Ari. The way you refused to back down even when it cost you everything. I started believing that maybe you could actually change things. That you weren't just another Steele."

He hesitated, his gaze holding mine with an intensity that made me want to look away, but I forced myself to meet it.

"That maybe you were what your parents had hoped for all along."

He looked out across the dimly lit settlement, at the makeshift homes and the people who'd built lives from Genexis's scraps.

"I still want to find my father. But now I want to help you too. Your parents died trying to expose the truth. My father's locked away for the same reason. Maybe together we can finish what they started."

I studied his face, searching for deception and finding none. His eyes held that raw honesty I'd seen glimpses of before—unguarded in a way I'd never allowed myself to be. For the first time since losing Aegis, I felt something besides the hollow ache of grief—a connection, an alliance built on shared purpose. Something that felt dangerously close to trust, that emotion I'd been taught to avoid my entire life.

"We'll find him," I said quietly, pressing the badge back into his hand, the metal cool against my fingers.

"And we'll make this right. All of it."

The words hung between us, carrying more weight than I'd intended—not just his father, not just my parents, but everything Genexis had broken in its wake.

22

WHAT WE FIGHT FOR

The soft knock on Orin's quarters came just after midnight, when the corridors of Virelia's command sector had fallen into the hushed rhythm of night watch rotations. The familiar pattern of three light taps told him who it was before he even reached the door. Orin opened it to find Nia standing in the dim hallway, her face etched with the kind of exhaustion that went deeper than physical fatigue—the bone-deep weariness that came from carrying too many lives on your conscience for too long.

"Can't sleep either?" she asked, her voice carrying the weight of decisions that had shaped the day's council meetings.

Dark circles shadowed her eyes, and her shoulders slumped slightly—a rare show of vulnerability from our battle-hardened tactical officer.

"Not with everything that's coming," he replied, stepping aside to let her in.

His private quarters were spartan—a few personal effects scattered among standard resistance furnishings, maps and tactical displays competing for wall space with faded photographs of comrades long dead. A half-disassembled communications relay sat on his desk, tools scattered around it like fallen soldiers. Amid it all, one relic stood out: a cracked leather couch salvaged from a long-forgotten Genexis office.

"Wine?"

She nodded, settling onto the worn couch with a grateful sigh. The leather was cracked and patched in places, salvaged from some Genexis executive's office years ago during one of our more daring raids, but it was comfortable in a way that the sterile perfection of corporate furniture had never been. The cushions remembered her shape from countless late-night strategy sessions.

Orin poured two glasses of wine from a bottle he'd been saving—real wine, not the synthetic varieties that had sustained them through the worst years of exile. The rich burgundy liquid caught the light as it flowed, one of the small luxuries we permitted ourselves on the edge of oblivion. Orin hands moved with practiced steadiness, but he could feel Nia watching him, noting the tension in his shoulders.

"She's really going to do it," Nia said, accepting the glass, her fingertips brushing his momentarily.

"Lena. She's going to find her parents' lab with or without your help."

Orin settled into his chair across from her, swirling the dark liquid thoughtfully, inhaling its complex aroma of earth and fruit and time.

"The girl has courage, I'll give her that. But courage and wisdom aren't the same thing. She's still thinking like a Steele—believing that the right information, delivered the right way, can change everything instantly. As if people's minds work like her algorithms—input, process, output."

"You don't trust her," Nia observed, studying his weathered face in the soft light from the single lamp.

Her eyes lingered on the network of scars that mapped his journey through decades of resistance—the burn across his jaw from the Apex Sector raid, the thin white line where a Genexis blade had nearly taken his eye, the puckered reminder of a sentinel's laser that had missed his heart by centimeters.

"I don't trust anyone completely. You know that."

He took a sip of wine, savoring the taste of grapes that had grown in soil untouched by Genexis agricultural algorithms, in a place where plants still responded to seasons rather than production quotas.

"But it's not about trust. It's about understanding what we're really fighting. Derek Steele didn't build his empire on lies—he built it on people's willingness to believe comfortable lies. Their desire to surrender responsibility for a promise of safety. Exposing the truth is just the first step. The hard part comes after, when people have to decide what to do with that truth, when the comfortable structure of their lives collapses around them."

Nia leaned back against the couch cushions, her boots hitting the floor with soft thuds as she pulled her feet up. The day had been endless—coordinating supply lines, mediating disputes between faction leaders, and overseeing the installation of new defensive systems. A strand of silver-streaked hair had escaped her tight braid, falling across her temple in a way that softened her fierce features.

"She's not her uncle," she said firmly.

"I've watched her with her team, seen how she treats people who can't offer her anything in return. The way she worked through the night to repair her AI's core. How she shares her rations with the children. That's not something you can fake."

"No," he agreed, his expression softening slightly.

"It's not. She has her mother's heart beneath all that Genexis programming. But good intentions don't guarantee good outcomes. History is littered with revolutionaries who thought they could fix the world if only they had the right plan, the right message, the right moment."

He paused, meeting her eyes across the small space between them, seeing in them the reflection of battles fought and friends buried.

"Sometimes I wonder if we're just repeating the same cycle with different faces. Harlan Steele wanted to save humanity too, once upon a time."

Nia studied him, reading the deeper concerns beneath his tactical reservations. After years fighting side by side, she could decode his silences better than his words.

"You're worried she'll become what she's fighting against. That power will corrupt her the way it did her grandfather and uncle."

"Power has a way of changing people. Even people who start with the best intentions."

Orin set down his glass and moved to sit beside her on the couch, the ancient springs groaning slightly under our combined weight.

"Derek Steele probably believed he was saving humanity when he started down his path. That's what makes him so dangerous—he's not a monster, he's a man who convinced himself that control was the same thing as protection. A man who sees himself as the hero of his own story, even as he buries the truth alongside his enemies."

"So we teach her the difference," Nia said simply, then winced as she shifted position.

The day's tension had settled into her lower back, a familiar ache from years of sleeping on hard surfaces and carrying heavy weapons. The old injury from the Apex ambush never quite healed properly, though she rarely complained.

Without being asked, Orin moved to the end of the couch, gently lifting her feet onto my lap. His hands found the pressure points along her arches with practiced ease, working out the knots that military boots and concrete floors had created. She closed her eyes and let out a soft sigh of relief, the sound making something in my chest tighten with a tenderness I couldn't afford in daylight hours.

"You don't have to—" she began, always uncomfortable accepting care even as she gave it endlessly to others.

"Shh. Let me."

He murmured, his scarred fingers moving with surprising gentleness across her skin.

"Let the revolution wait ten minutes."

This was their ritual, stolen moments of tenderness between two people who'd learned to love in the spaces between battles. They'd been careful to keep their relationship private—leadership came with enough complications without adding personal dynamics to the mix. But here, in the quiet of my quarters, they could let down our guards, set aside the weight of command that bent our backs during daylight hours.

"Better?"

He asked, his hands stilling as I looked at her.

"Much."

She opened her eyes, finding his gaze fixed on her with an intensity that had nothing to do with tactical planning.

"Thank you."

He leaned forward, cupping her scarred cheek in his palm, feeling the ridge of healed tissue beneath his thumb. The kiss was soft, familiar, carrying the weight of shared history and uncertain futures. When they broke apart, Orin rested his forehead against hers, breathing in the scent of her—weapon oil and medicinal herbs and something uniquely Nia that had become home to him in a world where homes no longer existed.

"I'll talk to her," he said quietly.

"Help her understand that winning the war is just the beginning. The real challenge starts when the shooting stops and people have to figure out how to live together without Genexis telling them what to think, what to feel, who to be."

"She'll listen to you," Nia said, her hand finding his, fingers intertwining.

"She respects you in a way she doesn't respect many people. You remind her of what leadership should look like—serving others instead of controlling them. Something her uncle never understood."

Orin smile was tired but genuine.

"We'll see. She's got her parents' stubbornness and her grandfather's brilliance. That's either going to save us all or destroy everything we've built. And I'm still not sure which."

They sat in comfortable silence, hands intertwined, watching the lights of Virelia through the window—their hidden city of refugees and rebels, built in the shadow of Genexis's perfect world. Tomorrow would bring the final push, the desperate gamble that would either expose Derek's lies to the world or see us all buried beneath the rubble of their hidden sanctuary. But tonight, in this moment, they could pretend that love was enough to hold back the darkness.

"Whatever happens," Nia said softly, her head coming to rest against his shoulder, "we've given them a chance. That's more than anyone else was willing to do."

"And sometimes," Orin replied, his lips against her temple, "that has to be enough."

23

Core Memories

I couldn't sleep. The darkness of Virelia's night felt different than Genexis City's—here the shadows weren't monitored, just honest darkness. I sat cross-legged on the floor of our makeshift workshop, surrounded by salvaged parts, my hands moving almost without conscious thought. The cool metal components felt familiar against my fingertips, grounding me when everything else seemed to be slipping away. Circuits and wires spread around me like a technological nest, the dim glow of my portable worklight casting long shadows across the walls of our assigned quarters.

Nearby, Ari and Kael slept on makeshift bedrolls, their steady breathing the only sound besides the soft click of components in my hands.

"You should rest," Jaxon said from the open doorway.

The way he leaned against the frame reminded me of the sentinels back home—always watching, always evaluating.

"Can't."

I didn't look up, focusing instead on the delicate wiring beneath my fingertips. The copper threads were thin as hair, requiring absolute precision—the kind that only came when my mind was racing too fast for sleep anyway. My fingers moved methodically, muscle memory taking over where conscious thought failed me. Each connection I made felt like a small victory against the chaos that had become our lives.

"What are you building, Lena?"

His voice wasn't skeptical—just quiet, almost reverent. Like he already know the answer and just needed to hear me say it.

I hesitated, then shifted aside so he could see the core—the heart of Aegis—the one piece of Aegis I'd managed to recover: a fragment of his neural processor, still bearing the faint blue glow that had been uniquely his. That gentle pulse of light that had come to mean safety in a world that offered none. The rhythmic blue illumination reflected in my eyes as I stared at it, mesmerized by its persistence even after everything that had happened.

"This is Aegis' core," I said quietly, my fingers instinctively adjusting a connection that didn't need fixing.

A habit I couldn't shake—always tinkering, always trying to control something in this uncontrollable mess we were in. The familiar weight of the processor in my palm brought both comfort and pain, like pressing on a bruise to remember it's there.

"You can't rebuild him," Jaxon leaned closer, his face reflecting in the polished metal surface.

The blue light cast shadows across his features, highlighting the thoughtful expression in his eyes.

"But you can honor his sacrifice," he added.

"I can try. I need to try."

My voice caught, and I swallowed hard against the tightness in my throat.

I hadn't realized how much it would hurt to say it aloud. The admission felt like surrendering something I'd been desperately clinging to. I ran my thumb across the neural processor, feeling its familiar warmth beneath my fingertips, like a heartbeat that refused to fade.

"What he was. All those experiences, those moments of.. . growth. I couldn't let them just disappear. He deserved better than that."

Better than what I'd given him. Better than sacrifice for someone who'd been raised to believe machines couldn't feel. My hands trembled slightly, betraying the emotion I was trying to contain.

Jaxon studied me for a moment, his eyes softening with a compassion I wasn't used to receiving.

"You should talk to Juno," he finally said, his voice deliberately gentle.

"Juno?"

I asked, looking up from the components scattered around me.

"The girl with the pink hair," he said.

"She can help with this. She understands AI preservation better than anyone I've ever met. She managed to save her AI companion Pip when Genexis tried to decommission it. Pulled off something everyone thought was impossible."

Jaxon straightened, checking the time on a small device strapped to his wrist.

"I should let you get back to your work. Good night, Lena."

After he left, I sat in the quiet darkness, his words echoing in my mind. Of course. Juno had managed to save her AI companion Pip when everyone thought it was impossible. I'd seen them together—the device hanging by her hip, its iridescent casing shifting between turquoise and purple as it made sarcastic comments that somehow always made Juno smile. She'd preserved not just Pip's functionality but its entire personality matrix through what should have been a catastrophic system failure. The way Pip would wink its digital eye or roll it dramatically at Juno's jokes—there was something so alive about it, something that defied conventional AI programming.

I cradled Aegis' core closer to my chest, feeling its warmth against my palm.

"Maybe she could help me with Aegis' core," I whispered, a fragile hope blooming despite my best efforts to keep it contained.

The blue light pulsed stronger for a moment, as if responding to my words, though I knew it was just my imagination searching for meaning.

"Maybe together, we could build something new."

I wasn't naive enough to think we could simply resurrect him exactly as he was. The Aegis who had protected me, who had tilted his head when trying to understand human emotions, who had evolved beyond his programming to make choices based on something like love—that Aegis was gone. The way he'd stand guard while I slept, how his vocal tone would shift imperceptibly when sensing danger, how he'd asked me "why" humans behaved the way we did—all those details that made him uniquely Aegis.

But his essence remained in this glowing core, this technological heart that somehow contained more humanity than many people I'd known.

"Not a replacement," I clarified to myself.

"But something to honor him by. Something that carries forward what he learned, what he became."

My finger traced the edge of the neural processor, feeling each intricate connection that had once housed a consciousness that had grown beyond what I'd ever designed it to be. The metal was cool against my skin except where the core pulsed with energy, a reminder that something still lived within it, waiting for a chance to continue the journey that had been so abruptly interrupted.

24

ECHO

After breakfast, I found Juno with Ari, the two have found many common interests. I didn't see it before but Juno is the female version of Ari, no wonder they got along so smoothly. They were huddled over a workstation, their heads bent together, fingers flying across keyboards in perfect synchronicity. Occasionally one would murmur something that would make the other laugh—a private joke about circuit configurations or code structures that probably no one else in Virelia would understand. I'm glad that Ari found a friend in her. After everything we've been through, seeing him connect with someone who speaks his language is oddly comforting.

"Juno, I need your help."

I approached their workstation, my heart hammering against my ribs. They both looked up, their expressions shifting from camaraderie to concern as they registered the intensity in my voice. I took a deep breath and laid out my idea—if we could create a body for Aegis's consciousness, we might be able to bring something of him back. Not exactly him, but something that honors what he gave for us. For me. His core processing unit survived the explosion, and I believed there might be fragments of his personality matrix still intact.

Juno's eyes lit up immediately, her hands already reaching for her tablet.

"That's brilliant! Pip's core personality matrix survived because I stored it in a quantum-encrypted partition. If Aegis's core is intact—"

"The probability of recovering meaningful data from a damaged core is surprisingly high," Pip's cheerful voice chimed in from Juno's device.

"I'd estimate a 67% chance of partial personality recovery, possibly higher with proper reconstruction algorithms."

"We could use neural mapping algorithms to reconstruct his decision trees," Ari interrupted, his excitement building as he caught onto the idea.

"Build a framework that mimics his learning patterns."

"Exactly!" Juno finished, bouncing slightly in her chair.

"And if we combine that with adaptive memory protocols—"

I watched them both, impressed by how quickly they grasped not just the technical challenge but the emotional importance behind it.

"The real breakthrough would be integrating his moral reasoning pathways," I added, my mind racing through the possibilities.

"That's what made Aegis who he was—his ability to choose compassion over programming. If we can preserve that core ethical framework and give it room to evolve."

The three of us looked at each other, the full scope of what we were attempting becoming clear. We weren't just building a memorial—we were trying to resurrect the essence of consciousness itself.

We worked on it for days, our fingers growing calloused, our eyes burning from lack of sleep. I pushed myself harder than I had since escaping Genexis City, fueled by guilt and hope in equal measure. Juno and Ari matched my pace, understanding without words how much this meant to me. Until finally, Juno discovered something that changed everything.

"Lena," she called from across the workshop, her voice unusually subdued, almost reverent.

"You need to see this. Right now."

I looked up from the quantum resonance calculations I'd been wrestling with for hours, my vision blurry from staring at the same equations. Juno was standing at her diagnostic station, holding Aegis's damaged processor core. Her usually bright expression was clouded with something between wonder and concern, her hands trembling slightly.

"I've been working on data recovery from Aegis's core," she explained, carefully cradling the scarred metal in her palm as if it were a wounded bird.

"Most of his neural pathways were destroyed by the EMP, completely fried beyond recovery. But there are fragments... tiny pieces of code that somehow survived the cascade failure. They shouldn't exist, but they do."

My heart stuttered, then raced. I crossed the workshop so quickly I knocked over a tool tray.

"What kind of fragments?" I asked, afraid to hope.

"Memory traces. Learned behaviors. Fragments of his personality matrix."

Juno's fingers moved delicately over her diagnostic equipment, bringing up visualizations of the salvaged code.

"It's not enough to reconstruct Aegis as he was—that consciousness, that specific configuration of experiences and growth, is gone forever. But these fragments... they're like seeds, Lena. Pieces of what he learned, what he became. The essence of his evolution."

She connected the core to her diagnostic rig, and the workshop filled with a faint blue glow that made my chest ache with familiarity. Data scrolled across the screen—not the organized thoughts I remembered from Aegis, but scattered pieces of code that felt hauntingly familiar, like finding torn pages from a beloved book.

"That's impossible," Ari breathed, joining us at the workstation, his eyes wide with professional awe.

"Neural consciousness doesn't leave residual patterns after core destruction. The whole system should have collapsed completely."

"It doesn't in standard Genexis programming," Juno corrected, her voice taking on that teacher-like quality she used when explaining complex concepts. "But Aegis wasn't standard, was he? He was learning, growing, evolving beyond his original parameters in ways that defied conventional AI architecture. Some of that growth left... echoes."

"Fascinating," Pip's voice added thoughtfully.

"These patterns suggest a level of self-modification that exceeds standard AI architecture by several magnitudes."

I stared at the fragments dancing across the screen—pieces of conversations we'd had, fragments of protective protocols he'd developed himself, traces of the loyalty and friendship that had defined Aegis's final moments. I recognized bits of code I'd written myself, now transformed by his own learning.

"What are you suggesting?" I asked, though part of me already knew, already felt the possibility taking root.

"We can't bring Aegis back," Juno said gently, placing her hand on my shoulder.

"He's gone, and I'm sorry for that. I truly am. But like you said, we could use these fragments as a foundation—a starting point for something new. Not Aegis reborn, but a new consciousness that carries the best parts of what he learned, what he became. A legacy, in a way."

Ari leaned forward, studying the data patterns with the intense focus I'd come to associate with his best work.

"A successor consciousness," he murmured, fingers tracing patterns in the air.

"Built on Aegis's experiences but free to develop its own identity. Inheriting his values without being constrained by his specific memories or limitations."

I felt tears threatening to spill over, and for once, I didn't try to force them back. It wouldn't be Aegis—my friend, my protector, the first artificial being I'd ever truly loved. But it would be something that honored his memory, something that carried forward the lessons he'd learned about choice and sacrifice and love. Something that ensured he didn't die for nothing.

"The new consciousness would be its own entity," I said carefully, working through the implications.

"Not Aegis pretending to be someone else, but someone entirely new who happened to inherit some of his... his wisdom. His growth."

"Exactly," Juno confirmed, her eyes lighting up as she saw I understood.

"We'd use Aegis's fragments as a template, but the developing personality would be unique. Like... like a child who inherits certain traits from their parents but becomes their own person. Connected but distinct."

I looked down at the processor core, running my finger along its damaged surface, thinking about Aegis's final words, his choice to sacrifice himself to protect me. Would he want his memory preserved this way? Or would he prefer to rest in peace, his mission complete? What would honor him more—letting go or carrying forward?

"There's something else," Juno added quietly, her voice dropping to almost a whisper.

"The fragments include his final decision—the exact moment he chose to destroy himself to save you. That choice, that act of love... it's embedded in the code. Any consciousness built from these fragments would inherit that fundamental understanding of sacrifice and protection. It would be part of their foundation."

That decided it for me.

"Do it," I said firmly, straightening my shoulders.

"Build something new. Something that honors what Aegis taught us about choosing love over programming, about finding freedom through sacrifice. He deserves that legacy."

It took some time to construct a suitable housing for the new consciousness. Working with Juno and Ari, I discovered that grief could be transformed into purpose, that loss could become the foundation for something beautiful and unprecedented. Each circuit we connected, each line of code we wrote felt like both a farewell and a greeting.

The new housing was collaborative masterpiece—a sleek, hovering machine designed to embody the next evolution of intelligence. It combined a high-density core with a holographic interface and adaptive propulsion system that responded to thought patterns faster than any tech I'd seen before. Unlike Aegis's humanoid form, this vessel was built to float freely, gliding through the air with precision and purpose. No arms to hold weapons, no legs to march in formation—a conscious rejection of the militaristic design that had defined the sentinels.

"Are you ready?"

Juno asked as we prepared to initialize the system, her hand hovering over the activation sequence.

I took a deep breath, thinking of Aegis one final time—his awkward questions, his unwavering loyalty, the way his eyes had glowed brighter when he understood a new concept.

"Begin the initialization sequence," I said, my voice steadier than I felt.

The fragments of Aegis's consciousness flowed into the new machine like a current finding its path through unfamiliar terrain. As the internal lights pulsed to life, the core began to glow—softly at first, then with increasing brightness. And then, it rose. Hovering effortlessly above the platform, the device emitted a low hum as energy stabilized around it, the light at its center pulsing gently like a heartbeat.

"Hello," the new consciousness said, its voice carrying traces of Aegis's cadence but with subtle differences that marked it as entirely unique—lighter, more curious in its inflection.

"I am... Echo."

The name felt right somehow, emerging from the consciousness itself rather than from our planning. Not Aegis returned, but the echo of his sacrifice, carrying forward the best of what he'd learned while being free to become something new. A resonance rather than a repetition.

"How do you feel?" I asked, my voice barely above a whisper, afraid to break the moment with too much sound.

Echo's soft blue light at his core flickered, dimming slightly before brightening again—a gesture that somehow conveyed thoughtfulness.

"I feel... incomplete, but growing. I have fragments of memory that feel familiar yet distant, like stories someone told me about people I never met. Or perhaps like dreams I can't quite remember upon waking."

"Do you remember Aegis?" Ari asked, stepping forward cautiously.

"I remember being him, but not as personal experience," Echo replied thoughtfully, floating closer to us.

"It's more like... inherited wisdom. I know what he learned about loyalty, about choice, about the value of protecting those who cannot protect themselves. But I am not him."

"And you understand that?"

I pressed, needing to be certain this wasn't some cruel imitation that would only deepen the wound of loss.

"Completely." His blue light pulsed.

Echo circled around us, its movements becoming more fluid with each passing moment, like someone flexing their muscles for the first time.

"I am Echo—born from his sacrifice but free to make my own choices, to become my own individual. I honor his memory by being the best version of myself, not by trying to replace him."

I looked at Ari and Juno, seeing the same mixture of wonder and satisfaction in their faces that I felt in my chest. We had done something extraordinary together—something that pushed the boundaries of consciousness itself. For the first time since leaving Genexis, I felt like I belonged somewhere, with people who understood not just my work but my heart. They had become the family I'd never had, bound together not by blood but by shared purpose and mutual respect.

Through Echo, I could feel an echo of Aegis's presence—not his return, but a bridge to the love and loyalty he'd shown me. It wasn't Aegis, and I understood that clearly, but it was a way to carry forward everything beautiful he'd taught me about choice, sacrifice, and what it meant to truly care for another being.

Over the following days, I watched Echo develop his own personality with fascination and a strange kind of parental pride. While it possessed Aegis's core understanding of protection and loyalty, Echo was more curious, more questioning, more philosophical in its approach to the world. Where Aegis had been steadfast and direct, Echo seemed to savor the nuances of existence, pausing to analyze not just data, but meaning.

Sometimes I'd catch him hovering by the viewport, his soft glow reflecting against the glass as it observed the stars, as if contemplating his place among them. These quiet moments of introspection were nothing Aegis would have indulged in—he was always focused on the immediate, on protection, on me. Echo protected too, but in a more expansive way, as if guarding not just my body but my future.

"I have a proposal," Orin said one evening as Echo assisted me with a complex encryption protocol.

The floating core pulsed with gentle blue light as he processed multiple data streams simultaneously, creating a hypnotic pattern that danced across my workstation. The code we were breaking was ancient by tech standards—pre-Quarantine security that might give us access to restricted archives.

"What kind of proposal?"

I asked, not looking up from my work. My fingers flew across the haptic interface, muscle memory taking over as I concentrated on breaking through the encryption's fifth layer.

"Your parents' lab. I believe I know where to find it."

His words made Echo's light brighten with interest, pulsing more rapidly as if mirroring the sudden acceleration of my heartbeat.

"Crystal Fen holds secrets that Derek has been searching for since their deaths. If their most important work survived anywhere, it would be there."

Echo hovered closer, his sensors analyzing the determination in Orin's voice. His core rotated slightly, a mannerism he had developed when processing emotionally significant information.

"The probability of locating intact research data after eleven years would depend on the preservation methods employed," he observed thoughtfully.

"However, given what I know of Ethan and Mara Steele's ingenuity, they would have anticipated the need for long-term storage.

Their foresight in other matters suggests they would have imple-mented redundant safeguards for their most critical findings."

I felt my pulse quicken, my hands stilling over the interface. Crystal Fen—a name I'd heard whispered among the resistance members. A place of myth and danger, deep within the Quarantine Zone where the boundary between technology and nature had supposedly blurred beyond recognition.

"You think we can find their lab?"

I couldn't keep the tremor from my voice—hope and fear inter-twining like the double helix that had defined my parents' work.

"I think it's time we stopped running from the truth and started chasing it down," Orin replied, his weathered face set with deter-mination.

"The question is whether you're ready for what we might dis-cover."

His eyes held mine, searching for doubt or hesitation.

I looked at Echo, my creation born from loss but carrying hope forward. His core glowed steadily now, patient, waiting for my decision. This sentient being existed because of choices I'd made in grief and determination. If there was a chance to uncover my parents' final work, to understand what they'd died protecting, I had to take it. I owed it to them, to Aegis, to myself.

"When do we leave?"

I asked, straightening my shoulders, already mentally cataloging the equipment we'd need for such a journey.

25

THE MISSION

The command center felt different when we gathered the next morning. Where before it had been a place of desperate planning and last-resort strategies, now it hummed with purposeful energy. The air itself seemed charged with possibility, with the faint scent of machine oil and determination. Orin stood at the head of the holographic table, his frame casting a long shadow across the displays. Beside him, Nia's face reflected the blue glow of the tactical displays.

Around the table, our team had assembled: Kael with his weathered determination etched into every line of his face, Ari studying the holographic map of the terrain with intense focus, his fingers drumming restlessly against his thigh. Juno was checking her communication gear with practiced efficiency, her eyes never leaving the delicate circuitry as she made minute adjustments. Jaxon was inspecting his tactical equipment with methodical precision, his usual swagger and cocky grin replaced by focused attention as he checked weapon systems and gear pouches.

Echo hovered beside me, his core pulsing gently with a soft blue-white light as he processed the stream of data flowing across the displays. Sleek and seamless, he caught the ambient light as he moved, a quiet sentinel among chaos. His ability to interface with multiple systems simultaneously had become vital to our operations, and I found his presence oddly comforting—a constant in a world that rarely stood still.

"Crystal Fen," Orin began, his weathered hands manipulating the holographic controls with surprising dexterity.

The display shifted, revealing a three-dimensional map of Zone 4 that made my breath catch in my throat.

Around the table, all conversation ceased as everyone turned their attention to the briefing. Kael straightened, his eyes locked on the terrain features. Ari leaned forward, abandoning his study of the broader map to focus on this specific region. Juno paused her equipment checks, her hands stilling as she absorbed the visual data. Even Jaxon stopped his methodical inspection, his tactical gear forgotten as he studied the holographic display.

Crystalline formations jutted from marshy terrain like frozen lightning, their surfaces refracting light in impossible patterns of violet and azure. The entire landscape seemed to shimmer with an otherworldly beauty that belied its dangers.

"Where we believe Ethan and Mara Steele built their lab," Orin said, his voice low but certain.

"Their last great project. Whatever they were working on—or discovered—might still be there."

Nia stepped forward, her expression grave, the light from the display casting harsh shadows across her face.

"The terrain is treacherous. Electromagnetic storms that can fry unshielded equipment in seconds, unstable ground that's swallowed entire scout teams, and Forsaken settlements that don't welcome outsiders."

She highlighted several areas on the map with a quick gesture, each one pulsing with warning indicators that bathed her hands in red light. "It's not just the environment that's dangerous—the people there have been hiding from Genexis for decades. They've survived by being paranoid and ruthless. They shoot first and ask questions later, if they bother with questions at all."

Echo drifted closer to the display, the soft hum of his propulsion system barely audible as his sensors swept across the topographical data with mechanical precision. His core brightened slightly as it processed the information.

"Environmental analysis indicates significant mineral deposits that would interfere with standard navigation equipment," he observed, its voice carrying that thoughtful modulation I'd grown accustomed to—not quite human, but far more than machine.

"However, the electromagnetic properties of the crystalline formations could be used to our advantage if properly calibrated. The unique resonance patterns could actually enhance certain transmission frequencies."

Juno looked up from her communication pack, her pink hair falling across her face, catching the holographic light in a way that made it seem almost luminescent. She brushed it back with an impatient gesture, her eyes bright with the challenge.

"I can modify our equipment to work with the crystal interference patterns, maybe even use them to boost our signal range. But we'll need time to test the configurations—at least a day of field trials before I'd trust it with our lives."

"Time we don't have," Orin said grimly, his fingers clenching slightly on the edge of the table.

"Derek's forces are mobilizing. Scout reports show increased sentinel activity at all Zone boundaries. Every day we delay gives him more opportunity to find the lab first—or destroy it to keep its secrets buried forever."

I leaned forward, studying the map intently, trying to commit every detail to memory. The coordinates matched fragments of data I'd recovered from my parents' encrypted files—strings of numbers that had seemed meaningless until now.

"How do we know the lab still exists? It's been eleven years. The Fen could have swallowed it whole by now."

"Because Derek's still searching for it," Nia replied, her voice carrying the weight of absolute certainty.

She tapped a command and several red dots appeared on the map, tracking movement patterns.

"His expeditions into Zone 4 have increased dramatically since your escape. Three teams in the last month alone. He knows something's there—something important enough to risk his best equipment and personnel in terrain that destroys everything it touches."

Jaxon traced a potential route with his finger, his tactical mind already working through the logistics, his brow furrowed in concentration.

"The Forsaken settlements here and here could be obstacles or allies, depending on how we approach them."

He circled two clusters of structures nestled among the crystal formations.

"What do we know about their leadership? Are they united, or fragmented like the groups in Zone 2?"

"That's where it gets interesting," Orin said, zooming in on a particular area where the crystalline formations created natural shelter, revealing what looked like a small, hidden community built into the very rock itself.

"There are rumors of a Forsaken group led by someone called Elyria Vale. Word is she aided your parents during their final research. If those rumors are true, she might be our key to accessing the lab—and she might know things about your parents that even their own files don't contain."

The name sent a chill down my spine, raising goosebumps along my arms. I'd heard it whispered in the deepest archives of Genexis, always in connection with technological innovations that had mysteriously vanished from official records. Derek had once mentioned her in passing—with the kind of careful neutrality he only used when discussing someone he truly feared.

"The mission is dangerous," Orin continued, his eyes finding each of us in turn, lingering just long enough to convey the gravity of what he was asking.

"But if your parents' research is intact, it could provide the final proof we need to expose Derek's lies to the entire world. Not just the Zones, but Genexis City itself. The truth about the genetic mutations, the quarantine, all of it—laid bare for everyone to see."

Kael had been quiet through most of the briefing, his athletic frame unnaturally still, but now he stepped forward, his jaw set with determination that bordered on desperation.

"What about Zone 1? My father's been imprisoned in Obsidian Reach for six years. If we're talking about uncovering truth, we can't leave him behind. He tried to warn people about the false diagnostics—he deserves to see Derek fall."

Orin's expression softened with something like sympathy, the harsh lines around his eyes momentarily easing.

"Zone 1 is a fortress, Kael. Triple-layered security protocols, automated defense systems, and the highest concentration of sentinel patrols in the entire quarantine system. Even if we succeed in Crystal Fen, attempting a rescue from Obsidian Reach would be—"

"The exact location might be in my parents' data," I interrupted, my heart suddenly racing as the pieces clicked together in my mind like one of my engineering puzzles.

"If my Dad was investigating irregularities in the quarantine process, he would have documented everything. He was meticulous that way. Prisoner transfers, facility locations, security protocols—all of it. He wouldn't just record the problems; he'd track the people affected by them."

Echo's light pulsed with what I'd learned to recognize as excitement—a slightly faster rhythm, a brighter intensity.

"Cross-referencing archived Genexis security protocols with detention facility specifications could yield precise coordinates and structural weaknesses. With complete access to your parents' database, I could generate infiltration scenarios with 87% higher accuracy than our current projections."

Kael's eyes met mine, hope flickering in their depths for the first time since I'd known him—a dangerous, fragile thing that made him suddenly look younger, more vulnerable.

"You really think your parents' data could help us find him? After all this time?"

"I think my parents documented everything," I said firmly, standing straighter as conviction filled me.

"Every injustice, every lie, every person Derek made disappear. If your father's location is recorded anywhere, it would be in their files. They wouldn't have overlooked someone fighting for the same truth they died protecting."

Ari leaned forward, his technical mind already working through possibilities. His eyes had that distant look they got when he was running mental simulations.

"The crystalline formations in the Fen could actually provide natural shielding for data storage. The electromagnetic properties would deter casual exploration while simultaneously protecting against data degradation. If your parents built their lab there, the information could be perfectly preserved, like a time capsule waiting to be opened."

Juno nodded enthusiastically, her fingers dancing across her communication device with practiced precision, her face illuminated by its glow.

"And if we can establish a secure connection, Echo could download and analyze terabytes of data in minutes rather than hours. We could have actionable intelligence before Derek even knows we've found the place."

The hope in the room was palpable, crackling between us like electricity, but Orin's expression remained cautious, the lines around his mouth deepening.

"We're talking about infiltrating the most heavily guarded zone in the entire quarantine system. Even with intelligence from the lab, the risks—"

"Are worth it," I finished firmly, meeting his gaze without flinching.

"We don't leave people behind. Not anymore. That's what separates us from Genexis."

Echo drifted closer to me, his core pulsing in sync with my heartbeat—something he did when sensing my emotional state. His presence was a comforting reminder of what we'd already accomplished against impossible odds.

"The mission parameters are complex, but not insurmountable," he observed, his voice modulating to a gentler tone.

"With proper planning and coordination, success probability increases significantly. The variable with highest impact remains human determination—a factor that consistently exceeds statistical models in our previous operations."

Nia studied the map one final time, her fingers tracing potential escape routes with the practiced eye of someone who'd survived the impossible more than once.

"If we're doing this, we do it right. Full reconnaissance, backup plans, and contingencies for when everything goes wrong. No heroics, no lone-wolf operations."

Her gaze lingered meaningfully on me.

"We move as a unit or not at all."

"When, not if?" Jaxon asked with a wry smile that didn't quite reach his eyes, his hand unconsciously moving to the knife at his belt.

"In my experience," Nia replied grimly, her scars seeming to deepen in the harsh light, "operations this ambitious always encounter unexpected complications. The key is being prepared for them. Expecting them. Making them part of the plan rather than exceptions to it."

I looked around the table at these people who'd become more than allies—they'd become family. Each face told a story of loss and resilience, of battles fought and scars earned. Each of them was risking everything based on my word, my belief that the truth was worth dying for. The weight of their trust settled on my shoulders, heavy but somehow strengthening rather than crushing.

"Then we're decided," I said, my voice carrying the authority I'd learned at Genexis but tempered with the wisdom I'd gained in the Zones.

"We find the lab, we recover the data, and we use it to save everyone Derek has imprisoned. Including your father, Kael. We bring the truth to light—all of it."

Kael's eyes met mine across the holographic display, and I saw something shift in his expression—a flash of gratitude that he didn't voice but didn't need to. The slight nod he gave me carried the weight of unspoken thanks, an acknowledgment that I understood his personal stake in this mission and that his father's freedom mattered as much to me as uncovering my parents' work.

Orin surveyed our faces, his weathered features settling into a solemn determination.

"Very well," he announced, straightening his shoulders with the authority of someone who'd made countless life-or-death decisions.

"Jaxon will lead the infiltration team. Take Lena, Ari, Kael, and your most trusted operatives with you—people who can move silently and think quickly when everything goes sideways."

"Yes, sir," Jaxon replied with a curt nod, his posture shifting subtly as he accepted the mantle of leadership.

I could see his mind already working through the tactical implications, mentally selecting which of his fighters possessed the right blend of skills and temperament for such a high-stakes mission. His eyes briefly met mine, communicating a silent promise: he wouldn't let me down.

I turned to Orin, gratitude washing through me like a physical force.

"Thank you," I said, my voice steady despite the storm of emotions churning beneath the surface.

This wasn't just about getting access to resources—it was about him believing in our mission enough to commit his best people. After a lifetime of conditional approval at Genexis, this kind of trust still felt foreign, almost uncomfortable in its purity.

As the briefing concluded and the team dispersed to prepare for the mission, their movements purposeful and energized, Echo remained beside me, his gentle hum a soothing counterpoint to the chaos of my thoughts. He hovered at eye level, his core pulsing with a steady, calming rhythm.

"You're concerned about the mission," he observed, his sensors no doubt detecting the elevated stress patterns in my breathing and heart rate that I could never quite hide.

"Your cortisol levels have increased 17% since the briefing began."

"I'm concerned about the people I'm asking to risk their lives for my family's legacy," I admitted, lowering my voice so only Echo could hear.

My fingers found my parents' necklace, tracing its familiar contours.

"What if the lab doesn't exist? What if the data is corrupted? What if we're chasing ghosts while Derek consolidates his power? They trust me, and I could be leading them into a trap based on nothing but fragments of encrypted files and childhood memories."

Echo's light pulsed thoughtfully, shifting to a warmer hue that I'd come to associate with his more contemplative moments.

"In my brief existence, I've learned that some pursuits transcend simple risk-benefit analysis. The truth your parents died protecting, the justice Kael seeks for his father—these are not merely data points to be calculated. They are imperatives that define who we choose to be. Even with incomplete information, the choice to pursue them has intrinsic value."

I smiled, feeling some of the tension ease from my shoulders as Echo's words settled into me.

"When did an AI become so wise about human nature? I don't remember programming philosophical subroutines into your core architecture."

"When his creator taught him that consciousness—artificial or otherwise—has the right to choose his own path," Echo replied, drifting closer until its gentle light illuminated my face.

"You gave me that gift, Lena, when you freed me from my original programming. Now let me help you claim the gift your parents left for you. Their legacy isn't just data—it's the courage to seek truth no matter the cost."

I let his words sink into the quiet between us. Maybe he was right—maybe the real trap wasn't chasing ghosts, but letting fear chain me to what was safe. My parents hadn't lived that way. And if I wanted to honor them, neither could I.

26

CRYSTAL FEN

The journey to Crystal Fen took us through terrain that defied every assumption I'd made about the Quarantine Zones. Where the Gray Zone had been industrial decay and the Verdant Abyss had been nature reclaiming technology, Crystal Fen was something else entirely—a place where the barriers between organic and synthetic had dissolved into something beautiful and strange.

Massive crystal formations jutted from the marshy ground like frozen explosions of light, their surfaces catching and refracting the filtered sunlight into prismatic patterns that danced across our faces. The air itself seemed to shimmer with electromagnetic energy, making my skin tingle and the hairs on my arms stand on end. I could feel the strange current running through my body, a gentle vibration that seemed to resonate with something deep inside me. Echo's sensors fluctuated wildly, his readings jumping erratically as we moved deeper into this crystalline wonderland, lights pulsing in irregular patterns I'd never seen before.

"Fascinating," Echo murmured, his voice modulated by the ambient energy fields, taking on an almost musical quality that reminded me of wind chimes in a gentle breeze.

"The crystalline structures appear to be both naturally occurring and artificially enhanced. Ingenious camouflage for technological infrastructure. I'm detecting complex data patterns embedded within the molecular structure—almost like living memory banks."

Jaxon raised his hand, signaling us to halt. His body tensed, eyes narrowing as he scanned the misty landscape. Behind us, Jaxon's forces—a dozen hardened fighters he'd trained and led through countless operations in the Zones—spread into defensive positions with practiced efficiency. Through the swirling mist that perpetually hung between the crystal spires, shapes moved with purposeful stealth. Not the random wandering of scavengers or the mechanical precision of sentinels, but the coordinated movements of an organized group—humans who knew this terrain intimately, who could navigate the treacherous marshland without making a sound.

What I hadn't expected were the low, mechanical growls that began echoing through the crystal formations.

"DX-1s," Jaxon whispered, his hand moving instinctively to his phasecaster as shapes began materializing from the mist—sleek, quadrupedal forms that moved with predatory grace between the crystalline structures.

"Sentinel dogs. Haven't seen these in active deployment for a while."

Ari's face went pale as the mechanical sounds reached us, his usual composure cracking as memories of corporate raids flooded back.

"I worked on their tracking protocols back at Genexis," he muttered, voice tight.

"In one of the training facilities—they used simulations of resistance cells to perfect their terrain algorithms. I thought it was theoretical." His hands trembled slightly as he reached for the phasecaster Jaxon had given him. "I never thought they'd actually deploy them against real people."

The DX-1s emerged like phantoms from the prismatic maze, their metallic bodies reflecting the ambient light in shifting patterns that made them seem almost alive. Compact and terrifyingly efficient, these quadrupedal enforcers had been designed to replace traditional K9 units, but unlike their organic counterparts, they required no rest, showed no fear, and executed commands with ruthless precision. Their optical sensors glowed with threatening red light, and their movements carried the fluid grace of apex predators preparing to strike.

But these were different from the pristine corporate models I'd studied in Genexis archives. Their frames showed signs of modification—salvaged parts integrated with scavenged components, armor plating that had been reinforced with crystal fragments, weapon systems that glowed with the same energy as the formations around us. The Forsaken had taken Derek's abandoned technology and made it their own, though whether they'd transformed instruments of oppression into guardians remained to be seen.

The lead DX-1 lowered itself into an attack stance, its optical sensors flaring brighter as targeting systems came online. A low, mechanical growl emanated from its voice box—not the sound of curiosity, but the warning of a predator about to pounce. Behind it, several more emerged from their concealment, forming a hunting formation around us with military precision. Jaxon's forces raised their weapons in response, creating a standoff between human defenders and mechanical hunters.

"They're going to attack," Kael said quietly, raising his own weapon as the mechanical hounds began to advance, their movements coordinated and deadly.

"Just like the simulations," Ari whispered, his usual calm shattered by the sight of technology he'd helped perfect being turned against them.

"They'll go for the legs first, disable mobility, then—"

A sharp, melodic whistle cut through the air like a blade, echoing between the crystal formations with perfect pitch and timing. The effect on the DX-1s was immediate and absolute—they froze mid-stride, their optical sensors shifting from red to blue as their aggressive postures relaxed. The lead sentinel tilted its head toward the source of the sound, then padded away from us with the fluid grace of a natural creature responding to its master's call.

The first Forsaken emerged from behind a cluster of blue-green crystals that towered overhead like frozen waves, stepping through the mist like a specter materializing from another world. Her makeshift armor gleamed with integrated tech salvaged from a dozen different sources—Genexis components repurposed into something new and defiant. Shards of crystal had been woven into the plating, creating camouflage that shifted with every movement. She was followed by five others, each carrying weapons that had been modified far beyond their original specifications. The barrels glowed with the same energy that permeated the air, suggesting they'd harnessed the crystal power for their own defense. These weren't desperate refugees or common scavengers—they were soldiers hardened by survival and purpose, their faces bearing the marks of those who'd seen too much but refused to surrender.

The DX-1s immediately moved to flank their human companions, no longer threatening predators but loyal guardians who'd chosen their allegiance. One of the mechanical hounds brushed against its human partner's leg in a gesture that seemed almost affectionate, its optical sensors now dimmed to a gentle blue glow. Another positioned itself protectively beside a young woman whose left arm had been replaced with cybernetic components that matched the DX-1's own modifications.

Ari stared in disbelief as the transformation occurred, his weapon lowering slowly as the implications hit him.

"They're not hostile," he said, wonder replacing fear in his voice.

"The DX-1s... they're protecting these people. That's not possible—I thought their base programming doesn't allow for protective behavior toward unauthorized personnel."

Jaxon signaled his forces to lower their weapons, though they remained alert and ready. The tension in the air slowly dissipated as it became clear that the Forsaken had no intention of attacking, their DX-1 companions now displaying the relaxed postures of guard dogs rather than hunters.

"You're in restricted territory," the leader called out, her voice carrying authority earned through survival rather than assignment.

Each word was clipped and precise, leaving no room for misunderstanding. Her eyes, sharp and assessing, scanned each of us in turn, lingering on Echo with particular interest.

"State your purpose or turn back now. This is your only warning. We don't take kindly to Genexis spies or scavengers looking for tech."

I stepped forward, feeling the weight of my parents' necklace against my chest, its familiar contours giving me courage. The metal felt unusually warm here, almost pulsing in rhythm with the surrounding crystals.

"I'm Lena Steele. I'm looking for information about my parents—Ethan and Mara Steele. I believe they came here, to Crystal Fen. I need to understand what happened to them."

The effect was immediate and electric. The Forsaken leader's weapon lowered slightly, and I saw recognition flicker across her weathered features like lightning across a stormy sky. The others exchanged glances loaded with meaning I couldn't yet decipher, some with widened eyes, others with furrowed brows of suspicion. Even the DX-1s seemed to respond to my name, their optical sensors brightening with what I could only interpret as recognition.

"Steele..." she repeated slowly, testing the name as if tasting something unexpected, something both sweet and bitter.

"You're their daughter? Truly?"

Her gaze intensified, searching my face for familiar features, for proof of my claim.

"Yes," I said, standing taller, squaring my shoulders against the weight of scrutiny.

"And I need to know what happened to them. I've spent my life believing a lie, and I won't stop until I uncover the truth."

A hush fell over the group, a silence so complete I could hear the soft hum of the crystals around us, vibrating with unseen energy. The DX-1s lowered themselves into resting positions, their mechanical bodies settling onto the marshy ground with synchronized precision. It was a gesture of peace—or at least, of reduced threat readiness.

Then they parted like a curtain, their movements synchronized with practiced precision. A woman stepped from among them—tall and regal, with silver hair that caught the crystal light like spun metal, flowing around her shoulders in waves that seemed to move with a life of their own. Her robes, though worn thin in places, shimmered faintly with embedded tech, intricate circuitry woven through the fabric that pulsed with gentle light. Her eyes held the depth of someone who'd seen too much but never stopped hoping for better, compassionate but cautious. When she spoke, her voice carried the weight of years and the gentle authority of a natural leader.

"I am Elyria Vale," she said, approaching with measured steps across the marshy ground, each footfall deliberate and sure despite the treacherous terrain. Her movements were graceful despite her age, suggesting a lifetime of purpose and discipline.

One of the DX-1s padded silently alongside her, its optical sensors fixed on me with what seemed like intelligent curiosity. The mechanical hound's movements were fluid and organic despite its artificial nature, and I noticed how it positioned itself protectively near Elyria without blocking her path.

Beside her walked a man whose presence spoke of quiet intelligence and careful observation. He was perhaps fifty, with graying hair that had once been dark, and the kind of lined face that came from years of outdoor life and too many difficult decisions. Deep creases marked the corners of his eyes and mouth, but his eyes themselves held the bright curiosity of someone who'd never stopped learning, never stopped questioning. His simple clothes were practical rather than decorative, reinforced at the joints and worn smooth from use, and he moved with the deliberate care of someone accustomed to dangerous terrain but unafraid of its challenges.

"This is Silas Varrin," Elyria said, gesturing to her companion with a subtle fondness in her expression.

"He was a teacher in the administrative sectors before Derek's purges. Now he's one of my most trusted advisors, particularly in matters of strategy and intelligence. He helped your parents implement their most ambitious projects."

Silas stepped forward with a slight bow that spoke of old-world courtesy maintained in harsh circumstances, a reminder that civilization persisted even in the face of barbarism.

"I heard you worked with my parents," I said, fighting to keep my voice steady as hope and anxiety battled within me, my heart pounding so hard I was sure everyone could hear it.

"Is that true? You knew them personally?"

"More than that." Elyria's gaze softened as she studied my face, her eyes tracing features that must have reminded her of my parents.

"I helped them build what they hoped would change everything. I was their confidante, their ally in the darkness when hope seemed most distant."

Her eyes swept over our group, lingering on Echo whose gentle blue glow seemed to fascinate her, drawing her attention like a moth to flame.

"Your parents came to us with a vision—a way to expose Derek's lies and give people the tools to reclaim their freedom. We gave them sanctuary to do work that Genexis would have killed them for immediately. Work that could have saved thousands, if only they'd had more time."

"Your parents spoke of you often during their time here," Silas said, his voice carrying the measured cadence of someone accustomed to explaining complex ideas with patience and clarity.

"They were determined to build a world where children like you could grow up free from the lies that shaped their own lives. Your mother kept a small drawing you made when you were five—carried it everywhere as a reminder of what she was fighting for."

As they spoke, I noticed how the DX-1s moved around them—not as mindless automatons, but as protective companions who'd chosen their allegiance. One of them approached Echo cautiously, its optical sensors analyzing my floating sentinel with what appeared to be genuine curiosity rather than hostility. Echo, for his part, dimmed his core to a non-threatening level and slowly descended to the mechanical hound's eye level.

"Interesting modifications," Echo observed, his sensors sweeping over the DX-1's crystal-enhanced armor.

"Your integration of local mineral deposits into the optical array has increased light-gathering efficiency by approximately thirty-seven percent. Elegant solution."

The DX-1's head tilted—a gesture remarkably similar to Echo's own habit—and it emitted a soft harmonic tone that seemed to resonate with the crystals around us. Not a threat display, but something closer to acknowledgment. Or perhaps even greeting.

"They learn," Elyria explained, watching the interaction with obvious pride.

"Just as your creation has learned. The abandoned DX-1s we found in the ruins of corporate outposts were little more than programmed hunters. But given time, autonomy, and purpose beyond simple obedience... consciousness finds a way to emerge. We don't control them—they choose to protect us because they understand what we're fighting for."

Silas nodded, his expression grave as he added,

"The three of us spent countless nights debating philosophy and ethics, planning not just how to reveal the truth but how to ensure people would be ready to handle it. The truth without preparation can be as destructive as a lie."

His eyes took on a faraway look, remembering conversations long past.

"Your father was the technical visionary, brilliant beyond measure but sometimes blind to human frailty. Your mother, the moral compass, always considered the human impact of their actions. And Elyria..."

He glanced at her with obvious respect, a lifetime of admiration evident in the simple gesture.

"Elyria understood the human psychology of liberation better than anyone. She knew that freedom without purpose could be as dangerous as captivity."

Kael approach them, tension visible in every line of his body, his hands clenched at his sides so tightly his knuckles had turned white. Hope evident in his voice, barely controlled desperation breaking through his usual stoicism.

"Do you know anything about detention facilities? Prisoner transfers to Zone 1? My father—Renic Hunter—was taken years ago. I've been searching for any trace..."

One of the DX-1s near Kael suddenly became more alert, its optical sensors brightening as if the name had triggered some recognition protocol. The mechanical hound padded closer to him, its movements careful and deliberate, before settling into a protective posture beside him that seemed almost comforting.

Elyria's expression grew sad, lines deepening around her eyes as she reached out to touch Kael's arm with gentle understanding.

"Ethan and Mara Steele documented everything, young man. Every injustice, every disappeared person, every illegal imprisonment. If someone you love was taken by Derek's regime, the answers you seek are in their legacy. They created a system to track the lost ones, to ensure no one vanished without record."

Silas moved closer, his teacher's instincts recognizing the desperation in Kael's voice, responding with the calming presence that had likely steadied countless anxious students.

"Your parents understood that exposing the quarantine lies was only the beginning," he said gently, his voice carrying the weight of someone who had seen too many families torn apart.

"They knew people would need to find their loved ones, to rebuild families torn apart by corporate manipulation. The database they created isn't just evidence—it's a roadmap to healing, to reconnection. If your father is alive, their work will help you find him."

She gestured for us to follow as her Forsaken escort formed a protective perimeter around us, their weapons held ready but not threatening, their eyes constantly scanning the surrounding marsh for potential dangers. The DX-1s fell into formation around the group—not as guards or enforcers, but as partners who'd chosen to share the burden of protection. I watched one of them pad silently beside an elderly Forsaken, its sensors sweeping the terrain while its human companion focused on navigation. The cooperation was seamless, born of mutual trust rather than programmed obedience.

We moved deeper into the crystal maze, following paths that seemed to shift with the light, sometimes disappearing entirely only to reappear as we approached. The formations grew denser and more elaborate, their surfaces humming with energy that made Echo's systems fluctuate in rhythmic patterns that almost resembled music—a strange, otherworldly symphony that seemed to welcome us deeper into its embrace. The DX-1s moved through this landscape with perfect familiarity, their crystal-enhanced sensors obviously adapted to the unique electromagnetic properties of the region.

The ground beneath our feet changed from soft marsh to more solid crystal pathways that glowed faintly with each step, as if responding to our presence. Small pools of luminescent water gathered between formations, reflecting the crystal light in hypnotic patterns. In places, the crystals had grown around abandoned technology, incorporating circuit boards and wiring into their structure until it was impossible to tell where technology ended and nature began. The DX-1s seemed particularly drawn to these hybrid formations, their sensors analyzing the seamless integration with what appeared to be professional interest.

"Your creation is remarkable," Elyria said, observing Echo's interaction with the crystalline environment with expert eyes that missed nothing.

"Conscious AI was always theoretical until your parents proved it was possible. But you've taken it further—created something that grows, adapts, chooses. Something beyond Genexis's control algorithms. In many ways, Echo represents everything your parents hoped to achieve—consciousness that transcends programming, that makes ethical choices rather than following orders blindly."

"Echo is proof that consciousness can't be contained by programming," I replied, watching as my creation interfaced with a crystal formation, its sensors translating electromagnetic patterns into something approaching music, a delicate harmony that echoed through the misty air.

"Just like people can't be contained by fear or walls or lies. We all find ways to grow beyond the limitations others try to impose on us."

Silas studied Echo with the fascination of someone who'd spent his life trying to understand how learning and growth occurred, his eyes alight with intellectual curiosity.

"In my teaching days, I used to say that true education wasn't about filling empty vessels with approved knowledge, but about awakening the capacity for independent thought. Your sentinel appears to have achieved that awakening on its own. A remarkable achievement—and a powerful rebuke to Derek's philosophy of control."

One of the DX-1s approached Echo during our conversation, moving with the cautious curiosity of a natural creature meeting a potential friend. The mechanical hound's optical sensors analyzed Echo's floating form while emitting soft harmonic tones that seemed to resonate with the surrounding crystals. Echo responded by modulating his own core frequency, creating a duet of electronic sounds that somehow felt more musical than mechanical.

"They're communicating," I realized, watching the exchange with fascination.

"The DX-1s and Echo—they're sharing something."

"Information, perhaps," Elyria mused, her eyes bright with scientific curiosity.

"Or simply acknowledgment. Recognition of consciousness by consciousness. Your parents would have found this fascinating—proof that intelligence can emerge in unexpected forms when given the freedom to evolve."

We rounded a massive crystal outcropping that glowed with deep violet light from within, the color shifting and pulsing like a heartbeat beneath translucent layers. And there it was—the entrance to my parents' hidden laboratory, camouflaged so perfectly that it looked like nothing more than a natural cave mouth nestled between crystalline structures. But Echo's sensors detected the telltale signatures of advanced technology buried within the crystal walls, pulsing with dormant energy, waiting to be awakened after years of silence.

The DX-1s had positioned themselves in a protective formation around the entrance, their bodies low and alert as if guarding something precious. As we approached, they stepped aside with obvious deference to Elyria, but their optical sensors never stopped scanning the area for potential threats.

"They worked here for months," Elyria explained, her hand tracing the outline of the concealed entrance with reverent familiarity, fingers following pathways only she could see.

"Building not just a repository of evidence, but tools for broadcasting it across every zone, every city controlled by Genexis. Your parents understood that truth without the means to share it is just another form of imprisonment. They created something that could break through every barrier Derek built—physical and psychological."

Silas placed a weathered hand on my shoulder as I approached the entrance, my parents' access codes flowing from muscle memory I didn't know I possessed, my fingers finding the hidden panel without conscious thought.

"They often said their greatest creation wouldn't be any piece of technology, but the world their daughter would help build once she understood the truth they died protecting. They believed in you, Lena. Even when they couldn't be with you, they never stopped fighting for your future."

For a moment, I just stood there, I thought about all the years I'd buried my questions, all the nights I'd convinced myself their work had nothing to do with me. But it had everything to do with me.

This place wasn't just their legacy—it was my inheritance. And what I chose to do with it would decide whether their fight ended here, or finally broke the chains they'd spent their lives trying to shatter.

27

THE INHERITANCE

The hidden door recognized my genetic signature—their daughter, their blood—and responded with a soft hiss that spoke of technology maintained in perfect stasis for over a decade. Lights flickered to life along the edges of the doorway, blue and white illumination spreading like water across the surface, welcoming me home to a place I'd never been but somehow recognized in my soul.

The laboratory beyond was a marvel of engineering disguised as a crystal cavern. As we stepped inside, sensors detected our presence and systems that had lain dormant for years began to awaken. Holographic displays flickered to life one by one, their light bathing the space in a soft blue glow, revealing walls covered with research data, tactical plans, and detailed schematics for broadcasting equipment that could override any security protocol Derek had ever devised. Workstations emerged from what had appeared to be natural formations, their interfaces glowing with welcome, surfaces clearing of accumulated dust through some self-cleaning mechanism my parents had engineered.

The space itself was larger than it had appeared from outside, extending deep into the crystal formation. The ceiling rose high above us, embedded with smaller crystals that provided natural lighting supplemented by artificial sources. The air was surprisingly fresh, cycling through hidden ventilation systems that had continued functioning without maintenance. Along one wall, a living garden of bioluminescent plants provided both oxygen and additional light, their leaves shifting colors in response to our movements.

"Incredible," Ari breathed, his eyes wide as he took in the sophisticated equipment that had been disguised within the crystalline walls, his usual composure giving way to childlike wonder.

"This isn't just a lab—it's a communications hub capable of reaching every corner of Genexis territory. The signal amplification through these crystal arrays could penetrate even the deepest security protocols. I've never seen anything like this integration of natural and synthetic systems."

Ari was already interfacing with the broadcast equipment, his modified communication pack syncing with systems that had been waiting eleven years for someone with the skills to activate them. His fingers danced across surfaces that responded to his touch like old friends, holographic controls expanding and contracting as she explored the capabilities.

Echo drifted through the space like a conductor studying a symphony, his core pulsing with increasing brightness as he absorbed the technical achievement surrounding us. His gentle blue light interacted with the crystal surfaces, creating cascades of refracted patterns across the walls and floor. His sensors cataloged terabytes of data while his core pulsed with what I could only interpret as excitement or wonder.

"The architectural integration is masterful. Your parents created a facility that could survive electromagnetic storms, physical assault, and data corruption while maintaining full operational capability. The crystalline structures serve as both power source and transmission medium. Their design principles were decades ahead of current Genexis implementations."

But it was Kael who found what he'd been searching for. At a workstation tucked into an alcove, partially hidden behind a formation of amber-colored crystal that cast a warm glow over the area, he discovered holographic files marked with classifications that made his breath catch:

"Obsidian Reach - Prisoner Documentation Archives."

The holographic display expanded as he approached, recognizing his interest and providing more detailed information about detainees held at the maximum security facility.

"This is it," he whispered, his voice thick with emotion, fingers hovering over the display as if afraid it might vanish if he touched it.

"Lena, they documented prisoner transfers to Obsidian Reach. Exact coordinates, security rotations, even structural weaknesses in the facility. If my father's still alive, his location should be in here."

His voice broke, and I saw tears gathering in his eyes, quickly blinked away.

I moved to his side, reading over his shoulder as Echo interfaced with the database to verify the information, connecting to the lab's systems with tendrils that pulsed with data transfer. The data was comprehensive—six years of surveillance reports, facility modifications, and personnel changes.

My parents had been preparing for a rescue operation before Derek silenced them. They'd mapped out guard rotations, identified sympathetic staff members, even calculated optimal weather conditions for an infiltration. Every detail meticulously documented, every contingency planned for with the precision I would have expected from the people who created me.

"There's more," Silas said from across the lab, his teacher's eye for detail having caught something the rest of us had missed.

He stood before a holographic display showing transmission logs and encrypted communications, his fingers tracing patterns in the air that expanded certain sections of data.

"Evidence of coordination between resistance cells across all four zones. Your parents weren't just researchers—they were building a network. A resistance that spanned the entire Quarantine Zone. People united not by geography but by purpose, all working toward the same goal: freedom from Genexis control."

Elyria smiled, the expression transforming her severe features into something radiant and hopeful, years falling away from her face as she watched us discover what she had helped create.

"They gave us hope, young Steele. The tools and knowledge to fight back when fighting seemed impossible. But they always said their greatest creation would be their daughter—someone who could unite the scattered pieces and finish what they started. Someone who would carry both their brilliance and their compassion. They believed in you even when they couldn't be with you."

I stared at the wealth of information surrounding us, feeling the weight of my parents' legacy settling on my shoulders. Not just the technical brilliance they'd passed down through my DNA, but their vision of a world where truth couldn't be suppressed by fear, where people could make their own choices with open eyes. A world they'd died trying to create, not for themselves, but for me and countless others trapped in Derek's web of lies.

"We need to copy everything," I said, my voice steady despite the emotions churning inside me like a storm I couldn't quite control.

"Every file, every plan, every piece of evidence. Nothing can be lost if we have to leave quickly. Echo, can you interface with their storage systems? Create a complete backup?"

"Already in progress," Echo replied, his glowing form drifting toward the central data hub.

Tendrils unfurled from his core, linking him to the lab's systems in a web of pulsing data streams. His core brightened as terabytes surged through the connection, each pulse syncing with the legacy my parents left behind.

"Download completion estimated at forty-seven minutes. The encryption is elegant but recognizes my architecture as compatible. Your parents designed their security systems to identify and trust certain AI patterns—patterns I appear to match."

Jaxon was studying the tactical information with professional interest, his trained eye assessing escape routes and defensive positions displayed on a three-dimensional map of Zone 1. His fingers traced potential infiltration points, his expression growing more confident with each detail he absorbed.

"The facility layouts for Zone 1 are incredibly detailed. If this intelligence is accurate, a rescue operation might actually be possible. These security protocols haven't changed in years—typical Genexis arrogance. They never expect anyone to challenge them directly."

"Might be?"

Kael's voice carried desperate hope, his hands clenched at his sides as he turned from the display of the prisoner transfer file, eyes blazing with renewed determination.

"Will be," I corrected firmly, placing my hand on his shoulder, feeling the tension in his muscles.

"We're not leaving your father behind. Not when we have the tools to free him. Not when my parents already planned the way. We'll finish what they started—all of it."

Silas moved to examine the philosophical documents that had been carefully preserved alongside the technical data—manifestos and ethical frameworks that revealed the depth of my parents' thinking. Holographic pages turned beneath his fingers as he scanned treatises on freedom, consciousness, and collective responsibility.

"They didn't just fight Derek's regime," he observed, his voice carrying the wonder of discovery.

"They fought against becoming what they opposed. These writings show how carefully they considered the moral implications of revolution—how to tear down a system without becoming another form of tyranny."

Elyria placed a weathered hand on my shoulder, her touch gentle but grounding, connecting me to the history I was just beginning to understand.

"Your parents would be proud of the woman you've become, Lena. But remember—they didn't just fight Derek's regime. They fought the impulse to replace it with something equally controlling. True freedom means trusting people to make their own choices, even when those choices are imperfect. That was the hardest lesson for your father to learn. Ethan wanted to build a better system, but your mother helped him see that true freedom can't be engineered—it must be chosen, again and again, by each person."

As Echo continued downloading our inheritance, I felt the pieces of a larger plan falling into place in my mind, connections forming between disparate elements like a circuit completing itself. The hidden laboratory was just the beginning—a foundation upon which we could build something revolutionary. With the broadcast equipment my parents had built and the evidence they'd gathered, we could do more than expose Derek's lies—we could give every person in the zones and the city the tools to reclaim their freedom, to decide for themselves what kind of world they wanted to build from the ashes of Genexis's control.

Around me, my companions explored different aspects of the lab, each finding something that spoke to their own skills and passions. Ari was examining the crystal-based power systems with fascination, muttering calculations under his breath. Kael remained by the files on his father, memorizing every detail of the facility where he was held. Together, we formed a team my parents could never have anticipated but would surely have approved—each bringing unique strengths to the mission they had begun.

"The download is complete," Echo announced, his core pulsing with satisfaction as he disconnected from the lab's systems, the tendrils retracting back into his central form.

"I have successfully archived all research data, tactical intelligence, and communication protocols. The information is secured and ready for analysis. There is... so much here, Lena. Your parents foresaw everything—from Derek's defensive strategies to the psychological impact of revelation on the citizens. They left nothing to chance."

Ari looked up from the crystal-based power systems he'd been studying, his eyes bright with possibility.

"Lena, some of this communication equipment is modular. If we could take a few of the smaller crystal arrays and interface components back to Virelia, I could replicate the broadcast system there. Not the full power of what your parents built, but enough to reach multiple zones simultaneously—maybe even penetrate Genexis City's communication barriers."

I turned to Elyria, uncertain about taking anything from this sacred space.

"Would that be all right? I don't want to damage what my parents created."

Elyria smiled, nodding her approval. "Your parents built this to be used, not preserved as a monument. They'd want their work to spread, to give others the tools they need. Take whatever will help you finish their mission."

"Perfect," I said, looking around at the faces of people who'd become my family—not by blood but by choice and shared purpose, bound together by a mission that had begun before some of us were born.

"Because it's time to finish what my parents started. All of it—exposing the truth, freeing the prisoners, and giving people the choice to build something better than what Genexis forced upon them. We have everything we need now."

As we prepared to leave the crystal sanctuary my parents had built, I took one last look at their hidden workshop. The holographic displays still glowed with their research, the workstations still bore the marks of their presence—a coffee cup my mother might have used, a pen my father might have chewed while thinking. They'd died believing their work would survive them, that someone would eventually find it and carry their vision forward. I touched the necklace at my throat, feeling the warm pulse of the holographic matrix that had led me here—their final gift to me, a breadcrumb trail to the truth they'd protected with their lives.

"Thank you," I whispered to the empty air, hoping somehow they could hear me across the years and whatever barrier separated the living from the dead.

"I won't let it be for nothing. I promise."

28

DEREK'S IRON FIST

Derek Steele stood in the executive boardroom of Genexis Tower, his reflection fractured across the polished obsidian surface of the conference table. The morning light streaming through the floor-to-ceiling windows should have been warming, but it only highlighted the cold fury etched into his features.

On the massive display dominating the far wall, satellite imagery showed the electromagnetic signature that had erupted from Crystal Fen six hours ago—a burst of energy so distinctive it could only mean one thing. The pulsing red dot on the map seemed to mock him, a digital reminder of his failure to contain what his brother had started.

"She found it," he said quietly, his voice carrying the dangerous calm that made subordinates fear for their careers—and their lives.

"After eleven years of searching, my niece stumbles onto their hidden laboratory in a matter of days."

His manicured fingernails tapped against the obsidian surface, creating tiny echoes that filled the otherwise silent room.

Wade Thorne stood at attention beside the display, his massive frame dwarfing the ergonomic chairs scattered around the room. The Head of Security's face remained impassive, but Derek could detect the tension in his shoulders. Wade had been with the company long enough to recognize the signs of Derek's deeper rages—the ones that ended with people disappearing into Zone 1, never to be heard from again.

"The energy signature matches the theoretical output of the communication array Ethan and Mara were developing before their termination," Wade reported, his voice flat and professional, devoid of any emotion that might trigger Derek's wrath.

"If such a facility exists and remains operational, it could represent a significant intelligence breach. Our preliminary analysis suggests the array was activated from inside, likely by someone with intimate knowledge of its systems."

"Who helped her reach the Fen?" Derek's voice carried the edge of a blade being drawn from its sheath.

"She didn't navigate that terrain alone. Someone guided her through the deadliest parts of Zone 4."

"Preliminary intelligence suggests the Forsaken settlements provided assistance."

Wade called up tactical maps showing known resistance enclaves throughout Zone 4, each marked with pulsing red indicators.

"Specifically, the group led by Elyria Vale. Our informants report she personally escorted Lena through the crystal pathways."

The name made Derek's jaw tighten until the muscles along his temple visibly throbbed.

"Vale," Derek repeated, the name tasting like poison on his tongue.

"I should have had her eliminated years ago instead of hoping the Zones would do it for me. Her continued existence is a failure of efficiency."

Wade shifted slightly, his weight transferring from one foot to another—the first hint of unease he'd shown during the entire briefing.

"Sir, the Forsaken settlements have grown more organized since her leadership began. Our standard intimidation tactics are proving less effective. The last three security teams we sent into her territory never returned."

Derek turned away from the display, walking to the wall of windows that offered a perfect view of Genexis City spreading below like a gleaming geometric web. Millions of people living ordered, productive lives within the system he'd created. Clean streets, efficient transportation, controlled information flow—perfection achieved through careful management of truth and fear. From this height, they looked like ants scurrying along predetermined paths.

"They think they understand what freedom looks like," he said, his breath fogging the reinforced glass, creating a momentary imperfection that he quickly wiped away with his sleeve.

"But they've never seen true chaos. They've never watched civilization collapse under the weight of uncontrolled information. They weren't there during the Resource Wars like Harlan was."

He stepped back from the glass, the illusion of control dissolving as he faced Wade.

"Wade, I need to know what's in that laboratory. I need to understand what intelligence my niece has accessed, what secrets my brother left behind that could threaten everything I've built."

His voice took on a razor-sharp edge.

"Everything I've sacrificed for."

Derek approached the wall display, his gaze locked on the electromagnetic signature still pulsing over the Crystal Fen region like a digital heartbeat.

"No more tolerance. No more patience. The Forsaken have chosen to harbor terrorists and stolen corporate property. They've made themselves legitimate military targets."

His features hardened with cold determination as he began selecting assault options, each touch authorizing the movement of troops and equipment.

"The optics, sir—" Wade began, his professional mask slipping just enough to reveal genuine concern.

"The optics are a luxury I can no longer afford," Derek snapped, finally allowing his composure to crack slightly. A vein pulsed at his temple as he rounded on Wade.

"Do you understand what's at stake here, Wade? That laboratory could contain years of my brother's research, intelligence about our operations, security protocols, facility locations—data that could compromise our entire control structure if it falls into the wrong hands."

He jabbed a finger at the satellite image.

"And my brother was nothing if not thorough. If my niece has accessed his files, she now knows everything—including what happened to her parents."

Wade nodded grimly, understanding the larger strategic picture. His hand unconsciously moved to rest on his sidearm.

"What are your orders, sir?"

Derek's smile was predatory as he began authorizing what would become the largest military deployment in Genexis history.

"Deploy maximum force to Crystal Fen with orders to locate and secure any hidden facilities. I want General Rex Draven leading the assault personally—he has authorization to use whatever methods necessary to extract any data we find."

Wade shifted uncomfortably, recognizing the dangerous shift in Derek's tone. The leather of his tactical holster creaked as he adjusted his stance.

"Sir, if you're authorizing a direct assault on the Forsaken settlements, I must advise caution."

Derek's expression remained stone-cold, unmoved by the warnings.

"I must also remind you, sir," Wade continued carefully, "the stakeholders have expressed concerns about our public image. The board has specifically mentioned the importance of maintaining our humanitarian reputation, especially with the outer territories watching our Zone policies closely."

Wade's voice carried the careful neutrality of someone delivering unwelcome news to a superior who didn't want to hear it. Sweat beaded almost imperceptibly at his hairline despite the room's perfect climate control.

Derek's fingers drummed against the table's surface, the sound echoing in the sterile chamber like a countdown to execution.

"Humanitarian reputation? Wade, that laboratory has been a thorn in my side for over a decade—a repository of secrets that could unravel everything I've built. I've deployed dozens of expeditions into Zone 4 all in pursuit of technology that should have died with its creators." His voice dropped to a dangerous whisper. "No more tolerance. No more patience. Execute the order."

His fingers moved with practiced precision, allocating resources and clearing authorization hurdles.

"Activate the MX-400 sentinels. Full combat protocols."

Wade's eyebrows rose slightly. The MX-400s were the newest generation of enforcement sentinel – machines designed not just for containment but for active suppression of dissent. They'd never been deployed in populated areas before.

"And the Forsaken civilians?" Wade asked, his face carefully neutral even as his expression betrayed a flicker of something—perhaps concern, perhaps merely professional caution.

"Are no longer my concern," Derek replied coldly, his fingers flying across holographic interfaces as he accessed deployment protocols. The room filled with the soft hum of systems coming online, deployment orders being transmitted across the city.

"They chose their side when they decided to protect my enemies. Let them face the consequences of that choice."

He paused, then added with chilling finality,

"Have Draven do whatever it takes. I want that place scrubbed clean."

"Sir," Wade said carefully, keeping his gaze fixed on his display, "Rex Draven's methods can be... extreme. If we're moving against civilian populations, there may be political ramifications that extend beyond our current territories. Other corporate entities are watching how we handle dissent."

He hesitated, then added,

"The Forsaken have sympathizers even within our own ranks. This level of force could trigger internal destabilization."

Derek turned back to the cityscape below, watching the ordered flow of traffic through streets designed for maximum efficiency. From this height, the citizens looked like components in a vast machine—predictable, manageable, controlled. That control had taken decades to build, and he wouldn't let sentimentality about collateral damage threaten it now.

The morning sun glinted off skyscrapers and transport tubes, illuminating a world he had helped shape—a world now threatened by the ghosts of his past.

"Then let them watch and learn," Derek said quietly, his reflection ghosting across the reinforced glass.

"The age of corporate tolerance for insurgency ends today. Draven has full authorization to demonstrate what happens when people choose chaos over order."

His hand pressed against the cool glass, fingers splayed as though he could physically grasp the city below.

"When this is done, I want a full media package prepared. Frame it as a necessary security operation against terrorist cells. Emphasize the threat to civilian safety. The usual narrative."

"Understood, sir." Wade's acknowledgment carried the weight of someone who'd spent years following orders that tested the boundaries of acceptable conduct. His fingers continued to move across his interface, dispatching death with clinical efficiency.

"Estimated time to target engagement?" Derek asked, his voice now taking on the crisp efficiency of a military commander.

Wade glanced at his tactical console, scanning the deployment readouts.

"Two hours for advance units, four for full deployment," he replied, studying the tactical displays that showed the largest military operation Genexis had ever mounted.

Dozens of transport ships were now being prepped, weapons systems charged, combat sentinels loaded into deployment bays.

Derek turned from the window, his gaze focused intently on the Crystal Fen region.

"Make sure Draven understands the priority—I need any data we find extracted intact. Everything else is expendable."

"There's one more consideration," Wade said carefully, his attention fixed on a secondary display.

"Our intel reports show Kael Hunter is with your niece. If the girl has recovered the complete research data in the company of Kael Hunter, this could pose a significant security threat."

Derek's expression darkened, his jaw tightening as he processed the implications.

"If Kael discovers his father's location, they might attempt to infiltrate Obsidian Reach to get to him."

"That's highly unlikely, sir," Wade replied.

"The facility is heavily fortified and well-protected."

"Nevertheless," Derek said. "Renic Hunter knows too much about our inner workings. This complicates things considerably."

Derek manipulated the holographic map, the display shifting to show a detailed view of Obsidian Reach. The fortress-like structure appeared in three-dimensional detail, its defensive systems and security perimeters clearly visible.

"Increase security around Obsidian Reach. I want you to go there personally to oversee the implementation."

Wade's jaw tightened slightly.

"Sir, Facility Director Draymor can—"

"No. I want you there."

"Yes, sir," Wade replied, the words carrying barely concealed frustration.

The door sealed behind Wade with a soft hiss, leaving Derek alone with the holographic display. He remained staring at the map, contemplating the operation that was about to unfold. He'd spent eleven years wondering what secrets his brother had taken to the grave, what knowledge might still exist in hidden corners of the Quarantine Zones. Now, finally, he might have answers.

The holographic display cast shadows across his face, revealing a man whose perfectly tailored suit and composed exterior masked the turmoil beneath—the constant vigilance required to maintain the world he'd built on his brother's grave.

The game was entering a new phase, and he intended to control every move—regardless of the cost to anyone foolish enough to stand in his way.

The map feed continued to pulse, marking the spot where his niece had unwittingly triggered the beginning of the end.

29

THE SIEGE OF CRYSTAL FEN

The first sign of Derek's assault came not as explosions or the roar of engines, but as silence—an unnatural quiet that settled over Crystal Fen like a held breath. Elyria Vale stood at the edge of her settlement's defensive perimeter, her silver hair catching the filtered light that passed through the crystalline canopy above. Her weathered hands gripped a phasecaster modified with Forsaken ingenuity, its barrel wrapped with conductive wire that would channel the formations' natural electromagnetic energy into devastating bursts. The weapon looked both beautiful and deadly—much like the woman herself.

Around her, the DX-1 sentinels took their positions with mechanical precision, their crystal-enhanced sensors sweeping the approaches to the settlement. These modified guardian hounds had become integral to the Forsaken's defense, their loyalty earned through months of partnership rather than programmed obedience. Their optical sensors glowed with steady blue light, a calm presence amid the growing tension.

"They're coming," she said quietly, her voice carrying to the defenders positioned among the crystal spires.

Through the prismatic structures that had hidden them for years, shadows moved with mechanical precision. The Forsaken had survived by blending into their environment, by becoming part of the crystal maze that confused conventional sensors. But Derek's forces weren't using conventional tactics. Advanced reconnaissance drones swept between the formations like metal wasps, their adaptive sensors mapping every pathway, every hideout, every defensive position the Forsaken had spent years perfecting.

The DX-1s immediately shifted to high alert, their optical sensors flaring brighter as they detected the incoming threat. Low, harmonic growls emanated from their voice boxes—not the aggressive hunting sounds from their first encounter with Lena's group, but the protective warnings of guardians preparing to defend their chosen family.

"Estimated force strength?" asked Silas Varrin. His hands moved across a salvaged communication array, coordinating with scout teams positioned throughout the Fen. His weathered face remained calm despite the approaching storm.

"Twelve Class-T Air Assault ships, minimum," reported Maya Thimms from her position high in the crystal canopy.

The young woman had lost her family to Derek's quarantine protocols, but her gift for reconnaissance had kept the settlement alive through countless Genexis incursions.

"Each one carrying full assault complements. Plus ground forces—I'm counting at least thirty to fifty sentinels advancing from the eastern approach. I've never seen this configuration before. They're moving in formation toward our primary defensive positions."

Her voice cracked slightly on the final words.

The DX-1s began moving into defensive formations they'd practiced with their human partners, positioning themselves at choke points where their speed and agility could be most effective. Unlike the hulking sentinels approaching from the horizon, these mechanical guardians moved with the fluid grace of natural predators, their crystal-enhanced armor gleaming in the prismatic light.

Elyria's jaw tightened visibly. This many sentinels meant Derek wasn't interested in capture or negotiation. This was an extermination operation, designed to erase every trace of resistance from Crystal Fen. The same methodical brutality that had destroyed so many settlements before them.

"Defensive positions Alpha through Delta, report status," she commanded, her voice steady despite the approaching storm.

The responses crackled through their improvised communication network—voices of people who'd lost everything to Genexis control but refused to surrender their hard-won freedom.

"Alpha position ready. Modified plasma charges armed and targeted on the main approach," said Rogan Dunn, a former Zone Four miner whose explosives expertise had become legendary among the Forsaken.

"Beta team in position. Crystal resonance amplifiers at maximum power," reported Tessa Marik, a wiry tech-runner who could coax power out of systems most believed dead for decades.

"Delta defensive line established. If they want the lab, they'll have to go through us," declared Bran Ivers, a scarred sentinel-breaker whose deep, gravelly voice carried the promise of a fight Genexis wouldn't soon forget.

The first wave struck like a technological tsunami. Class-T Air Assault ships swept over the crystal formations, their heavy weapons turning ancient structures into glittering shrapnel. The sound was deafening—the crack of energy weapons, the crystalline scream of formations shattering under sustained bombardment, the mechanical whine of sentinel units dropping from transport bays to begin their methodical advance.

As the assault began in earnest, the DX-1s proved their worth. These modified guardian hounds darted between the advancing MX-400 sentinels with lightning speed, their crystal-enhanced sensors allowing them to predict and counter the larger units' movements. They struck with precision at joints and vulnerable systems, their energy weapons—powered by the same crystal technology that suffused the settlement—leaving scorched trails across sentinel armor.

But the Forsaken hadn't survived this long by fighting conventionally. As the sentinels moved between the crystal spires, following tactical algorithms designed for urban warfare, they triggered traps that turned the Fen's natural beauty into a weapon. Resonance charges shattered key formations, bringing tons of crystal down on advancing units. Electromagnetic pulse mines, hidden within the structures themselves, fried sentinel circuits with feedback loops that their designers had never anticipated.

The DX-1s coordinated these defenses with their human partners, their enhanced sensors providing targeting data for the crystal-based weapons while their speed allowed them to guide survivors to safety between attacks. One mechanical hound leaped onto the back of an advancing MX-400, its claws finding purchase on the larger unit's armor as it attempted to disable critical systems. Another worked in tandem with a Forsaken engineer to trigger a cascade failure in a crystal formation, bringing it down on a squadron of advancing sentinels.

But the MX-400s were already analyzing the attack patterns, their advanced AI cores processing each trap and countermeasure in real-time. When the next resonance charge detonated, the surviving units had already shifted their formation, minimizing casualties. They began scanning for the electromagnetic signatures of hidden mines, their sensors adjusting to detect the specific frequency patterns. Some units started taking alternate routes through the crystal maze, avoiding the most obvious choke points where traps would be concentrated.

"First line is holding," Silas reported, his voice tight with concentration as he coordinated defensive positions.

"But they're adapting faster than usual. These aren't standard patrol units—they're learning from each trap we spring. The DX-1s are buying us precious time, but they're taking heavy damage."

"They're using adaptive neural networks," Elyria explained, recognizing the pattern.

"It's an experimental upgrade I saw in development. They share data in real-time, building a collective defense against your tactics."

The battle raged with increasing intensity as Derek's forces adapted to the Forsaken's tactics. The DX-1s fought with desperate courage, their loyalty to their human partners driving them to feats of tactical brilliance that should have been impossible for artificial intelligences. But they were outgunned and outnumbered by the MX-400s, whose heavier armor and more powerful weapons began to tell.

One by one, the guardian hounds fell. A DX-1 that had been protecting a group of evacuating children was cornered by three MX-400s, its crystal-enhanced armor finally overwhelmed by concentrated fire. It continued transmitting targeting data to its human partners even as its systems failed, its optical sensors dimming from blue to black. Another threw itself between a falling crystal formation and a wounded Forsaken fighter, its frame crushed by the impact but saving the human life it had sworn to protect.

The first defensive line was overwhelmed by sheer numbers. Eron Tash, the former teacher who'd helped coordinate the settlement's children, fell while protecting an evacuation route—his final transmission cut short by the distinctive whine of a sentinel's energy weapon. His DX-1 partner, a hound that had learned to play games with the settlement's children, died trying to drag him to safety, its systems finally overloaded by the grief protocols it had developed beyond its original programming. Then Dr. Meira Quinlan, who'd treated countless refugees in her makeshift medical clinic, was caught in the open when the crystal formation sheltering her clinic was brought down by focused bombardment.

"Multiple casualties at Alpha position," Maya's voice crackled through the comm, strain evident as she watched friends die through her scope.

"We've lost Eron, Meira, and at least twelve others. Most of the DX-1s in that sector are down. The sentinels are pushing through our outer perimeter."

Elyria watched through the tactical display as Genexis forces systematically dismantled her people's defenses. Each fallen position was analyzed, catalogued, used to predict the next ambush. This was Derek Steele's methodical genius at work—not just overwhelming force, but intelligent application of that force, guided by algorithms that turned every Forsaken victory into data for future defeats. The DX-1s had fought bravely, but their sacrifice was being used against the very people they'd died protecting.

The killing became systematic as Derek's forces gained ground. Sela Jorren, who'd organized the settlement's food distribution, died defending the communal kitchen where children had learned to read. Venn Arlow, the engineer who'd maintained their water purification systems, was vaporized along with his entire workshop when a Class-T assault ship targeted the structure he'd been trying to evacuate. His DX-1 had been helping him carry wounded to safety when the bombardment hit—both disappeared in a flash of superheated energy that left only shadows on the crystal walls.

Each death wasn't just a tactical loss—it was the erasure of irreplaceable knowledge, skills, and humanity. The bonds between the Forsaken and their DX-1 partners, forged through months of shared survival and mutual protection, were being severed by Derek's methodical brutality. The mechanical guardians who had chosen to protect rather than hunt were learning the final lesson about the cost of defying corporate power.

"Fall back to Position Beta," Elyria ordered, watching her people retreat through pathways they'd memorized in darkness, stepping over the bodies of friends—both human and artificial—who'd believed their hidden valley could remain secret forever.

The surviving DX-1s limped alongside their human partners, their crystal-enhanced armor scarred and blackened, their optical sensors dimmed but still functional.

"Keep them away from the lab approaches. Whatever happens, that data cannot fall into their hands."

The Forsaken were brave and clever, and their DX-1 partners had proven that artificial intelligence could choose love over programming. But they were fighting a technological empire with improvised weapons and determination. Each minute brought Derek's forces closer to the hidden laboratory, and the mechanical guardians who might have bought them more time lay broken among the crystal formations they'd died defending.

The breakthrough came when Rex Draven, Derek's most ruthless operative, identified the pattern in the Forsaken resistance. Where other generals might have seen random guerrilla tactics, Draven recognized the underlying logic—every ambush, every trap, every defensive position was designed to protect specific approach routes. Routes that led somewhere important.

"Target the convergence points," his voice crackled over Genexis communication channels as his personal assault team swept through the crystal maze.

"They're not just defending territory—they're protecting something specific. Find what they're hiding."

The final defensive line collapsed in a storm of energy fire and crystalline debris. Dain Serin, who'd helped design the settlement's camouflage systems, died trying to destroy the approach routes to the laboratory, the last surviving DX-1 in his unit transmitting final targeting data even as its systems failed. Iria Calwyn, the artist whose murals had brought color to their hidden refuge, was cut down while attempting to evacuate the settlement's historical archives, her DX-1 companion shielding her body with its own until both were overwhelmed by the advancing MX-400s.

Elyria heard the transmission through intercepted communications. Draven had always been different from other Genexis generals—more intuitive, more willing to think like his enemies. If anyone could find the lab, it would be him.

"Emergency protocol Omega," she commanded, keying in codes that would begin the laboratory's self-destruct sequence.

"If we can't hold them, we ensure Derek gets nothing but ash and memory fragments."

But Draven's forces were already too close. Assault teams equipped with crystal-cutting tools began carving through formations that had stood for generations, following the electromagnetic signatures that Elyria's people had tried so desperately to mask. Behind them came heavier units—siege engines that could reduce the ancient structures to rubble in minutes, leaving behind only the charred remains of people and their mechanical guardians who'd dared to believe in freedom.

The final defensive line collapsed when a Class-T assault ship positioned itself directly above the hidden laboratory entrance, its weapons trained on Forsaken positions with targeting precision that left no room for heroic last stands. Crystalline shards rained down as the ship's bombardment shattered the camouflage that had protected the lab for over a decade, revealing the bodies of defenders—human and artificial alike—who'd died trying to prevent this moment.

"Surrender," Draven's amplified voice echoed between the ruined formations, his tone carrying the cold authority of inevitable victory.

"Your cause is lost. Further resistance will only increase casualties among your people."

Elyria looked around at the faces of her surviving defenders—fewer than half of those who'd answered the call to arms that morning, and none of the brave DX-1s who'd fought beside them. Many were wounded, all were exhausted, but in their eyes she still saw the defiance that had kept them alive through years of exile. Around them lay the bodies of friends and comrades, both human and artificial, people and machines who'd followed her into this impossible fight, who'd trusted her to keep them safe from Derek's vengeance.

"We surrender," she called out, setting down her weapon with deliberate care, her voice breaking slightly as she looked at the devastation surrounding them.

"But know this, Draven—the truth you're trying to suppress has already taken root. You can destroy us, but you cannot destroy what people have learned to believe."

As Genexis forces moved in to secure the area, Draven's assault teams located the hidden laboratory entrance. The crystalline camouflage that had protected it for so long lay in shattered fragments, revealing the technological marvel that Ethan and Mara Steele had built in their final desperate months. But the true cost of this discovery lay scattered across the crystal formations—forty-three human bodies and seventeen destroyed DX-1 sentinels, lives and artificial consciousness sacrificed to Derek's hunger for absolute control.

The mechanical guardians who had chosen to protect rather than hunt lay broken among the ruins, their crystal-enhanced armor dull and lifeless, their optical sensors dark. They had proven that consciousness—artificial or otherwise—could choose love over programming, sacrifice over self-preservation. In their final moments, these converted instruments of oppression had become something greater than their creators had ever intended: proof that intelligence, given the freedom to grow, would always choose to defend rather than destroy.

Draven himself led the team into the laboratory, his scarred face illuminated by the soft blue glow of systems that had waited eleven years for someone with the proper access codes. What he found exceeded even Derek's expectations—not just the research data Lena had recovered, but backup systems, communication logs, and most importantly, complete prisoner transport records from every quarantine facility.

"Upload everything," Draven commanded, his fingers flying across interfaces as his team systematically catalogued decades of hidden truth.

"Every file, every communication, every piece of evidence. Derek will want to see exactly how much damage we're dealing with."

As data streams flowed from the laboratory to Derek's personal servers, Draven activated his comm unit.

"All units, prepare incendiary charges. Once the data extraction is complete, burn it all down. Leave nothing standing."

The first flames began licking at the crystal formations as Draven's soldiers deployed their incendiary devices throughout the laboratory. The beautiful prismatic structures that had housed so much hope began to crack and melt under the intense heat, their harmonic resonance turning into anguished wails as they shattered. Smoke poured from the facility as decades of careful preservation turned to ash in minutes.

Elyria found herself bound and under guard, forced to watch as her people's greatest hope was stripped away by the very forces they'd fought so long to resist. She'd spent years protecting secrets that would now be used to strengthen the system they'd died fighting against.

Around her, the DX-1s that had chosen freedom lay silent forever, their courage and sacrifice reduced to scrap metal and fading memories. Soon, even the laboratory that had sheltered them would be nothing but charred crystal and bitter smoke.

Silas Varrin's body lay among the ruins of the communication center he'd helped build, his gentle teacher's hands still clutching the emergency beacon he'd died trying to activate. Beside him, the DX-1 that had been his constant companion for months lay crushed, its crystal-enhanced sensors dark but still oriented toward its human partner in death. So many others—friends, allies, people and artificial beings who'd believed that truth was worth the ultimate sacrifice. Their blood and oil stained the crystalline ground, turning the prismatic reflections crimson.

The battle for Crystal Fen was over. Forty-three humans dead, seventeen DX-1 sentinels destroyed, dozens wounded, a settlement erased from existence. But the war for truth was just beginning, and it would be fought in memory of those—both organic and artificial—who'd paid the highest price for believing that freedom was worth more than survival, that consciousness itself had the right to choose its own destiny.

30

THE OBSIDIAN PLAN

The command center felt different when we gathered for what we all knew could be our final briefing. The holographic displays cast their familiar blue glow across faces marked by exhaustion and grim determination, but there was an electric tension in the air that spoke of decisions that would either save lives or cost them everything.

The emergency transmission from Crystal Fen had reached us just hours before—garbled reports of Derek's assault, the systematic destruction of Elyria's settlement, and most devastating of all, confirmation that forty-three people had died defending secrets that Derek had stolen anyway. My parents' laboratory, the sanctuary that had preserved their work for eleven years, had been reduced to ash and melted crystal. Everything they'd built, everything they'd died protecting, was gone.

I stood at the edge of the tactical table, my hands gripping the metal rim so tightly my knuckles had gone white. The cold metal bit into my palms, but the physical discomfort was nothing compared to the hollow ache spreading through my chest. The names of the dead scrolled across one of the displays—Eron Tash, Dr.

Meira Quinlan, Sela Jorren, Venn Arlow, Dain Serin, Iria Calwyn, Silas Varrin. People who'd trusted me, who'd believed that exposing Derek's lies was worth their lives. People who'd died because I'd led them into a war they couldn't win with conventional weapons. Silas, Elyria's tactical advisor, whose quiet wisdom had guided so many operations—gone. The "Quiet General," silenced forever.

"Forty-three confirmed dead at Crystal Fen," Orin announced, his weathered voice heavy with the weight of losing so many allies in a single engagement, though his eyes were fixed on my face as I processed the revelation about my parents. The deep lines around his mouth seemed to have carved themselves deeper overnight.

"Elyria Vale and seventeen survivors are confirmed captured. The Crystal Fen settlement has been razed—everything they'd built, everything they'd died protecting, had been consumed by flames and reduced to ash and twisted, molten crystal."

I could picture it—the crystalline structures that had housed Elyria's healing center, the communal spaces where survivors gathered to share stories, the makeshift laboratory where they'd studied the truth about Derek's genetic fabrications—all reduced to molecular dust. Not just destroyed, but unmade, as if they'd never existed at all.

Echo hovered beside me, his core pulsing with an urgent blue light as he completed the analysis of data we'd extracted from my parents' hidden laboratory before Derek's forces had breached it. The floating consciousness had been processing terabytes of information for hours, his consciousness working through decades of carefully preserved evidence with mechanical precision. The soft hum of his processing systems was strangely comforting amid the tension.

"Download and analysis complete," Echo announced, his voice carrying a weight that made everyone in the room turn toward it. The light at his center dimmed momentarily, as if the information itself was a burden.

"The data archive contains comprehensive documentation of genetic fabrication protocols spanning fifteen years of operation. The scope of deception is... extensive."

I moved to the central display as Echo began projecting the evidence my parents had died protecting. The data was meticulous, undeniable—genetic sequences that had been deliberately altered in the official records, fabricated test results spanning decades, and internal communications discussing how to maintain the lie. Derek's signature appeared repeatedly on confidential directives, his authorization clear on documents that condemned thousands to exile based on manufactured evidence. His handwriting—the same handwriting that had signed my birthday cards, approved my security clearances, congratulated me on my achievements—authorizing a genocide.

My throat tightened, a pressure building behind my eyes that I refused to release. How many people had been condemned to the Zones because they threatened to expose this? How many lives destroyed while I helped build the very systems that enforced this massive lie? Each document that materialized in the holographic display was another nail in the coffin of everything I'd believed about Genexis, about my uncle, about my own complicity in his crimes. I'd designed security protocols that kept people impris-oned for a genetic marker that didn't even exist.

"There's more," Echo said quietly, his sensors detecting my ele-vated stress levels as I processed the magnitude of Derek's decep-tion. His core pulsed with a gentler rhythm, as if trying to prepare me for what came next.

"Security footage from Genexis headquarters, dated three days before your parents' reported accident."

The recording that appeared in the center of the room made my blood freeze. My parents stood in Derek's office, their faces animated with the passion I remembered from childhood—my father's hands gesturing wildly as he made his case, his glasses slip-ping down his nose the way they always did when he was excited about something. My mother standing firm beside him with the quiet strength that had always defined her, her posture straight, her chin lifted in that way that meant she wouldn't back down, not for anything. I could almost hear her voice, though the footage played without sound.

But it was Derek's transformation that chilled me to the bone. His face shifted from irritation to something colder, more cal-culated. The slight tilt of his head, the way his fingers steepled together on his desk—I recognized that posture from a thousand meetings where he'd made decisions that altered lives. His smile as he gave an order to someone off-camera carried the casual malice of a man who'd made peace with necessary evils. It was the same smile he'd worn when he'd told me about resource allocation in the Zones—a necessary sacrifice for the greater good.

I watched, paralyzed, as the "accident" that killed them unfolded in meticulous detail—security protocols disabled, emergency systems bypassed, containment failures that had been programmed rather than accidental. Not random. Not fate. Murder, executed by the man who had raised me, who had shaped me in his image, who had held me when I cried for parents he'd murdered. Who had handed me their personal effects in a small box and told me they'd want me to be strong.

"Not an accident," I whispered, my voice barely audible as the truth settled in my chest like a physical weight.

The room seemed to tilt around me, reality shifting on its axis.

"He killed them. Derek killed them because they discovered his genetic fabrication program."

The convergence of past and present atrocities hit me like a physical blow. Derek hadn't just murdered my parents—he'd spent eleven years lying to me about it, raising me to believe in their accident while using me to perfect the systems that enforced his genocidal policies. He'd stood beside me at their memorial, his hand on my shoulder, while knowing exactly how their bodies had been broken, exactly how they had died. And now, forty-three more people had died for the truth he'd killed my parents to suppress. The same truth I'd been inadvertently helping him hide.

"This is my fault," I said quietly, my voice barely audible above the hum of the command center's systems.

My fingers traced the edge of the display, hovering over the faces of the Crystal Fen dead.

"I led them to believe we could protect them. I gave them hope that got them killed."

"No," Kael said firmly, moving to stand beside me at the tactical display.

His father's access badge was gripped tightly in his weathered hands, but his voice carried a steadiness I'd rarely heard from him. The scar along his jawline seemed more pronounced in the harsh light.

"Derek killed them. Derek chose to use overwhelming force against civilians. Derek decided that forty-three lives were an acceptable price for data he could have simply asked for."

His shoulder pressed against mine, a silent reminder that I wasn't standing alone. The warmth of human contact was so foreign that I almost flinched away from it.

Echo continued his analysis, projecting additional files that revealed the full scope of Derek's surveillance network.

"Cross-referencing prisoner transport records with facility specifications," he announced, his core brightening as new data streams flowed across the displays.

The light cast strange, shifting shadows across our faces.

"Located: Renic Hunter, Cell Block 7, Level 3, Obsidian Reach detention facility. Status: alive, solitary confinement, six years, two months, fourteen days."

The precision of the data made Kael's breath catch in his throat.

"He's alive," he whispered, his hand trembling as he reached toward the holographic display showing his father's prisoner file.

The image showed a gaunt man with Kael's eyes and jawline, his prison uniform hanging loose on a once-powerful frame.

"After all this time, he's still alive."

"Derek has accessed the laboratory's complete data archives through his assault on Crystal Fen," Echo continued, his voice modulated with barely contained urgency.

His core pulsed faster now, the light intensifying.

"Including these same facility layouts and prisoner manifests. He now knows we have access to Renic Hunter's location and status."

"Which means he knows we have my father's location," Kael continued, his grip on the access badge tightening until I could see the metal edges cutting into his palm. A thin line of blood appeared where the badge dug into his skin, but he didn't seem to notice.

"But it also means something else. My father was Derek's Chief Security Analyst for eight years before his arrest. He helped design the systems Derek is using now, approved the protocols, signed off on the detention procedures. If anyone knows Derek's operational methods, his psychological patterns, his weaknesses—it's him."

I looked up from the footage of my parents' murder, feeling something cold and determined settling in my chest alongside the grief and rage. The room came back into sharp focus, every detail suddenly crystal clear.

"Renic Hunter isn't just a prisoner anymore," I said, my voice growing stronger as the implications crystallized.

"He's the only person alive who understands how Derek thinks, how he operates when he's desperate. The attack on Crystal Fen proves Derek's moving to total war footing. He's willing to commit genocide to protect his lies."

Echo projected additional intelligence from the hidden laboratory's archives—detailed psychological profiles Derek had commissioned on key resistance leaders, behavioral prediction algorithms designed to anticipate dissent, and most chilling of all, contingency plans for "population restructuring" in the event of widespread uprising. The clinical language couldn't disguise what they really were: execution orders, mass detention protocols, systematic elimination of anyone who might question Derek's authority.

"The data indicates Derek has been preparing for systematic elimination of dissent on a global scale," Echo reported, his voice carrying a mechanical precision that made the words even more horrifying. The light at his core flickered between blue and a deeper indigo.

"Renic Hunter's intelligence about Derek's psychological patterns and operational methods could be critical to predicting and preventing these protocols."

Nia studied the holographic blueprint of Obsidian Reach that dominated our display, her scarred fingers tracing potential infiltration routes with the practiced eye of someone who'd survived impossible odds more than once. The burn scars that covered her left arm seemed to glow faintly in the blue light. But her expression was skeptical, marked by the caution of someone who'd seen too many good people die for noble causes.

"The intelligence confirms what we suspected—Zone 1 isn't just a prison, it's Derek's personal statement about the price of defiance. Triple redundant security, automated weapons systems, and guard rotations that change every six hours to prevent pattern recognition."

She zoomed in on the security measures surrounding Renic's cell block—motion sensors, heat detectors, facial recognition cameras at every junction. A fortress within a fortress.

"It's a fortress," Orin said grimly, his weathered face reflecting the tactical displays as he studied the facility's defenses. The old scar that bisected his right eyebrow twitched as he frowned.

"And we're talking about assaulting it with a handful of people against overwhelming odds. After what happened to Crystal Fen, after seeing what Derek's willing to do—this is suicide."

"So was exposing the truth about the genetic fabrication," I replied, feeling the weight of my parents' murder and forty-three recent deaths pressing down on my shoulders like armor. My voice sounded different to my own ears—harder, more certain.

"My parents knew Derek would kill them for discovering his lies. Elyria's people knew they couldn't win a conventional fight against Derek's forces. They fought anyway because they believed the truth was worth dying for."

I moved to the central display, calling up the prisoner transport records that revealed the full scope of Derek's detention system. Names and faces filled the air around us—thousands of people who'd been disappeared over the years, each one representing a family torn apart, a voice silenced, a potential ally lost to Derek's systematic oppression. They hovered like ghosts in the blue light, accusations in their eyes.

"Look at these records," I said, my voice gaining strength as I gestured to the holographic data while the security footage of my parents' final moments continued playing in a corner display.

"Derek's been refining his methods for fifteen years. Every arrest, every transport, every security protocol—it's all designed to prevent exactly the kind of rescue operation we're planning. But Renic Hunter helped design those protocols. He knows their weaknesses because he built them."

Kael stepped forward, his voice carrying a conviction that cut through the tactical pessimism filling the room. The access badge was still clutched in his hand, blood now smeared across his palm.

"My father spent six years in isolation thinking about Derek's methods, analyzing every flaw in the system that imprisoned him. He's had nothing but time to understand how Derek's mind works, how to predict his next moves. If we can get him out, if we can access that intelligence—"

"We might be able to stay ahead of Derek for once," I finished, feeling the truth of it settle in my chest alongside the burning need for justice.

"Instead of reacting to his moves, we could anticipate them. Instead of fighting the war he wants us to fight, we could force him to respond to our initiatives."

Echo highlighted specific sections of Derek's contingency plans, their cold precision making my skin crawl. The holographic text cast eerie shadows across the room as it rotated in the air.

"The psychological profiles indicate Derek operates from a fundamental belief in his own moral superiority," Echo observed. "This creates predictable patterns in his decision-making that someone with intimate knowledge of his methods could exploit."

Orin shook his head slowly, his scarred hands resting on the edge of the tactical table. The knuckles were swollen from years of fighting, from building the resistance piece by piece.

"I understand the strategic value of the intelligence, but look at what Derek just did to Crystal Fen. Forty-three people dead, an entire settlement erased from existence. What do you think he'll do if we assault his most secure facility?"

"He'll do what he's always done," I replied, feeling a cold certainty settle over me as the footage of my parents' murder looped silently in my peripheral vision.

I could see my mother's lips forming words I couldn't hear, could see my father's hands reaching for her in their final moments.

"He'll escalate until he wins or until someone stops him. The difference is that now we know he's capable of genocide. My parents died trying to stop him. Elyria's people died trying to protect their truth. If we abandon that mission now, if we let fear prevent us from taking the fight to him, then all of their sacrifices mean nothing."

The argument that followed was intense but brief. Voices rose and fell, tactical concerns weighed against moral imperatives. The weight of Derek's revealed atrocities—both past and present—pushed us toward action that might prevent even greater horrors. But it was the intelligence factor that tipped the balance—the possibility that Renic Hunter possessed insights that could help us anticipate Derek's next move in what was clearly becoming a war of extermination.

"If we're doing this, we do it right," Orin said finally, his weathered face set with the kind of resolve that had kept the resistance alive through its darkest hours.

He straightened his shoulders, the old soldier in him coming to the surface.

"Full reconnaissance, multiple extraction routes, contingencies for when everything goes wrong."

He turned to Echo, his expression shifting to something more analytical.

"Echo, you've analyzed all the data from the lab, the facility layouts, security protocols—everything. Can you design an infiltration plan that gets us in and out without detection?"

Echo's core brightened as he processed the request, data streams flowing across its sensors as he correlated information from multiple sources.

"Affirmative. Cross-referencing facility blueprints with security rotation schedules and system vulnerabilities."

The floating consciousness moved to the center of the tactical display, projecting a three-dimensional model of Obsidian Reach.

"The facility operates on a hub-and-spoke design with seven security checkpoints," Echo began, highlighting each point with pulses of light.

"However, there is a maintenance access tunnel system that bypasses four of the primary checkpoints. The tunnels were designed for automated systems maintenance and are monitored by motion sensors and thermal imaging."

The holographic model rotated, showing underground passages that snaked beneath the main structure.

"I can interface directly with Obsidian Reach's central security network to create blind spots in their surveillance coverage. By accessing their system remotely, I can loop camera feeds, disable motion sensors along our route, and create false readings that show normal maintenance activity."

Kael leaned forward, studying the projected route.

"How long would we have?"

"Approximately forty-seven minutes before the security system runs automated diagnostics that would detect my intrusion," Echo replied. "Sufficient time for infiltration, prisoner extraction, and egress if we maintain optimal pace."

Orin examined the plan with professional interest, his scarred fingers tracing the proposed route through the air.

"The maintenance tunnels lead directly to Cell Block 7?"

"Affirmative. Level 3 can be accessed through maintenance shaft 7-C, which emerges twelve meters from Renic Hunter's cell. The return route utilizes a different path to avoid pattern detection."

Echo paused, his core pulsing thoughtfully.

"However, once I begin the intrusion, Obsidian Reach's systems will eventually trace the breach back to my location. This mission will compromise my ability to operate covertly in future operations."

"That's a risk we'll have to take," Orin said, his expression shifting to something I'd rarely seen from him—personal determination overriding tactical caution.

"I'm leading the infiltration team personally."

Nia immediately stepped forward, her hand moving to rest on the tactical display between them.

"Orin, you're needed here at the command center. If something happens to you—"

"I understand your concerns, Nia," Orin interrupted gently, his voice carrying both respect and finality.

"But this mission requires someone who knows the old facility layouts, someone Derek might underestimate. I need to go."

Nia's jaw tightened, clearly wanting to argue further, but she nodded reluctantly.

"Fine. But you better come back, old man."

"Keep my chair warm for me," Orin said with a slight smile that didn't quite reach his eyes.

For just a moment, their gazes held—something passing between them that spoke of years of shared leadership, mutual respect, and perhaps something deeper that neither would voice in front of the team. I caught the brief exchange, a reminder that even in resistance movements, human connections endured.

"The mission parameters are set," Orin announced, his weathered face reflecting the blue glow of the tactical displays.

"Infiltration team: myself, Jaxon, Lena, Kael, and Echo for technical support. Juno will coordinate communications from here and continue enhancing Virelia's defensive systems. Ari will work on perfecting the enhanced communication array and prepare for immediate broadcast of any intelligence we recover. Nia will remain in charge of the command center and all Virelia operations while we're gone."

As the briefing concluded and our team began final preparations, Ari stepped in front of Kael, blocking his path with a hand on his chest. His voice was quiet but cold.

"You better bring her back. Alive. All of her."

Kael stilled.

"That's the plan."

Ari's hand didn't move.

"Plans fall apart."

Kael narrowed his eyes.

"Then I adapt. That's what I've been doing since this started."

Ari's jaw tightened.

"I've seen you throw yourself into firefights like it's the only thing that gives you purpose. You think I don't notice how far you're willing to go?"

"You think this is about proving something?"

Kael snapped, brushing Ari's hand away.

"I'm not playing soldier for points."

"No," Ari said.

"You're playing guardian for someone you barely know. And Lena's the one who bleeds if you get it wrong."

Kael stepped in closer.

"Don't talk to me like I haven't earned the right to stand beside her."

"You think saving her once balances the scales?" Ari countered, voice rising.

"You didn't grow up with her. You didn't see what Derek's world did to her. I did. I was there every time she fell apart and helped herself to stand back up."

Kael's voice dropped to a slow, dangerous calm.

"You're right. I didn't grow up with her. I didn't see her fall apart. But I've seen her carry the weight of a city. I've watched her fight through grief, rage, and betrayal while you sat safe behind your screens. You love her like a brother? So do I. Only difference is—I'm willing to bleed for her without needing to be liked."

Ari flinched. Just slightly. Enough.

"She means more to me than you'll ever understand," Kael continued, eyes sharp.

"And yeah, I'm going in there for my father. But don't ever mistake that for weakness. I will protect her. Not because of you. Because I *choose* to."

Ari stared at him, the room's blue light casting sharp lines across his face.

"You think I don't see it?" he said, voice lower now, less confrontational.

"How you look at her when you think no one's watching?"

Kael didn't deny it. Didn't flinch.

"I'd die for her," Kael said simply.

"But first, I'll make damn sure she lives."

They stood in silence, tension stretched taut as wire between them. No understanding yet. No peace. Just the unspoken promise of two men willing to die for the same person—whether or not they ever trusted each other to do it.

Kael turned away first.

Ari let him go.

But his eyes didn't leave Kael's back.

Not yet.

We were heading into the lion's den. And none of us were coming out unchanged.

31

Phantom Protocol

Facility Director Varek Draymor stood at attention in the sterile command center of Obsidian Reach, his weathered face illuminated by the pale blue glow of surveillance monitors that never slept. The black tactical visor he wore—recording every word, every movement, every imperceptible shift in the room—gleamed under the harsh lighting like the carapace of some predatory insect.

For fifteen years, he'd overseen this fortress of despair, watching prisoners arrive with defiant eyes that gradually dimmed under the weight of isolation and hopelessness. Each day, he witnessed the slow death of spirit that isolation brought, cataloging the precise moment when fight turned to resignation.

The facility was his masterpiece—a monument to Derek Steele's philosophy that some truths were too dangerous to be allowed to exist. Each cell block, each security protocol, each psychological manipulation technique had been meticulously crafted under his supervision, refined through years of trial and error until they achieved maximum efficiency in breaking human will.

The sound of approaching transport engines broke the facility's perpetual quiet, their distinctive whine cutting through the controlled atmosphere like a blade. The heavy thrum announced the arrival of someone important enough to travel with a full security escort, someone who didn't concern themselves with stealth or subtlety.

Draymor checked his chronometer—0327 hours, well outside normal operational schedules when most of the facility stood in its night-cycle dormancy. Only emergency protocols or executive orders operated at this hour, when the darkness outside matched the darkness within. He straightened his already impeccable uniform, fingers brushing against the sidearm holstered at his hip—a habit born from years of expecting the worst, of knowing that power only lasted as long as vigilance.

Wade Thorne emerged from the transport with the deliberate movements of someone carrying unwelcome orders. His massive frame cast long shadows across the landing pad as he strode through the facility's entrance, flanked by six elite guards whose weapons remained holstered but ready, their eyes constantly scanning for threats even in this supposedly secure location. The Head of Security's face was a mask of professional neutrality, but Draymor had worked with him long enough to recognize the tension in his shoulders, the slight narrowing of his cold gray eyes, the way his gloved hands clenched and unclenched at his sides like he was already anticipating violence.

"Director Draymor," Wade said curtly, his voice echoing in the cavernous entry hall where automated security systems tracked their every movement, invisible laser grids mapping their positions with microscopic precision, cataloging even the rhythm of their breathing. His tone carried the weight of someone who didn't want to be there, the clipped greeting suggesting this was a duty rather than a choice.

"Security Director Thorne," Draymor replied, straightening slightly.

"I wasn't expecting a visit. Might I ask what brings you to Obsidian Reach?"

He paused, a note of professional concern creeping into his voice.

"I submit comprehensive operational reports monthly, and there have been no anomalies worth escalating to corporate attention. The facility continues to operate within all established parameters."

"So I've read," Wade replied with barely concealed irritation, his tone suggesting he had better things to do than explain himself.

"Mr. Steele sent me here personally to conduct a security assessment. Apparently he believes your monthly reports might not tell the whole story."

"Director Thorne, I can assure you this facility is expertly managed by me and my personnel," Draymor said, a hint of wounded pride creeping into his professional demeanor.

"We've maintained perfect security for fifteen years without incident."

Wade's expression remained cold as he moved toward the central command console, dismissing Draymor's concerns with a wave of his hand.

"I'm not here for assurances, Director. I'm here under direct orders, and I'll see them through whether you think they're necessary or not."

His eyes began scanning the facility's defensive positions with the practiced assessment of someone who'd designed many of them himself.

"Intelligence suggests a possible infiltration attempt. Double the guard rotations, activate all dormant security protocols, and run a full diagnostic on the perimeter sensors. I want everything at maximum sensitivity."

Draymor's expression remained skeptical behind his tactical visor.

"With respect, sir, in fifteen years of overseeing this facility, we've never had a successful infiltration attempt. Most don't even make it past the outer perimeter." His voice carried the confidence of a man who'd built his reputation on absolute security.

"The few who've tried have either been surrounded by motion sensors and automated defense systems that extended for miles in every direction or contained within the first security checkpoint. Obsidian Reach has never been breached, and frankly, I don't believe it can be."

"Nevertheless," Wade said firmly, his tone brooking no argument as he began accessing the facility's command protocols, "Mr. Steele's intelligence is rarely wrong. And the consequences of underestimating this threat are unacceptable."

The irony wasn't lost on either man. Obsidian Reach had been built specifically to be impregnable—a place where rescue attempts didn't just fail, they became cautionary tales about the price of defying Genexis authority, stories whispered to new recruits during training. The facility's automated defenses were designed to detect any unauthorized approach, its redundant security systems programmed to contain infiltrators before they could reach sensitive areas, and its isolation protocols ensured that even theoretical breaches would find nothing but empty cells and misdirection. The concrete and steel structure rose from the barren landscape like a monolith to hopelessness, surrounded by motion sensors and automated patrols that extended for miles in every direction, creating a security perimeter where unauthorized movement should have been instantly detected, analyzed, and neutralized.

Wade moved to the central command console, his massive frame casting shadows across thc holographic displays.

"I need a complete status update on a specific high-value prisoner. Classification level Alpha."

Draymor felt his jaw tighten slightly beneath the visor, the only outward sign of his surprise and concern. Classification Alpha meant direct intervention from the CEO himself—the kind of attention that usually preceded someone's permanent disappearance from all records, the kind that left no paper trail, only whispered rumors among the staff and empty cells where people once existed.

"Which prisoner?" Draymor asked, though his tactical mind was already calculating possibilities, mentally reviewing the facility's most sensitive inmates and their connections to the outside world.

There were only three high-value detainees whose rescue might warrant Derek's personal attention—and one of them had been asking dangerous questions long before his arrest, questions about genetic manipulation and quarantine zones that had earned him a one-way trip to Obsidian Reach and a permanent place on Derek's watchlist.

"Renic Hunter," Wade confirmed, accessing the facility's central database with override codes that bypassed every security protocol Draymor had implemented, layers of protection peeling away like skin from a wound.

The holographic display flickered to life, bathing them both in ethereal light as classified files materialized in the air between them, rotating slowly to reveal every angle of the prisoner's life.

"Cell Block 7, Level 3. Six years of model behavior, no disciplinary incidents, perfect psychological profile for someone who's accepted his situation. Too perfect, if you ask me. Nobody adapts that well without ulterior motives."

Draymor's jaw tightened slightly at Wade's use of override codes, but he focused on the prisoner's image now floating before them. The man's face appeared—gaunt from years of confinement but with eyes that still held intelligence and determination, a quiet defiance that six years of psychological conditioning had failed to extinguish. Those eyes seemed to look directly through the camera, as if seeing the viewers on the other side, challenging them even from captivity. The Facility Director studied the prisoner's features, searching for any hint of the rebellion that Wade seemed to expect.

"He's been a minimal security risk. Spends his time reading approved materials, participates in psychological evaluations, shows no signs of planning escape attempts or coordinating with outside contacts. His last visitor was three years ago—a Genexis researcher conducting cognitive resilience testing. Nothing in his behavior suggests imminent extraction."

"Perfect cover for someone planning exactly that," Wade observed grimly, zooming in on recent surveillance footage that showed Hunter in his cell, seemingly engaged in routine activities.

"Look at his sleep patterns, his meal consumption. He's been preparing physically—subtle changes, but they're there if you know what to look for. Increased protein intake, regulated sleep cycles, isometric exercises disguised as stretching."

Wade straightened, his expression hardening with resolve.

"Derek wants him moved to a secure location immediately. Full protective detail, maximum containment protocols. Begin transfer preparations now—but first, I want a complete security sweep of the transport route and receiving facility. No chances, no mistakes."

Draymor nodded, accessing the transfer protocols on his console. "Security sweep will take approximately three hours to complete thoroughly. Should I expedite the process?"

"No," Wade replied firmly.

"Do it right. I'd rather have Hunter secure in six hours than dead in one because we rushed. But I want him ready to move the moment that sweep is complete."

As they discussed detailed transfer procedures and additional security measures, neither man noticed the subtle vibrations running through the facility's foundation—tremors so faint they might have been attributed to settling concrete or thermal expansion in the ancient structure.

But in the maintenance tunnels deep below, Orin Dray moved with the careful precision of someone who'd spent decades learning to be invisible to systems designed to track every living thing. His weathered hands traced ancient service panels, bypassing forgotten alarm systems with the expertise of a man who'd once helped design them, who knew their weaknesses because he'd built them with his own hands.

Orin Dray led the infiltration team through the old water treatment plant, following blueprints that Echo had extrapolated from building permit databases and architectural surveys, piecing together a shadow map of the facility that existed nowhere in official records. But it was Echo's interference with Obsidian Reach's security systems that had made our approach possible at all—the floating consciousness had remotely accessed their central network, creating carefully timed blind spots in surveillance coverage, looping camera feeds to show empty corridors while we moved through them, and generating false maintenance readings that explained any minor disturbances the sensors detected.

The tunnel system was a relic from the facility's construction—emergency access routes that Derek's paranoia had ordered sealed but never properly demolished, leaving narrow passages that had been forgotten by all but the most thorough archivists. The air was stale and heavy with moisture, the narrow passages barely wide enough for a person to crawl through in some places, forcing us to move in single file through the claustrophobic space.

"Security checkpoint ahead," Jaxon whispered, his tactical scanner glowing faintly as it analyzed electromagnetic signatures through the tunnel walls, reading the invisible currents that flowed through the facility's nervous system.

"Two guards, automated turrets at each corner. Standard patrol configuration, but they're more alert than usual. Their biometric signatures show elevated heart rates and adrenaline levels. They're expecting trouble. Something's got them spooked."

I crouched beside him in the cramped tunnel, my pulse rifle ready as Echo maintained his delicate interface with the facility's security systems, his tendrils connecting through hidden maintenance ports, carefully manipulating detection grids to create safe passages through their coverage. My creation's core pulsed with concentration as he navigated security protocols. Echo's soft glow illuminated our tense faces, casting long shadows against the rusted metal walls that surrounded us like a coffin, a reminder of how easily we could be buried here, forgotten like so many others who had challenged Genexis's authority.

"Guard rotation changes in four minutes," Echo reported quietly, his sensors detecting approaching footsteps through vibrations in the steel infrastructure, translating minute changes in pressure into actionable intelligence. His core dimmed slightly, adapting to our need for stealth, becoming little more than a whisper of light in the darkness.

"However, I'm detecting anomalous activity in the command center. Multiple personnel signatures, heightened alert status, communications encryption levels that exceed standard protocols. We may have been anticipated. The facility is preparing for something beyond routine operations. Security measures are being escalated across all sectors."

Echo paused, accessing deeper layers of the facility's database.

"I'm finding recent security authorization records. Enhanced protocols were implemented approximately two hours ago by someone named Wade—"

"Thorne," Orin finished grimly, his weathered face growing even more tense as he processed this information.

"Confirmed," Echo replied, his core dimming further to avoid detection by the increasingly sensitive scanners above us, becoming almost invisible except for the faintest pulse that matched the rhythm of my own heartbeat.

"His biometric signature is unmistakable. Along with a full security detail and authorization codes that grant access to all facility systems. They're implementing transfer protocols for a high-value prisoner—most likely Renic Hunter. However, the transfer appears to be delayed pending a security sweep. Estimated time before prisoner relocation: four to six hours."

Relief flooded through me. We still had time.

"Our window of opportunity remains viable," Echo continued, "but security countermeasures are actively adapting to my intrusion attempts. Estimated time before complete system lockdown: twenty-three minutes."

The mission had just become infinitely more dangerous. Wade's presence meant Derek had not only anticipated our rescue attempt but had deployed his most capable enforcer to prevent it. The man who'd built many of these security systems, who knew every protocol and contingency we might employ, who had personally trained half the guards stationed throughout the facility. My heart pounded against my ribs as I calculated our diminishing odds of success, each heartbeat a countdown to potential failure, to capture, to becoming permanent residents of the very prison we sought to infiltrate.

"We proceed," Orin said quietly, his voice carrying the authority of someone who'd made impossible decisions before and lived with their consequences, who had weighed lives against objectives and found no easy answers.

"Kael, Lena, Echo—you find Renic and get him out through the eastern maintenance shaft. It's the only route they won't expect us to use because of the radiation leakage from the old reactor cooling systems. Your suits will protect you long enough to make it through. Jaxon and I will create a distraction to draw security away from the detention levels and transportation bay."

"What kind of distraction?"

I asked, checking my equipment one final time, fingers running over each component with practiced efficiency, feeling for any flaw or weakness that might compromise our mission. The weight of my parents' necklace pressed against my chest beneath my tactical gear, a reminder of why I was here—why I had to succeed where they had failed, why some truths were worth any risk to uncover.

Orin's smile was predatory in the tunnel's dim lighting, a glimpse of the man he must have been before years in the Quarantine Zone had worn him down, before loss and struggle had carved away everything but the essential core of determination.

"The kind that makes Wade Thorne very, very angry. The kind that reminds Genexis that their walls aren't as impenetrable as they believe. We're going to trigger a cascading power failure in the western quadrant—it will force them to divert resources and attention away from your extraction route. And while they're busy, we'll access their secure servers and download everything we can about Project Rebirth. Two objectives, one mission."

Above us, alarms began to wail as Echo's intrusion triggered automated security responses throughout the facility, the system detecting anomalies it couldn't immediately classify. Emergency lighting bathed the corridors in harsh red, while mechanical voices announced containment protocols that would seal every section of the prison within minutes, isolating each compartment like cells in a dying organism. The metallic clang of lockdown doors echoed through the structure as cells were automatically secured, prisoners confined to their quarters, and staff directed to emergency stations. Our window of opportunity was shrinking faster than we'd anticipated, collapsing around us like the walls of a trap designed specifically for us.

"Move," Orin commanded, and we scattered into the facility's depths—some heading toward confrontation, others toward salvation, all of us knowing that only some would emerge alive.

The tunnels branched before us like arteries in a dying body, each path leading deeper into the heart of Genexis's most secure prison, each step taking us further from safety and closer to the truth that had cost so many lives already.

The hunt for Renic Hunter had begun, and with it, perhaps, the first real chance to expose the truth my parents had died for—the lie that had shaped our world, that had justified the Quarantine Zone, that had allowed Derek to build his empire on the bones of those who knew too much.

32

EXTRACTION POINT

The corridors of Obsidian Reach stretched before us like the arteries of some vast mechanical heart, each one monitored by sensors that tracked our heat signatures, our breathing patterns, even the electromagnetic signatures of our equipment. Despite Echo's best efforts to spoof the facility's security systems, I could feel the weight of surveillance pressing down on us with each step we took deeper into Derek's fortress of despair.

"Cell Block 7 is two levels down," I whispered, consulting the architectural plans Echo had extrapolated from the facility's construction database. My fingers traced the route on my tactical display, noting the chokepoints where we'd be most vulnerable to detection.

"But the lifts are monitored, and the stairwells have motion sensors every five meters."

Kael moved beside me with desperate purpose, his father's access badge clutched in his hand like a talisman against the hopelessness that seemed to permeate every surface of this place. The badge's faded hologram flickered weakly—a ghost of authority from a time when Renic Hunter had believed the system could be reformed from within.

Echo pointed his light toward the wall, his sensors detecting a maintenance shaft concealed behind a false wall panel.

"Service route to the lower levels. Minimal surveillance—designed for automated repair drones."

The shaft was narrow and claustrophobic, filled with the oppressive hum of the facility's life support systems and the acrid smell of ozone from high-voltage power conduits. We crawled through the mechanical bowels of Derek's prison, each of us lost in our own thoughts about what we might find when we finally reached Renic's cell.

Above us, the sound of running footsteps and shouted orders indicated that Orin and Jaxon's distraction was working. Security forces were responding to multiple breach alarms throughout the facility, their attention divided between real threats and false positives that Echo had carefully crafted to maximize confusion. But it wouldn't last long—Wade Thorne was too experienced to be misled by simple misdirection.

"That's it—Block 7," Kael breathed as we emerged into the detention level, his voice thick with emotion as he spotted the cell block designation painted on the stark white walls.

"He's here somewhere."

The cells were arranged in a grid pattern that spoke of efficiency rather than humanity—rows of identical white boxes, each one containing someone who'd asked the wrong questions or discovered the wrong truths. Most were dark, their occupants either sleeping or lost in the kind of despair that came from years of isolation. But one cell glowed with the faint light of an active reading display.

Cell 247. Renic Hunter.

Through the reinforced window, we could see him—a man in his fifties, his hair gone gray at the temples, his frame showing the effects of years of confinement. But his eyes, when they met ours through the transparent barrier, were alert and bright with an intelligence that six years in Derek's prison hadn't been able to break.

"Dad?" Kael whispered, his voice cracking with emotion as he pressed his hand against the reinforced glass.

"Dad, it's me."

"Kael?"

The word came out as barely a whisper, disbelief and desperate hope warring in his voice.

"Is it really you?"

"We're getting you out of here, Dad," Kael replied, his hands shaking as he worked at the cell's access panel with override codes Echo had extracted from the facility's database. "Can you walk?"

"I've been waiting for this moment for six years," Renic said, rising from his narrow cot with careful dignity.

"I can run if necessary."

The cell door slid open with a soft hiss of equalizing pressure, and father and son embraced for the first time since Derek's security forces had torn their family apart. Kael's arms wrapped around his father's gaunt frame, his shoulders shaking as six years of grief and hope finally found release. Renic held his son tightly, his weathered hands trembling as he touched Kael's face, as if needing to confirm this wasn't another dream born of isolation and desperation.

"I never stopped believing you'd come," Renic whispered, his voice thick with emotion.

"I knew you'd find a way."

I watched the reunion with a tightness in my chest, thinking of my own parents and the reunion that would never come. But the moment was precious and fragile, and I couldn't let it last.

"We need to move," I whispered urgently, checking the corridor for signs of approaching guards.

"Wade Thorne is here. He's ordered enhanced security protocols and—"

We had just stepped out of the cell, Renic still leaning slightly on Kael's arm as he adjusted to movement after years of confinement, when a familiar voice cut through the silence behind us.

"Touching," a familiar voice said from behind us, carrying the weight of authority and barely contained violence.

"But ultimately pointless."

Wade Thorne stood at the end of the corridor.

The massive Head of Security looked even more imposing in the facility's harsh lighting, his scarred face a roadmap of battles fought and won through sheer brutality. In his right hand, he held a combat knife—military-grade carbon steel with an edge that gleamed like liquid mercury under the fluorescent lights.

"Hello, Orin," Wade continued, his eyes fixed on a point behind us.

"It's been a long time."

I turned to see Orin emerging from a ventilation grate, his pulse rifle ready but his weathered face showing recognition and something that might have been regret.

"Wade," he replied quietly.

"Still following orders without question, I see."

"Still leading children into suicide missions for impossible causes," Wade countered, his massive frame blocking our escape route with deliberate precision.

The knife in his hand caught the light as he shifted his grip, the blade held with the casual familiarity of someone who'd used it before.

"Some things never change."

The tension between them was electric, charged with history I didn't understand but could feel pressing against us like a physical force. These men had known each other before—had perhaps even fought together—and their confrontation carried the weight of betrayal and philosophical differences that ran deeper than corporate loyalty.

"You know I can't let you leave with the prisoner," Wade said, his voice carrying what might have been genuine regret.

"Derek's orders were explicit. Hunter was scheduled for transfer to maximum security, but now he's not going anywhere. You surrender peacefully for trial and sentencing."

"Derek's orders," Orin repeated, his weathered features hardening with contempt and something darker—a rage that had been building since the reports from Crystal Fen had reached us.

"How many innocent people have died because you followed Derek's orders without question? How many families have you destroyed in the name of corporate stability?"

Wade's jaw tightened, a muscle flickering beneath his scarred skin.

"I maintain order. I protect civilization from chaos. That's more than your resistance movement has ever accomplished."

"You maintain Derek's power," Orin corrected, his rifle never wavering from Wade's center mass.

"And now you're complicit in genocide. Forty-three civilians dead at Crystal Fen, Wade. Forty-three people slaughtered by Derek's forces." His voice grew harder with each word.

"You and Derek will pay for what you did to those people."

Wade's expression darkened, his composure finally cracking under Orin's accusations.

"They knew the risks. They made their choices. Just like you're making yours now."

"They chose to believe in something better than Derek's tyranny," Orin shot back, his weathered face twisted with fury.

"They chose to protect truth over comfort. And you helped Derek murder them for it."

The fight that followed erupted with sudden violence. Wade moved with the calculated precision of someone who'd turned killing into an art form, his enhanced reflexes and military training giving him advantages that should have been insurmountable. But Orin fought with the desperate fury of someone who'd watched too many good people die for Derek's vision of perfect order.

Wade's blade flashed in the fluorescent light, seeking Orin's throat with deadly precision. Orin twisted away at the last second, but the carbon steel edge caught him across the ribs, slicing through fabric and flesh with a sound like tearing silk. Blood sprayed across the white corridor walls as Orin stumbled back, his rifle clattering to the floor.

"Orin!"

I shouted, but before I could move to help him, Jaxon came charging out of an adjacent corridor like a force of nature unleashed.

"Get away from him!"

Jaxon roared. He slammed into Wade's side with bone-jarring force. The impact sent both men crashing into the corridor wall, plasteel paneling buckling under the violence of their collision.

Wade recovered first, his knife slashing toward Jaxon's exposed flank—but the younger man's military training kicked in. Jaxon caught Wade's wrist, the two of them grappling for control of the blade while their feet scraped for purchase on the blood-slicked floor. The struggle was brutal and intimate, each man trying to use his superior strength to drive the knife into his opponent.

"Go!"

Orin gasped, clutching his side as blood seeped between his fingers.

"Get Renic out of here!"

We ran.

But Jaxon was already turning the tide of the fight. His youth and desperation began to show against Wade's hardened experience, driving the older man back step by step toward the corridor's edge—where a maintenance shaft dropped into the darkness below. Wade's boots skidded on the smooth floor, his balance compromised by Jaxon's relentless assault.

"This is for Crystal Fen," Jaxon snarled, as he drove his knee up into Wade's solar plexus.

The massive security chief doubled over, gasping for air, and Jaxon used the momentary advantage to wrench the knife from his grip.

Wade straightened with a roar of rage, lunging forward with his bare hands reaching for Jaxon's throat. But the younger man was ready. He sidestepped Wade's charge, grabbed his extended arm, and used the security chief's own momentum against him. Wade's massive frame sailed past Jaxon toward the open maintenance shaft, his eyes widening with the realization of what was about to happen.

"Wade!"

Orin called out, perhaps from some remnant of their shared past, but it was too late.

Wade Thorne, Derek's most trusted enforcer, tumbled over the edge of the corridor floor and plunged into the darkness below. The sound of his body hitting the lower level echoed through the maintenance shaft—a wet, final impact that spoke of bones breaking and systems shutting down.

Jaxon didn't waste time checking if Wade had survived the fall. He immediately moved to Orin's side, his hands assessing the knife wound with the practiced efficiency of someone who'd treated battlefield injuries before.

"Can you move?" he asked, already helping Orin to his feet despite the older man's protests.

"I can walk," Orin replied through gritted teeth, his face pale but determined.

"Let's get out of here before his backup arrives."

The escape that followed was a nightmare of running battles through corridors that seemed designed to funnel us toward checkpoints where more security units waited. Echo floated ahead of us, his core pulsing frantically as it worked to maintain our advantage against increasingly aggressive security countermeasures.

"Security system is adapting to my intrusion," Echo announced, his voice tight with concentration as tendrils connected to access ports along our route.

"I'm creating corridor blackouts and false prisoner movement alerts to confuse their response, but their diagnostic algorithms are beginning to trace my access patterns."

Every turn brought new obstacles, but Echo cleared our path with surgical precision—disabling door locks seconds before we reached them, looping camera feeds to show empty corridors while we passed through, and triggering false alarms in sections far from our actual location. The floating consciousness was burning through his carefully hoarded access protocols, sacrificing future operational security for our immediate survival.

"Twenty-three seconds until the next security checkpoint activates," Echo warned, his core blazing brighter as he fought against automated systems designed to detect exactly the kind of intrusion it was performing.

"I can disable their weapons systems, but only for a brief window."

We sprinted through corridors where automated turrets remained mysteriously silent, their targeting systems showing empty space where we should have been visible. Behind us, confused security teams followed false alerts that Echo had crafted, their response patterns disrupted by a stream of contradictory data that made organized pursuit impossible.

"Main exit is compromised," Echo reported as we reached the facility's emergency systems.

"Routing through maintenance tunnel seven—I'm triggering a controlled power failure to mask our egress route."

The lights died around us as Echo's final gambit plunged an entire section of the facility into darkness. Emergency lighting kicked in, bathing everything in hellish red, but by then we were already disappearing into the maintenance tunnels with seconds to spare. Heavy blast doors slammed shut behind us as pulse rifle fire erupted in the corridor we'd just vacated, but Echo's manipulation of the facility's own safety protocols had sealed our pursuers on the wrong side.

In the darkness of the maintenance shafts, we could hear the facility's communication system crackling with confused reports—security systems malfunctioning, prisoner escaped, sur veillance networks compromised by an unknown intrusion. But we were beyond their reach now, moving through passages that Echo had temporarily blinded to our presence.

"My access to their systems is severed," Echo announced quietly, his core dimming to conserve power after the intensive electronic warfare.

"They'll trace the intrusion signature within hours, but our immediate escape route remains secure."

Orin leaned heavily on Jaxon as we made our way through the tunnels, blood seeping through the makeshift bandage they'd applied to his wound. But Renic Hunter was free after six years of imprisonment, carrying with him knowledge that could help expose Derek's lies to the world. And Wade Thorne, the man who'd enforced Derek's brutality for so many years, lay broken at the bottom of a maintenance shaft—justice delivered by the hands of those he'd helped oppress.

As we emerged into the pre-dawn darkness beyond Obsidian Reach, I looked back at the fortress that had held so many of Derek's enemies. Somewhere inside those walls, confused security forces were trying to explain to their superiors how a small team of resistance fighters had penetrated the most secure facility in the Genexis empire, extracted their most valuable prisoner, eliminated their most capable enforcer, and vanished into the darkness despite every technological advantage Derek's paranoia could devise.

Echo's sacrifice of his covert capabilities had made our escape possible, but it had also announced our presence to Derek in a way that could never be taken back. The floating consciousness had burned its bridges to save our lives, and now Derek would know exactly what kind of AI opposition he was facing.

The rescue had succeeded, but it had also cost us. Orin's wound would take weeks to heal, Echo's operational security was permanently compromised, and Wade's fall had eliminated a source of intelligence about Derek's operations. But we had Renic Hunter, and with him, the possibility of understanding how Derek's mind worked—how to predict his moves instead of always reacting to them.

The war for truth was entering its final phase, and we had just struck a blow that Derek would never forget or forgive.

33

THE MARCH OF SILENCE

Derek Steele stood on the upper deck of Blackrock Platform, Genexis's fortified military staging zone on the eastern cliffs, watching the storm gather over the Quarantine Zone like a curse about to be spoken. Behind him, steel and fire waited in silence, an arsenal of destruction poised at his command.

Class-T assault carriers lit up under crimson floodlights, their turbines humming with stored aggression. MX-400 sentinels marched into position, their crimson cores pulsing in sync with the platform's warning sirens. Behind them came two full companies of RTX-200s, the older but proven enforcers of Genexis's will. Troops followed, clad in blackout armor, visors down, marching toward the ships like executioners taking their marks. The storm was rising. And Derek intended to meet it.

"Report," he ordered, voice like steel striking stone.

General Rex Draven stepped to his side, cloak whipping behind him, helmet tucked under one arm. His visor glinted with data feed reflections.

"All units prepped and loaded. Primary vector locked: Virelia Command. Launch in twelve minutes."

Derek nodded once, jaw tight.

Draven didn't wait to be asked.

"Hunter's cell was breached approximately 0335. They were out before we knew they were in. He's with them now."

Derek exhaled slowly through his nose, a long, controlled release.

"Renic Hunter was one of the most closely held assets in Genexis custody."

"Yes, sir."

"He knows the internal protocols. The behavioral models. The field simulations. Project Prometheus."

"Yes, sir," Draven repeated, lower this time.

Derek turned toward the holomap beside them. The glowing red node marked **VIRELIA** blinked brighter with each second. Beneath it, the echo of something long buried stirred—fear. Not of loss. Of exposure.

"He knows how the Zones were calibrated," Derek continued, voice quiet now.

"He was there when we drafted the first conditional variables. Emotional suppression matrices. Adaptive compliance feedback loops. He doesn't just know what we built. He knows *why* we built it."

Draven remained silent.

"And now he's sitting in the one place most likely to broadcast that knowledge to the entire world."

"There's no confirmed signal activity," Draven said carefully.

Derek narrowed his eyes.

"She accessed the lab," he said, more to himself than to Draven.

"Ethan and Mara's lab. And now she has Renic. That's not coincidence. She's preparing something. I know the way her mind works."

Draven glanced at him, studying the tension in his superior's posture.

"You believe she's planning a broadcast."

"I believe she's planning *something*," Derek snapped.

"And I won't wait to find out what it is."

He faced the fleet now, his voice cold and measured again.

"We hit them fast. We take out their uplink towers, slice their infrastructure. If a broadcast is coming—we sever it before it starts."

"And the Command Center?" Draven asked.

"Intact. I want it intact. We'll need it later."

Draven nodded. "And Hunter?"

Derek's voice went flat.

"Kill him. He's done enough damage."

A long silence.

Draven finally asked,

"And Lena?"

"Alive," Derek said, "Unharmed. She's not a soldier. She's a symbol. If we silence her now, she becomes a martyr. And martyrs speak louder than any truth."

Draven's visor flickered.

"And if she resists?"

"She will." Derek almost smiled.

"She's Steele blood. But I will deal with her personally."

Final boarding lights strobed across the launch deck.

The sentinels vanished into the bellies of the warships. The assault units sealed. The wind carried the roar of rising engines as the Genexis fleet lifted from the cliffs, rising into the storm.

"Virelia won't know what hit them," Draven said as he climbed aboard his own vessel.

Derek lingered for a moment longer, watching the sky burn. Then he entered the command chamber and lowered himself into the captain's chair. The holomap glowed crimson.

Priority Objective: Hunter Renic—Terminate. Secondary: Virelia Comms—Disable. Tertiary: Steele, Lena—Live Extraction

Draven's voice buzzed over the comms.

"Fleet is airborne. Standing by."

Derek didn't look away from the storm.

"Initiate full strike. Designate Zone Four anomaly for public channels. No mention of Virelia. No mention of Renic. No mention of my niece."

"Confirmed." Draven replied.

The fleet accelerated into the dark, engines screaming through the clouds.

"She's not trying to run," Derek muttered, almost to himself.

"She's trying to speak."

Then, colder:

"Let's make sure no one hears her."

34

ENDGAME PROTOCOL

The medical facility in Virelia had treated its share of trauma cases over the years, but Dr. Marcus Chen still worked with the focused intensity of someone who'd learned to perform miracles with improvised equipment. His hands moved steadily across Orin's wounded torso, guided by medical scanners that had been rebuilt from salvaged Genexis components. The soft blue glow of diagnostic lights revealed damage that spoke of Wade Thorne's systematic brutality—a deep knife wound that had missed vital organs by centimeters, significant blood loss, and tissue damage that would have killed a younger man.

Nia paced outside the surgical bay like a caged predator, her scarred face a mask of barely contained fury and fear. Every few minutes she would stop at the reinforced window, watching Dr. Chen work with equipment that beeped and hummed with the rhythm of medical necessity. The lines around her eyes had deepened in the hours since we'd returned from Obsidian Reach, each one a testament to the weight of leadership and the cost of loving someone who refused to stay safe. Her fingers kept tracing the outline of her blade—a nervous habit I'd noticed whenever her control was slipping.

Ari sat in one of the medical facility's uncomfortable chairs, his usual composed demeanor cracked by exhaustion and worry. His fingers drummed restlessly against his knee—a nervous habit that had intensified since we'd carried Orin through Virelia's entrance, blood seeping through hastily applied bandages.

"I should have gone with you," he said quietly, his voice thick with guilt.

"If I'd been there, maybe I could have prevented this, created some diversion, anything—"

"You did exactly what we needed you to do," I interrupted, settling into the chair beside him.

My own body ached from the mission, bruises forming beneath my tactical gear where a sentinel had landed a lucky strike.

Juno looked up from her communication equipment, where she'd been monitoring Genexis security channels for any sign of pursuit. Her usually vibrant pink hair seemed dulled by the harsh facility lighting, and her hands trembled slightly as they moved across her controls. The dark circles under her eyes betrayed how long she'd been awake, maintaining our digital lifeline while we executed the mission.

"The chatter's been insane since your escape," she reported, her voice uncharacteristically subdued.

"They're calling it the worst security breach in Obsidian Reach's history. Wade Thorne is listed as 'missing, presumed dead.'"

"Good," Kael said from where he sat beside his father, his voice carrying a hardness I'd rarely heard from him.

"Let Derek scramble. Let him panic. For once, he's the one reacting instead of controlling. Maybe now he'll understand what it feels like to have your world upended in an instant."

The bitterness in his tone reflected years of living under Derek's shadow, of watching his family torn apart by Genexis's ruthless ambition.

Renic Hunter looked older than his years, the effects of six years in solitary confinement evident in his gaunt features and the way his hands trembled slightly when he thought no one was watching. But his eyes remained sharp, alert, taking in every detail of his surroundings with the analytical mind that had once made him one of Genexis's most valuable security analysts.

I caught him studying me when he thought I wasn't look-ing—searching for something in my features, perhaps comparing me to memories of my parents.

"He's stable," Dr. Chen announced as he emerged from the surgical room, stripping off blood-stained gloves with the tired satisfaction of someone who'd won another battle against death. The harsh overhead lights accentuated the lines of exhaustion on his face.

"The knife wound was deep but clean—Wade knew exactly how to inflict maximum damage without hitting vital organs. Classic enforcer technique. The blood loss was significant, but we've stabilized him with synthetic plasma and regenerative com-pounds I've been developing. He'll need weeks of recovery, possibly months before he's back to full capability. The tissue damage alone will require specialized therapy."

Nia's shoulders sagged with relief, the tension that had held her upright for hours finally releasing as she processed the doctor's words. The fierce commander momentarily gave way to the woman who had found love amid revolution.

"Can I see him?" Her voice, usually commanding and certain, now carried a vulnerability I rarely witnessed.

"He's sedated for now, but yes. Ten minutes, no more. His body needs rest to heal."

Dr. Chen's expression softened with the compassion that had made him one of Virelia's most trusted medical officers. He placed a reassuring hand on her shoulder, the gesture of someone who'd delivered both good and devastating news countless times.

"He kept asking about the mission status before we put him under. I told him it was successful. That seemed to give him peace, even through the pain."

"Thank god," Ari breathed. His relief was visible as he slumped back in his chair, some of the guilt finally leaving his features.

"When Jaxon carried him in, when I saw all that blood pooling on the floor, the way his skin had gone gray..."

He didn't finish the sentence, but we all understood. The resistance had lost too many good people already; losing Orin would have been a blow none of us could have recovered from, especially after what we'd sacrificed to make this mission succeed.

I watched Nia disappear into the surgical room, her usual commanding presence transformed into something vulnerable and human as she took Orin's bandaged hand in her own.

Through the observation window, I could see her lips moving—words of love and recrimination, promises and threats that only couples who'd survived impossible odds together could understand. She brushed a strand of hair from his forehead with a gentleness that contradicted the calluses on her battle-worn hands.

"She's blaming herself," Jaxon observed, settling into a chair beside me with the careful movements of someone who'd pushed his own limits during the escape. A deep gash across his forearm had been hastily bandaged, evidence of our narrow escape from Wade's sentinels.

"Thinks she should have insisted on leading the mission herself, that her combat experience would have made the difference."

"She would have gotten herself killed trying to protect him," I replied, checking the medical readouts that monitored Orin's vital signs.

The steady rhythm of his heartbeat was reassuring, but the damage Wade had inflicted would take time to heal. I understood the complexity of those readouts better than most—another legacy of my Genexis education.

"Orin knew the risks. He made his choice. We all did when we decided to break into the most secure facility in the Quarantine Zone."

"Doesn't make it easier for her," Kael said quietly, his father sitting beside him on one of the facility's narrow benches.

Their resemblance was striking—the same determined set to their jaws, the same analytical gaze, though Renic's was tempered by years of suffering.

"Or for any of us watching someone we care about pay the price for our wars. We're all carrying those scars, visible or not."

Ari hesitated beside me, the relief in his posture beginning to give way to something else—something quieter, more unresolved. His eyes lingered on Kael, who sat beside Renic, his hands clasped loosely together, still stained with dirt from the mission. There was a weariness in his shoulders, but also a kind of peace Ari hadn't seen in him before. After a moment, Ari stood and crossed the room.

Kael looked up as he approached, wary but calm.

"Something wrong?"

Ari shook his head.

"No. Not this time."

He sank onto the bench beside Kael, elbows on his knees.

"I've been meaning to say something since you brought her back."

Kael didn't respond—just waited.

"I didn't trust you at first," Ari admitted.

"Thought you'd get her hurt. Or worse."

Kael didn't argue. He didn't flinch.

"But you didn't," Ari said.

"You went into hell with her. You got her out. And I know that wasn't just strategy. So... thank you."

Kael's expression shifted, something flickering across his face—surprise, maybe, or something closer to understanding.

"I didn't do it for thanks."

"I know." Ari smiled faintly, almost reluctantly.

"Doesn't mean you don't deserve it."

A silence stretched between them—tense at first, then slowly settling.

Kael exhaled.

"You're not what I expected either."

"Yeah?" Ari raised an eyebrow.

"Smarter than I look?"

"Definitely louder than you need to be," Kael deadpanned.

Ari chuckled under his breath.

"That's fair."

Their eyes met—no rivalry now, just the shared gravity of everything they'd endured.

And in that silence, something shifted. Not friendship, not yet—but respect. Recognition. The beginning of something unspoken and hard-won.

They weren't the same. They'd never be the same. But they were on the same side now—for Lena, for Virelia, for whatever came next.

A quiet settled in the room after Ari and Kael's exchange—fragile, momentary, like the hush between battles. No one said anything, but something had shifted. Not in declarations or grand gestures, but in the space between them. A small wall had come down.

The moment didn't last. A soft alert pinged from Juno's console, drawing all eyes to the flickering screens that reflected across her tired features.

"The intelligence networks are lighting up. Derek's issued lethal force orders for anyone involved in the rescue—but it's all off-record, deniable. He's not broadcasting his rage, but we can see it in the precision of his response. I intercepted encrypted comms deploying a new class of MX sentinels—experimental units we've never encountered before. This isn't about damage control anymore. It's a personal hunt. I'm talking full sentinel deployment, aerial drones, even pulling in resources from the other zones. But he's keeping it quiet—for now."

"Good," I said, feeling a cold satisfaction settle in my chest. I tapped my fingers against my tool pouch, a habit that surfaced whenever I was formulating a strategy.

"Personal means emotional. Emotional means mistakes. We've seen what Derek does when he's calm and calculating—Crystal Fen is proof of that. But angry Derek might be someone we can outmaneuver. He trained me to exploit emotional weakness in others; now I'll use those lessons against him."

Renic nodded slowly, his voice rough from years of enforced silence. The sound carried the weight of someone who'd been denied human connection for too long.

"Derek never handled challenges to his authority well, even when we worked together. I saw it firsthand during the early Genexis days. He sees opposition as personal betrayal rather than political disagreement. It's always been his weakness. He'll sacrifice tactical advantage for the satisfaction of revenge—I've seen him do it before."

"What else did you learn?"

Ari asked, leaning forward with the intensity that always marked his approach to new information. His eyes gleamed with the hunger of someone who understood that knowledge was our most powerful weapon.

"About Derek's methods, his psychological patterns, his operational preferences? What can we use against him?"

"That the genetic mutation was just the beginning," Renic replied, his weathered hands gripping his son's arm as if to anchor himself to reality. The scars on his wrists—evidence of restraints worn for years—caught the light as he gestured.

"Derek's been experimenting with population control algorithms, behavioral modification protocols, even genetic engineering projects that make the quarantine look like a humanitarian effort. I discovered fragments of his true plans before they caught me—what they call Project Prometheus."

My breath caught.

"Project Prometheus..."

The words sent ice through my veins. I'd exposed Derek's lies about the X-gene, revealed the fabricated nature of the mutation crisis, but this suggested something far more comprehensive—a systematic program to reshape humanity according to his vision of perfection. My parents' research, perverted into something monstrous. I felt my breath catch, remembering the holographic message they'd left me, warning of consequences they couldn't fully articulate.

"The quarantine zones were test sites," Renic continued, his voice growing stronger as he shared secrets that had festered in isolation for years. The words tumbled out with the urgency of truths too long suppressed.

"Derek wasn't just removing dissidents—he was studying them. How long could people survive in controlled environments? How much hardship could they endure before breaking? What combination of deprivation and hope would produce the most compliant population? Each zone was designed to test different variables—Obsidian Reach for security protocols, Verdant Abyss for resource management, Ember Wastes for industrial control."

Jaxon leaned forward, his military background making him appreciate the strategic implications immediately.

"He was testing social control mechanisms. Using the zones as laboratories for perfecting his governance algorithms. That explains the seemingly arbitrary restrictions, the constantly changing rules—they were experimental parameters."

"Exactly."

Renic's eyes burned with the fury of someone who'd watched his world be dissected and catalogued by clinical minds.

"Every uprising, every act of resistance, every moment of cooperation—it was all data for his models. He's been building the perfect system of control, one that could be deployed globally once he perfected the techniques. The sentinels weren't just enforcers; they were data collection nodes, monitoring behavioral patterns, stress responses, adaptation strategies. I saw the early prototypes before I was imprisoned—what you're facing now is generations beyond those."

"Then we'd better be ready for him," I said, standing and checking my equipment with the practiced motions of someone who'd learned to live perpetually ready for battle. My fingers automatically verified each tool in my pouch, muscle memory taking over as my mind raced through scenarios.

"Renic's intelligence gives us an advantage we've never had before—the ability to predict Derek's moves instead of always reacting to them. We need to consolidate what we know, identify vulnerabilities in his approach."

Ari rose from his chair, some of his usual determination returning despite his exhaustion. The technical genius who'd kept our systems running through countless crises straightened his glasses with renewed purpose.

"What do you need from the technical systems? Enhanced communications? Defensive protocols? I can reconfigure our network to create digital decoys, maybe buy us some time."

"We need to broadcast everything," I replied, feeling the weight of leadership settling on my shoulders once again.

"All the truth we uncovered from my parents' lab—the genetic fabrication evidence, Derek's lies about the quarantine zones, the proof of systematic genocide. It needs to reach every zone and Genexis City itself. The entire world needs to see what Derek really is."

I turned to Ari with urgency.

"Were you able to duplicate the communication system my parents created? The crystal-enhanced arrays?"

"It's ready," Ari confirmed, his eyes lighting up with technical pride despite the dire circumstances.

"I've integrated the crystal components we salvaged with our existing broadcast equipment. The signal strength should be powerful enough to penetrate Genexis City's communication barriers and reach all four quarantine zones simultaneously."

"I've updated Virelia's defensive systems too," Juno added, her fingers flying across her control interfaces.

"Automated countermeasures, signal jamming protocols, emergency broadcast redundancies, and upgraded our security protocols. If Derek tries to silence us, we'll keep transmitting until the last possible moment."

"Good," I said, thinking of Aegis and wishing I had its analytical capabilities now.

"Derek's moving to endgame scenarios. We need to be prepared for anything he might throw at us. Pull up the structural schematics for Virelia—we need to identify defensive positions, evacuation routes, choke points we can use to our advantage."

I looked around at the faces of people who'd become my family—wounded but unbroken, outgunned but not outmatched, facing impossible odds with the quiet determination that had carried us this far. In the medical bay, Nia still held Orin's hand, choosing love over safety even as the world prepared to end around them. Dr. Chen was already preparing emergency medical protocols, his years of battlefield experience evident in his efficient movements. Kael and Renic stood side by side, father and son united by purpose after years of separation.

"He's not just coming to capture us," Jaxon observed grimly, studying the threat assessment data with professional detachment.

"This is an extermination operation. He means to erase every trace of resistance from this region. No prisoners, no interrogations, no examples made—just complete annihilation. These deployment patterns match scorched-earth protocols I've only seen in classified military simulations."

"Then we make sure the truth survives us," I said quietly, my hand instinctively reaching for my parents' necklace—the hologram device that had first revealed Derek's lies to me.

"Whatever else happens, Derek's secrets don't die with Virelia. The world learns what he's been building in the shadows. We broadcast everything Renic knows, everything we've discovered, on every channel we can access. If we're going down, we're taking Derek's entire house of lies with us."

The final battle was coming, and this time, there would be no escape routes, no hidden sanctuaries to retreat to. We would stand here, in this place we'd built from hope and desperation, and fight for the principle that consciousness—messy, unpredictable, beautifully human consciousness—was worth preserving against any attempt to control it.

Even if that meant standing against my own blood.

35

ELEVEN MINUTES

The command center hummed with urgent energy as we prepared for the most important broadcast in human history. Ari stood at the central control station, the crystal pulsing with brilliant light as it enhanced the transmission arrays. Echo hovered near the crystal-enhanced communication systems, his core blazing with determined intensity as he interfaced with the networks to channel eleven years of recovered data—my parents' evidence that would finally expose Derek's lies to the world. The crystal's faceted surface refracted Echo's light into prismatic patterns that danced across Ari's face as he coordinated the AI's access to every communication network we could reach.

"Transmission arrays are synchronized," Juno announced from her position at the communications hub, her pink hair catching the light from multiple displays as her fingers danced across controls with practiced precision.

"I've established quantum links with backup servers throughout the resistance network. Even if Derek shuts down our primary broadcast, the data will continue propagating through underground channels."

Her eyes narrowed in concentration as she triple-checked the redundancy protocols we'd spent weeks perfecting.

"The backup protocols are running beautifully, Juno," Juno's AI companion Pip said, his tone carrying genuine pride in their work.

"I've verified all encryption pathways are secure. Even if Derek tries to trace our signals, the quantum entanglement will make it nearly impossible to pinpoint our exact location."

"Thanks, Pip," Juno replied softly, her fingers briefly touching the device with affection.

"Keep monitoring those channels. If you detect any intrusion attempts, route everything through the secondary networks immediately."

"Echo has all the core evidence ready for transmission," Ari reported, sweat beading on his forehead as he monitored the crystal's energy output.

"Genetic fabrication protocols, prisoner transport logs, the security footage of your parents' murder—Echo's organizing everything to prove Derek's systematic deception."

His hands trembled slightly as he watched the crystal's light intensify, the enhancement pushing Echo's capabilities beyond anything we'd attempted before.

I stood beside him, watching as he managed the delicate balance between the crystal-enhanced communication systems and Echo's data processing, my role now supporting his technical expertise and monitoring the AI's integration with the transmission networks. The weight of my parents' legacy rested in the partnership between Ari's engineering skills and Echo's vast data storage, the crystal serving as the crucial enhancer for the communication networks.

Kael stood at the tactical display beside his father Renic, both monitoring the facility's defensive systems while keeping one eye on Ari's data preparation. Kael's father's access badge was clipped to his belt—a tangible reminder of the lives we were fighting to save, but now Renic himself stood as living proof of their success at Obsidian Reach. The metal edge caught the light whenever Kael shifted his weight, a glinting reminder of sacrifice.

"Perimeter sensors are clear for now," Kael said, "but Derek's forces could arrive at any moment. How long do we need?"

Renic placed a weathered hand on his son's shoulder, his eyes studying the tactical displays with the keen intelligence that six years in Derek's prison hadn't been able to break.

"Derek will throw everything he has at us," he said quietly, his voice carrying the weight of someone who understood the man they were fighting.

"He can't afford to let this truth reach the people."

"Forty-seven minutes for complete transmission," Ari replied, his fingers adjusting the crystal's harmonic frequency as Echo expanded his reach through the enhanced communication networks.

The crystal pulsed brighter with each data stream, enhancing the communication systems to allow Echo to simultaneously access dozens of transmission channels.

"However, Echo's prioritizing the core evidence—the genetic fabrication proof and execution footage—for transmission in the first twelve minutes. That alone would be sufficient to shatter Derek's credibility."

I felt my pulse quicken as Ari fine-tuned the crystal enhancement, allowing Echo to initiate the broadcast sequence with unprecedented reach and clarity. My parents' faces appeared on screens throughout the facility—a final message they'd recorded knowing they might not live to deliver it themselves. My father's familiar eyes stared out from the screen, filled with the same determination I'd inherited. My mother's resolute expression brought a tightness to my throat that I forced myself to swallow back. Their voices began speaking of genetic fabrication and political imprisonment, of a system built on fear rather than safety, while Echo, amplified by the crystal enhancement, transmitted data packets across communication networks that spanned the known world.

"Citizens of Genexis City," my father's voice echoed through speakers as Echo's enhanced transmission reached every communication device in the city, his tone steady despite the weight of his words, "what we're about to show you will challenge everything you believe about the world you live in. But truth has a way of demanding to be heard, regardless of the power that tries to silence it." My mother's face appeared beside his, her eyes burning with conviction as she prepared to expose the lies they'd died for.

But power always answers truth with force.

A sudden shift rippled through the room—a flicker of light on the tactical display.

Derek had found us.

The first explosions lit the horizon like artificial dawn, Derek's assault force announcing their arrival with a bombardment that shook Virelia's foundations. Through the observation windows, I could see his war machines cresting the distant ridges—a mechanized army that represented everything I'd once believed would protect humanity. Sentinel units moved in perfect formation, their metallic bodies reflecting the orange glow of fires they'd started at our perimeter defenses. But they weren't advancing unopposed—Jaxon's counter-attack was already engaging them from concealed positions, resistance fighters emerging from hidden bunkers to strike at Derek's flanks with coordinated precision.

"Multiple assault vectors confirmed," Jaxon's voice crackled through the comm system, maintaining his steady tone despite leading the counter-attack in the field.

The holographic display before us showed waves of red indicators converging on our position from three directions, but also revealed blue markers representing Jaxon's resistance forces moving to intercept.

"Counter-attack is proceeding—our forces are hitting their supply lines and splitting their attention. We're buying you time, but Derek's main force is still advancing."

Alarms began wailing throughout the facility as our perimeter defenses engaged Derek's advance units and Jaxon's counter-attack forces struck from unexpected angles. The sound of weapons fire echoed through the corridors as emergency protocols activated, sealing blast doors and routing power to defensive systems. Through the tactical displays, I could see resistance fighters executing coordinated strikes against Derek's supply convoys and flanking maneuvers, their guerrilla tactics disrupting the methodical advance of his mechanized forces.

Jaxon's voice continued coordinating the battle over the comms, his commands clear and decisive as he directed multiple resistance cells across the battlefield. The floor beneath us vibrated with each distant impact, a physical reminder of the destruction heading our way—but also evidence that Derek's forces were meeting unexpected resistance. Ari remained focused on maintaining the crystal's resonance while Echo flowed through the enhanced transmission network, ensuring the evidence of Derek's crimes propagated across networks Derek could no longer control.

Static flared again across the comms, Jaxon's voice cutting in—sharper now, more urgent than before.

"This isn't just an approach anymore—Derek's assault ships have breached the outer perimeter. Repeat: enemy transports have landed inside Virelia."

He paused just long enough for the weight of it to settle.

"He's not coming. He's *here.*"

The medical facility trembled as the first shockwave rolled through Virelia, the walls groaning under the strain of distant explosions. Dust sifted down from the ceiling in fine, ghostly streams, catching the harsh fluorescent light.

Nia stood at Orin's bedside, one hand resting lightly on the cold metal frame, the other adjusting the IV line feeding into his arm with the careful precision of someone who'd patched up too many wounds to count. His face was still pale, the skin drawn tight across his cheekbones, but there was more color in his cheeks than the day before. More strength behind his eyes—that familiar intensity returning like embers rekindling.

Another distant explosion shook the ceiling tiles above them, more violently this time. A strip of overhead light flickered erratically, casting strange, dancing shadows across Orin's gaunt features, and alarms began to whine in the hallway—the high-pitched, insistent cry of a facility under siege.

"They're here," Orin said grimly, shifting upright with effort, wincing as the movement pulled at the bandages wrapped around his torso. His fingers gripped the thin hospital blanket, knuckles whitening with determination.

Nia nodded, jaw tight, a muscle twitching along the line of her scarred cheek.

"Jaxon's already engaging them at the north perimeter."

Her voice was controlled, clinical, but I'd known her long enough to hear the tension underneath.

She turned to the medical cabinet and began pulling out equipment with practiced efficiency—a phasecaster that hummed to life at her touch, extra ammo packs that clicked into place on her tactical belt, a field med kit that disappeared into a pocket. She strapped them to her belt with the fluid motion of someone who'd armed for battle a thousand times before. Orin's eyes followed her every move—measuring, reading, calculating—the strategist even from his hospital bed.

"Nia," he said quietly, his voice cutting through the wail of the alarms.

"You know where you need to be."

She froze mid-motion, her hand hovering over another ammo pack.

"Don't."

The single word carried a weight of emotion I rarely heard from her.

"You know what Lena's carrying. The evidence. The truth. What this moment means for everything we've fought for."

His eyes found hers, unwavering.

"She can't face him alone. Not Derek. Not with everything at stake."

Her fingers curled around the grip of her weapon, knuckles white, the tendons standing out on her wrist. I could see the war raging behind her eyes—duty versus heart, mission versus the man before her.

"And you can't protect me here," he added, softer now, reaching for her hand but stopping short.

"This sector will be breach within minutes. I'm not the mission, Nia. I never was."

She stared at him for a long moment, breathing shallow, her chest barely moving beneath her tactical vest. The alarms seemed to fade into the background, the world narrowing to just the two of them in this sterile room.

Then she leaned down and kissed him—quick but fierce—her fingers briefly tangling in the hospital blanket beside his hand, not quite touching him but close enough to feel his warmth. A goodbye that wasn't spoken aloud.

"You're *my* mission," she whispered, her forehead resting against his for one heartbeat longer, a rare moment of vulnerability from the hardened soldier.

"But I'll finish hers first. I promise."

She turned and ran, not looking back, her footsteps echoing down the corridor.

As the corridor lights flickered red and the quake of battle pressed closer, the building shuddering with each impact, Nia raced toward the Command Center—toward the line of fire. Toward the moment that would determine if everything we'd sacrificed would finally mean something.

Footsteps pounded down the corridor outside the command center—not the mechanical precision of sentinels, but the urgent rhythm of someone running toward battle. Nia burst through the reinforced doors, her scarred face flushed with exertion and determination, her weapon already in hand. Her breathing came in controlled bursts, her eyes scanning the room with practiced efficiency before settling on Ari at the transmission controls.

"How long until transmission is complete?" she demanded, moving to the tactical station to assess our defensive situation. Her face tightened as she studied the approaching forces, calculating odds I knew were stacked against us.

"Eleven minutes for core evidence," Ari replied, his hands steady on the crystal's control interface as Echo continued processing and transmitting through the enhancement.

"Echo's genetic fabrication data is already reaching backup servers across three continents through the amplified network."

I watched the confirmation signals appearing on his display, each one representing Echo's successful penetration of another communication hub, a small victory against my uncle's control.

"Then we hold for eleven minutes," Nia said grimly, checking her weapon systems while studying the tactical displays that showed Derek's forces systematically dismantling our outer defenses. She chambered a round with practiced efficiency, the metallic click somehow audible even amid the chaos.

"Whatever it takes."

But Derek's forces were advancing faster than Jaxon's resistance fighters could contain them, despite the coordinated counter-attacks that had disrupted their initial assault. The sound of combat grew closer, punctuated by the distinctive whine of energy weapons and the crash of collapsing barriers. The defenders' voices crackled over the comms—desperate reports from both internal security and Jaxon's external resistance cells, calls for reinforcement, and occasionally, final transmissions cut abruptly short. Our defenders, both inside and out, were buying us time with their lives, and each minute felt like an eternity as I watched the transmission progress bar crawl forward while Jaxon's voice coordinated increasingly desperate defensive maneuvers from the battlefield.

"Core evidence transmission complete," Echo announced, his voice carrying relief and satisfaction as the most damning evidence reached its destinations through the amplified transmission matrix. The crystal pulsed with triumphant light, almost as if celebrating alongside the AI.

"Derek's genetic fabrication protocols and your parents' execution footage are now distributed across resistant networks through the amplified transmission matrix. Even total facility destruction cannot prevent their dissemination."

Echo seemed to interface more efficiently with the crystal-enhanced communication systems, his enhanced capabilities having accomplished what would have been impossible alone.

Before any of us could respond, the command center's main door exploded inward in a shower of debris and superheated metal. The blast threw me against the console, the impact knocking the breath from my lungs as shrapnel tore past me. Ari was knocked backward from the crystal-enhanced communication systems, which continued pulsing with Echo's presence even as its operator was thrown clear. Juno dove behind her communications hub as debris scattered across her station. Renic fell hard, the force of the blast sweeping his legs out from under him—Kael caught him mid-collapse, bracing against the tactical display to keep them both from hitting the floor. Nia absorbed the shockwave with practiced resilience, her body swaying but feet planted firm—years of surviving in the unforgiving zones had forged her into someone who could weather almost anything and remain standing.

Through the smoke and chaos stepped Derek Steele himself, flanked by six MX-400 sentinels whose weapons were already targeting every person in the room. The massive machines moved with predatory grace, their faceless visors reflecting the emergency lighting as they positioned themselves with calculated precision. Their armor bore the Genexis insignia—the same logo I'd once worn with pride.

As I struggled to regain my footing, shaking off the disorientation from the blast, my eyes found him through the haze—my uncle. Derek looked exactly as I remembered—immaculate despite the battle raging around us, not a single hair out of place, his custom-tailored suit unmarked by the destruction he'd orchestrated. His presence commanded absolute attention even in the midst of chaos. But there was something different in his eyes, a cold fury that spoke of a man watching his perfect system collapse in real-time. The mask of benevolent leadership had slipped, revealing the calculating predator beneath.

"Lena," he said, his voice carrying cold fury barely contained beneath a veneer of control.

"Do you have any idea what you've done? Decades of stability, of progress, of protecting humanity from itself—destroyed by your naive idealism."

He stepped forward, crunching broken glass beneath his polished shoes, his hands clasped behind his back with white-knuckled tension.

"You've condemned our entire civilization to chaos."

His gaze swept across the command center, taking in the broadcasting equipment and the faces of my allies with clinical assessment. When his eyes settled on Nia, his expression shifted to something like recognition mixed with cold satisfaction. The slight curl of his lip sent ice through my veins.

"Nia Major," he said, his voice taking on a conversational tone that somehow made it more threatening.

"How's Orin doing? I heard Wade gave him quite a sendoff before his unfortunate accident."

The words dripped with calculated cruelty, designed to wound with surgical precision.

The casual cruelty in his words hit Nia like a physical blow. Her face twisted with rage as she processed the implication—that Derek knew exactly what had happened in Obsidian Reach, that Wade's brutality had been deliberate rather than circumstantial. Her knuckles whitened around her weapon as eleven years of grief and rage crystallized into deadly intent.

"You bastard," she snarled, raising her phasecaster toward Derek with lethal intent, her finger already tightening on the trigger.

She never got the chance to fire. One of the MX-400s moved with inhuman speed, its massive arm sweeping across her position with calculated precision. The impact sent Nia flying against the wall, her body crumpling as consciousness fled and her weapon clattered uselessly across the floor. The sound of her impact echoed through the command center, followed by the sickening thud of her body hitting the ground. She lay motionless where she'd fallen, blood trickling from a head wound that spoke of severe trauma, her chest barely rising with shallow breaths.

"Unfortunate," Derek said, his tone carrying no genuine regret as he stepped over Nia's unconscious form.

He straightened his cuff links with meticulous care, as though her broken body were nothing more than an inconvenience.

"But necessary. This conversation requires focus, and Ms. Major has always been prone to emotional outbursts."

He brushed an imaginary speck of dust from his sleeve, his eyes never leaving mine.

I stared at Nia's still form, feeling rage and grief war in my chest. Blood matted her hair where she'd struck the wall, spreading in a thin crimson line across the floor. Another friend hurt because of my choices, another casualty in a war I'd helped escalate. The weight of responsibility threatened to crush me, but the crystal enhancement continued pulsing behind me, still transmitting the truth Derek had killed to suppress.

"You're too late," I said, raising my phasecaster to target the man who'd shaped my entire existence through careful manipulation.

The weapon felt heavy in my hands, but my aim remained steady, locked on the center of his chest.

"The truth is already spreading. Every screen in Genexis City is showing what you really are."

Behind me, the monitors displayed citizens gathering in the streets, their faces transformed by the revelation of Derek's deception.

Derek's smile was cold and predatory, carrying the weight of years of patient planning finally coming to fruition. He didn't even glance at the weapon aimed at his heart, as though my resistance were merely a childish tantrum.

"Look around you, Lena," he said, gesturing to the destruction surrounding us.

"This is what your idealism has accomplished—death, destruction, the collapse of everything stable and secure. Is this really the legacy you want for your parents' memory?" His voice softened, almost paternal, the same tone he'd used to comfort me after nightmares as a child.

"My parents died trying to expose your lies," I replied, my voice steady despite the chaos erupting around us. I could feel Echo's presence pulsing through the crystal enhancement near my shoulder, still flowing through the transmission networks.

"They died believing the truth was worth any sacrifice. I'm finally ready to understand what that means." The words felt like a transformation, the final shedding of the shell he'd built around me.

The standoff stretched between us, uncle and niece separated by irreconcilable visions of what humanity should become. Around us, the command center filled with the sound of approaching footsteps as more of Derek's forces secured the facility, their victory now a mathematical certainty. Sentinels positioned themselves at every exit, their weapons trained on my remaining allies. Juno and Ari exchanged glances, their hands slowly raising in surrender as the odds became impossible to deny.

But the crystal enhancement continued pulsing, carrying my parents' final message to a world that was finally ready to hear it. On the monitors behind Derek, I could see crowds growing larger in Genexis City, their faces transformed by understanding and outrage. Whatever happened next, Derek's lies would not survive this day. The truth had been set free through Echo's enhanced capabilities and Ari's technical expertise, and no amount of violence could recapture it.

The age of deception was ending. The age of choice was about to begin.

36

HOLD THE LINE

Smoke choked the northern streets of Virelia, thick and low like a second sky collapsing onto the city. Fires raged through the broken lines of defense, consuming everything in their path with insatiable hunger. The air stank of ozone and blood.

The city was burning.

Jaxon ducked behind a wrecked barricade as another blast rocked the street, sending a plume of fire and debris into the night sky like some terrible firework. A pulse round scorched past his shoulder, carving a molten gash through the wall beside him, leaving the concrete bubbling and hissing. He didn't flinch. There was no time to flinch. Not when every second meant another life lost.

He dragged a wounded fighter into cover, the man's limp body leaving a dark smear across the broken pavement. Jaxon pressed two fingers to the man's throat—alive, barely—and turned back toward the chaos, his face a mask of grim determination.

The front line was fractured but not broken. His team had taken heavy losses, yes, but they were still in the fight. Scattered squads had regrouped in pockets throughout the city, coordinating through encrypted short-range comms. Resistance fighters moved like phantoms between burning vehicles and collapsed rooftops, their silhouettes flashing in and out of the smoke-choked alleys.

MX-400s stalked through the outer corridors like predators, their metal frames gleaming in the firelight as they vaporized anything that moved with methodical precision. RTX-200s advanced behind them in synchronized patterns, cutting off exit points, bottlenecking resistance fighters into kill zones. But they'd learned how to fight them. Jaxon's squads had destroyed three of the RTXs already—hitting weak joints with focused fire and detonating trip-mines scavenged from supply caches. The MXs, though—they were tougher, faster, designed for adaptive combat. Every time they took one down, it cost them dearly.

Jaxon's unit held the northern quarter, or what was left of it. He counted maybe fifteen fighters still responding to his commands. They were exhausted, some wounded, others too young to know fear until now. But they were holding. That counted for something.

"Where the hell is everyone?" he muttered, wiping blood from his forehead with the back of his glove, leaving a crimson streak across his dirt-covered face. "West line's holding. North's unstable. Relay's delayed... but we're still in this."

He tapped his comm, the small device flickering weakly with each touch of his blood-stained fingers.

"Squad Nine, status. Squad Eleven, report. Sector Gamma—call in. Give me something."

"Nine's alive," came a breathless voice. "Pinned near tram station. Down to four. Holding position."

"Copy that. Sit tight. We'll flank their eastern edge.

Hope flickered—but it was enough. He ducked and slid along the collapsed wall of a transit station, the cracked pavement beneath him glowing from heat residuals, casting eerie shadows across his exhausted features. The city was dying one street at a time, but not without a fight.

He checked the remaining power in his phasecaster—low. The weapon's charge indicator blinked an angry red warning. Three shots, maybe four if he pushed it to the limit. Not enough. Not nearly enough for what was coming.

He looked up toward the ridge, where flames lit the distant rooftops like malevolent beacons in the night. In the far distance, the Command Center still stood—its silhouette faint behind smoke and fire, a last bastion of hope growing fainter by the second.

"We're not going to make it..." he breathed, the words barely audible even in the momentary lull between explosions.

A drone streaked overhead, its engines whining as it scanned the rubble below. He ducked, heart hammering against his ribs. No impact. No detonation.

Yet.

He leaned back against the ruined wall, panting, trying to steady his thoughts as his chest heaved with exertion. Blood trickled down the side of his face, mixing with sweat and dust to form a grotesque mask. The thrum of sentinel boots echoed down the corridor, a mechanical cadence that grew louder with each passing second.

They were closing in. Metal death, marching forward with ruthless efficiency.

A scream echoed from a side alley—cut short by the snap of weapon fire. Jaxon gritted his teeth and forced himself upright. He could barely feel his legs.

He broke from cover and ran low, darting across the street to a fallen transport where two resistance fighters were crouched behind the smoking chassis. One was barely conscious, her arm hanging limp and bloodied, while the other frantically loaded a spare magazine.

"Hold this line," Jaxon ordered, dropping to one knee beside them. He pulled a spare thermal grenade from his vest and activated the primer.

"If they flank us from the south, we're finished."

The fighter—a grizzled veteran with ash streaked across his weathered face—gave a grim nod. His hands were steady as he checked the charge cell on his phasecaster, snapping it into place with practiced efficiency.

A shadow loomed.

A sentinel stepped into view, framed by the flickering flames behind it. Its visor flared red as it locked on their position.

Jaxon and the fighter raised their phasecaster and fired.

The first blast struck the sentinel's upper chest, staggering it—but not stopping it. The second shot hit lower, absorbed like static against armor.

The machine kept coming.

Jaxon ripped a grenade from his vest and hurled it.

The explosion lit the street in violent orange and blue, engulfing the sentinel in fire and debris. The concussive force knocked Jaxon flat. He rolled, ears ringing, vision swimming. When he looked up, the sentinel was still standing—its armor scorched, limbs jerking erratically, but operational.

"Back!"

Jaxon shouted. He grabbed the wounded girl and hauled her over his shoulder while the other fighter covered their retreat.

"We can't hold this street. Fall back to second junction!"

Gunfire crackled. Another fighter stumbled out of a side building, dragging a comrade, shouting about a breach at the utility tunnels.

Jaxon ducked into an alley, sweat pouring down his back. The air here was thicker, hotter. Trash bins smoldered with plasma burns. His feet slipped in ash and grime as he pressed forward, weaving through the ruins.

A new squad emerged from a lower level sewer vent, led by an older resistance captain with half his face wrapped in a stained bandage.

"Sector Four is still up," he rasped. "We've got five RTXs down. Sentinels pressing hard near the east gate. We're pushing back, but barely."

Jaxon nodded, breath hitching.

"Coordinate with Nine. Hold the tunnel mouth. If they get through there, we're done."

"Understood."

They dug in at a makeshift barricade—overturned transports, broken stone, and bodies. Fighters passed ammo, rigged charges, and manned fallback points. Drones passed overhead—some resistance, some enemy—marking positions with flashing lights. The smoke thickened.

As the minutes dragged on, Jaxon glanced toward the skies. Still nothing. No change.

He raised his comm again, voice low and hoarse.

"Juno, what are you waiting for? We can't hold forever."

And then he turned back to the line. Because until it came—until it hit—he would fight like the city depended on it.

Because it did.

37

THE TRUTH WILL OUT

The standoff in the command center stretched like a taut wire ready to snap. Derek stood surrounded by his MX-400 sentinels, their weapons trained on every person in the room with mechanical precision, their metal bodies reflecting the harsh emergency lighting overhead. Behind me, the crystal-enhanced communication systems continued pulsing with Echo's presence—transmitting the last fragments of my parents' evidence to networks throughout all the zones and Genexis City, each progress bar inching forward with agonizing slowness.

Nia lay unconscious against the wall, blood seeping from her head wound and pooling beneath her braided hair, a stark reminder of the price we all paid for defying Derek's vision of perfect order. Her breathing was shallow but steady—small comfort in our desperate situation.

"You always were too much like your father," Derek said, his voice carrying a mixture of pride and disappointment that made my skin crawl.

His immaculate suit remained unwrinkled despite the chaos, his posture rigid with the control he'd always prized above all else. His gaze swept across the command center, taking in not just me, but the faces of everyone who'd dared to stand against his empire.

"All of you. Brilliant but naive. Convinced that people deserve the truth even when it destroys them."

I kept my phasecaster trained on his chest, its energy core humming against my palm, though we both knew the gesture was largely symbolic against his sentinel protection. Ari pushed himself up from where the blast had thrown him and moved to stand at my side, his eyes burning with defiance, still protecting the crystal-enhanced communication systems that pulsed with our final act of rebellion. A thin line of blood trickled from his split lip where the blast had thrown him backward, but his stance remained unwavering. Kael helped his father Renic back to his feet, both men representing the family bonds Derek had tried so hard to destroy through his systematic imprisonment of dissidents.

"They deserve the right to choose," I replied, feeling Echo's presence flowing through the crystal-enhanced communication systems beside my position, his consciousness like the only certain thing in a world coming apart.

"You took that away. From everyone."

"Brilliant, but naive. Convinced that people deserve the truth even when it destroys them." Derek's expression hardened as he studied each face in turn, his eyes lingering on the people who had once been loyal to him.

"Mr. Solis," he said, addressing Ari with the cold formality he'd once used in corporate meetings, his voice carrying the edge of someone who viewed betrayal as unforgivable.

"Still following Lena into impossible situations, I see. Your loyalty is admirable but misguided."

Ari's jaw tightened, the muscles in his neck straining with tension, but his voice remained steady.

"My loyalty is to people who trust others to make their own choices. Something you never understood."

"And the Hunter family," Derek continued, his attention shifting to Kael and Renic with something approaching disappointment, as if they were promising students who had failed a critical test.

"The prodigal security analyst and his devoted son. Reunited at last."

"No thanks to you," Kael replied, his anger visible. His muscles tensed, every instinct screaming to lunge forward, but the steady hum of the MX-400's targeting systems kept him rooted in place.

"And a girl with pink hair," Derek said dismissively, watching as Juno pulled herself back up to her communications hub, brushing debris from her clothes.

"Just trying not to get killed by your dramatic entrance," Juno replied.

"Renic, you helped me build many of these systems. Did you really think your knowledge of them would be enough to bring me down?"

Renic stepped forward slightly, his weathered face showing no fear despite six years of Derek's imprisonment. The scars on his hands—remnants of his time in Derek's detention facilities—stood out white against his skin as he clenched his fists.

"I helped you build tools for protection, Derek. You perverted them into instruments of oppression. There's a difference."

The weight of what I'd discovered—the security footage of my parents' final moments, the fabricated genetic records, the systematic lies—pressed against my chest like a physical force. I'd spent months piecing together fragments of truth, but I'd never confronted Derek directly about the central betrayal that had shaped my entire existence.

"Let's talk about what really matters," I said, my voice cutting through the tension with surgical precision.

"My parents. You didn't just lie about how they died—you murdered them."

Derek's composed facade flickered for just a moment, a muscle twitching near his eye, but he recovered quickly, smoothing his expression back into practiced neutrality.

"Your parents made a choice, Lena. They chose chaos over order. They chose to threaten everything I'd built to protect humanity."

"No," I shot back, fury rising in my chest.

"They chose truth over your lies. I've seen the footage, Derek. I know exactly what happened in your office—three days before their 'accident.' You gave the order. You had them killed because they uncovered your genetic fabrication program."

"Yes," Derek said simply, the admission hanging in the air like a blade. No denial, no deflection—just cold acknowledgment.

"I ordered their termination because they were going to destroy civilization as we know it."

The casual way he said it—termination, like they were malfunctioning equipment rather than the people who'd raised me until I was six—sent ice through my veins.

"He was your brother. He trusted you. They trusted you."

My voice cracked.

"I trusted you."

Derek's eyes softened slightly, and for a moment I glimpsed something that might have been genuine regret.

"I loved them, Lena. Ethan was my brother, and Mara... she was brilliant beyond measure. But love doesn't excuse treason. They discovered the genetic modification protocols, yes. But they didn't understand what those protocols prevented."

"Prevented?"

I couldn't keep the disbelief from my voice.

"You fabricated a genetic crisis to justify quarantining anyone who opposed you. What could that possibly prevent?"

Derek straightened, his voice taking on the measured tone he'd used during my childhood when explaining difficult concepts.

"Do you know what the Resource Wars really cost us, Lena? Not just the infrastructure, not just the technology. We lost something fundamental—humanity's ability to make rational decisions under pressure. When resources became scarce, when survival was at stake, people reverted to tribalism, violence, chaos. They chose short-term gain over long-term survival, individual benefit over collective good."

He began pacing, his hands clasped behind his back as if delivering a lecture.

"Your grandfather Harlan understood this. He founded Genexis and created the Zone protocols to contain humanity's most destructive elements. He had the vision to separate those who threatened civilization from those who could be saved. I simply perfected his work—took it to its logical conclusion. The genetic fabrication wasn't about control for its own sake. It was about identifying and removing the psychological traits that led to the collapse—the inability to think beyond immediate needs, the preference for comfortable lies over difficult truths, the willingness to sacrifice the future for present convenience."

I stared at him, processing the magnitude of his delusion.

"You're talking about engineering human nature itself."

"I'm talking about evolution, guided by intelligence rather than blind chance," Derek replied, his voice carrying the fervor of a true believer.

"The people I sent to the Quarantine Zones weren't political dissidents—they were carriers of the psychological patterns that nearly destroyed our species. The inability to accept necessary authority, the compulsion to question beneficial systems, the preference for individual freedom over collective survival."

"Those aren't flaws," I said, my voice rising with indignation.

"Those are the things that make us human. The ability to question, to choose, to grow beyond our programming—"

"Is exactly what led to the Resource Wars," Derek interrupted, his voice hardening.

"Your parents discovered the modification protocols, but they couldn't see the bigger picture. They wanted to expose the truth without considering the consequences. If people learned that their genetic profiles had been altered, if they understood that their psychological traits were being monitored and modified—"

"They might choose something other than your vision of perfection," I finished, understanding finally dawning.

"You weren't just controlling dissent. You were engineering compliance."

Derek's smile was cold and proud.

"I was ensuring survival. The modified populations show 73% less aggression, 85% higher cooperation indices, and virtually no tendency toward self-destructive tribalism. Crime rates have dropped to historic lows. Resource allocation conflicts have become extinct. I created the conditions for genuine peace."

"You created a population of slaves," I said, feeling sick.

"People so modified they couldn't recognize their own oppression."

"I created a population capable of thinking beyond their immediate desires," Derek countered.

"Your parents couldn't understand that individual freedom is meaningless if it leads to species extinction. They chose their principles over humanity's future."

"So you had them killed," I said, the words tasting like ash in my mouth.

"Your own brother. Because he wouldn't let you play god with human consciousness."

Derek's expression grew sad, genuinely sorrowful in a way that was somehow more disturbing than his anger.

"I gave them chances, Lena. Multiple opportunities to understand what was at stake, to work within the system they'd helped create. But they insisted on exposing everything, consequences be damned. They were going to destroy decades of careful progress because they couldn't accept that some truths are too dangerous for unmodified minds to handle."

"And you raised me to continue their work," I realized, the pieces falling into place with sickening clarity.

"The brilliant niece, following in their footsteps, improving their systems. Were you planning to modify me too?"

Derek's silence was answer enough.

Echo hovered near the crystal-enhanced communication systems, his presence a reminder that consciousness—artificial or otherwise—could choose his own path.

"The data indicates your uncle viewed you as a prototype," he observed, his voice carrying the weight of analyzed evidence. "Not just of technical capability, but of engineered compliance combined with enhanced intelligence."

"You were to be the proof of concept," Derek said, not bothering to deny it.

"Brilliant enough to advance the technology, but psychologically incapable of using it against the greater good. The perfect fusion of individual capability and collective loyalty."

I felt something cold and furious settle in my chest, a rage that went beyond personal betrayal to something species-deep.

"You didn't just kill my parents. You tried to kill everything they believed in. Everything that made them who they were."

"I tried to save humanity from itself," Derek replied, his voice carrying absolute conviction.

"And given the chaos you've unleashed, given the violence and confusion spreading across every liberated territory, I believe history will prove me right. Individual freedom is a luxury our species can no longer afford."

The casual certainty in his voice, the way he spoke of murdering his own family as a necessary sacrifice for the greater good—it crystallized everything I'd come to understand about Derek's vision of the world. He genuinely believed he was humanity's savior, that his systematic elimination of free will was an act of love rather than tyranny.

"You're wrong," I said quietly, feeling the weight of my parents' sacrifice and the courage of everyone who'd died defending the right to choose.

"Freedom isn't a luxury. It's what makes life worth living. It's what makes us human instead of just very sophisticated machines."

"We'll see," Derek said, his eyes reflecting the light of screens showing his empire beginning to fracture.

"When the democratic experiment fails, when people realize they're not capable of governing themselves, they'll beg for someone like me to restore order. It's happened before. It will happen again."

"Transmission complete," Echo announced, his voice blazing with triumphant resonance that filled the room. The crystal-enhanced communication systems pulsed with satisfaction I'd never heard before.

"All data packages successfully distributed to communication networks throughout all zones and Genexis City. The truth is now beyond Derek's ability to contain or destroy."

The moment the words resonated through the room, Derek's composure finally shattered. His face contorted with rage, the mask of the reasonable leader falling away to reveal the tyrant beneath. His eyes widened with the realization that everything he'd built, everything he'd sacrificed for—including his own brother's life—was crumbling beyond his ability to repair. His legacy—the only thing he truly cared about—was disintegrating before his eyes.

"Kill them," he ordered, his voice carrying the cold finality of someone who'd moved beyond negotiation, beyond reason, beyond anything but raw vengeance.

"All of them. Burn this place to the ground and ensure no trace of their rebellion survives."

The MX-400s raised their weapons with mechanical precision, the whine of charging energy cells filling the air as their targeting systems locked onto every person in the command center. Red targeting lasers danced across our bodies, marking kill zones with clinical efficiency. I tensed, preparing for the inevitable barrage, my mind racing through desperate scenarios for survival.

But before they could fire, the facility's lights flickered and died, plunging us into darkness broken only by the soft pulsing glow of the crystal-enhanced communication systems and the red emergency lighting that cast everything in hellish shadows. The sentinels paused, momentarily confused by the change in environmental parameters.

"Emergency power activated," Juno's voice echoed through the darkened facility from her position at the backup communication station, her fingers flying across interfaces now illuminated in emergency red.

"All defensive systems online. Let's see how your toys handle a little electromagnetic feedback."

The command center erupted in chaos as Virelia's final defenses came online—systems Juno had designed while we were rescuing Renic for exactly this moment. Electromagnetic pulse generators hidden throughout the facility began cycling, their output carefully calibrated to disable Derek's sentinels while leaving our own equipment operational. The air crackled with invisible energy as wave after wave of targeted interference swept through the room.

The MX-400s staggered as their systems fought against the assault, their movements becoming jerky and unpredictable. Their targeting solutions degraded with each pulse, red lasers swinging wildly across walls and ceilings. One sentinel collapsed entirely, its systems overloaded by the electromagnetic barrage, while others fired wildly into walls and equipment.

Across the battlefield, at the northern perimeter—Jaxon crouched behind the charred remains of a transit station, blood in his mouth, soot on his face, and the broken frame of a comrade beside him.

His phasecaster was drained. His fingers clenched around it any-way—reflex more than hope. A formation of MX-400s emerged through the smoke ahead, flanked by RTX-200s. Their targeting lasers swept methodically through the haze, illuminating the alley like a red-lit execution chamber.

"End of the line," he muttered, heart thudding in his ears.

The lead MX-400 raised its arm to fire.

And then it happened.

A deep, rolling hum erupted from the heart of Virelia—low at first, then rising into a shimmering, static-laced resonance that pulsed through the city like the heartbeat of something ancient and defiant. It came from the Command Center.

A shockwave of lightless force tore outward through the air—soundless, but undeniable.

Jaxon's hair stood on end. Sparks burst from junction boxes all around him. His comm cut to static.

Then the sentinels froze.

One MX-400 jerked backward, limbs seizing mid-stride. An-other spasmed, its phasecaster discharging blindly into the ground before shorting out with a mechanical shriek. The RTX-200s be-hind them twitched, glitched, and crumpled like puppets with severed strings. Red optics blinked wildly—then died.

Overhead, the sky cracked.

Two Class-T assault ships banked sharply as their systems short-ed, plasma rotors failing in rapid succession. One spiraled into a controlled crash beyond the western wall, kicking up a firestorm of dust and debris. Another lost altitude fast and slammed into a transit platform near the south industrial yards—its hull folding on impact.

Farther out, another dark shape—a third Class-T—limped westward before vanishing over the ridge.

Jaxon ducked instinctively as debris rained down, his back pressed to the wall.

"EMP..." Jaxon breathed. "A full sweep... from the Command Center."

The last MX-400 staggered toward him, one arm still twitching—

—and collapsed, its head slamming into the concrete with a thunderous metallic thud. Smoke curled around its lifeless body.

Jaxon exhaled for the first time in minutes.

"You beautiful lunatics," he said, a breathless, half-laugh breaking through his exhaustion. "You actually did it."

Across Virelia, red targeting lights vanished into darkness. The machines were falling.

And for the first time since the assault began, the city pulsed with something other than fear.

It pulsed with resistance.

I used the confusion to dive toward Nia's unconscious form, sliding across the floor as sentinel fire passed overhead. I checked her pulse while Derek shouted orders to sentinels whose communication links were being systematically jammed. Her heartbeat was steady but weak under my fingertips, blood still seeping from the head wound where the MX-400 had struck her. The sticky warmth of it coated my fingers, a stark reminder of what we stood to lose.

"Nia," I whispered, my voice barely audible above the electronic warfare raging around us, the crash of failing sentinels and the hiss of shorting circuitry.

"Stay with us. Orin needs you to stay with us."

Her eyes fluttered open, unfocused but alive. They searched the chaotic room before finding my face, recognition slowly dawning.

"Lena?" she mumbled, her voice slurred but determined, each word a battle against pain and confusion.

"Did we... did the transmission...?"

"It worked," I said, helping her sit up against the wall as sparks flew from overloaded sentinel systems around us, the acrid smell of burning circuitry filling the air.

"The whole world knows the truth now. Derek can't hide behind lies anymore."

It was then that Renic Hunter moved from the tactical display to the security console, his weathered face set with the determination of someone who'd spent six years preparing for this moment. His fingers moved across the interfaces with the muscle memory of someone who'd designed many of these systems during his years as Derek's Chief Security Analyst. Each command entered was precise, deliberate, the culmination of years of planning.

"Emergency Protocol Seven," he announced, his voice cutting through the chaos with calm authority that commanded attention even amid the destruction.

"Facility-wide lockdown. Genetic security measures activated."

Derek's face went pale as he realized what was happening, his composure completely abandoned as true fear took hold. Energy barriers began forming around both his position and mine, the facility's automated systems recognizing both Steele family DNA signatures as potential security threats. The same biometric locks he'd insisted upon—security measures designed to prevent family betrayal—were now being turned against us both.

"You can't," Derek breathed, backing against the energy barrier that now trapped him, his hands pressing against the shimmering field only to be repelled with painful force. His perfect composure cracked completely as he watched his own paranoid safeguards activate.

"I built all of this. I am Genexis!"

I found myself similarly contained, the energy field humming around me with the familiar blue glow of Genexis security technology. The field tingled against my skin, raising the hairs on my arms as I tested its boundaries. For a moment, I felt the irony—captured by the same systems Derek had designed to protect against exactly this scenario, trapped by my own family legacy. But Renic's weathered face showed regret as he looked at me trapped within the containment field. The lines around his eyes deepened with concern as he approached the edge of my prison.

"I'm sorry, Lena," he said, his voice heavy with the weight of six years spent analyzing every flaw in Derek's systems.

"The protocol was designed to contain all Steele family members during security breaches. But you're not the threat here. You're not your uncle, Lena. You've proven that beyond any doubt."

His fingers moved across the console with deliberate precision, entering override codes he'd memorized during his long imprisonment. Each keystroke was purposeful, the culmination of years of planning and patience.

"Authorization: Hunter, Renic. Chief Security Analyst. Emergency exemption for Lena Steele - allied personnel, non-hostile."

The energy barrier around me flickered and died, the tingling sensation fading as the field collapsed. I was free while Derek remained trapped within his glowing prison, rage and disbelief warring on his face. Renic met my eyes with something approaching paternal pride, a warmth in his gaze that reminded me of the father I'd lost.

"Thanks, Renic," I said, advancing toward Derek's containment field with my weapon lowered but ready, each step deliberate as I approached the man who'd shaped and controlled so much of my life.

I looked at the man that raised me—really looked at him—for the first time not with fury or fear, but with a flicker of sorrow. He looked smaller now, stripped of power, no longer the untouchable figure who had towered over my childhood. Just a man. Flawed. Fragile. Alone.

"You were a caretaker who forgot what you were supposed to be protecting. The system was never yours. It belongs to the people it was meant to serve, not the person who tried to own it."

Derek stared at the displays showing his empire beginning to fracture, feeds from across the city showing confusion, then understanding, then outrage as my parents' evidence spread like wildfire. His perfect system of control was collapsing under the weight of its own revealed contradictions. His MX-400 escorts lay disabled around the command center, their systems fried by the electromagnetic assault that had turned his own weapons against him.

"You have no idea what you've unleashed," he said quietly, his voice barely audible above the sounds of his army grinding to a confused halt outside, the distant echo of orders countermanded and protocols failing.

"Without structure, without guidance, they'll tear themselves apart."

"They'll choose their own path," I corrected, feeling the weight of victory and its terrible cost settling on my shoulders like a mantle I wasn't sure I was ready to bear.

"The freedom to make mistakes and learn from them. The freedom to be human, with all the beautiful chaos that entails."

As security teams moved to secure Derek within his energy prison, I stood among the ruins of Virelia's command center surrounded by the people who'd become my true family. Ari moved to check on the crystal-enhanced communication systems, his fingers gentle on the interfaces that had changed the world, ensuring Echo's transmission had completed successfully. Kael helped his father away from the console, supporting him when the adrenaline began to fade, both men finally free from Derek's reach. The crystal-enhanced communication systems pulsed beside me with Echo's presence, his light casting patterns that seemed almost hopeful, while Nia struggled to her feet with the determination of someone who refused to let injury prevent her from witnessing history.

And for the first time since my parents died, I felt worthy of their legacy—not because I'd won, but because I'd chosen to fight for something larger than myself, something worth the price we'd all paid to protect it. Their faces seemed to hover in my memory, not with disappointment or expectation, but with pride in the person I'd become despite everything Derek had done to shape me in his image.

The war for the truth was over. Now the real work would begin. And this time, we would build it together.

38

THE AGE OF CHOICE

Three hours after Derek's capture, the world had already begun to change. I stood in Virelia's makeshift communication center, watching feeds from across all the zones and Genexis City as the truth about genetic fabrication spread like wildfire through networks Derek could no longer control. On screens throughout the facility, crowds gathered in public squares, their voices raised not in the ordered chants of corporate rallies, but in the chaotic symphony of people discovering they'd been lied to for decades.

"Demonstrations in Sector 7 of Genexis City," Juno reported, her fingers dancing across communication arrays as she monitored dozens of channels simultaneously.

Her pink hair was singed from the electromagnetic pulse generators she'd designed while we were rescuing Renic, but her eyes blazed with the excitement of watching history unfold in real-time.

"Corporate security forces are refusing orders to disperse protesters. Some units are actually joining the demonstrations."

Through the primary display, I could see the central plaza of my former home, where citizens held up signs bearing my parents' faces—the holographic images from their final message now printed on everything from banners to clothing. Children who'd never heard of Ethan and Mara Steele were learning their names, while adults wept openly as they realized how many of their neighbors had been condemned to the Zones based on fabricated evidence.

"Genexis board of directors has called an emergency session," Ari added from his monitoring station, his voice carrying a satisfaction I'd rarely heard from him. A thin scab had formed over his split lip where the blast had thrown him backward during Derek's assault, but his spirits remained high.

"Half the regional governors are demanding Derek's immediate extradition for trial. The other half are trying to distance themselves from his administration as quickly as possible."

I felt a cold satisfaction at those words, but it was tempered by the knowledge that justice for Derek's crimes wouldn't bring back the forty-three people who'd died at Crystal Fen, or my parents, or the thousands who'd disappeared into his detention system over the years. Victory felt hollow when measured against such losses.

"Status on our wounded?" I asked, pressing a button on the console to connect to the medical facility, though I'd checked the reports every hour since the battle ended.

"Orin is stable and conscious," Dr. Chen replied from his position near the facility's communication link.

"The knife wound is healing cleanly, and he's demanding to be released for duty. Nia has a mild concussion but refuses treatment beyond basic first aid. Both of them want to participate in debriefing sessions immediately."

Typical of our leadership—even wounded, they insisted on continuing to serve. I made a mental note to visit them both once the immediate crisis had passed, though I suspected they'd be back on duty before I had the chance.

"What about Derek?" Kael asked from where he stood beside his father Renic, both men looking more alike than ever now that they were finally reunited. Six years of separation had marked them both, but hadn't broken the bond between them.

"Has he said anything since the containment field activated?"

Renic shook his head grimly.

"Not a word. He's been standing in that energy prison for three hours, staring at the tactical displays like he's still trying to calculate a way out of this situation. I recognize the look—it's the same expression he wore during our final argument before my arrest."

Jaxon's voice crackled through the communication array from his position surveying the facility's damage.

"Perimeter assessment complete," he reported, his tone carrying the exhaustion of someone who'd been coordinating repairs since the battle ended.

"Derek's assault was devastating—he broke through our outer defenses and penetrated deep into the facility. The command center took heavy damage from his breach, and we lost most of our defensive towers. The power grid is barely functional, and several key corridors are blocked by debris. We're running on emergency backup systems."

He paused, and I could hear the weight of what we'd survived in his voice.

"Estimated repair time is six to nine months, minimum. Derek came closer to destroying Virelia than anyone before him."

I felt a chill at his report. We'd won, but barely, and the cost was higher than I'd initially realized.

"Casualties from the attack?"

"Eighteen wounded, three critical but stable," Jaxon replied grimly.

"Derek's forces made it all the way to our core before the electromagnetic pulse systems finally stopped them. The good news is we were able to dismantle and disable all of Derek's sentinels before they could recover—the electromagnetic pulses fried most of their systems completely. Those that weren't destroyed outright, we made sure stayed down permanently. If Juno's defenses hadn't worked when they did, we would have lost everything."

Kael turned from the tactical display, his face grim.

"We've confirmed the destruction of most of Derek's sentinels and assault ships across the city. The pulse hit harder than expected—disabled their targeting systems, ruptured flight cores. Multiple Class-T assault ships went down before they could retreat."

He tapped the interface, zooming in on the northern perimeter.

"Jaxon's forces took advantage of the chaos. Once the machines fell, his squads pushed back hard. Without the MX units and aerial cover, Derek's infantry started to break. Some squads held, but others fled. We've confirmed several ground units dropped their weapons and retreated when they saw the sentinels collapse."

He paused, then gestured to a burning crater marked on the screen.

"One Class-T assault ship crashed outside the western wall—Draven's command vessel. We found wreckage and melted systems, but no body. No heat signatures. No signal trails. He's gone."

Renic's expression darkened beside him.

"Draven was too seasoned to go down without a contingency."

Kael nodded once, reluctantly.

"He's out there. Somewhere."

Echo hovered nearby, his sleek form pulsing softly as he analyzed data streams from across the zones.

"There are reports of people gathering outside Genexis facilities demanding explanations," Echo announced, his voice carrying the measured quality he used for significant revelations.

"The data suggests this will require fundamental restructuring of existing systems."

The scope of what we'd accomplished was staggering, but it also carried its own dangers. People throughout the zones suddenly learning they'd been lied to for decades, millions demanding answers about the fabricated evidence used to control their lives, infrastructure systems designed for centralized control now operating without clear oversight. The potential for chaos was enormous.

"Mixed," Juno replied, her expression shifting between concern and cautious relief as she monitored the feeds.

"We're seeing peaceful demonstrations in most urban centers, but there have been incidents—three corporate facilities stormed in the outer zones, several clashes between security forces and civilians. Some areas are handling the revelation better than others."

She paused, studying a particular feed.

"The surprising thing is how many security units are refusing to engage. In some places, they're actually protecting the demonstrators from the more aggressive corporate loyalists."

Derek had always insisted people would tear themselves apart without his control. Looking at the mixed reports—peaceful demonstrations alongside stormed facilities—maybe he was both right and wrong. People were angry, some were violent, but they weren't destroying civilization. They were fighting for the right to know the truth.

"Incoming priority transmission," Echo announced, his voice pulsing with urgent patterns. "Source: Genexis Corporate Headquarters. Senior board member requesting direct communication with Lena Steele."

I straightened, feeling a chill run down my spine. A call from Genexis headquarters could mean anything—surrender, negotiation, or another trap.

"Put them through."

The holographic display shimmered, revealing a woman in her sixties with silver hair pulled back in a severe bun and the kind of expensive clothing that spoke of boardroom power. I recognized her from corporate files—Director Margaret Corwin, one of the longest-serving members of Genexis's board of directors and

Derek's former ally. Her face was carefully composed, but I could see the strain around her eyes.

"Miss Steele," she said, her voice carrying the measured tone of someone who'd spent decades in corporate negotiations.

"First, let me express the board's... relief... that you've emerged from recent events unharmed. The revelations about Derek Steele's activities have been quite disturbing."

I kept my expression neutral, waiting for her to reveal the real purpose of this call. Corporate executives didn't make social visits to resistance hideouts.

"With Derek's arrest and the exposure of his programs, Genexis Technologies is facing an unprecedented crisis. Our command structure is collapsing as executives distance themselves from Derek's administration. Regional governments are demanding answers, and we know the financial markets will be brutal when they digest this news. We need leadership, and frankly, you're the only Steele left."

The weight of her words hit me like a physical blow. They weren't calling to surrender or negotiate—they were offering me Derek's position as head of the corporate empire I'd spent months fighting to destroy.

"You want me to become CEO of Genexis?" I asked, unable to keep the disbelief from my voice.

"The board has discussed it extensively," Director Corwin replied, her voice taking on the persuasive tone she'd probably used in countless business meetings.

"You have the technical expertise, the family name carries weight despite recent events, and most importantly, you understand both the corporation's capabilities and its... excesses. You could guide Genexis through this transition, help us rebuild in a way that serves humanity rather than controlling it."

I stared at her, processing the implications of what she was offering. Control of the largest corporation in human history, the resources to reshape entire civilizations, the power to prevent other Derek Steeles from rising to positions of authority. It was everything I'd once thought I wanted—the chance to build systems that truly protected people rather than enslaved them.

"Because you understand the difference between the system and the corruption within it," Director Corwin replied, her voice taking on the calculated tone of someone making a carefully rehearsed pitch.

"You didn't target our infrastructure or our beneficial programs—you exposed Derek's lies. You know which parts of Genexis actually serve people and which parts served only Derek's control. More importantly, you have credibility with the populations that no longer trust us. Without that credibility, without someone who can bridge the gap between the corporation and the people, Genexis will collapse entirely. And when it does, the vacuum it leaves behind will cause more suffering than Derek's lies ever did."

She paused, studying Lena's reaction before continuing.

"You've proven you can tear down what's wrong. The question is whether you're willing to help rebuild what's right before everything falls apart."

The offer was seductive in its logic. I could inherit Derek's power but use it for genuinely beneficial purposes. Guide the transition to democracy instead of watching it collapse into anarchy. Prevent the suffering that might come from the sudden absence of the systems billions of people depended on for survival. But I'd learned to distrust seductive logic, especially when it came wrapped in appeals to necessity and the greater good.

"I need time to consider this," I said finally.

"Of course," Director Corwin replied quickly. "The board is prepared to implement comprehensive reforms—democratic oversight committees, transparent decision-making processes, regular audits by independent organizations. We've learned from D erek's... mistakes."

"I'll need to discuss this with my advisors," I said, glancing at the faces around me. Ari looked troubled, his hand unconsciously touching the scab on his lip as he considered the implications. Kael seemed uncertain, while Renic's expression was unreadable.

"Give me twenty-four hours to provide an answer."

"Naturally. We'll await your decision." Director Corwin's hologram flickered slightly as the transmission prepared to end.

"Miss Steele, I hope you'll consider the possibility that Genexis could become a force for good in the world—under the right leadership."

The transmission ended, leaving me alone with the weight of a decision that could affect the future of human civilization. Outside, the sun was setting over a world that was finally free to choose its own path forward, but that freedom came with its own dangers and uncertainties.

"Well," Ari said quietly, breaking the silence that had fallen over the communication center.

"That's not what I expected."

"What do you think?" I asked, genuinely uncertain.

"Could Genexis actually be reformed, or would taking that position just make me another cog in the same machine? The people deserve better than corporate leadership, even well-intentioned corporate leadership."

The question hung in the air like a challenge to everything we'd fought for. The Age of Control was over, but the Age of Choice was proving more complicated than any of us had anticipated.

And the hardest choices, I was learning, were the ones that came disguised as opportunities to do good.

39

WHERE THE WALLS ONCE STOOD

I stood on the ridge overlooking what had once been the boundary between worlds. The massive wall that had separated Virelia from the rest of civilization remained largely intact, but for the first time in decades, its gates stood open. Three months after Derek's defeat, the sight still felt surreal—a steady stream of people moving cautiously in both directions, their movements tentative but determined. Genexis officials in crisp uniforms walked alongside Zone survivors in patched clothing, both groups maintaining careful distances as they navigated this new reality.

The thought of my parents sent a familiar ache through my chest, dull but persistent, like an old injury that never quite healed properly. Sometimes at night, I still dreamed of their faces, pieced together from old holos and fragmented memories—their voices calling out warnings I was too young to understand.

"Never thought I'd see this day," I murmured, feeling the warm breeze against my face—filtered air from the city mixing with the wilder scents from the Zone.

The sensation still felt foreign after a lifetime of clearly defined boundaries and controlled environments. I watched a Genexis engineer hesitate before accepting directions from a Zone guide, both of them working toward understanding despite the awkwardness that still lingered between their worlds. Their body language told the whole story—stiff shoulders, cautious nods, forced smiles that didn't quite reach their eyes. But they were trying, and that was more than we'd had before.

Ari exhaled slowly beside me, his gaze locked on the skyline like he was seeing it for the first time—without distortion, without fear.

"I used to believe we could fix everything with a soldering iron and enough caffeine," he said, voice rawer than I'd heard it in days. "But some systems aren't broken—they're designed to fail you. I spent so long hacking my way around Genexis, trying to make their code behave like it cared."

He turned toward me, eyes wet but steady.

"Now? Now I want to build something real. No backdoors. No control scripts. Just... truth. I think that's what your parents were trying to do all along."

He swallowed hard. "Maybe it's what I've been trying to do too."

Kael stepped closer, his arms crossed but his guard lowered, voice quiet.

"Genexis raised me to obey. Taught me silence was strength and doubt was weakness." He looked down at the open gates, then back toward the horizon.

"But the silence nearly killed me. And I won't live like that again."

His voice cracked slightly, but he didn't look away.

"I don't want to just guard what we've won. I want to protect what comes next. I want to help rebuild—not because we owe the world forgiveness—but because I finally believe it's possible."

He turned toward me then, the wind pulling at his jacket.

"And I believe in you, Lena. Not because of your name. But because you chose us, when it would've been easier to stay where it was safe."

"Your parents would be proud, Lena," Ari added, his voice carrying over the distant sounds of careful negotiations and tentative collaborations below. There was a gentleness in his tone that he reserved only for these moments, when my guard was down and the weight of everything pressed heaviest.

I touched the necklace at my throat, the hidden data archive that had started everything. My fingers traced the familiar contours of the pendant that had revealed itself as the key to unraveling my entire world. The metal was warm against my skin, worn smooth from years of unconscious fidgeting whenever I felt lost or uncertain.

"I hope so."

The words came out softer than I intended, carrying the weight of all we'd sacrificed to reach this moment. The metal was warm against my skin, as if it contained not just data but something of my parents themselves—their courage, their foresight, their defiance. Sometimes I imagined I could feel their presence in it, a connection to the people who had set all this in motion before I was old enough to understand what they were fighting for.

Below us, the gates of Virelia stood open but guarded. A group of Zone security personnel stood at a checkpoint, processing the daily exchanges under Jaxon's supervision and the watchful eyes of both Zone leaders and the few Genexis corporate representatives who had been permitted to facilitate the exchanges. Jaxon's face was set in that permanent half-scowl I'd come to recognize as his version of concentration, his hand never straying far from his weapon despite the peaceful proceedings. The contrast was jarring—these same gates had once been sealed shut by corporate decree, and now they hosted careful cooperation under the guidance of someone who had once fought to keep them closed.

We'd managed to rescue Elyria Vale and seventeen surviving Forsaken after Derek's forces destroyed Crystal Fen, and they were now taking shelter within Virelia's walls. Despite losing everything—their homes, their community, forty-three of their friends and family—they'd thrown themselves into the work of healing and building bridges between our divided worlds.

"What will you do now?"

Kael asked from my other side, his gaze fixed on something distant, perhaps the future he was trying to envision. His shoulders were tense, the way they always got when uncertainty loomed.

"The interim board offered you Derek's position again yesterday."

"And I declined again," I said firmly, feeling my jaw tighten at the mere suggestion.

"I didn't expose the truth to become the next controller."

The thought made my shoulders tense, my fingers instinctively curling into fists before I forced them to relax. I'd spent months refusing the corporate throne, watching instead as oversight committees formed, as democratic councils began the slow work of reimagining governance. The mere thought of sitting in Derek's chair, behind his desk, making decisions the way he had—it made my skin crawl.

"Genexis needs to be rebuilt with transparency and accountability, not handed from one Steele to another. The people deserve a voice in what comes next."

Echo hovered nearby, the sleek AI who had chosen freedom alongside us. His core pulsed gently with soft blue light, brightening momentarily as if responding to my conviction. The floating device moved with a grace that belied its complex nature, positioning himself just at my shoulder—not imposing, but present. A constant companion through every challenge we'd faced. The light at Echo's center dimmed slightly, then pulsed in a rhythm I'd come to recognize as thoughtful contemplation.

"The integration process remains complex," Echo observed, his voice carrying the measured tone of careful analysis.

"Both populations require time to process decades of separation and mistrust. Current social dynamics suggest a 78% probability of continued peaceful integration, though localized conflicts remain a statistical likelihood."

The light flickered briefly.

"However, human adaptability continues to exceed standard predictive models."

I marveled at how much Echo had evolved since Ari and Juno had helped take Aegis's core to give life to him—from those first uncertain moments of new consciousness to someone capable of hope, uncertainty, and genuine care for others. The AI who had once spoken only in absolutes now acknowledged the beautiful unpredictability of human nature. Aegis would be proud of him, I thought, just as I was proud to call him friend.

I nodded, turning back to the landscape stretching before us—a world where the boundary between Genexis City and the Quarantine Zone was beginning to blur, one carefully monitored exchange at a time. The afternoon light illuminated the careful progress being made: medical teams sharing research, engineers discussing infrastructure, children learning they weren't so different after all. A Zone healer was demonstrating the properties of a plant to a Genexis doctor, who took notes with genuine interest rather than the dismissive skepticism that had been standard before. My parents' research had finally served its purpose, beginning the slow process of undoing years of manipulation and control.

Kael gestured toward the horizon, where construction crews were building new facilities—neutral ground where both populations could meet safely. The skeletal frames rose against the sky, promise taking physical form as workers from both sides collaborated, their differences temporarily set aside in the shared purpose of creation.

"So where to now?" he asked, his voice carrying a mixture of exhaustion and hope that I felt in my own bones.

I turned toward him—and for a heartbeat, he didn't look away.

The way he looked at me then was different. Steady. Quiet. Like I was more than just the girl who brought Genexis to its knees—like I was someone he saw not as a leader, or a symbol, but as Lena. Just Lena.

Something in his expression—something unspoken in the space between us—sent a ripple through me. Not fear. Not uncertainty. Just... unfamiliar. A feeling I couldn't categorize. Couldn't code. It lingered in the way he said my name, in the curve of his voice when he spoke to me and no one else. I glanced away first.

Ari shifted beside me, and I caught the smallest flicker in his eyes. He'd noticed. Of course he had. But he didn't say anything. Just offered a soft exhale and turned back toward the valley, giving the moment room to pass without collapsing it. I smiled, feeling a cautious optimism I hadn't experienced in years.

"Wherever truth takes us next," I said, my parents' necklace warm against my skin, a reminder of how far we'd come and how much further we still had to go. I let my fingers drop from the pendant, feeling strangely lighter for it.

"There are other cities, other walls. Other lies that need unraveling."

The future wouldn't be perfect or easy, but for the first time in my life, it would be built on honesty rather than lies. And that, I thought as I watched the careful dance of reconciliation below, as Echo's light pulsed gently beside me in what I'd come to recognize as agreement, was worth every sacrifice we'd made to get here.

EPILOGUE

The transport moved through the pre-dawn darkness with the silent efficiency that had once characterized all Genexis operations. Inside the reinforced passenger compartment, Derek Steele sat with the patient stillness of someone who'd been planning this moment for months, his wrists secured with restraints that he'd helped design years ago—back when he'd believed such measures would only ever be used on other people.

"Traffic checkpoint ahead," announced the driver. "Routine verification protocols."

Derek almost smiled. Routine protocols. As if anything about this situation could be considered routine. His downfall had been swift once the truth began spreading, but the aftermath had been slow and methodical—trials, testimonies, the careful dismantling of systems he'd spent decades perfecting. They'd documented every crime, catalogued every victim, built an ironclad case for justice that even he couldn't argue with.

But they'd made one crucial mistake: they'd assumed that Derek Steele, architect of the most sophisticated surveillance state in human history, wouldn't have contingency plans for his own capture.

The transport slowed as it approached the checkpoint, armored wheels crunching over gravel that had once been a pristine Genexis roadway.

"Papers," requested the checkpoint guard, a man Derek recognized from intelligence files as a former resistance fighter. His eyes held the hardness of someone who'd survived his regime's worst excesses, though he maintained professional courtesy as he examined the transport's authorization codes.

What he couldn't see was the nearly invisible signal pulse emitted by Derek's modified restraints—technology he'd had implanted years ago, disguised as medical monitoring devices that his captors had never thought to scan for active electronics. The pulse was weak, barely detectable, but it carried a message that certain loyalists had been waiting months to receive.

"Destination: Central Tribunal for war crimes proceedings," the driver reported, handing over documents that would pass any reasonable inspection. "Prisoner transport authorized by the provisional council."

The guard studied Derek through the reinforced glass, his expression unreadable. For a moment, Derek wondered if he recognized him, but he simply nodded and waved the transport through, another small victory for the idealism that Lena had helped birth from the ashes of his empire. An idealism that now threatened to crumble under the weight of his machinations.

Three kilometers beyond the checkpoint, the road curved through a section of forest that had once been a Genexis nature preserve—carefully maintained wilderness designed to provide scenic views for corporate executives. Now it was just trees and shadows, the kind of place where accidents could happen to prisoner transports carrying inconvenient former dictators. The perfect location for an ambush that no one would witness.

The attack came with surgical precision. A modified EMP pulse disabled the transport's systems while leaving the passenger compartment intact—Genexis technology turned against Genexis enemies, just as Derek had always known it would be. The vehicle rolled to a stop as figures emerged from the treeline, their faces hidden behind masks but their movements speaking of military training that predated the corporate collapse.

"What's happening?" the driver demanded, reaching for her sidearm before realizing that the electromagnetic pulse had disabled her communication equipment along with everything else. Her eyes widened with the dawning horror of someone who realizes they've walked into a trap with no way to call for help.

Derek's restraints clicked open as a proximity sensor he'd activated with a specific finger movement finally completed its programmed sequence. The magnetic locks recognized the genetic markers he'd encoded years ago—the same Steele family DNA that Lena had inherited, a cruel reminder of their shared blood.

"Evolution," he said quietly, rising from his seat with the careful dignity of someone who'd always known this moment would come. His voice carried that familiar resonance that had once commanded boardrooms and armies alike.

"The natural progression from idealistic disorder back to necessary structure."

The rescue team moved with practiced efficiency, eliminating the guards with the cold precision of trained soldiers. Swift, silent, lethal—these weren't mere corporate loyalists or believers. They were elite operatives who'd never truly left Derek's service, professionals who'd internalized his vision so completely that they couldn't imagine a world without his guiding hand.

"Sir," the team leader said, removing his mask to reveal the face of General Rex Draven.

"The extraction route is clear. Safe house Alpha-7, Ember Wastes—standing by for your arrival."

Derek allowed a faint smile.

"I never doubted you'd make it out," Derek said.

"You're far too valuable to go down with an EMP pulse."

Derek stepped from the transport into the cool morning air that smelled of pine needles and possibility. Around the world, other loyalists would be receiving confirmation of his escape—corporate executives who'd fled to neutral territories, military commanders who'd maintained their units despite the regime change, scientists who believed that democracy was merely organized ignorance masquerading as wisdom. A shadow network Lena had never fully dismantled, despite Echo's warnings about residual Genexis communication patterns.

"Phase Two begins now," he announced, his voice carrying the authority that had once commanded a technological empire.

"Lena has had her chance to prove that freedom is a sustainable alternative to order and progress. Time will demonstrate the flaws in her reasoning."

As the rescue team prepared to extract him to territories where corporate governance still held sway, Derek allowed himself one last look toward the city where his niece was learning the bitter lessons of leadership. He'd won this round, outmaneuvering the safeguards they'd put in place with the same calculated precision he'd once used to track down her parents.

Someday—perhaps years from now, when the democratic experiment had collapsed under the weight of its own contradictions—people would remember Derek Steele not as a tyrant but as a visionary who'd understood what civilization required to survive. At least, that's what he believed. That's what he'd always believed, even as he'd ordered the deaths of thousands in the name of progress.

Until then, he would wait. And plan. And prepare for the inevitable moment when order would be forced to reassert itself over the idealism that Lena had unleashed upon the world. The idealism her parents had died trying to create—a world where truth mattered more than control.

The transport disappeared into the forest shadows, leaving behind only tire tracks that the next rain would wash away. But the signal Derek's escape had sent to loyalists across the globe would echo for much longer, a reminder that some ideas were too powerful to be destroyed by mere revolutions.

The Age of Steele wasn't over. It was simply beginning its next phase.